J. Eden

HARDSCRABBLE BOOKS—*Fiction of New England*

J. Eden

A NOVEL BY

Kit Reed

University Press of New England   Hanover and London

UNIVERSITY PRESS OF NEW ENGLAND
publishes books under its own imprint and is the publisher for
Brandeis University Press, Dartmouth College, Middlebury College Press,
University of New Hampshire, University of Rhode Island, Tufts University,
University of Vermont, Wesleyan University Press,
and Salzburg Seminar.

University Press of New England
Published by University Press of New England, Hanover, NH 03755
©1996 by Kit Reed
Printed in the United States of America   5   4   3   2   1

Library of Congress Cataloging-in-Publication Data
Reed, Kit.
    J. Eden: a novel / by Kit Reed.
        p.   cm.—(Hardscrabble books)
    ISBN 0-87451-746-X (alk. paper)
    I. Title. II. Series
    PS3568.E367J18   1996
    813'.54—dc20   95-40885
    ∞

Amelia Manning's book
as promised
and with love

SPRING

1

Chad

It's amazing and sad, how you set out to do one thing and end up doing another. Your synapses misfire and you hit delete instead of save, or yell when you mean to be sweet. You start laughing uncontrollably on your way to a funeral, singing in the cab the way we did, forgive us, the way we did in September, after everything was done. One day you touch her arm to say, *I'm sorry*, and against your will your eyes roll and your lips curl back in an accidental grin. One morning you turn over in bed and reach out for the one you love most and find that person gone.

Listen. What you're doing and what you think you're doing are not always the same thing. The farm was supposed to be a safe house for our kids; they could run like puppies while the eight of us sat on the porch in the long summer evenings, getting down in the soft country air. Or that's what Leslie said. We could make our own time in the country, do our own thing. We could leave the windows open and not worry, sleep like stones with all the doors unlocked. She was sick of the exigencies of the city: dead bolts and doormen, sitters, daycare. Gentle question periods. Somebody touched you on the subway? They touched you where?

We were all edgy that spring, tired and embattled. It seemed right to circle the wagons against whatever was to come.

She stormed me when I least expected it, beautiful Leslie,

who lives from scheme to scheme. She'd already found a place so far from the city that we could forget who we were supposed to be and be ourselves. The house was in a depressed area in Massachusetts, the kind of place where locals come out on the front porch to watch the sun go down—no nearby ski areas, none of your Tanglewood chic, so it was cheap. In that little valley, deep country still seemed like a possibility, and if some of us had day jobs and it took hours to get there from the city, it made no difference to Les.

She waited until she had me in a vulnerable position. Don't ask. Before I could apologize for what happened, much less lay out my top ten reasons not to spend a summer that far from the city, she said sorry, our friends were coming at five to sign the lease.

It was already ten of. The champagne was chilling and the crabmeat was on ice in her grandmother's crystal bowls. She had the au pair Windexing the last fingerprints off the glass and chrome in the living room. We were in the bedroom fighting, and if there was a subtext, we were afraid to touch it. If she didn't mention it, neither would I.

"Massachusetts! I can't go to Massachusetts. I have this TV project." I think I can name one thing that was the matter with us that year—Zack and Calvin and I. I can't speak for Stig. Life's clocks had started ticking loud enough to hear. If the producers liked my treatment, I wrote the script instead of some TV writer who'd get paid ten times what they put down on my book.

She said heartlessly, "I'll get you a fax."

"I can't leave my job."

"You just don't want to," she said. Leslie couldn't understand the pressure: turn away for a minute and you lose your place in line. "You could use your vacation. Take some of your comp time."

"No I couldn't."

"Then go in once a week and modem the rest. If you loved

me, you'd do it." Her face was smeared because of the things we'd said to each other that very afternoon. "You know you would."

I wanted to hug her and beg her to stop. I wanted us both to forget about everything, how I accidentally hurt her, which I wouldn't mention if she didn't bring it up. I hurt my wife. She fights back with real estate. I wanted to grovel and kiss Leslie until she laughed; I wanted to make her grin but all I could do was yell, "I can't, I'm on deadline." Not the first time I used this to win our arguments. Then I made a mistake. I said, "You can do whatever you want, but I have to work."

"You've got your work." She stepped away and looked at me. "And what do you think I have?"

"God, Leslie. You have . . ." I wanted to make her feel good and I didn't know what to say. I said, "You have *all this*." I waved around. She did: penthouse on Riverside, espaliered fruit trees on the balcony, ancestral paintings, beautiful life. Not my money, her grandmother's, and this is another thing. She knew I hated her using Lavinia's money. Then I looked at her and knew. Whether or not she bought my answer, this discussion was academic. Thank you, Lavinia. Her grandmother had already put money down on the farm.

Her lips seemed to be melting. "What do I really have?"

I looked around our beautiful room. The question beggared me. "Oh, Les!"

She said it anyway. "I don't have a life."

I heard a new voice. "Dad."

"You have your damn work," she said, "you have your car and you have your goddamn little—"

"Dad . . ."

I put up my hand to hush her. "Don't, Les!"

"Mom! Shut up. *Stop barking.*" It was our son. Lucky. Leslie didn't hear him; she was too intent on winning, crying, "And me? I don't have anything!"

"Wait a minute, Mom." Timothy Chadbourne Burgess—excuse me, Lucky. Our son Lucky was hanging there in the doorway with this killed-in-action look.

She didn't see him, either; she said, "Not a thing."

"Mom, that isn't true!"

He was about to cry. I wanted to grab him and cover his ears but he backed away. I didn't know how to reach him; from the beginning we'd been like this, a complex of missed connections. There was more going on than he saw, that I needed to keep from him. Right, it was Leslie who was yelling, but in this round, I was the perp.

She whirled on me. *How long has he been listening?*

I said over her head, "I'm sorry, Tim."

"Lucky, I-told-you-never-to . . ." She shouted, "Frieda!"

The girl took forever to come. We waited with the fight smearing our faces while Lucky bobbed in our bedroom doorway like an angry ghost. When our au pair appeared she was yellow with humiliation, rubbing her thumbs across those watery blue eyes. "Oh, Mrs."

Leslie wailed, "Frieda, you're supposed to be watching him!"

I said, "It isn't her fault."

"Oh, Mrs!" When she got here from Finland, poor Frieda seemed surprised that we didn't speak her language, and sad that the winter sun didn't go down at 1 p.m. Her face was so miserable that I couldn't bear to look.

"That will be all, Frieda." Leslie spoke clearly—you know: If I can only say it loud enough she'll understand. "Take Timothy into the kitchen and give him some cookies."

"I don't want any . . ."

"Just go." Frieda reached out but Lucky hung back. The poor girl was transfixed with embarrassment. Apron, crown of braids, who told her she would be happy in New York? Who told her she would be just like a member of the family in the new land, when she was being sent to people who *were not like her?* When

Frieda lingered, Leslie spoke in her grandmother's tones. "I said, *that will be all.*"

With that ghastly, bucktoothed grin, Frieda grabbed Lucky's hand and let him lead her away.

By that time I was feeling rotten. "I'm sorry."

"Oh God," Leslie said, looking in the mirror, "look what you've made of me!" She did look bad, for Leslie—eyeliner smudged, eyes red, beginning lines at the corners of her mouth.

"If the farm means that much to you, for God's sake let's go ahead with it." That made her smile. This time I hugged her until she hugged back.

We made up. I got stuck answering the door. The Petersons were first. I heard somebody knock. When I first looked out the hall was empty. I'm not used to short people, which is another way of saying I've never been easy with kids. (Leslie at the end, glaring: "You never saw him. Why in God's name couldn't you ever look *down?*")

"Hi Mr. Burgess." This chrysanthemum head was bobbing at waist height—Zack's little towhead, looking up at me out of his father's face. "Mr. Burgess, it's me. Gabe. Gabe Peterson?" What had Zack said? Said Gabe wanted to grow up to be a writer, said he was too embarrassed to ask me how. Gabe stood there with this uncomplicated, kid's grin, waiting for me to let him in.

I should have thought of something writerly to tell him but all I could think was: *I wish Lucky was . . .* and couldn't finish the thought. "Gabe. Cool. Come on in."

The Petersons rounded the corner looking like the Blue Fairy and Father Bear, straight out of some sixties popup book. It didn't matter what Zack put on, he always looked like a walking futon—sort of, you know, slept on. Even Permapress rumples on Zack, which may be why he teaches college instead of running with the sharks in an Armani suit. His wife Polly bought all her clothes in this hopeful blue that matched her eyes.

Zack stood back so she could go into the living room and

when we were alone he bellied up to me, asking, "How's business?" as if we were in the same business.

I had development money for a miniseries based on my book on runaways. The producers and network people were talking spinoff, a story a week. These days at lunches, when I looked around the table and met anybody's eye, that person automatically smiled. But facing Zack in my front hall, I shrugged and said, "About the same," while my friend slitted his eyes, trying to see far enough into me to find out if I had secretly triumphed and was hiding it from him.

"Great," he said hollowly. He was like Calvin that year. Like me, I'm afraid. At some point when we weren't looking this had turned into a race. At the end of parties we used to huddle around the gemlike flame and set deadlines—BY THE TIME WE'RE FORTY: you know. This was getting hard for me. I had banners on the front of *Vanity Fair* and *New York Magazine*. Book contracts. More to come. I kept my secrets and hunkered down with my friends, pretending we were all still moving at the same rate. I sensed a flicker of envy, and wondered how much longer we'd be easy together.

Even though Zack hadn't asked, I said, "It's no big deal."

"Easy for you to say. Did I tell you about my deal?" He had. Some fly-by-night independent producer had scoured Columbia, turning out English professors willing to update the classics on spec. Zack thought if I could get big bucks for writing a script, anybody could. Like him.

"You did. It sounds great." I didn't have the heart to tell him how many of these projects go up in smoke or how hopeless this one was—rewriting Dracula, when the vampire business is maxed out. I don't know why he was so desperate to change his life. One call returned from some kid executive's car phone and another from Vail and Zack started talking like an insider— treatment this, pitch that, when recycling bins are filled with dead screenplays and every clerk in the Beverly Center has a script. His students loved him, he was a great professor, and all he wanted was something he probably can't have.

I was relieved when Stig Fenton came in and Zack grimaced and moved on. Stig's wife Roseann gave me a kiss, drifting by in a bodysuit and chiffon skirt and so many bracelets that I should have guessed something was up. Their little girl slipped in behind them in matching chiffon and wouldn't look at me. Stig ducked his head and headed for the living room without saying anything beyond hi.

Jane Darrow came in last, apologizing because she was seeing patients until the last minute and by the time she started calling, it was too late to get a student to stay with the kids.

"It's OK," I said. "It's kids' day."

She grinned. "Every day is kids' day." My best friend Calvin's two sons rolled in from the hall where they'd been fighting. I was struck by how tough they were, tough and sturdy and loud. The little one hit the big one and when the big one hit back, the little one started to yell. Jane tried to shut them up, but I could see she was proud. "You guys!"

"Go find Lucky," I said. Next to these two, Lucky seemed so *quiet.* "He's in back."

"Cal's going to be late. He has a meeting." Jane added with a pleased look, because she always puts his business before her own, "at the Yale Club." I don't know why this was such a big deal, except that Cal secretly wished he'd gone to Yale.

Leslie materialized. The tears were gone. She looked perfect.

Plain Jane's face broke in a big smile. "You look *great.*"

Leslie hugged her, lying. "So do you."

I let Leslie pull Jane into the living room while Frieda herded the boys into Lucky's room, where my wife had laid on pizza and a cooler of Cokes and Dove Bars for the masses. Frieda was under orders to keep everybody out of sight. We buy silence at any cost.

But the Fentons' kid was still drifting in the foyer, looking like the blown flower Roseann had named her for. She was the same age as the others, around eleven, but with a look on her pretty, triangular face so complex that she could have been eighteen, or forty. I don't know why I went looking for her instead of following the others into the living room. Maybe I didn't want the afternoon to start. I spoke to her. She froze for an odd moment, studying me with violet eyes. I even remembered her name. "The guys are waiting, Hyacinth."

"Don't call me that." She gnawed her knuckles. "Speedy. Please."

"Speedy." I shooed her. "Why do you kids all hate your names?"

I went into the living room. It was everything Leslie intended: perfect. Late afternoon sunlight crashed through the long windows and bounced off the Hudson to pool on our white ceilings. Light was everywhere, catching in people's hair and warming her polished woods and shining glass surfaces. In my wife Leslie's rooms there were always freshly cut flowers; our kitchen looked like a stage set where no food came; she had a gift for keeping everything in its place. Her man. Our son. Even our friends, the major players of that summer, were arranged like ornaments in her beautiful living room. We could have been early Americans in a Grant Wood painting, sitting with our heads bent in the late afternoon light, waiting for the service to begin.

Walking cold into the group, you wouldn't necessarily place us in any age bracket. We could have been anybody, handsome, easy in shaggy sweaters, trendy jeans. Childless. Single. Young. Listen, a girl at the magazine told me I still looked like a thirty-two-year-old guy. I didn't disabuse her. When I looked in the mirror I didn't see a guy with an uptown life and an eleven-year-old that he couldn't talk to. The same kid I'd been at the beginning was still there in the mirror, looking back at me.

From the back room, thumps came. In spite of which the grownups looked untrammeled, gracefully disposed around

Leslie's sunny living room like figures in a Seurat. There were no outward signs of currents tugging underneath, or what might be running on ahead.

If we didn't see the future already written, how were we supposed to know? We were children of the late fifties turned out in millennium territory, proceeding without marching orders or a map. Tell yourself you're still young, turn your back for a second and the next generation springs up like dragon's teeth. Twenty-five-year-old kids running the show, with their unreadable kid faces and six-hundred-dollar suits. *If you're over forty,* one producer told me, *I don't return your calls.*

We still looked young. We looked fine. We were still OK, at least I thought we were, but somewhere just beneath the surface, assumptions were moving like seismic plates, about to shift and crack. We were at the moment when the camera tilts. You know that everything that comes after is going to be strange.

How were we supposed to know? The seven of us sat there dreaming along in the sunlight, suspended in of one of my wife's careful, beautiful arrangements, waiting for whatever came next. Zack and Polly were on the leather sofa, sitting close, while Jane spread out in a side chair in her big shirt, smiling her big smile, while I sat on the radiator, waiting to see where Leslie would sit to conduct this scene.

Next to Roseann on the love seat, Stig Fenton looked dull as usual in his banker's suit, but there was something different about him that day—beginning stubble, disrupted hair. Stig has always been as safe as houses, the kind of guy you would count on to make your money sprout, but that day he could have been put together in a factory that had sent him out badly assembled. Either the starched collar had gotten too big or my friend's neck had shrunk. His hair stood up in back. Roseann squirmed in Stig's shadow, with blue paint stuck in her hair. She was taking night classes in painting somewhere downtown. She flowed toward Stig in such a blur of good intentions that I should have known. When Leslie started showing pictures of the farm, even

I would be startled by the look the Fentons exchanged—the camera tilting, right?

But waiting for Leslie, drowsing in the sunlight on that pretty afternoon she had wrenched into existence with her bare hands, none of us focused on disorder. I sat with the sun warming my head and waited. For the first time in a long time, I was relaxed.

Don't think you know what the people sitting down with you are thinking, because you don't.

Leslie came in with stemmed glasses on a tray and smiled at me. I went to the kitchen and came back with champagne. Grave and quiet as a good boy, I poured Blanc de Noir while she held the tray with her head tilted, so the descending sun struck gold lights in her hair. Yes she was beautiful; yes she was still mad at me. And nobody would have known that, either.

"To us," somebody said, and my Leslie turned with that brilliant smile, correcting the toast.

"To continuity. To the summer." She looked into the bubbling surface of the champagne and then she flashed that smile on me. It was like a bank of klieg lights going on. "Chad?"

I was playing this scene with Leslie's suspicions between us, nothing proved, mind you, nothing definitive said, but if I was being judged here, this seemed only fair. "Me?"

She was waiting. "We're drinking to the farm."

"The farm . . ." Everybody was looking at me, and I understood that at such moments, when your world is tilted and vibrating underfoot, ready to slide you out of your life and into the next century, you hold yourself in place with existing forms. Somebody gives a party, you smile. Somebody toasts, you return the toast. Glowing with pleasure at the afternoon she had created, Leslie had made the first move. It was my turn. If things between us were going to be mended, it would begin with me bending to the occasion. Completing the toast. I smiled back. I said, "To the farm."

2

Summer's Lease

We were buzzed on champagne. The kids were stashed. Leslie had everyone's attention. She was lovely in the same way her rooms were lovely: simple, expensive, the best. *Oh don't dress up, it's just us,* she'd told her friends and then walked into her closet and walked out in one of those fuck-you costumes she put on like armor—silk shirt, concha belt. Next to the others, she shimmered.

Oh God, I thought, looking at her. *Oh, God.*

"About the farm," Leslie said. "We were in the country last weekend. I took the Darrows up to Massachusetts, prospecting. We found this farm? It's so deep in the country that nobody'll find us unless we want them to. The tourists haven't found this town, there aren't any skiers pushing prices up so the owners don't have a clue as to what it's really worth. Four bedrooms, plus one off the kitchen. It has a barn." She could have been proposing marriage; her eyes shone. "It's perfect for us, right Jane?"

"Just right."

"Look!" She passed the pictures around. "Jane's going to fill you in."

On cue, Jane beamed. "Twelve acres. Reservoir, where we can swim. We're getting it for a song. What do you think?"

I'd already seen the pictures. I cleared my throat.

Leslie silenced me with a look. She had that don't-start set to her delicate jaw. "Jane has all the details."

Blushing, Jane shifted in her seat. We could have been at the Bradys' house, with this motherly-looking smart woman playing Best Friend. Today Jane had put on self-effacing shades of brown—rumpled linen shirt, big brown-flowered skirt to hide her bottom half, squashy shoes. It was as if she'd been rehearsed. "We take it for three months with an option to buy, and if it works out . . ." Her face shone. "If it works out . . ."

Stig Fenton's mouth moved, but if words came out, we didn't hear. Leslie snapped, "Of course it will work out. If it works out . . ."

Jane flushed as if she and Leslie really were proposing marriage. Her face shone. "We can have it for as long as we want."

Completely innocent of all futures, my wife Leslie laughed. "If we like it, we could even move up and live there for good."

Jane laughed too. "Closed corporation."

Oh, Leslie! She said, "Together against the world."

While the rest of us sat with our heads bent in the sunlight like a good congregation waiting to be blessed. It made sense at the time. At the time it looked as though we were all trying to do the same thing, stay in love for life, bring up great families and have major careers. We'd come out of the same childhoods, played the same rock groups in the same years, marched on Washington together and gotten drunk in all the same places. We knew most of the same people and all the same gag lines. Was it Leslie's fault that she assumed we must all want the same things? When nobody jumped, Leslie prodded. "What do you think?"

Jane said, "Calvin's stuck at a meeting and he's going to be late but he wants you to know we've already signed the lease."

I looked at Leslie. "So it doesn't matter what we decide, it's already decided."

"Chad, be cool." Zack was so full of Hollywood dreams that everything looked good to him. "It could be a good place for all of us. This script I'm doing—I can make it an emblem for the turn of the century. I can make it big. If I can only get the time." He was serious and joyful. "Guys. I have work to do!"

To which Polly responded stiffly, "Maybe I do too."

Leslie prompted Zack. "You know. The pottery."

Polly had worked Zack's way through graduate school, and now he patted her pretty hair and said dutifully, "Right, the pottery."

"If I can get galleries to take my work, maybe I can quit teaching third grade."

When you teach college maybe it's built in that you condescend to people who teach third grade. Zack said, "Don't count your chickens yet."

Polly whipped her head around, but Zack just went: *Pretty Polly, there there,* silencing her with a pat on the thigh. Her curse was looking like a Barbie with a body perm. Unlesss it was teaching third grade.

Jane held out both hands. "You can do anything you want."

"I can do anything I want," Polly said.

"That's the whole thing about the farm." Leslie's eyes were too bright. "We can all do anything we want."

Yes I should have been warned.

Somebody said, "It'll be great for the kids."

"Get them out of the damn city where people keep ripping you off." Who was Zack selling, himself? Me? "Street gang took Gabe's bike last week—mugged him on the way to a birthday party. Kids!"

"Exactly. I'm scared to let Lucky go to the park." My wife had the papers on a plexi clipboard. "This is a lease with an option to buy. House. Outbuildings, everything. Each couple owns a fourth. If you want out later the rest of us buy you out."

From the love seat where he and Roseann sat with fingers linked, Stig said, surprisingly, "A third."

Now Roseann shifted in her seat. She looked lovely but haunted in her chiffon with wild blue paint flecking her hair;

she and Stig clung as if aroused by the fact that they were just about to be exquisitely unhappy

Leslie did not pick up on this. "You aren't committing to buy right now; all you're committing to is the rent."

Stig muttered, "We're not committing to anything."

"No way I won't finish this script." Zack caught me looking and pounced. "Chad'll read it for me. You'll read it for me, right?" As if he thought success was something you could catch.

"Sure," I said, but I was unsettled and conflicted. I hate being that far from the water. Hills make me feel shut in. I'd seen the pictures. The house was a wreck. Dark green shadows marched down on the farmhouse. The mountainside above was riddled with caves. Crevasses. Places where you could fall. There was probably some long-dead farmer hanging himself from a rafter in the shed chamber, or hurtling downhill on his tractor and wiping out on a rock. I was overcommitted and I couldn't be there much. The night Leslie came back from the farm she and I fought for hours, but then we made teeth-rattling love. I didn't know.

In the course of human events I had managed to forget or suppress a couple of things. You had to, just to keep on getting up in the mornings. Like the phoenix rising up I said, "Why not?"

Jane said, "We're good together."

I forgot everything, remembered Leslie's body. "We are."

Zack laughed. "We really are. Together we can . . ."

I knew what he meant—that old line from the novel *V*. "*You see, there are thirteen of us and together, we rule the world.*"

Leslie's look made it all almost worth it. "Oh, Chad."

Polly said, "We can share the chores."

I said, not too drily, "Brook Farm." I loved that she was smiling at me after the day we'd put in but I already heard the *ting* of a distant warning bell.

"We're going to be so *happy*," Leslie said.

I was aware of the decibel level rising in the hall that led from the back of the apartment, where the kids were stashed. I was aware of a clatter of bracelets: Roseann and Stig Fenton stirring on the love seat. They were drawn and feverish, swelled with importance and gathering themselves like stunt fliers about to take off.

Leslie thrust the clipboard at them. "What do you think?"

Once more, Stig tried to begin. "Listen, we . . ."

There was a stir in the hall; simmering kids coming to a boil.

Then Calvin blew in. "Hi gang." He was like a parade, so full of himself that everything stopped. *Miles gloriosus,* straight out of "A Funny Thing." Successful man, entering. At Doyle Dane, he brought in more income than anybody else, and while Jane wore the same old thing Cal dressed the part: blazer with gold buttons, crisp shirt, funky tie. He gusted past Leslie and hugged Jane, who went pink with pride. With a careless, expansive gesture my friend Calvin turned his wife into an instant beauty and something in me twisted in loss. Leslie and I were nothing like this. Before our eyes that plain woman became: Jane the cherished. I knew that more than anything, Calvin Darrow wanted what I had, but I felt the warmth and in that instant, I envied him.

"Oh Calvin," Leslie said, whirling. "All systems are Go!"

Stig and Roseann subsided. Their moment, whatever it was, had passed. The afternoon was aloft. Everybody started talking at once, hardly noticing the champagne at work, laughter drowning out the sounds of disorder from the back hall. Whatever our children were doing to each other back there, our sad, homesick girl Frieda would just have to cope. Leslie's hands flew as she described the garden she was going to put in. She produced the crabmeat, pâté. Some party. It was going to be like this all summer; it was going to be . . .

This of course was when the festivities fell into a shambles, Leslie's crystal surface shattered by the kids. The sequence began when Jane and Cal's two sons started fighting, tough, hardy, all-American siblings rolling down the hall in a wholesome tangle, solid Rocky on the bottom and his temperamental Alfred on top. Then Gabe Peterson piled on and Hyacinth call-me-Speedy followed, snowballing in a knot that collected kids like the tarbaby and rolled into the living room, toppling ornaments and smearing Leslie's pâté into the rug.

Leslie cried, "Oh lord."

Jane said, "Oh, Alfred!"

Both boys said, "I didn't start it, he did."

Everybody else said, "Oh shit."

"Cut it out!" Quick and angry, Calvin separated his Cain and Abel: Rocky fell silent while angel-faced Alfred combed those red Orphan Annie curls with his fingers and howled with remorse. For no apparent reason Gabe hit his head on the corner of the glass coffee table and started to bleed. Polly, who had two other boys away at school, applied pressure and stopped the bleeding without turning a hair. Glad to be the center for once, Gabe bowed his head with a gratified grin. Children milled, screaming with excitement, reminding those assembled that no matter who we thought we were, we were parents after all.

Leslie fretted over the wreckage while distanced from it all, our only son leaned against the walnut end table with a look that made it clear that whatever was happening, he had somehow started it. Next to the others Lucky looked pale and weedy, like a flawed Leslie. He was too smart, was one problem. The other was, he knew this, and it embarrassed him. I thought: *God, I love him. God, I don't know why I don't like him more,* if like was what I meant. I thought, *Maybe if I'd asked for him.* The baby was Leslie's idea, and on and off the books he was really Leslie's kid.

("Listen," I said, the first time she brought it up. We faced off over it, me home from a long day at the *News.* My first job. "I can't do this and that too." She accused me, "That job is more important to you than I am." How could I explain? My Leslie, rattling around our first apartment, which she'd filled and polished to perfection. She cried, "I've run out of things to do." I pleaded with her, "We're too young to start a family." She was. I shouldn't have let her quit college to marry me. I was astounded by her anger. "That's all right for you to say." On the spot she set the rhetoric for the rest of our lives together: "You have your job. I don't have anything.")

I gave in. How could I know it was going to put me on the front lines? When you have a kid there's never a time in your life that you can with any confidence put that person down and say, *There.* You can't pat them in place and expect them to stay.

You start hearing the clock. It's your—what? Intimation of mortality. Living yardstick, measuring you off. You have a son to remind you that no matter how beautiful the setting and no matter how tightly organized your schemes, you are split seconds away from accidents and surprises, disruption and chaos. Getting old.

I should have felt sorry for Leslie—all this confusion in the middle of her beautiful, carefully laid scene, but it was somehow vindicating, watching kids boil into her perfect living room, wrecking things. Alfred was blaming Rocky, blaming Gabe, blaming the dog, while poor Frieda scooped up the pâté, cross-eyed from trying to pick out the fuzz, and call-me-Speedy bent over the glass coffee table like a wilted flower. With her back to her parents she was moving the ashtray like the counter on a ouija board, and call-me-Lucky bent over her, rattling off imagined notes from the spirit world. I wanted to grab them both and shake: *What is it with you?*

Lucky said, "It says, Friends, Romans, countrymen . . ."

Rocky joined in. "It says mene, mene, tekel upharsin."

Little Alfred was still in a red haze: face red with anger, angry red hair.

"Oh, shh," Jane said, but she was laughing.

Leslie tried hard to preserve what she had wrought, as if getting the right names in the right order on her designer clipboard would demonstrate that the disruption was only temporary. Once she had everybody signed up, they could take their kids and go. She rushed Zack with the lease while our humiliated au pair tried fruitlessly to take control and everybody else assessed damages, rehearsing parental speeches for later.

Not, perhaps, the best time for Stig to clear his throat and say, from the doorway, "I'm terribly sorry, but we can't."

"Oh shit," I said, so fast that I didn't know how I knew.

Leslie wheeled on Stig. "Of course you can."

But it was a holding action only; she'd lost control of the afternoon Snowballing into my wife's carefully constructed urban Eden, the kids had raised the possibility of disorder, releasing Stig to disrupt Leslie's scheme. Enabled, he said what he had not been able to say from the depths of Leslie's velvet love seat, with sunlight in his hair and his mouth fizzy with Leslie's champagne.

Forms. I wondered. Without the kids' mess, the noise and confusion, would Stig and Roseann have gone along and signed the lease like good sheep and therefore kept it together? Would he and Roseann have stayed married for good?

Stig blurted, "We can't." Once it was out in the open, his sorrow expanded. Embarrassed, he said, "We need our space."

"You can at least afford August." Leslie rushed him with the clipboard.

"Don't, Les." Zack put out an arm like a traffic cop. "Give him a break."

Stig was miserable. The guy who looked as safe as houses couldn't even protect his own. If you studied his calm banker's surface you could see that it had already begun to fissure; there was a different kind of Stig stirring behind the comfortable facade and now, under pressure, that person was about to emerge; he said too loud, "Listen, OK?"

We could have been the children, sitting quietly while Stig broke the news like the dad in the old pop song: *You'd better sit down, kids. And listen to me.*

Feeling strangely consolidated, I thought: Oh, right, Leslie's mad at Stig, not me. Had safe, dependable old Stig turned out to be a rat? He was earnest and cryptic, with his voice dry, his face too grey. Cough. Ahem. "Not everything is the way you think it is, OK? So . . . Ah." He coughed. "We're working it out. Right, Roseann?"

So it was Stig Fenton who breached the surface of our assumptions, driving the first wedge.

"Oh, you bastard," Leslie said under her breath.

Ever the professional, Jane offered, "Maybe counseling . . ."

This is how Stig surprised us. He bared his teeth. "Don't think you can see into somebody else's marriage, because you can't."

Roseann's voice was light. "Don't look so upset everybody, it's just a temporary thing. We're getting our heads together, no biggie."

Jane said gently, "Tell us all about it," and Stig's eyes got wet. I clenched my teeth because there was the agonizing possibility that they would.

But Roseann turned on her old friend and snapped: "Back off."

Leaving Stig to say, "Sorry to wreck your summer plan, but we have our priorities. So if you'll just bear with us . . ."

By this time Roseann's eyes were like crumpled violets with water standing in them. She went soft. "We just need some time."

Stig said, with genuine suffering, ". . . and try to understand."

Leslie put her arm around Roseann in an open demonstration of solidarity. Polly murmured there there and so did Jane; if we had to take sides, the women would line up with Roseann.

At the end, when the afternoon had crashed and we were all in the foyer assembling coats, kids, sweet-looking Roseann let the elevator doors close on Stig and their hyacinth girl Speedy and sent them down to the lobby alone. Then, before we even guessed what she was up to, she stirred in a jangle of bracelets like a helicopter about to lift, and began. "I hate not going to the farm."

Leslie said the right thing. "We hate your not being there."

Jane offered, "You can always come up and visit us."

Surprise! Roseann said, quick as that! "Can't. I'm tied up."

"All summer?"

Instead of answering, she blushed. "I'm really sorry about it, I mean, I don't mind about me, but poor Hyacinth. She was counting on it so much!"

Roseann wanted Leslie or me to say, No problem, we'll take care of her! But there is a myth all parents know. If you accept responsibility for somebody else's baby, even for an hour, you may get stuck with it. Accept someone else's child and it's yours for life. It stops being their responsibility. It becomes yours.

I saw the whites of Leslie's eyes flash as she shook her head.

Polly shamed us all. Hugging Zack, she turned to Roseann. "If it'll help, we can take Speedy to the farm."

Before she even finished, Roseann pounced. "For the summer?"

In the old movie *Land of the Pharaohs,* somebody cuts a rope and far away, huge blocks of stone start an inexorable passage that is not immediately apparent to the principals. One by one we thudded into place with a shudder, sealing the pyramid. When the women freed Roseann, something stirred and tore the first cord. Somewhere near the periphery the first stone of that summer came loose and started to move . . .

Wait a minute, I thought uneasily. Hey, wait. But in seconds Roseann had lodged Speedy for the summer, like, *That's that.* If she thought it was a simple logistical problem, easily handled, she was wrong. At the time she thanked us all like a grateful guest leaving a party. "Leslie. Polly. You guys are wonderful. I thank you, Hyacinth thanks you, Derek thanks you . . ."

"Derek!"

"Oops!" Too late, Roseann stuffed her hand in her mouth to keep from smiling that odd, secret smile.

Surprise, the rat was never Stig. It was Roseann.

3

Rocky

Rocky got up early because he couldn't stand Alfred. Mom
and Dad had all the groanies over for pizza after the thing at
Lucky's house. They stayed late and left after 1 a.m., going,
thank you Jane, thank you Calvin. Mrs. Burgess was thin and
chic but there was so much glass in her living room that even the
grownups were afraid of breaking her stuff. Grandma Darrow's
great big squashy chairs and sofa lay around in Rocky's living
room, waiting for you to fall into them. His friends could jump
up and down on the kingsized bed and nobody would yell at
him. Besides, everybody liked Jane better. So after the pizza the
groanies hung out in the living room and the kids spied on
them. It sounded like they were having fun in there. They stayed
up late so everybody was still sleeping, even Alfred. If Rocky
sneaked, he could have the house to himself for once.

On Saturdays the rules were you could do anything you
wanted at Rocky's house, as long as you were quiet. You could
put M&Ms and peanut butter in your Cap'n Crunch if you
wanted to, or eat all the cookie dough ice cream. You could take
your dish in the living room and eat in front of the color TV. You
could play Nintendo or set fire to the sofa as long as you didn't
wake up Mom and Dad. Rocky could sit and just *be* without
Alfred bothering him.

He squeezed Pop Tart frosting on his peanut butter toast and
took it in the living room. He had the new *Watchman* comic

book. He loved the silence. He loved that the day was border-line—not really light out, not exactly dark.

The trouble was, there was a dad left over. Speedy's father was laid out on the Darrows' living-room sofa with his head stuck under Jane's Guatemalan serape pillow to make him think he was alone in here. Rocky thought maybe Mr. Fenton got so drunk that Mom was afraid he was going to stagger out and get hit by a car, but the truth was he probably slept over because he didn't have anyplace else to go. They heard last night the Fentons were Having Problems, but Speedy just laughed and jumped up and down on the king-sized bed with her hair flying up and nobody mentioned it because it was so embarrassing.

It was embarrassing finding Mr. Fenton here. Rocky tried to tiptoe out backward, but somewhere in there, Mr. Fenton heard him. He rolled over and the pillow fell off. So there he was, plopped in the middle of Saturday morning like an extra piece of furniture, this big messy heap smack in the middle of this hour when Rocky had expected to be alone for once. He slept facing the TV, looking ruined in his T-shirt and boxers, and the worst thing was, the boxer fly fell open and this sleeping dork was lolling out? It was limp and terrible, embarrassing. Mr. Fenton's pink face was blurry, rumpled as if he'd been crying in his sleep. The worst thing was, the two naked parts of the guy that showed right now both looked kind of alike. Like, essentially spoiled? Pink crumpled penis, pink crumpled face. It was humiliating. Rocky wanted to wake up Mr. Fenton so he could apologize for seeing it.

Then, shit. Alfred stumbled in. "You ate all the ice cream."

"Shut up."

"What's that?"

Rocky hissed, "Shut up."

But Alfred was bending over Mr. Fenton. He was bending so close that his breath ruffled Mr. Fenton's face. Rocky grabbed him. "Don't wake him up."

Alfred got louder, "What are you doing?"

Rocky tightened his fingers. "I said, Shut *up*."

"I will not. Ow, you're hurting me."

He jerked Alfred away, grinding his knuckles into Alfred's neck. "You. You think you can get away with anything."

"I want to watch TV." Alfred knew what he was doing and he did it anyway. "I WANT TO WATCH TV."

"You're going to get us killed."

"I'M NOT DOING ANYTHING."

So Rocky thought, *Fuck you. Fuck all baby brothers everywhere.* Everything bad that ever happened to Rocky started with Alfred. For the first year he was all alone in the garden with the Mom, the Dad, happy as the three bears. At Valentine's Mom made three interlocking paper dolls with bears' faces and round bear ears and big bear smiles and put their names on them: Jane, Calvin, Rocky. He still has them somewhere. Then one day the snake came in. They were so proud when they came home with it and showed him the thing in the blanket. "Look, you have a baby brother. His name is Alfred," this squirming little ugly *thing*. Other people live their lives without being bothered, but every day Rocky did battle with the enemy, who came late and had his number.

Alfred knew just exactly what to say and do to drive Rocky up the wall. Like turning on the TV with Mr. Fenton just lying there. Rocky barked so loud it made Mr. Fenton jump. "Don't do that!"

"I SAID I WANT TO WATCH TV." Alfred turned it on anyway. What did he have to lose? He never got blamed for anything.

Rocky whispered, "What are you *doing*?"

"I'M WATCHING CARTOONS."

"Shut up, it's only six-thirty!"

This pebbly voice said, "It doesn't matter." It didn't. Mr. Fenton was awake.

Rocky was scared to look, but he did. Thank God the dork was covered up.

Alfred had this grin that made grownups think he was some

kind of cherub. "I told you not to turn it on, Rocky." Louder. "Mr. Fenton, I told Rocky not to, but he said he didn't care what you wanted, it was his house and his TV."

"It's cool." Mr. Fenton rubbed his hair with a wonky grin and went off to the bathroom. He didn't care if Alfred lied or not. He just came back with a beer and sat on the sofa and watched cartoons with them, eating leftover crusts from last night's pizza. After a long time he said, "I guess your folks are still asleep."

Rocky didn't say anything. If Mr. Fenton was that hungry, let him get his own damn cereal.

But the guy wouldn't take care of himself. This guy Stig, supposed to be a grownup, he just sat on the sofa in his underwear and gnawed crusts and watched cartoons with them. Dumb Stig, if he'd only shut up it would have been OK, but when they were getting into the new Batman, he started. "I bet you guys are bored."

Nobody wanted to answer. He said, "I know Hyacinth gets bored to death on Saturdays when I'm asleep and..." He was a grown man, and he thought they didn't hear his voice wobbling? ". . . her mom is still asleep. Ah. The difference is. Ah. Poor Speedy doesn't have any nice brothers or sisters to keep her company."

Nice brothers, right.

Alfred went, Hee hee. He looked like a rubber troll with the Dynel orange curls and that smarmy smirk; Rocky wanted to smash it off his face.

But Mr. Fenton was fishing for something. "I mean, like you guys?" He sounded like he was about to cry. "You're never alone. I mean, you have each other, right?"

Rocky gave Alfred the finger. Mr. Fenton didn't want to see. All Mr. Fenton wanted was to make Rocky and Alfred help him get it together, even though he was the grownup. "So I'm going to do you guys a favor, OK guys?"

Rocky and Alfred skidded backward on their butts, too late.

Mr. Fenton gave them this party smile. "You can make as much noise as you want at my house."

He said they were all three going over, forget the subway, he'd pay for a taxi to the west side and pick up some Dunkin' Donuts for everyone. Speedy had a new video she was waiting to watch until she had some company to watch it with. When they asked him what was it he didn't exactly answer; he said, "Something, you know, that one you all wanted to see?" and when Alfred said, "You mean the new Batman?" he went yeah yeah, that's probably the one. He said they were going to have fun. They didn't want to go but he wrote a note and made them get dressed and sneak out so they wouldn't wake Mom and Dad. It turned out Mr. Fenton was scared to go into his own apartment all by himself, but he wouldn't say that to Rocky or Alfred. He said he was taking them away so their folks could sleep, but that was a lie. He said they were doing Speedy a big favor by going to play with her, but that wasn't the truth either.

He said, "She doesn't have anything to do while her mom's sleeping."

He said, "Her mom isn't herself, lately. She's been. Ah. Sick."

He said, "I'll get you guys Blimpies for lunch."

He said, "If you want to, I'll get two quarts of Cherry Garcia."

At least they went in a cab.

It was dark in the Fentons' apartment because all the shades were down. Alfred said, too loud, "This is creepy."

Mr. Fenton cleared his throat. "The cleaning lady couldn't come this week."

"That's too bad." Rocky knew they didn't have a cleaning lady. It was like walking into a swamp. The living room was messy; it was like a kid's room right before the Mom comes in and gives them hell for not cleaning up. Some of the furniture was broken. There were clothes and papers everywhere, overflowing ashtrays, smeared glasses, plates with dried food on them; it looked old. This wasn't party mess, and as it turned out it wasn't kid mess either. It came from a slow buildup—days, weeks, months of layers, grease and cigarette butts and stains where the dog had peed. The dog had dragged plants and dirt out of their pots; there was a dirty bra under the TV.

At least Mr. Fenton had stopped pretending he was doing something nice for them. He said, to nobody, "She gave up on this place when she gave up on me."

Mr. Fenton paddled through the dirty clothes, wading mournfully toward the groanies' bedroom. Rocky grabbed Alfred before he could say anything and dragged him back to Speedy's room. The big difference here was that Speedy's room was clean. She had also made her bed with the flowered quilt and she was sitting on it in her pink fur bathrobe with her feet pulled up like a person on a raft, watching cartoons on the little black-and-white TV.

Speedy looked up. "It's He-Man and She-Ra."

"Neat-o."

Across the hall, a conversation started; Speedy just scrunched up her face and turned up the volume. They watched until Rocky and Bullwinkle came on. They had to ignore the yelling. It was Mr. and Mrs. Fenton plus some guy. Speedy had her shoulders hunched and her collar pulled up to cover her ears so she wouldn't hear. Rocky would never say anything, but Alfred.

God damn Alfred said, "What's that?"

"Nothing."

"Yes it is."

"Shut up." Rocky squirmed. Was Alfred so stupid he didn't know? But he wouldn't shut up. "Who is that other guy?"

"Nobody."

Alfred got louder. "I hear another guy."

Speedy groaned. "It's Derek."

Rocky punched him. "Shut *up!*"

"Who's Derek?" Alfred said anyway.

"My mother's boyfriend, OK?" Speedy's eyes were grey. Her face was so smooth Rocky could almost see his reflection in it.

"Oh." Typical Alfred; when he got into these things, he couldn't stop. "Maybe we ought to call our folks or something?"

Speedy said, "Never mind."

"I mean, Mr. and Mrs. Fenton are having a fight."

"Forget it."

"Or the super?"

"Don't be an asshole, Alfred."

"SPEEDY, YOUR PARENTS ARE HAVING A FIGHT."

Rocky had no choice: he hit Alfred hard. They tangled, and because there weren't any grownups around to give Rocky hell for fighting with his baby brother, he could let him have it for real.

Then there was this big noise out in the hall. Speedy slammed the door and turned up her television.

At the end, Mr. Fenton left so fast he forgot he had brought over extra kids. Rocky wanted to run out of the apartment after him yelling, Wait for me, anything to get out of that dim place, but Speedy was looking at him hopefully. "Want a Pop Tart?"

It was a bribe.

Alfred said, "I want to go home."

"Pop Tart?" Rocky straight-armed him. "Sure."

"I want to go . . ."

"I would love a Pop Tart."

Alfred said, "With Marshmallow Fluff."

Speedy looked like he'd smacked her in the face. "We're out of Marshmallow Fluff."

Rocky said quickly, "Whatever, OK? Whatever it is, it's fine."

They got Pop Tarts out of that filthy kitchen and then they sat on Speedy's bed watching TV until the phone rang. When nobody picked it up Speedy went out in the hall to answer, and when she came back she said, "It's your mom. She wants you to come home." Her face smoothed out. "She says I should come with you guys."

When they went out, the door to Mrs. Fenton's bedroom

was open. They were still in there, Speedy's mom and this guy Derek snuggled under the covers, he guessed they were sleeping; Rocky thought the name sounded sharp, like the blade of an axe. He gave Alfred a push and they went by the door fast, without looking in.

God he was so scared; it was like there was a big black pit and he had to walk across it on a wire.

On the crosstown bus Rocky could feel his teeth getting jagged. He felt like the werewolf in the middle of the change. What if the bus crashed and they all got killed? What if Con Edison was secretly digging and the street collapsed and they fell into a pit? What if he threw up here right in front of everyone? What if they got home and there wasn't any building, just a smoking hole?

Then they got home and home was still there. Mom was cooking, and Rocky's mouth flooded with gratitude. Good old frozen pizza. Good old brownies. Good old Mom. She said after lunch she was taking them to *Batman Forever* at the Trans Lux. Again. Even though it felt like he and Alfred had been gone for years, nobody's hair had turned white while they were at the Fentons'. They looked the same and the apartment was exactly the same. His mom had picked up Mr. Fenton's pillows off the sofa and taken away the dirty glasses from last night and rearranged the Indian throw to cover up the burn Mr. Fenton's cigarette had made in the upholstery. His dad was watching baseball like always, and typical Dad, Calvin was working on a new layout for one of his accounts at the same time, moving things around on the screen of his laptop in front of the TV. The house smelled the same and in the kitchen Mom had the opera going just the way she did every Saturday.

When they sat down to lunch, their mom had their old *Spiderman* placemats on the table along with the Bruce Lee mugs. It didn't matter how many same things he numbered, Rocky couldn't stop squinting. He had to make sure there was nothing new or different. He was a little crazy with it, but in the end he thought everything was probably fine.

In spite of which, when Jane came in to tell him and Alfred good night Rocky heard this tumbling out of his mouth. "Mom, when you get divorced I'm going to spend six months with Dad and six months with you."

As she hugged him hard, he shot Alfred a triumphant look over her shoulder: *the first-born*. It's me she hugs. But Rocky kept holding her tight, demanding assurances. "Right Mom?"

Kissing his hair, she said, "Don't be an asshole."

4

The Kids

So for Easter we were all going up to Massachusetts to try out this farm? Some kind of summer preview.

"Aren't you excited?"

Not like you'd think. We would've been just as happy if they'd gotten the five of us our own apartment. We were together all the time anyway, this just made it easier.

Mom and Dad were more excited about it than we were. It sounded too far away from everything. They were all, "Wait'll you see how great this part of New England is," so you wanted to know what was the matter with it. Unspoiled, they said, no Four Flags near Eaglemont, Mass., no sir. No cineplex, no malls trashing up the landscape, not one McDonald's or Wendy's. Like, what's the *point?* "Caves," they said. "Think *Tom Sawyer.*" You couldn't go, "Wait," and if you went, *"No malls,"* they'd get all hurt and say, "We're doing this for you," like this farm was our big present.

Look, there would be chickens and pigs this, hayloft that, hills to climb and a reservoir to swim in, oh by the way, TV reception sucks up there because of the mountains but you guys are going to have so much fun outside that you'll never notice. OK, they were bringing a VCR and some tapes in case we freaked with no TV. Then they promised us new bikes so we would have fun up there all summer, when what they meant was they'd buy us anything if only we'd go off and play and not bother them.

Everybody knows that even if you have a ton of stuff, it's never the right stuff.

That year we had Power Rangers and Mr. Potato Head and Slime; we had Pop Rocks and Play-Doh and Creepy Crawly and Incredible Edibles and Silly Putty and Bubble Stuff. Lucky had the most expensive toys, from a Skeanateles set to this knight's helmet out of real tin with yellow ostrich plumes and the matching sword and shield, the kind of thing his great-grandmother buys. Gabe had a Lionel train set handed down from his big brothers, and about a million Legos and a chemistry set. We had Koosh balls and Slinkies and all the Power Rangers stuff, and Speedy had a Barbie that Alfred had put a GI Joe head on it. We had Etch-a-Sketch and astronaut helmets, some of us, and the ones whose folks thought toy guns were cool had the laser pistol that shot water or the plastic Uzi that rattled like a real one. Alfred still had all his stuffed animals. People were always telling us to pick up our toys and get our junk out from under the beds. We kept our old bikes and sleds and skates in the back hall, along with discarded training wheels and skateboards and springs you strapped on like roller skates so you could jump around, sprong sprong; some dad was always going: I told you to move that stuff so we can still get out of the apartment in case of fire.

We were always over at each other's houses.

At the Darrows' house Alfred and Rocky could do anything they wanted as long as they didn't bother their mom while she was with her patients. She heard their troubles in her office behind the dining room and after she told them what to do she came out and made cookies for us, except she always ate half of them. At Lucky's house we got Entemann's and ice-cream sand-wiches from the au pair girl, who had a chapped nose from cry-ing all the time, and when Frieda locked herself in her room you could drop water bombs off the terrace balcony. We didn't play at Speedy's much after her mom moved out, it was too creepy. Gabe's mom gave us cocoa and Pop Tarts no matter what time of day it was and then she let us play with clay in the maid's room, which she kept calling her studio. We got Flintstones vitamins and Ninja Turtles cereal even after everyone was sick of them. We got Cap'n Crunch and Quake at home, Lucky Charms and Count Chocula and Eggos because our moms wanted us to have a good breakfast. When we were together we had Hot Pockets or frozen pizza for lunch, depending on whose house it was, and milk or Cokes, depending on which mom was deciding. We had hot dogs, a lot; frozen pot pies if the groanies were having a party and desserts made from a mix if we had to eat early because somebody was sleeping over and our folks were going out.

For school we wore what you wear, except for Speedy, whose mom had this thing about flowered skirts that Speedy just hated. Our jeans went out at the knees before they ever faded right, and they turned into highwaters in no time, all except Lucky; his mom threw out clothes as soon as they started looking like you wanted. Nobody's socks matched. Everybody's hair was growing out except for Lucky, whose mom stood over him while the person at Bergdorf's cut it. As soon as he got outside he hid it with a headband, that was cool. Speedy's hair was pale and long enough to sit on; she was a space case even before her folks broke up. Rocky was the handsomest, Lucky the smartest and Gabe the mellowest; Alfred was the leader, nobody knew why except he wanted it so bad.

We messed around a lot. Once we put Mrs. Burgess's *crème de menthe* and Pernod on top of ice cream and got all weird. Stupid Frieda thought we were delirious from the flu. Mrs. Burgess was OK about Alfred throwing up on Lucky's bed but when she found out how much liquor was gone, she wouldn't let us come over for a month. At Speedy's we made dopey phone calls and the next time we were allowed to go to Lucky's we put broken Coke bottle in all the underwear. We were going to put aspirin in the moms' birth-control things but they were too big for the little pink holes.

Our folks said, Be careful what people try to give you. Pills are the most dangerous because you don't know what's in them. They said, There is a lot of bad stuff going down. When you're out playing, don't take anything from anyone you don't know, no transfers that could be acid tabs, don't take anything they say will make you feel good. They said, Don't ever smoke pot, it will only lead to a lot worse things, but everybody knew Mr. Peterson did grass with his students and Lucky smelled something funny at his parents' big parties, and Mrs. Darrow had this kitchen window box that she said it was all herbs for cooking? Mr. Peterson was in a psych experiment at Columbia; they gave him L.S.D. and a notebook. He was supposed to write down what he thought. Lucky's mom took Valium for some reason and Gabe's mom had it for muscle pains in her back from bending over the pottery bench and the moms talked a lot about Prozac because they had friends that it had saved their lives. Alfred and Rocky's dad took all these pills at breakfast. We were in fifth grade before we figured out it was vitamins.

The 'rents said, Be good and have fun and most important, try never to hurt anybody. They said, We want to be your *friends,* but when we got in trouble, they spanked us all the same, and when we tried to hang out with them, they said, Why don't you go watch TV?

Our parents said, Would you turn that thing down?

They said, Go away and play, but other times they liked hanging out with us. We watched TV football with Mr. Burgess and Mr. Darrow at the Darrows' house, they got into it and yelled a lot. Mr. Peterson was writing this vampire movie that was going to take him to Hollywood so we got to watch all his horror tapes with him, he kept going, What do you think about this part? Are you scared yet? The moms took us to movies. Sometimes the 'rents were as good as big kids, we'd fool around together until we forgot which words it was *not* OK to use in front of them, hanging out until we started having too much fun and forgot who they were. Then the marker went up: Grownup here.

Wait till we grow up. Then we'll be in charge. Grownups can do anything they want.

Since it was Easter they bought all this Easter stuff to take up to the country. We had plastic grass and jellybeans and candy eggs in the car, along with shrink-wrapped chocolate bunny-rabbits that Lucky's mom bought to put at each person's place for the Easter brunch—we ate everything before we ever got off the Taconic. They got us gliders and Mylar balloons and laser tag, they brought Monopoly and Twister, water guns, plastic models that we'd never have time to put together; they brought comic books, malt balls, speckled eggs with chocolate inside and Gameboy and puzzle books and Pustafix. The only thing they refused to bring was Nintendo, but they brought everything else they could think of to keep us happy, by which they meant, anything to keep us quiet.

The trip took forever.

You went up the Taconic to the throughway and headed for the Mass Pike and drove and drove. After too long you turned off and started heading back down, on this back road that took you into deep Massachusetts. Here's how deep: you could drive and drive without seeing one thing you were used to seeing. It was all broken trees and run-down houses, overgrown shacks with rusting cars and things like fridges submerged in the mud in front of them. We stopped thinking it was going to be great and went to sleep. When we woke up we were on some desperate country road with rocks rising on either side. Even though it was warm that day there was leftover snow bunched in the dirt and ice like Elmer's Glue running down the rocks in places, so it was like driving back into winter. We sat up, going, Are we there yet? Are we there yet? Are we ever going to get there?

Finally the road straightened out and Lucky's father stopped. We all stopped. Off to the right we saw a tilted post with an old-fashioned mailbox: J.EDEN.

Then one by one the cars nosed onto the dirt driveway and we came down the hill into the last valley. Big old house with a

shaggy roof and its paint worn off so the naked wood shone
through, giving way to a shed that gave way to this big old barn.
Our folks took forever making a turn at the last big tree and
parking in the turnaround. They said, "This is it."

We yelled, "The barn!"

Mom said, "You'll freeze out there."

"We don't care."

"Take your coat," Mom said and wouldn't let us go until we
did. Alfred hit the ground first because he has to be first at
everything; Rocky came after, trying to look like he wasn't running, but everybody was. Speedy and Gabe both fell out the
tailgate of the Petersons' Volvo wagon and Lucky came out of
his father's car, he was so sick of riding in the back with dumb
old Frieda that he fell down and scrambled up already running,
he could hardly wait to get away from her. If that's what he was
running away from.

Mrs. Burgess was going, "Chad, how do you like it?"

Sure they expected us to help carry stuff inside, but except for
Mrs. Burgess, who was standing there stressing because Mr.
Burgess hadn't said anything, the groanies were clumped in the
turnaround, hanging out and laughing because the best thing
about long car trips is when you finally stop. Mr. Darrow and
Mr. Burgess were opening beers for everyone, so we thought we
were going to get away without being noticed. Then Lucky's
mom yelled, "Wait!" and came running after him. She snatched
him so suddenly that his eyes bugged and his tongue stuck out
like a Goo-Goo doll's.

"Timothy. Not so fast." She would not let go. "Somebody's
going to get hurt."

He gave her a weird look. "What are you so mad about?"

"I'm not mad," she said. "I'm just. I just want you to be careful." Then she said the dumbest thing. "We'll have an egg hunt
on Easter if you guys promise to be good."

Even Alfred stopped.

What was that about?

But Lucky shook loose with this embarrassed grin and took off for the barn while his mom stood there in the turnaround getting all pink for no reason and looking ready to cry. We followed him. The barn was dark and mouldy. It looked like it was falling apart. She would never follow us in there.

Inside, we forgot everything. It was like going through the wardrobe into Narnia, or coming down in the cyclone and landing in Oz. We saw humongous dead farm machinery and we heard small things rustling in the straw, rats maybe, unless it was birds. It was dark and smelly in there and still cold from the winter, but then Lucky found the light switch and we saw the loft.

Somebody whispered, "It looks like a stage."

Everybody wanted to be first in the loft. Alfred pushed Rocky out of the way. "Fuck you, Rocky. You're just oldest, not first."

Rocky shrugged and let him go ahead. "Fuck you too."

Speedy was next up the ladder, and if she was quiet that day it was because her folks weren't even coming this weekend, she'd had to ride up to Eaglemont with Gabe and the Petersons when everybody else was stuck with their parents—the mom, the dad, one of each. When she went in the house to go to the bathroom Gabe told Lucky that Speedy put her head down and pretended to go to sleep in the car because she wanted to cry without anybody finding out. It was like being around a sick person; you were still their friend but everything was different, like they might have gotten something you could catch.

Never mind. Rocky went next, and then Gabe went.

Finally we were all up there hanging over the edge except for Lucky, who stood down there in the straw with his arms spread, looking up at us. He grinned.

"Are you coming or what?"

He stood down below looking up at us with this goofy grin. He didn't climb up. He didn't say anything. He just threw his arms out and started spinning around.

"Lucky?"

He looked so happy! "This is great." So nobody could say what it was with Lucky, except that Friday afternoon he was happy and Saturday morning he was something else.

"Look," Alfred started prancing around. "A stage! What if we give a play?" But it was only stupid Alfred, so we hung back and pretended not to hear.

But Lucky heard. He stopped spinning and looked up. "A play?"

Alfred curled his fingers and turned. You'd think he was already wearing the cape. "Right, a play. I'm gonna be Batman, and you can be Superman."

"A play." Something clicked inside Lucky. He grinned. "Why not?" That got him up the ladder and into the loft. He started pacing off the space, figuring. "Hey, guys!"

"What?"

"Let's give them a bitchin' play." He squatted and pulled us into a circle. He was looking, what, tickled to death. "If the groanies like it, they'll let us do anything we want."

"The groanies?"

He laughed. "Like we're giving it for ourselves?"

We all had our agendas even though we couldn't have told you what they were. Of course we wanted the groanies there.

Alfred was all over it. "Batman. Let's do Batman."

Gabe said, "Bats. I'm sick of bats."

"Whatever," Lucky said.

Alfred started with his goddam Batman tryouts, he was going to make us all jump out of the loft and land in poses, so we'd be forced to admit he was the best Batman. He was first; he flew down and came back up so he could judge the rest. Lucky went next; he landed in the hay and started to laugh. Then Speedy went, even though Alfred was already sneering, like, "Who ever heard of a girl Batman?" Rocky is cool with heights, but Gabe is not, so he ended up stalled at the edge. He was the very last one.

We said, "Come on, Gabe, jump."

Alfred walked up his heels. "Jump or you'll never be Batman."

Gabe lied. "I don't even want to be Batman."

But Alfred was crowding him and going: "Chicken, chicken, puck puck puck."

Gabe just stood there on the edge, hunching his shoulders and looking miserable.

Then Lucky swarmed up the ladder like a pirate boarding a ship. He said, "Fuck you, Alfred," and pushed Alfred off.

So in the end Lucky played Batman, and he made Rocky be Robin because they were best friends. Alfred went back to the house and found a high-school cheerleader's megaphone in the shed chamber where we were all supposed to sleep. He brought it back and played director until we murdered him. Speedy did all the girl parts and Gabe was in charge of sets and lights.

When they called us in for dinner it was dark, and as we ran across the strips of light falling out of the kitchen windows Lucky grabbed Rocky's arm. Air came out of Lucky; he was half laughing, half whispering, "I wish we could stay here forever and ever and never have to go back."

Rocky was Lucky's best friend so he had to say, "Right!"

At dinner that night everything was warm. The room was warm, the colors were warm, the glow in the fireplace was warm. The food was warm and rich-looking, piled up on the table in plates and serving bowls. It it was like being on TV. We all sat down at one big table with our heads bent like a farm family, seriously mellow. When they sent us to bed it sounded like a rerun of *The Waltons.* "G'night, Ma," "G'night, Pa," and if the shed chamber was cold and a little creepy because it was the first time we slept in there, well, hey.

In the morning we took food out to the barn, chocolate bunnyrabbits and Doritos and Count Chocula, never mind rats. We hurt ourselves a lot, falling off things and getting scratched on rusty nails, but we would never tell, partly because nobody wanted the tetanus shot but partly because nobody wanted to stop. Lucky brought out what looked like the tag end of a joint, and if he was a little *weird* Saturday, we thought it was because of that.

The dads offered to drive us into town in Eaglemont, we thought why not, but Lucky got this funny look, like we were deserting him. He said, "We've got to do the play," making it sound like a game we had to win. So we stayed back and rehearsed. He made us rehearse even after we got sick of it; by the end of the day he was so strung out on it that he wouldn't let us quit.

At the last minute Alfred decided to put himself in the play. He said he was the director, and the director always got his own way. He played the Penguin. The trouble was he kept padding his part, so we had to keep adding stuff to say back to his stuff. It was a great play. Who knew it was getting too long? We could hardly wait for dinner to end so we could give the show.

We swept the barn underneath the loft and put benches for the audience, and after coffee they came. The groanies were mostly in a good mood, laughing and bumping into each other in the dark. Lucky's folks came in first and took the special chairs he had put out for them, you would think they were the king and queen, his mom in a beautiful white sweater with a white hood and his dad in a mood. Gabe's folks and the Darrows and dumb old Frieda sat on the benches, and everybody except Frieda was more or less mellow from whatever they were drinking. It wasn't that Frieda didn't drink. Like practically everything, drinking made her cry.

Everybody was excited because the groanies had on silly hats they'd pulled out of the farmhouse closets, so they knew our play was something you dressed up for. When Gabe doused the light they all snuggled together to keep warm, laughing in the dark. We were all happy and the groanies seemed so totally cool with everything that even when we whispered about it afterward nobody could sort it out—who really wasn't happy and who was.

Our play started out funny but we had a problem we didn't know about. It got too long. You know how it is when you're talking and talking and you suddenly notice nobody is listening? That's what it was like. We could hear them getting bored, but so what. Nobody minded but Lucky, whose face was stretching out of shape with it—when we came backstage and they hardly clapped, he hissed, "We're wrecking it!"

But out front Alfred had started another Alfred speech and somebody had to answer back.

Which is how we got stuck in the play.

"Oh shit," Lucky said, maybe too urgently. "If we only had a curtain we could ring it down."

But Alfred pranced downstage and made up another speech.

We heard Lucky groan, "Not tonight."

We didn't know how to make it end. Every line we said was a curtain line, but there was no curtain to bring down. Finally Lucky lunged for Gabe's tape recorder and punched it on. He just grabbed it and began to sing. You'd think he was alone out there, bellowing and grinning so hard that his face looked peeled. It was awful. Embarrassing. We all fell back. So Lucky was alone out there, shuffling away in the straw with his elbows flapping, yelling this raunchy song he had written to the tune of "Batman," so crazy to please the parents that he would do anything.

We were dying but the 'rents didn't see, they just began to laugh and clap as Lucky came downstage backward, kicking high, and lost track of what he was doing and fell backward off the edge. He rolled and tried to spring up but he couldn't exactly; he'd landed so hard he knocked out all his breath. He was giving these deep gasps, going, uck, uck, uck.

Some dad went, *Oh my God.*

We came down to see was he OK but Mrs. Burgess was already on top of him going, "Are you all right? Are you all right?"

When he could breathe Lucky kept asking, "Did you like it?

Did you?" And when she didn't answer, he went, "Mom, was it all right?"

"Oh Timmy, good lord!"

"Did you? Like it?" Lucky's face was bare and laid wide open; he didn't care if we saw him cry. "Did Dad?"

5

Chad

When Leslie and I first started fighting, we surprised ourselves. We kept doing awful things. We were like Rock 'em Sock 'em Robots. I did things I'm ashamed of. She did things back.

The week before Memorial Day she pushed the television out the window just to get my attention. She needed to hear the crash. It landed in the terrace flowerbox but did not implode, which disappointed me. These things ought to destruct with a bang. But the TV just thudded into the dirt. It lay there in the geraniums like a reproachful corpse while I followed her outside and begged her to tell me what was the matter.

"You," my wife said, standing on the terrace in a blue thing with that soft hair flying. She looked like a fugitive from a Pre-Raphaelite painting, lovely and pearly and mad. "How could you?"

I looked at her and all movement stopped: birds in midflight; cars twenty stories below, crawling along Riverside, her breath, mine. Everything in me shimmered and coalesced. *My God, I really do love you.* She had no evidence, so we would not have to act on her suspicions. She had no proof. I admitted everything, I admitted nothing. "I love you, Les. I love you more than anything."

We tugged back and forth over the TV, "I'll carry it in," "No,

I'll carry it in," until I saw Lucky watching: how long have you been here? I saw him watching with his jaw clenched and his hands working as if by sheer force of will he could gather up all the separate parts of his life—his mother, me, the TV—and force them back in place.

He caught me looking. "Mom, Dad!"

I wanted to put a bag over his head so he wouldn't see. "It's nothing, OK? Now go watch TV."

Lucky. I felt prickling at the backs of my eyes. When Leslie's parents were killed her grandmother took over, so my first, best love learned everything she knew from a woman from another generation. It was like being brought up by a Martian. She looked into our son's crib as if she'd never seen a baby. "Beautiful mother, handsome daddy, what a lucky boy," Lavinia said with exquisite irony, so it was Leslie's grandmother who named him. Like the good fairy at the cradle. Or the bad one. Leslie said it made him sound like a gangster and she hated it, so naturally he took to it. It may be the only real gift Lavinia ever gave him. On his sixth birthday she sent our son a dozen roses and made him cry. When Leslie reproached her, she was furious: "How am I supposed to know what children want?"

He was still standing there.

"I'm just helping your father," Leslie said, too loud.

"Are you going to get divorced like the Fentons?"

"For God's sake, no!"

Leslie hissed at me, "Now see what you've done."

So I had to promise to come for Memorial Day at the farm, part of a pledge to be there with her all summer.

I had my doubts, driving in.

Eaglemont was grim, one of those depressed New England towns with its abandoned gas stations, closed Sears and vacant Woolworth's building, leaving only a diner and a string of distressed storefronts with perpetual GOING OUT OF BUSINESS sales posted in the windows and an inventory you wouldn't want to see. Everywhere else it was broad daylight but there were long shadows in the one main street. Think Transylvanian villages where you know things are going to be strange.

When we rolled in that May the locals came out to the road to have a look at the people who were taking the Eden place; we saw dirty schoolkids and pinched swamp Yankees shaking their heads: Not like us, nope. Not with sunglasses and late-model cars. Upscale shirts from Land's End and Patagonia. Not like us. Outsiders, ayuh. Ayuh, spend a little money in our town.

And I looked at them and I thought, Boy, do we ever not belong.

In spite of which we moved in for the summer, with our laptops and cellular phones, Cuisinarts and bocce sets and breadmakers, with our kids singing backup and Frieda as kid wrangler, to keep them out of our hair. Taken singly, we were only people. When we moved out like that, as a group, we made waves. We could have been pioneers in the millennium, circling the wagons against the apocalypse.

Right!

You see, there are thirteen of us, and together we rule the world.

So by the time we came downhill through the woods into the little valley and saw the farmhouse, I was feeling pretty good. But before I could even park Leslie started dividing up real estate: utility shed down there by the big tree for you, pigshed for you, chicken house for Zack, all the farmer's outbuildings scattered like Monopoly houses on either side of the dirt road.

"They'll look great after we fix them up. All that private space. You can do all your work right there in the utility shed. I'll get it wired." As if I had already promised to forget everything and move into her scheme.

I hung a left by the big tree and pulled into the turnaround.

"Right, Chad?"

"If you say so." I would have done anything to please her.

The house was old, with a deteriorating Palladian window above the front door and granite steps that must have been dragged in by sledge two hundred years before. The shingles were no color, and the thing looked moored to the ground by heavy shrubbery and overgrown vines. Since April, the farmer had painted the sheds the same red as the barn. Also in our honor, he had blacktopped the turnaround in front of the house and planted geraniums in rubber tires cut up and painted to look like urns.

"Oh look," Leslie said. "Just look!" She squeezed my hand. We were far from Riverside Drive with its exigencies. Out from under Lavinia, the doyenne of East End Avenue. Jerked out of your environment like that and set down in a new world that's yours for the summer, a person just might believe it was possible to forget everything that went before. Just then I saw what Leslie saw. We really could start over. New people in the brave new land.

"Right!" I jumped out of the Benz. What did I think I was doing? I think I wanted to get out there and claim the land. I left Leslie and the kid and the au pair to grapple with everything she thought we needed, wardrobe changes and electrical kitchen toys and high-tech garden tools, everything brand new down to the Kitchen Aid; I don't know what moved me, I only know what I said. "Hey, this is it!"

Calvin heard me. He rolled out of their Buccaneer with his hopes and his vintage Olympia portable that he'd bought because he thought that was how you wrote great books. He stood in the turnaround with his shoulders back and his chest filled, standing there like Brigham Young, or was it stout Cortez. "We are the people."

Poor Stig yelled, "Right!"

Zack grinned that big Zack grin. "And this is the place."

And I, *me,* T. Chadbourne Burgess, I heard myself saying, "Maybe it is."

God we were young.

But it did seem right: clearing underbrush, making a run into town for everything we'd forgotten, collaborating on a danger-

ous soup. When we sat down at the table for dinner that night
we really were good together. We the grownups of that summer
sat around the head of the table like pilgrim fathers and good-
wives with Frieda riding herd on the kids at the far end. After
dinner we put the kids to bed in the shed chamber. As if you can
put kids down somewhere and say *there,* and expect them to stay.

"Look," Leslie said to Lucky when she handed him his sleeping bag. "It's going to be so much fun!"

We collected in the living room. Stig opened the port. Zack
lit a fire. For the moment, it was.

So the summer could have gone on OK, but there was more
to it than text or context: there was too much driving us.

The women drifted off to bed. Zack and Stig went tramping
into the moonlight to walk the boundaries, leaving Calvin and
me alone by the fireplace. It was then that we set the parameters
for the summer: what we were afraid of, what we hoped to have.

I don't know what made Calvin get down with me the way
he did. Usually he is guarded, as if we are in a footrace and he's
scared of telling me anything that'll help me get ahead. He waited until it got quiet and then he waited some more and after too
many Scotches, he looked at me and said, "So, Chad."

"Yeah."

This is when my old friend dropped his guard and let me see
the wheels grinding away. "So what it is," Calvin said, sounding
depressed. "Ah. What it is is, we're coming up against it."

"What?"

"You know. The cut."

"I don't know what you mean." I did.

"Yes you do. The cut. Like there was in junior high school."
He was sounding pressed, like somebody up against a deadline.
"They watched you all season while somebody up there decided
whether you were good enough to make the team."

I didn't say anything.

He said, "You know?"

Sure I knew. I just didn't want to talk about it. Instead I laid back and waited for Calvin to get tired of waiting for me to feed him his next line and go on to something else.

But he just kept on. "You know. Whether you get to play or not. Whether you're going to spend the rest of your life on the bench."

"I've gotta go," I said. "I'm dead beat."

"The cut," he said anyway. "In high school it was the spring playoffs."

"Don't be an asshole, there isn't any cut."

"The hell there's not. You know better than I do that it's cut-off time." He looked at me. "The big Four Oh."

If he was right, my personal alarm clock was going off August thirtieth. "Do we have to talk about this?"

"Miss the cut and it's over," he said. "What am I going to do?"

I was uncomfortable with even thinking about whether my good friend Calvin had made it, or if he ever would. I was all *there there,* when I secretly thought that Calvin was doing OK for his age and weight and class, but the deep truth was he had definitely missed the last train for the coast. Finally I said, "Nothing's that cut and dried." It was the best I could do.

He wouldn't quit. "But I can still write a bestseller, right?"

When you can't even finish a short story? "Sure."

"If I can only get the time."

This is how I bought my friend Calvin off, with lies. "If you want to, you can." And before he could make me tell any more lies, I went out for a walk.

It's not what you're doing, it's what it looks like you're doing that strikes the difference. When Roseann started stepping out on Stig Fenton, she used to get up every Sunday morning and walk to the Catholic church and slide into the front pew; she sat up straight and sang every hymn. It made perfect sense to me. For me that first weekend, the farm was supposed to be some of the same things. Not to monitor. To structure. Keep me in line, like church.

This was weeks after pretty Luann started coming on to me. She was a paid intern at the magazine, with an ambition so naked that it was arousing: *I want what you have.* She was quick in sex and just as quick to judge. Tick-tick, man. Measure your life. She was ten years younger; she had her tongue in my ear before we even said hello. Luann made me feel eighteen. Leslie didn't have to know. I thought: *Why not?* I wasn't tired of Leslie, I was tired of my life.

There was no way Leslie could know.

At midnight Cal and Zack and I put Stig on the sofa and went upstairs. We looked in on the kids in the shed chamber—you guys asleep?—and lingered in the hall, saying good night like hicks out of that W. C. Fields flick: "Don't forget to open your window a little bit." "Don't forget to open yours a little bit too."

Leslie and I were in the so-called master bedroom with the farmer's feather bed and the oleograph of naked Psyche in butterfly wings. I loved that bed. Never mind that she was pretending to be asleep. I would slide in and we could bury ourselves in feathers. We'd make great love and let the past be forever past. Before I could even get my shirt unbuttoned Leslie stirred and sat up.

So we were alone in the bedroom at the farm in the country, where we'd come to find peace. We faced off while the kids dreamed in the shed chamber and Stig snored on the sofa and lonely Frieda slept in the room off the kitchen below. Our good friends the Darrows and Petersons were bedded down behind thin bedroom walls on either side of us and for all I knew, fucking, I had my cuffs unbuttoned when Leslie got out of bed, standing so close that her naked feet warmed my toes. "How could you?"

"How could I what?"

"You know."

I did. I couldn't tell her that when Luann twined her strong legs around me I felt like Conan the Barbarian, so I didn't tell her anything. I stood on my dignity. "No I don't, Les."

She just handed me my binder with the script. I opened the folder and found a black lace bikini bottom neatly folded between the first and second acts: Luann's underpants. "You know damn well," she hissed. Shaking with rage, my only wife stuffed the lacy object into the waist of my jeans, shoving it down as if she could make me contain everything: the evidence, what I'd done, the way she felt.

It was weird, playing Leslie's carefully planned scene with my not-even-a-girlfriend's underwear stuffed down my front. "Where did these come from?"

"Don't you dare ask me where these came from."

"Oh Les, don't look at me that way. You make me feel awful."

"How do you think I feel?"

"Don't worry, I love you. It's over."

She whirled, raging. "Then there really was something." Q.E.D.

"Oh Leslie, it was nothing."

"It was something to her. She FedExed these to the house." Leslie turned a pale face with slitted eyes and her mouth set in a line I did not recognize. "It's something to me."

"Don't be like this. I love you."

"If you love me, how could you?"

Forgive me I said, "Oh Leslie, it was an accident!"

She rose up. Her voice was trembling. "Get out."

This is how your life splits in two. All at once. You're going along, everything OK, almost fine. Then something like this happens and you look down. You see the chasm. One false move and you plunge. One wrong step and you find yourself looking back over this gulf at a part of yourself you can never retrieve.

"Look," I said. "I love you. This fucking farm. Didn't I come with you? Didn't I say I would stay?"

Then she whirled on me, setting the tone for the summer. Her throat was so tight I could barely hear. "Don't do me any favors."

"Fine. If you want to know the truth I can't afford the time."

"Now go away."

"No." What could I do? I put my arms out and she walked into them. We fell down and made love.

So that night we set the pattern for the summer. The farm was her thing. I'd come back, but only when she let down the bars.

Now I can't stop going back. I wake up nights with it.

Somewhere in there while nobody was paying attention, we arrived at the fulcrum, the point where you teeter, poised in the second before you start the long slide into the last half of your life.

In the terrible vacuum of 4 a.m. my eyes pop open and I am back in Eaglemont, trying to put it together. What we did there. What we should have done.

SUMMER

6

Calvin

"Look, son," Alfred said to Rocky in the back seat, and their father started laughing. "Look out over the hills. Some day all this will be yours."

Rocky mashed Alfred's face against the inside of the car window and Jane laughed. Even Alfred laughed. Memorial Day was only the season opener. This weekend they were moving in.

"You guys," Jane said, and Calvin loved her all over again.

Driving in past other farms with their collapsing outbuildings and fields studded with broken-down farm machinery, Calvin wondered, Do we really think we can change the face of New England? People have worked and died here over generations, trying to yank a living out of these tough, rocky fields.

But these poor people started from nowhere, and we have— when he considered, their riches staggered him. Laptop with portable printer, Cuisinart and Nordic Track, breadmaker, Rolodex, Kitchen Aid, upscale educations not available in these parts. Money, which we can only feel good about here in the valley if we spread it around. In less than two weeks they and the others have paid out hundreds to local contractors to clear the woods and rototill the garden and clean out and paint the sheds. We've bought rollers and roller pans at the dry-goods store so we can paint over the flowered wallpaper in the living room. It's ours as soon as we take down J. Eden's tacky repros and hang a few things of our own. And then. He was aroused by the thought. I'm going to write the novel that will kill the world.

Guilty, he thought, Do we really think we can get more out of this place than we're bringing to it?

But this is not what Calvin meant. He meant: Do we really think we're better than the generations who tried and failed on this farm? *Not better,* he told himself, turning off the main road, but ambition leapt in Calvin like a silver fish. It showed itself, swift and savage as a shark. *Different.*

These people have tried over time to make sense of this countryside; now it's our turn.

What Calvin wanted, swamp Yankees couldn't even imagine, not the local realtor and certainly not the absent J. Eden and his family, who moved over to Worcester to take jobs in the mill. But rolling out of the woods and into the turnaround in front of the ramshackle farmhouse, Calvin could smell it: F. Scott and Bunny, or was it Nathanael West and S. J. Perelman, getting famous together on the farm.

Thus Calvin Darrow, coming into the territory. A current of excitement kicked inside him. High blood pressure of the soul. He wanted Chad to see him like this; he wanted Chad to see lucky Calvin with Jane glowing beside him and his two big, strong, handsome, uncomplicated kids. Broaching—OK, he'll admit it, broaching the prime of life.

"This really is the place."

Jane felt for his hand. "And we are the ones." His boys peeled off almost before the car stopped, ready to lay waste and pillage. *My sons.* We're first, Calvin thought. We could go inside and fuck. "Let's get moved in."

But Jane held back. "We can't. Leslie has the keys."

"Fuck keys." He was crazy to get inside and put his mark on the place before Chad got here in his goddamn Mercedes Benz. "We can break in."

The kids roared down from the toolshed with a pair of cowhorns. When they charged, Calvin did a Veronica with his jacket, yelling "Olé!" or was it "*basta, basta,*" as Jane whirled like a picador, so that when Chad's old convertible came over the crest they would be discovered laughing and grappling, family tableau. Perfect. Everything was potential then.

They heard the blat of a diesel horn, one of Chad's expensive jokes. The Burgess family came down the hill in Chad's Nazi command car, a vintage Mercedes with the top down. Laughing, he and Leslie waved like celebrities while the frazzled-looking au pair girl clung like a shipwreck survivor and Chad's boy Lucky sat up in the back on the folded canvas top, with his hands locked over his head, bowing like an astronaut. He was weedy and withdrawn and pale. He was not like the others, but Chad's kid had style.

Calvin always met his best friend with ambivalence. He'd had to struggle for everything he had, but things came easily to Chad. Never mind that Chad earned peanuts compared to what Calvin brought in at the agency. Chad had everything he wanted, and Calvin could not stop thinking: Why you? He had the byline in *Vanity Fair,* name on books, upcoming miniseries ("Peanuts, Cal, it's no big deal"); for all Calvin knew, upcoming fucking Pulitzer Prize. When he goes into midtown restaurants he is known. And when he goes into those places Chad puts on his wife like an accessory, lovely, sleek Leslie, who is so stylish and so cool.

In spite of this ambivalence, Calvin and Chad were friends for life. They grew up ambitious, shared a walkup their first three years in the big city, before Calvin's income went upscale. They wanted the same things. Calvin was going to be the new Norman Mailer and Chad by God a famous journalist—the great gulf fixed, between art and life. They used to get drunk and laugh about it. Chad was in the right place at the right time. He picked up a job on the *Daily News,* and even though Chad wasn't making much, Calvin felt pressed. *Getting ahead. Chad is getting ahead.* Unlike Chad, he understood that certain things were measured in money, so he bagged the novel and sold out. Which was how everybody thought of advertising when they grew up and how Calvin could afford his life, and Chad? He married money. So Calvin's last marker was negated, as easy as that.

Look at them coming, the Burgess family. They spilled out of the car, leaving blonde little Frieda stranded, blinking like a foreigner. Calvin was struck by the contrast between his own handsome tough guys and this ghost of a kid with his mother's face. Chad's boy Timothy, or Lucky, as he would have it, was, maybe, too special? Too clean, as if somebody still laid out his clothes. Calvin thought with a little flicker of superiority: In this department, at least, I'm way ahead. My sons are tough. Look at them.

Then his kids lunged at his ankles in a tackle, dragging him down. He couldn't walk; it was funny but it wasn't funny, Calvin shouting *"Raus," "Prego," "Omerta,"* hauling these two dead weights clamped to his feet while Chad stood in the turnaround free as a bird, with that careless grin. Kicking loose, he thought, Story of my life.

Calvin didn't know the details, but Chad was here against his will, dragooned into country weekends in one of those complicated transactions couples make. You're best friends, you think you know everything about a person and then you find out there's something about the marriage that you don't know. He thought they had been fighting in the car. As Leslie tried to thrust the family baggage on Chad his best friend turned to Calvin, and as if this friendship mattered more, fell on his neck in that familiar thud of flesh crashing. Friends.

"Cal! Let's check out the woods."

Leslie said, "Aren't you going to let us in?"

But Chad turned, looking over his shoulder. "Are you with me or what?" Did he even know he was holding the farmer's keys? He seemed not to hear Leslie, who, with the cold air of the person who is paying, would wait.

Calvin was torn. His friend—the house. The new world! He

needed to claim his space, but Chad waited as if nothing in this place was important except getting away.

"I *said,* aren't you going to let us in?" Leslie said, "Chad!"

Didn't he see this really *was* the place? Calvin was filled up with it and jittering, but Chad just shimmered in place like Captain Kirk fixing to beam up. They'd still be standing there if Calvin hadn't yelled, "Asshole, the keys."

Chad looked at the key ring, surprised. "Catch!"

Calvin snatched them in midair and charged the door.

Jane said, "For God's sake Cal!"

"First come, first served, *n'est-ce pas?*" but even though he was first inside, the fun had gone out of it. When they came back out Chad was standing right where Calvin had left him. So what if Calvin was first; Chad didn't give a fuck. He stood with his thumbs hooked in the back pockets of his jeans and his feet planted, like an indifferent kid.

Leslie was trying to move them toward the cars in this bright voice, like the mother in *Lost in Space.* "Let's get organized."

But Chad headed for the hill. Calvin followed. They were best friends before he even met Jane. What could he do?

"Cal," Jane cried, "our things!"

"Let Zack carry the heavy stuff." So much for their provisions against the summer. Luggage. Bikes. This was a new world. Everything in it was new. Calvin too.

"Where are you going?" Lucky came up out of nowhere, bobbing up and down at Calvin's elbow. "Can I come?"

Calvin grinned. "Guy stuff." If he comes, all the other kids will . . . Chad didn't seem to notice Lucky, maybe because your own kids are a constant, like Muzak or wallpaper, but Calvin was struck by the kid's contorted, anxious grimace. It cut the gap between this kid and his own sons, and this made Calvin generous. "Another time."

The kid's face was skewed with hope. "Now?"

"Ask your father."

"He's gone."

There were in fact times when you didn't want kids along. Was this one? Chad was halfway up the hill. He was climbing out of reach; if Calvin didn't start now he might never catch up. So he had to say, more or less kindly, "Not this time, OK?"

Lucky turned away with that raw look kids get when they're disappointed and Calvin said, "Next time, I promise, OK?" and as he loped after Chad he was astonished by what he thought but did not say. *Not yet, kid. It's still my turn.*

Unencumbered, he and Chad charged the hill, laughing and crunching brush. They didn't care where they went. When they got back the chores would be done. Reliable Zack Peterson would have rolled in from his safe academic job. He was like his standard faculty Volvo: navy blue and so tight and sturdy that when you slammed the doors your ears popped. When you thought about it, Zack's soul was probably navy blue. Conservative. Dark finish, conceals spots. Like boys, he and Chad could count on Zack to do all the father things, carry the heavy stuff, start the water heater, lay a fire. Dinner would be cooking by the time he and Chad got back to the farmhouse and in the spirit of tradeoff, which the men would forget as soon as they'd eaten, Calvin would promise to clean up.

They didn't stop running until they reached the lip of the ridge. Calvin stood with his blood humming, watching Chad climb a rock so he could get a good look at the house. Best friend. Calvin said, "You're pissed at Leslie." Why did he need Chad to say yes?

Chad sat down on a fallen log, blinking as if he hadn't understood. "What?"

"This arrangement." Calvin did not have to say: Leslie's grandmother's money, Leslie's plan.

"Oh, this." Chad's eyes were empty. "I don't care."

"Then what's the . . ."

Chad took the cap off the rum and proffered it as if to soften what he said next. "When I finish this TV project I'm out of here. I'm going to go to Tahiti, spend a year in a shack."

"On what?"

Chad's blue eyes were like marbles—clearies, but the pupils made black holes. Usually he kept his triumphs secret, like a doctor reluctant to tell a patient the worst, but he was distracted today. Without even knowing, he stuck in the knife. "Listen. With what I'm making—I can afford anything."

"What you're. . . ." Bastard. You've been *sparing* me. Somewhere inside Calvin, the worm stirred; gotcha. In time it was going to chew him to pieces. *Down, damn you. Back.*

Chad didn't notice. "I can afford anything I want."

Jealousy gave Calvin an instant erection. "You have a deal?"

At which point graceful, careless Chad Burgess saw that he had stuck the knife in his friend Calvin and this was twisting it. His face went through a series of possible expressions: *Who, me? Deal? It's no big deal.* Calvin didn't know which bothered him more, hearing about Chad's triumph in the race of life or Chad trying to spare his feelings by not telling him.

His reticence was borderline condescending; "Oh hell, it's going to be in the papers anyway. Book contract on the strength of my new series, all I have to do is write an introduction. BOMC main selection. Paperback for many hundreds of K, OK? This one may be a real movie. Big screen, which if it is, I write." Calvin could have handled it if Chad hadn't been so goddam apologetic. "Even without screen rights I'm going to break a mill."

Ow! Calvin's insides spasmed. "Amazing. That's great."

Chad was indifferent; he'd probably be surprised to know that success gave him a sheen. "I finish the book this summer and then cut out."

"I could get into that." This left Calvin squirming like a kid in a whorehouse—starting over! Success! "What are you going to do?"

"I may go to the coast."

Calvin was sitting on his hands like a randy teenager, aroused by the possibilities. He and Chad had been in a footrace from the beginning and until today he'd imagined they were neck and neck; in the sons division, Calvin was ahead. But now.

Jealousy aroused him. More: *If Chad can, I can.* It was so close. Everything seemed possible. He could not let Chad know what he was thinking, and in his distracted state did not attend to the logic of what he said next. "Me too," Calvin said; a lie! "I have a book deal cooking you wouldn't believe."

"That's great."

Below them in the bowl, afternoon shadows were rising; lights went on in the farmhouse and it glowed. He saw Zack trudging back and forth from the cars, dutifully unloading things for the women and, God help him, he thought condescendingly, God help all starving academics on a night like this. *Poor Zack.*

At dusk the kids spilled out of the barn like bats at twilight, swooping around the yard with their arms spread. The little boys and Stig Fenton's daughter were picking their way across the clearing, making their way up the hill without knowing they were being watched. As they got closer, Chad hooted as an owl hoots. Then he and Calvin lapsed into spooky noises, baiting the kids until Alfred located the sound and led them charging up the hill. As Calvin yipped his two savages lunged; kids swarmed over them, trying to pull them down. Emboldened, Lucky threw himself into the tangle, hurling himself at his father with a crazy, lovelorn look.

At the kitchen door Jane beat the triangle and they came downhill in a loud jumble, Chad and Calvin, their sons, shrill and bumping and rebounding, with Calvin's two taking the lead.

But Calvin had the will to win, which meant he had to outrun them; he would outrun them all. He and Chad were the soon-to-be famous, two peers coming in at twilight to talk futures; Nathanael West and S. J. Perelman all over, F. Scott and Bunny, getting famous together, unless they were Scott Turow and some even bigger fish graciously melting fondue for their women over the fire, *noblesse* . . . a little something for you girls. And as they did Zack gave them the look of the hopelessly domesticated, the big professor in his hopelessly untrendy plaid shirt and big-guy jeans.

They pushed tables together in the big kitchen to make room for everyone, grownups at this end with the Finnish au pair girl marooned with the kids at the far end. Poor Frieda kept jumping up and down to clean up mashed food or spilled milk dribbling into cracks between the floorboards; she had to get the ketchup or mayo, anything Leslie had forgotten, and she was expected to break up fights. She kept wiping her hands on her Nordic sweater without seeing what she did while the rest of them expanded in the glow from the outsized stone fireplace. They were sitting on long benches with their heads bent— happy farmhands after a hard day's work. This time Calvin took the head. Once he'd established his place he thought by God it was wonderful: frontier family eating off the land, Jane's chili, Polly's bread and exotic things from Zabar's thanks to Leslie, spare no expense, early Americans celebrating in the new land.

His Jane had on one of those fisherman's smocks that hid everything; she'd skewered her hair with a wooden ornament. She was rosy and Calvin knew he and Jane would have good times that night. Polly hadn't bothered and looked fine and Leslie had, good grief, Leslie had put on an evening skirt, a little bit of *Vogue* or *Town and Country* here among the common folk. Elegant, but as far as Chad was concerned she could have been wrapped in a Hefty bag. But did she not tuck in her cashmere sweater and touch her hair when Stig Fenton walked in like fucking Lazarus looking for a free feed.

In a way Calvin thought the trouble began with Stig. He said, "What's *he* doing here?"

Loving Jane covered his mouth. "Shh."

Since Roseann split with this kid junk sculptor, Stig Fenton had put on an untended look. His shirt was rumpled and his chin had gone to seed, either Gary Oldman chic or neglect. He hugged blushing, angular little Speedy and put a flower in her hair, grinning at the rest of them. "Hi kids."

Calvin muttered, "Freeloader."

Chad surprised him with a kick. "We can afford it." He could have been reminding Calvin that they had their health.

Stig said, "Don't get up."

At the same time Calvin felt Jane's finger in his palm; final countdown to bedtime, making promises as she got up to tend to Stig. He thought: I have my woman.

We can indeed afford it. Chad's right.

So it was Stig who started everything, tagging along unwanted in their summer—unless it was Stig's ex, Roseann. Roseann said she was into art, but that wasn't what she meant. She was into the artist; she was modeling, she said, getting naked for this retro auto-bumper sculptor, chrome teeth gnashing, chrome tongues protruding from squashy red velvet throats, for this she had to get undressed?

In the Final Days this spring, Roseann met Calvin downtown for lunch. She leaned across the table with her mouth wide open, as if she expected Calvin to take the plunge. Her moist mouth made him think: Stig is a fool, although later he had cause to wonder. Meanwhile Stig went around with that wounded, doggy look, with his hair curling over his collar; poor bastard had to shower at the gym and sleep in his office until Roseann went South with this Derek and he got his apartment back. She took off for the Carolinas, some earth-toned artists' colony where she could play eighteen-year-old while the new boyfriend crapped up entire pastures with auto bodies and got photographed for *The Voice*.

I could have had that, he told himself. Poor Stig.

But count ten and watch the women springing up like dragon's teeth to comfort him. Stig Fenton running around Manhattan like an eighteen-year-old. *Heey.* The man had everything—attention, freedom. The possibilities made Calvin shiver. *Wuoow.*

What's more the guy had walked into this weekend too late to buy food but in plenty of time to eat, coming to their feast with his dirty laundry and a bottle of cheap wine pulled out of the bargain case he and Roseann had bought for Easter. When Calvin went back for more pie he was too late; the women had consoled Stig with the last piece. He got extra dessert, extra everything. Calvin didn't know why the wives were in mourning for the marriage, or why Jane felt personally affronted.

It was as if the Fentons had trampled Eden, tracking mud and presaging upheavals to come. "They seemed so *right* for each other," Jane said mournfully; "you'd think they would at least *try,* get counseling, what is this going to do to poor Speedy? And, oh!" Thus she drove in the knife, "Poor Stig." Cooking tonight, she'd said unexpectedly, "Stig's allergic to garlic. I'm leaving it out in case he comes." Clara Barton had nothing on these wives, Nurse Edith Cavell, Florence Nightingale. They would have insisted it was the mother instinct, but Calvin saw what was in their faces; for some women there's no greater aphrodisiac than a man's suffering.

Stig. Who asked him? Where did he spring from? In the new arrangement Stig had opted out of the lease. Without paying a cent, after dinner he got the place nearest the fire, Lazarus stoked on the biggest pile of spare ribs, his mouth smeared with marshmallow and chocolate. Chad had spent an hour melting junk on graham crackers over the fire, which still stank of burning sugar. The farmer who had wrecked upstairs with extra walls and layers of linoleum had done one good thing. In the spirit of destroying the past he'd turned two parlors into one big living room, where the summer settlers had collected because on farms, now as in the old days, this was what you did. Bonded, they adhered to their mates, even Chad to that cold gorgeous woman of his. Everybody belonged except Stig, but it was solo

Stig who belched with satisfaction because, in love with loss, the women had forked over the lion's share.

Poor sod, Calvin thought, he'll get put to bed on the sofa in the end. All alone while upstairs the rest of us are fucking.

Who knew?

It was late.

They were in a tight circle on the floor, kids tumbling in the background while Frieda wept over the dishes and Calvin sat with his arm around Jane. To his surprise he found himself sizing up the others—Stig, looking puffy from neglect, and rangy Chad, who was lean but out of shape. Calvin was a runner; in a true collision of bodies he knew he could take most of them, and Zack, big as he was, Zack was soft; he could definitely take Zack.

What struck Calvin next may have been the result of Chad's rum, too much jug wine at dinner, brandy afterward; it was by no means an acid trip, but it was weird. As he had been on the hill, Calvin found himself aroused and squirming with a vision, but this time it was not of success. Instead he was sucked into a cosmic vision of bodies—his own and all of theirs, obsessed by it—the way the asses and crotches, the bellies and boobs in that close circle felt inside the varieties of cloth—nylon bikinis, jockey shorts, the poor sod's dingy boxers, what the clothes contained; he did not so much feel as know what each of the various couples had done together, and what they intended to do after the lights went out tonight.

All his nerve-endings seemed to be on his outside instead of his inside, which meant he did not so much see as *feel* fingertips touching the owners' mouths, the back of the hand on the forehead, the rub of nipples inside sweatshirts, denim, wool, Leslie's cashmere. He knew from within how each body felt and what it wanted, what were the ingrained patterns of movement, the individual, distinctive smells, and he knew how remarkably different each one was. He did not so much observe the owners of these bodies as *become* them in a fugue or vision both complete and overwhelming, bizarre because he knew that when they lay down at night it would not be willy-nilly but in the accustomed, timeworn pairs, happy couples except for Stig linked in what he was going to have to call determined uxoriality. Nobody could tell him it was not a word.

It was. It is what they were: uxorial, something pertaining to *ux*, he thought—I mean *us*.

In the next second he heard voices: Calvin to himself, person to person in a still tone he stifled with a guilty start: *Don't you ever get bored?*

Of course the kids disrupted Calvin's vision; his mistake for thinking he was autonomous. From the beginning all their lives were interwoven—parents' and kids', his and his sons'—and even though his boys loved him unqualifiedly they tumbled into the circle around the fire and landed hard on his weak spot, diffusing his intense sexual vision as they barked. "Daaad." "Hey Dad." "Da-ad!"

At Alfred's shriek he jumped, cooling and strangely relieved, bereft. In the curve of his arm Jane sighed. "Your turn."

So Calvin had to break out of the circle and separate the boys, while Lucky looked out from behind his sheaf of pale hair like Br'er rabbit from the briar patch. He had Chad's long body, Leslie's mouth, but none of it went together right. He skimmed his parent's faces like a speed reader cramming for exams. Maybe being an only child had exaggerated his faculties; no matter what secret thoughts you nursed, when Lucky looked at you, he knew. He told Calvin, "They drowned your laptop."

Rocky snorted. "In the well."

"You threw my laptop down the *well?*" Something inside Calvin cried out: *My unwritten novels!* But it was only a joke.

"And your laptop too." Lucky jogged Chad, who grinned absently; he didn't believe it—if he heard. "So, Dad. Aren't you mad?"

It reminded Calvin of the old joke: the masochist begs the sadist to hit him and the sadist says no. So sadistic Calvin shrugged off the suppliant extra boy, attacking his own sons with paternal joy. "My *laptop.*" But it suddenly went sour because if he had to, Chad could buy a dozen laptops, so Calvin's whole career might just as well be at the bottom of that well. "Shit!" His hand flew up; he accidentally hit Alfred, he hit him too hard.

Furious, Jane grabbed the sobbing boy with a how-could-you glare. "Don't!"

Then Calvin went cold, thinking: If we ever played Crash in real life, who would my wife choose? If this woman had to decide which of us to save, would it be me or would she push me out and save the kids?

Hastily she reached for his hand, murmuring, "Sorry," but it was too late. The smell of the other women present, whom he did not know and who had not borne his children, was rich in Calvin's nostrils, flooding his open mouth.

The evening was over the hill as far as Calvin was concerned, rank and beginning to brown at the edges. The entire weekend was getting old. The Petersons were exhausted from the long drive; everybody was. All Jane's threats or promises of joyful sex were going to have to wait for another night. They shooed the kids into the shed chamber and took turns going in to issue threats to shut them up. They opened the sofabed for their local Lazarus, which meant tomorrow they would have to pussyfoot around a sleeping Stig. There began the ritual pillow finding, blanket search, the dousing of the fire which Stig half-heartedly promised to stay awake and watch. (Jane murmured to Calvin, "Poor Stig needs his sleep." Right Jane, he thought; poor Stig needs his sleep.) There were goodnights, followed by sporadic goings back and forth from the single bathroom, men and male kids going out back to piss. For his own peace of mind Calvin lay quietly, waiting for the last one to finish; he needed to know where everybody *was.*

It took a long time for the house to go to sleep. Later Calvin could not be sure he'd slept at all; it was too much! He flattened himself and drifted, comprehending his position in the bed, how the bed lay in their room, the placement of the room in the house. Intent on the design they made, he understood how all the others' beds stood in relation to the rooms they slept in, which way the sleeping occupants' feet pointed in that loosely constructed house, where sound was as pervasive as thought. In the master bedroom he knew Chad and Leslie lay with their heads at the wall, their feet aimed at the front window and the hill beyond. In the room next to them Zack and Polly slept at right angles to Chad and Leslie, delicate Polly in her flowered flannel nightgown with the lace which Calvin had glimpsed coming back in from peeing against the big tree; he'd been aware of the flirt of flowered ruffles as pretty Polly bumped him in the hallway, squeaked and popped back into her room. He and Jane lay in the back room with their feet pointing toward the front of the house, parallel to the shed chamber, where the children stirred. Like Chad and slender Leslie, Jane and Calvin slept with their heads to the north and their feet pointing south, and beyond all of them Calvin did not so much sense as see the outer walls of the house, the way it sat on its small hill in their perfectly round valley; he saw how the outbuildings were disposed beyond, sheds marching up to the surrounding ridge, and in an extraordinary feat of orientation he comprehended the relationship of the valley to the road, the highway, the town, the world.

He lay awake too long, thought the whole house was sleeping, everybody but him.

The profound silence was only an absence of voices. Everywhere things stirred; people sighed in their sleep. He heard woods noises, creaking as of stairs or bedsprings, sounds that could have been couples murmuring in love or only the settling of the old farmhouse. In the cubicle off the kitchen, he imagined Frieda the au pair weeping with frustration or homesickness and in one crazed moment thought how easy it would be to slip downstairs and have his way with her: Shh, there there.

Then under his bedroom window he heard water—Stig peeing off the steps, perhaps after boffing Frieda, Calvin thought. This made it necessary for him to think old-fashioned thoughts: *Aha, you rascal, you sly dog,* and then, God, lying next to the body he knew, he could not stop thinking about the bodies he did not know—poor Frieda's—Polly's, the absent Roseann's. Leslie's, even though Chad was his best friend.

They were many things in this house, artists, survivalists, but Calvin was before anything a husband and father; he was by God a husband and father first. Here they were, three married couples with kids. Plus Frieda. Plus Stig. They were, mostly, solid, physical, handsome married people, which was why Calvin had to move in full knowledge and pleasure of his body, sure, right, but with care. If he was going to make it through this summer in this house he would have to make the effort—try to be just us folks together, men and women in only this one context, and in all the others just pals, chaste as priests and nuns.

He was, he had to be: OK. Listen, there had to be constraints. In fact, it put the edge on things, all those bodies, off limits to him, and so close.

I do love Jane, Calvin thought. Did. Do, but without sleep he was edgy and susceptible; he heard a voice he could not silence.

—Don't you ever. Get.

Back, down. Cut it out. Stop that.

—Don't you ever get. Bored.

Listen. He could've had Roseann Fenton that day they had lunch, to hell with Stig; there were pink parts of her falling out on the table, but he didn't, would not. Not a bit of it. He was a husband and father, right? Faithful to Jane. Damn Roseann with her big boobs and alternative lifestyles, rolling around on a tatami mat somewhere *right now* with who knows who. Damn Stig, surrounded by misguided angels of mercy, Stig, who could go back to his empty apartment in the city and have a different woman every night.

Then in the completeness of his vision Calvin saw the children, unwrinkled, unspoiled, with everything still in the future—kids like angels, blazing and naked, walking hand in hand through Eden without any fear of snakes. It was this perfect vision, finally, that overturned him.

He was thunderstruck and left trembling. God he envied them. They could be anything they wanted, Calvin thought. Anything. Why shouldn't I . . .

Oh! Calvin thought he heard the world crack. It fell open, just like that. The old constraints were gone. Forget moral or ethical considerations; he sat up in the dark. "Oh my God!"

Sleeping Jane stirred but did not wake.

Next to her in the bed in that room in the old farmhouse on its little rise in its containing valley outside Eaglemont, miles in from the Mass Pike in the middle of rural Massachusetts, Calvin Darrow meditated on the unfairness.

What he, Calvin, had been forbidden, his sons would take. You hear about something you can't handle and you go, *Heeey.* Then you think about it, and you go, *Wuoooww.*

He didn't sleep that night; there was too much on his mind: what everybody else in the house might be doing; what his good buddy Chad possessed—in his bed that night, in his life, everything he was going to get. Lord, Calvin was miserable, riding that unfamiliar bed through the hard night. Near dawn he moved his hand on sweet Jane's haunch and she stirred and rolled toward him without waking—he looked into her good face and he was back at his fifth birthday party, bawling, "Oh my God, is this all I'm going to get?"

Everything in Calvin shuddered to a stop. *So this is how these things happen.* First you go, *heeey*, and then you go, *wuooowwww.*

Like dropping a stone into a web. Just to see it quiver.

Then you just go, What the fuck?

7

Alfred

Drop a stone into the web of lives and watch it tremble, shivering along the threads at every intersecting point, vibration telegraphing the message to the far ends of every skein. The web flexes to accommodate the movement. It begins to change. Even at the periphery you can feel it. No matter how far you are from the center, you know.

Alfred knew something was happening.

He didn't know what, exactly, only that it made his ears itch and his teeth ache with excitement.

Something had changed. It charged the air in the farmhouse kitchen and made the moms cross and giggly and the dads too loud. What it was, Alfred couldn't say exactly. The youngest here, he was too little to recognize the hum of finely tuned nerves.

It's this stupid place, he thought. Always being last.

He scuttled from one place to another, testing—his mom's love, Gabe's patience, Rocky's temper. What could he get away with before somebody bashed him or told him to shut up? He tried to push Speedy aside and take her place—be next on the tire swing, steal the silver crayon, get the snake kite into the air. He attached himself to Lucky, hung on like a deer tick until even Lucky noticed he was in the way.

People were always trying to go places without Alfred finding out. Kids whispered behind his back and when they saw him coming they stopped. They crept off to the barn without telling him; they went with the moms to the reservoir and he had to bang on Frieda's door and yell until she got her damn bike and towed him over there. The more they tried to get away from him the more he hung on.

By the end of June the summer patterns were established: which kids were best friends and which were not. Everybody had a best friend but not always the same one. Except for Alfred, who was always left over. He got sort of, desperate? Ready to try anything. "I know. Let's give another play."

Rocky said, "Go away, Alfred, we're playing cards." They were playing poker and they wouldn't deal him in.

"Wuow," he said, looking over Rocky's shoulder, "all jacks and queens. Why don't you bid five clubs?"

So Rocky hit him in the head.

Even Gabe, who was usually nice to him, growled. "This isn't a kid game." It wasn't fair! He might be a year younger, but Rocky was sick for a year and in September they were all going into the same grade.

"Baby, baby, wash your head in gravy."

He went to Mom. "Let's go home. I'm sick of here."

She tousled his hair like an absent-minded mom in a book. "Not now, sweetie, not now." Mom had furloughed her patients for the summer to get back in touch with herself. At least that's what she said. This meant she was reading a lot, and if she didn't look up it wasn't because she didn't love him, it was because she had something more important on her mind.

"*Mom.*" When she jumped he pounced. "You're not think-ing about me at all."

"Yes I am," Jane said and for the first time since they got here she hugged him. Alfred explained and she said, "When lives were handed out, you just happened to be last in line. Remem-ber Avis, Alfred. You may have to try harder just to keep up, but you'll make it. You can do anything you want to do."

Well he was sick of trying harder. He just wanted to be first for once. Listen, they could all go to hell, he was first. He knew something they didn't know.

He didn't see which grownups went rattling around after bedtime last Saturday, or who was outside making noises in the night, but he was the first to hear. There was something going on. If he couldn't be friends with everyone, he was going to be the first to know.

Alfred, the spy.

He made a chart. He learned the groanies' schedule. Jane in the garden mornings and in the living room studying most afternoons and in the kitchen by five o'clock because of all the moms, she loved to cook. His dad in the city four days a week. When Calvin rolled in on Thursday nights Rocky laid back, but Alfred climbed his father like a tree. Dad hooted and thumped Alfred on the back and then he put him down and went for his laptop. He would spend the hours before dinner and half the weekend typing in the living room and you'd better stay out of there or he would get really pissed.

The other groanies had their own routines. Gabe's pretty mom spent the mornings out in the tool shed messing with big hunks of clay while Mr. Peterson holed up in the pigshed working on his movie script, he used an old-fashioned electric typewriter with a big long cord out from the house. When Alfred's dad said why didn't he use a laptop he said he needed to hear the keys bite off the words and chew them up, but Alfred heard this stupid clackclackclack all on one note that sounded more like Xing out.

Lucky's mom went shopping like it was her job. Every day Leslie came back with new food and some pretty thing they didn't need, like a blue vase to put daisies in, or a chiffon shirt that was way too fussy for the farm. When nobody was around Alfred put it over his face and looked out at a world smeared with big tropical flowers. Lucky's father hardly ever came, but Speedy Fenton's dad was around all the time. The moms all made a fuss over Mr. Fenton. He told the kids, "Call me Stig," but you wouldn't do that. The moms were like fourth-graders with the class bunny, let me pet him, no, let *me* pet him. Speedy was like, You have your own dads, just leave mine alone. Well she could have him. Alfred liked Speedy OK, but he hated Stig's big bunny eyes and his weak bunny mouth.

Frieda's schedule was she spent a lot of time in her room. Her job was the kids but they didn't get along with her that well so she stayed in her room and wrote letters and cried. She was supposed to make kid breakfasts and lunches and take kids places and be in charge while the moms and dads were out running around, but she wasn't old enough to come on strong. They got her number the first week. "Freaky Frieda," "Feely Frieda," you know. When the groanies weren't around she hid out in her room a lot, and they would go get her when they heard the cars come back. You could do whatever you wanted as long as nobody came home and caught you and you didn't get into their space.

Now for the first time all summer Alfred had his own space.

As a matter of fact, he had the entire farm. The house was empty, except for Alfred. It was Thursday. Everybody was pissed at him. Again.

The moms had gone antiquing and left Frieda in charge, but while the kids were in the barn a car came up and now Frieda wasn't anywhere. Lucky had been in the loft drawing comic books with Rocky, and when Alfred said he wanted to use Rocky's colored Pentels they said he should get his own damn Pentels. Then Alfred got mad and started grabbing, and when that didn't work he scrawled big purple wings on this Batman comic Rocky was drawing. Lucky kicked him out, Lucky, his own best friend. Gabe had his friend Kofi up from the city for the week and he and Speedy and Kofi were out riding bikes. They wouldn't stop even when Alfred tried to pull Speedy down, yelling, It's my turn. Shit, it was Alfred's bike. So he had to do what he did. He wouldn't have done it if they'd been nice to him. He waited until they were having lunch and then he sneaked back into the loft and wrecked the rest of Rocky's comic. He drew big black Magic Marker cockroaches all over it.

Now nobody would talk to him.

So what? When Mr. Peterson came out of the pigshed to take everybody swimming, Alfred just stayed back. If the kids were going to be that way, he didn't want to waste his time at the stupid reservoir. He'd stay here all by himself. That would show them.

The trouble was, they didn't even notice! Well they could go to hell. He thought by the time the Volvo wagon cleared the drive somebody would miss him and the guys would come begging, but they didn't. Well Alfred didn't care, he could do anything he wanted now. It was exciting. He could run around and set the place on fire if he wanted, he could pour jam into Mr. Peterson's typewriter, to keep him from finishing his movie before Dad got his novel done. But last night Mr. Peterson rumpled his hair and told Alfred he would be borrowing the department camcorder next month, they might even shoot some scenes up here on the farm. Listen, Alfred could be a star! Alfred figured Mr. Peterson needed all the typewriter he could get.

OK, he could practice with the cape. When they got back he'd swing out of some tree and scare them shit. He could make brownies all by himself. Then they'd have to be nice to him. He could build a club house in the big tree and keep everybody out. But it would take two people to move the extension ladder and besides, Lucky would never come up there unless he let Rocky in. He could count the groanies' pills and find the mothers' diaphragms. If he wanted to, Alfred could belly up to the bar and get drunk on Lucky's father's rum. Then he'd read all the groanies' mail looking for secrets, and when they came back he'd tell everyone. Time to check the groanies' bedrooms. He was looking for extra doors or rope ladders coiled in the closets. Clues.

Something was going on that he didn't know about.

The thing ate him up: who was sneaking around after bedtime, what made those noises that he kept almost hearing in the night, that yanked him out of sleep when he didn't want to come. It was creepy; he woke up scared, too groggy to know anything for sure. He had to find out.

The kitchen was so quiet he could hear the refrigerator hum.

He was in Frieda's room going through her dresser when he heard voices and somebody getting out of a car. Then he heard the car going away. He slammed the drawers plenty fast. There was nothing in there anyway, just flowery, foreign-looking clothes and pictures of Finland and snapshots with lipstick-y fingerprints and letters in this weird alphabet that looked like something else. If he stared at them long enough he might learn something, but Frieda would kill him if she came back and caught him here.

He could hear her voice out front: *"Oh please."* Oh shit, would he fit under the bed?

Turned out, it didn't matter. He heard Frieda crying and then he heard her footsteps crunching across the gravel turnaround and then, surprise, he heard her footsteps going away. By the time Alfred got to the kitchen door she was halfway up the driveway, heading for the road. He knew better than to yell; he couldn't tell if she knew he was here. She hesitated but did not turn. He saw her wipe her hand across her eyes and hunch her shoulders like a retreating soldier. Then she headed on up the hill. He also saw that she had a blanket over her arm.

Naturally he followed her.

When he wanted to be, Alfred was a good spy. He'd seen all the best spy movies and practiced the parts. Today he was sneaky, subtle, quiet and amazing, skulking through the underbrush alongside the driveway, running low through the trees and keeping pace with the au pair stumbling along in her sandals with the flapping straps. Every once in a while Frieda would turn as if she heard something following, but couldn't figure out what. She shrugged: *Oh, it's only . . .* Right, Alfred the farmer's dog, or was it Alfred the fox? When she got to the mailbox,

Alfred laid back while Frieda crossed the tarry road and started up the narrow road that zigzagged its way up Scarth Peak.

"Wuoow!" She'd have heard Alfred if a truck hadn't roared by, wiping out his voice. He counted thirty and scuttled across the road. Then he held his breath and counted sixty and started after her. Climbing, Alfred could hear Frieda crunching along ahead, and he thought he heard her sob. He put his feet down carefully, rocking on his sneakers until he had his footsteps synchronized with hers. There was so much natural sound—birds, squirrels, raccoons lumbering—all this fucking nature! that he doubted she would have heard him anyway. Power lines hummed nearby and there was the drone he would forever associate with this summer, of farm machinery tearing up fields and distant chainsaws clearing more.

Then, my God, the two-track road pooped out into a path and just when he was about to think she was leading him nowhere, Alfred came out into a little clearing. Frieda was heading toward a—he didn't know! It looked like a big black hole ripped in the hill. It was partly boarded up and protected by barbed wire—it was a . . . When the kids found out about this, oh, wow!

Staggered, Alfred read the sign tacked over the opening. "Scarth Cave!"

He could hardly wait to tell Lucky. He would show him this *neat place* and then Lucky would forget about Speedy and Gabe and dumb old Rocky and play with only Alfred. Only Alfred would get to play with him. They could be best friends.

But Frieda heard. She dropped the blanket she'd been spreading under a bush and whirled on him. Her blonde hair flew and her watery eyes opened so wide you'd think he'd hit her in the face. She yelled. "Alfred!"

He stopped cold.

Tears and phlegm clogged Frieda's throat but she was raging as she lunged for him. "Alfred, you little . . . you . . ." She bore down, pounding him with her fists.

He was too surprised to dodge. "Don't!" *Oh, Frieda.* He didn't know what he expected up here, but when he saw there was nobody coming out of the cave to do things with her on the blanket, Alfred was glad, really, surprised and grateful. "If you want to be alone I'll let you alone!" Shouting in relief. *It's only dumb Frieda sneaking around.*

But Frieda was hammering on him, railing and weeping. When she finally let go and he started to run, her words came up like vomit and followed him down the hill. "Alfred, get out! Go away you dirty, dirty boy!"

8

Leslie

It was Leslie who'd organized the farm. It made her proud, but it was embarrassing because this was the first thing she'd ever organized. She'd lined up the place and sold her friends on the idea and with her bare hands she had made it a pretty summer, buying earthenware plates in bright colors and Haitian primitives to hang in the kitchen because she was determined to make this summer hers. She'd brought sandwashed silks and chiffon skirts for summer evenings and now she was like a forgotten hostess, wringing her hands at the front door with a fading party smile while her friends went on with their lives with little thought for what she'd created here. Everybody had an agenda except her.

The contrast made her miserable. Everybody else was doing their own thing. Except for the business of this summer, she didn't have a thing lined up to do. It was her guilty secret that at Vassar she bought brides' magazines because when your mother dies and you are brought up by your grandmother, your expectations are formed in a different world. After Leslie was born her mother left home and after that she died and so Leslie grew up in her grandmother's house. Lavinia was the only mother she'd ever had.

Leslie thought: *You create what you don't have.* Of course she married young. When she quit college to marry Chad all she wanted to do was have his child. As soon as she got pregnant she quit her job. "Family comes first," she said to her friends, as if she needed to apologize. "It's the most important thing." She knew what Jane thought: *Women didn't die on the barricades for you to keep house,* but Jane was too nice to say it. She begged Leslie to take night classes and finish her B.A. Grandmother said, "Night school? Your grandfather didn't work all his life to have his granddaughter in night school." Her friends were too polite to ask but she saw it in their expressions: *What are you doing with your life?* Never mind, Grandmother was delighted; it was all Lavinia ever wanted for her. Beautiful house, beautiful child, handsome man.

The trouble is that Timmy got too old to be a full-time job and Chad was tied up in his work. Her friend Roseann, who was most like her, even Roseann Fenton was down south with this kid Derek, who had zero talent and beautiful eyes, said she was doing field work in art history. And Stig? What did he care what Roseann did? He hung out on the farm most weekends, rough-haired and redolent of freedom. Zack Peterson was wrapped up in this movie he was supposed to write, which Leslie noted with a twinge because she knew she was smarter than Mr. Chips, but when the chips were down Mr. Chips would always get the job. Polly, who taught, was aggressively busy in her pottery studio and on Tuesdays, she went to the city for classes at CCNY. Everybody had a project; Calvin was planning a bestseller. Jane was reading post-Freudian psychiatrists, working on a paper for a national meeting of shrinks, and Leslie?

She felt like Eeyore in the mud puddle, floating in helpless circles on her back. She let her hair grow and tied it back with one of her grandmother's double damask dinner napkins. She was waiting for something to happen; she didn't know what.

Meanwhile, she had her son. This summer that she'd created with her bare hands was for him. Quality time for him and Chad. Lucky could throw the ball around with his dad; they would get close.

But Chad was tied up in the city and Lucky slouched around like a felon and only spoke when spoken to; lord, when he was Timmy she used to take him *shopping* and now he wouldn't talk to her.

Chad was afraid to touch the baby; if Leslie put him in his father's arms Chad stiffened, grinning miserably until Timmy began to cry. When she took him away, the baby would stop. "See?" Chad said, "He wants you." She doesn't know what made Chad so diffident. Babies feel that kind of thing and they know.

So it was Chad's fault, she thought, that Lucky was so different. Until she saw Lucky with the other kids—it was so strange! Leslie was in the kitchen one morning when they clattered down for breakfast in a happy tangle; she was brushing her teeth in the sink. She watched the Darrow kids smearing peanut butter, Gabe slathering Marshmallow Fluff; she saw Speedy strewing Count Chocula as if she didn't have a care in the world while Lucky kept his distance, aloof, a little wry. Leslie had just come in from—never mind what she had just come in from. She was wide awake, alert, and in that moment she was stricken by the *difference* in their faces—these kids, and her smart, anxious boy.

Oh Lord, what have I done wrong?

Clearly her friends' children were not nearly as wonderful as hers but they were rosy, tough small animals judging her. Lucky was set apart. If family was a career, she'd messed up on the job.

There were other things rushing at her heels. Frieda stumbled around the kitchen with red eyes and a runny nose, which she took as a threat. Leslie didn't know what hulking country lout was making her cry but it was only a matter of time before she'd be begging Leslie to let her go home to Finland, raising another spectre.

Lord, what if this really was Brook Farm? Leslie was the only woman who wasn't, quote: Doing Something. She might end up being the maid. If Frieda went she'd get stuck with the chores.

To keep the au pair happy, she made festivals. For the Fourth of July she let Frieda plan the decorations, bought bootleg fireworks and put Lucky in charge of dessert. She found checkered tablecloths and borrowed picnic tables from the locals; she went into the city and raided Zabar's. Chad was coming for the first time in weeks. Chad. This made her mouth dry and her belly tight. She was remembering his hands.

Chad came out Thursday, looking like a foreign correspondent in the khakis and the safari jacket, pale from working indoors but glamorous. Leslie wanted to run her hands down his familiar body; she moved close. "Oh, Chad."

"Hey, babe." At least he grinned. It had been weeks and this is all he had to say to her. "I have front money. It's going to be a real movie, not just TV."

Leslie hugged him hard, pushing with her pelvis; it had been so long! "That's wonderful."

Yes Chad pushed back, but he was distracted. Did he sense some difference in her? Was there a difference in him? Their big day and all he did was bury his face in her hair. "Mmm. How are you?"

"I'm fine," Leslie said. So if there was a difference in her, too, Chad couldn't tell the difference. *Whew.* One less thing to worry about. Or was it one thing more? If Leslie was indeed different, Chad wasn't noticing. Did he not pick up on it because he was boffing somebody on the side? Was he that much in love with his work, or was it something in town? That girl Luann again? She didn't know, could not help wondering. But Leslie had something more pressing on her mind. She had news to break to him.

"Oh Chad, something awful has happened. Grandmother's coming."

He stiffened. "Why the fuck didn't you tell her no?"

(Lucky had come running around the corner of the house as soon as he heard the Mercedes. Passionately bashful, he scraped one foot against the other leg, muttering, "Dad.")

"I tried. She's spending the Fourth with us. Polly offered their room."

"Great," he said without conviction. "So much for sticking her in the Eaglemont Motel."

"Chad, she's practically eighty years old."

(Lucky was quivering. He had something to show. "Dad.")

Leslie groaned. "You know how she is." She was taut as a trout line, desperate to bind Chad with the old request. "You won't let her get at me, will you?"

Chad shrugged. "She only gets at you because you let her."

("Daddy.")

"Chad?" Not his fault she had to beg.

He just rubbed his cheek against her hair. "Be cool. She's only your grandmother."

"My fault for not having a mother," Leslie said with a flicker of pain.

"Dad, I found these arrowheads?" Lucky had grabbed the two of them below the waist, linking his family in a three-way hug, but Chad was looking at something far over his head.

All the child's life Leslie had been like a marriage broker, trying to push these two together. In Chad's stead she reached down to tousle Lucky's hair and prompted her husband, lover, everything but loving father: "Chad, Lucky has something special to show you."

"You want to see?" Her boy's beautiful face was off-kilter, his mouth stretched in an anxious trapezoid. He probably already knew that whether or not his father looked at the handful of arrowheads and the potshard he had dug up on the hillside, Chad would be benign about it, smiling without seeing. He might not notice rubies if Lucky brought them ("Of course I love him. He's only a kid.") and Lucky spent his life trying to make Chad proud of him. "Dad, do you want to see what I found?"

"It's really amazing," Leslie prompted, giving Chad a push. *Some mother I am, I can't even bring this off.*

Obedient Chad looked down as if mildly surprised by the arrival of a pet he loved but didn't know very well. "Sure, son. What did you find?"

With his face blazing, Lucky opened his hands.

"Great, Lucky."

Like any successful marriage broker, Leslie stepped back and let this rare, sweet moment happen. She would have been surprised to know that like Dolly Levi, she was wringing her hands. She'd brought her man and his son together; so for a minute or two, she had her small success. But like a farmer who knows there will be a hailstorm during haying, she knew she wouldn't have it long.

Lucky said hopefully, "It's arrowheads?"

Chad lifted his head, listening for something. Then unexpectedly, he said, "Arrowheads! Let's go see if we can find some more. Come on, kid, let's go." Before Leslie could guess why, Chad rushed him away. They were—they were escaping!

"Wait." Bastard. She should have known. "Chad . . ."

"Later, Les." Rat. He'd heard the approaching car.

A town taxi came over the crest and down the dirt track and it would not turn back until it had disgorged its passenger, bag and Vuitton baggage, ruining everything: *Don't leave me now!* Desperate to keep her ally against her grandmother, her only hostage, Leslie cried, "Wait. The party!"

On the hill, the two of them turned, cut from the same cloth, father and son in that reckless posture of departure. Lucky shot her a giddy wave and right before he plunged ahead, making good his escape, Chad shouted, "Lucky and I have fish to fry."

Left to face what was coming, Leslie trailed off, "I haven't told you about the party . . ."

Then over his shoulder her departing son threw her a triumphant look—a father-son thing, at last!—but at some level Timothy Austin Burgess was still her friend. Leslie softened because he called in that light voice, "If you want to, you can come."

But her grandmother was getting out of the taxi and Leslie had to turn and face the fact. She had to comb her hair with frantic fingers and try to smile and try to look glad.

Her big weekend. Her big weekend with Chad, the first time Leslie had gotten him here since early June and here was her grandmother—the red flag to Chad—Lavinia Austin approaching with her head high and her white hair freshly rinsed and that dreadful manufactured smile. Unarmed, Leslie turned to greet her and her insides clashed. Grandmother alone was hard enough; Grandmother in enclosed spaces with Chad—it was more than she could contemplate.

She couldn't forgive Chad for taking off with her one and only hostage. Leslie could never undo all their old negotiations, hers and her grandmother's, but she could make them more tolerable by putting her son between them. Lavinia adored him. Removed by a generation, Lavinia saw her granddaughter as a female child, flawed because she was not a son, flawed and in need of improving. Whenever Leslie put Lucky in front, Lavinia's aloof, judgmental smile crumpled into a look of unqualified love. He was too young to disappoint her expectations. He was a boy. She didn't understand boys, so she didn't criticize. She didn't have to improve him at all.

Smiling, Lavinia crossed the circle, an elegant martinet with her exquisite manners and impeccable toilette: raw silk traveling costume and careful makeup and, God, the lavender hair.

Even though it was too late Leslie called: "Timothy Burgess, come back and say hello to your grandmother."

Lavinia said mildly, "They have better things to do. Men."

"Grandmother, how wonderful. I can't wait for you to see the farm."

This was true. Putting together the summer, Leslie had thought: this will show her. Defined by the series of men she had married, Lavinia had brought Leslie up to believe that alone, she was no one in particular. Without a man, she couldn't do anything. Well, Leslie had chosen this place without Chad's help and furnished it without Grandmother's advice. There were no family portraits, no unwanted heirlooms here—nothing of her grandmother's taste and none of Lavinia's informative gifts—the kind women give to improve other women's standards of living. Lavinia would see that without her contributions Leslie could make beautiful arrangements—the kitchen, with new steel cookware and bright pottery; pumpkin pine floors and new rag rugs. Lavinia would envy Leslie the warmth she had created, the talented friends she had assembled to make her shine.

Maybe they could start over: *Leslie, I never dreamed.*

Instead Lavinia said, "Is this it?"

"I'm so happy you're here." They hugged. Once again she was aware of the difference in their bodies: her grandmother's contained, cool and remote. Then she stood back so Lavinia could see what wonders she had done here.

All she said was, "Oh, Leslie. Your poor hair!"

Leslie's face cracked. She was unarmed and disassembled. All she could do was smile and smile.

Helping Leslie make this a good show for her grandmother, Polly and Zack had offered to take the hide-a-bed so Mrs. Austin could sleep in their room. Stig could sleep in the barn. They offered because Leslie was so distraught—Chad's first long weekend, wrecked by Lavinia, the red flag. Polly helped Leslie clean the room and change the bed. Even though it was unnecessary she'd sent in Frieda to clean again in anticipation of the Princess; if Lavinia couldn't find a pea under the thousand mattresses, she'd grow one—God! They put fresh flowers on her bedside table; as a special gesture, Polly had hand-washed and ironed the priceless Wedding Ring quilt she'd picked up at Mrs. Wisset's for a song and put it on the bed.

At least Lavinia approved of the kitchen; she and Frieda played Maid and Mistress, automatically falling into roles from a dead era, Lavinia gracious, Frieda eager to please. Acting their parts, they suggested that even in this rough setting they, at least, knew how things were done. It baffled Leslie, but as long as it pleased her grandmother, she was content to let it run. Later, Frieda would brew tea in the Minton pot and take a tray to Lavinia. The stairs were swept and waxed; from the landing, at least, the living room looked tidy and rather chic, with its mirrorwork pillows and new Noguchi shades. Lavinia even said, "How nice."

Proudly, Leslie led her to the Petersons' room and threw open the door. "And this is your room."

As her grandmother moved inside, Leslie stood in the doorway admiring the spare beauty of the Wedding Ring quilt, the flowers, the sweet simplicity and, in an expansive moment, her handsome grandmother with the sunlight outlining her patrician profile and the silvery aureole of hair. She was close; Lavinia even smiled.

"Oh Leslie, it's lovely," she said. All their preparations had made her expansive. "And now I know what to send you as soon as I get back to the city."

Leslie jammed her knuckles against her teeth. Kleenex, she thought. I was so busy trying to remember everything that I forgot her Kleenex. It didn't matter what you did for this woman; what counted with Lavinia was what you forgot. The muscles in her neck turned to stone. "A present. How lovely, Grandmother. What?"

Thus Lavinia demolished all their efforts, blinking sweetly. "Why, I thought I'd go to Bloomingdale's and get you a pretty new comforter to perk this place up. You need a little color in here."

So Leslie kissed her grandmother and said she must be exhausted after the trip, and Lavinia sniffed the pillowcases for freshness and said yes, she thought she might like a little rest. The trip—this place—it was too much for her. Lavinia wavered, aging as Leslie watched. The weekend was already ruined.

If she and Chad screwed under this roof tonight, Grandmother would know it. Whether or not she knew, they would hear her pattering to the bathroom just as Leslie reached the top of the long hill and prepared to let go and scream; even if Lavinia slept like a stone she would be present, perched on the head of their brass bed.

Thank God she'd already taken to her bed. At least she was out of Chad's way when he and Lucky came back downhill. He was angry enough as it was. "You never told me she was coming."

"It came up at the last minute." Leslie's heart dissolved. "Oh Chad, I didn't tell you because I knew you wouldn't come."

"You know what you get like when she's around. You get so crazy you don't even know who I am."

She slipped a hand under his arm and moved closer, saying, furrily, "I know who you are. I had to lie to get you here."

At dinner Lavinia blotched her copybook. While Leslie crumpled, she said Leslie's boeuf bourguignon was lovely but rich food disagreed with her, she'd just have toast. Chad kept his mouth shut even when she complained about the noise in the bedroom, the walls are like *paper* my dear; they all pretended to ignore her comment about insect life.

Chad managed to keep his silence until she said the sagging mattress had misarranged her back. Then he sprang. Leslie blanched, knowing she would pay for this later. "I'll help you pack."

Hurt, Lavinia blinked at Chad. "What on earth do you mean?"

"If you don't like it, don't stay."

"I never said . . . it's lovely!"

"Why torture yourself?"

"Chad, please." Chad knew as well as Leslie who'd have to pay; Lavinia would never get back at him. Lucky was gnawing his lip with a twisted scowl and Frieda looked ready to cry.

"Leslie, your husband!" She was too genteel to deal directly.

"Shhh, Grandmother. You're just tired. Everybody's tired," she said; where did it come from, the kindergarten-teacher tone? "Just wait till you see what Timmy's made us for dessert!"

The old lady's mouth began to work. "Dessert?"

Lucky was at Chad's elbow like a puppy begging for attention. "Dad, your favorite."

"Oh," Chad said distractedly. "That's great."

"Imagine," Lavinia said. "My grandson, a cook."

Leslie knew it was cheap, but it worked; once again she had put Lucky in the front ranks.

In bed she and Chad were tense; Lavinia made them furtive. The lovemaking was rushed, Leslie guessed it was OK. She got up and combed her hair. "When I get old I'm not going to be like that."

"You don't know what you're going to be like," Chad said.

Thank God Zack was wonderful with old ladies, and so was Jane. Stig and Calvin rolled in Saturday morning so there were enough men there to make Lavinia feel girlish and enough kids to create a dozen diversions, and so they survived the holiday, fetching up at supper in what Leslie supposed was an ideal state, tired from working in the sunshine, rosy, relaxed. Calvin and Stig had done their work so well that Lavinia was expansive, grateful for the attention, for their making her feel like a girl, while Zack fed her showbiz details, which she received like so many floral tributes. They sat down to eight cold salads and half a smoked salmon from Zabar's, and in case nothing they had agreed with Mrs. Austin ("my digestion"), Frieda's chicken soup. Blushing, Jane produced a cake. They were going to finish with champagne.

As Chad popped the first cork, the mystery guest blew in.

When they first heard the motorcycle tearing up gravel out front, Lavinia flinched as if a fleet of Hell's Angels had arrived. The door crashed open. Like a traveler bringing back tales from a foreign country, a strange boy clumped in, giving off exotic scents and bearing the news that the world outside wasn't as orderly as they thought. Jane and Polly exchanged looks: *Where did he come from?*

Lavinia shrieked. "Help!" Clutching Zack, she shrank even after Frieda jumped up from the table with her arms wide.

Frieda's look was loving, confused. "Dave!"

Leslie was never gladder to see anybody. Here was Frieda's rough-looking raison d'être, with leather wristlets and a muscle shirt and impressive tattoos, probably exactly what kept her crying all the time. A boyfriend! And he was local. She could count on this Dave to keep their au pair happy down on the farm five thousand miles from downtown Finland. Love blew in like a saving grace. *Now you'll stop crying, right?*

Lavinia shrank. Who did she think this was, Conan the Barbarian? Leslie said, as you would to a deaf person, "This is Frieda's boyfriend, Grandmother." Frieda whispered to Leslie, who passed on the mitigating information. "He's a student at U Mass."

"Oh, dear!"

Ah but they had only the champagne and cake to get through; Lavinia loved a party. She rose to it. Leslie was almost home free when she accidentally let a silence fall. Calvin moved in with a friendly question. "Well, Mother Austin, how do you like our farm?"

"My goodness," she said. "You're all so isolated." Calvin was beaming helpfully, but the woman couldn't stop. She dredged up an old fear from their deep group memory. "The Sharon Tate murders. Remote house, helpless people." Her head trembled; even she must have realized what she looked like to them: Old. A joke. "Anything can happen here." The others were muttering but she hardly noticed; "Anything."

Understand, in all these cases Leslie was the one who would pay. But the old lady's surface was deceptive; sometimes Leslie would be strung taut, worrying, and nothing would happen. She was like a slow volcano; you never knew when. Poor thing, exhausted as she was, Lavinia was so polite that she sat up with Leslie and Chad and the other couples well past her bedtime. She looked so forlorn clinging to the edge of the sofa while everybody sprawled and drank and talked and forgot her that Leslie said, "Would you like a hot water bottle to take up?"

She gave Leslie one of those disarmingly grateful looks: "Oh darling, yes."

Everybody rallied except Chad. "Good night, Mrs. Austin." "Sleep well, Mother Austin." "If the kids bother you, just yell."

When they reached the room Leslie's grandmother was spent; still Leslie thought she might emerge unscathed and indeed, Lavinia waited until she'd pulled back the covers for her grandmother and put her things on hangers and hung an extra blanket over the window to shut out the morning light and then she said to the unwary Leslie, in that familiar for-your-own-good tone,

"Darling, you've let yourself go."

"Yes Grandmother. Good night."

It should have been enough but wasn't. With blue eyes watering with good intentions Lavinia said, "I'd be more than happy to pay for you to take a day at Elizabeth Arden. Darling, my treat." That sigh! "Be careful or you'll lose your looks, and then . . ."

It came to Leslie suddenly: The fact that no matter what she did, she could never please this woman—that except as a complement to Lavinia's own life, she didn't matter! She heard what she was saying and she knew what Lavinia was trying to do to her, but after a lifetime of trying to please her, Leslie was released.

Whether or not Lavinia ever found out, Leslie had already defeated her. She had killed her grandmother dead. It was as sure as shooting her in the head. Lavinia didn't even know. She snapped. "Mother, that's enough!"

But Lavinia blundered on in a welter of good intentions. "If you lose your looks, you'll lose your handsome man . . ."

It was interesting. Leslie could not afford to let Lavinia see what she was doing, but the truth was, nothing could touch her now. "Oh Grandmother, you don't know anything."

Fixing Leslie with those ice-blue eyes, she finished, twisting the knife. "And what will happen to you then?"

"Good night," Leslie said, too fast. She could feel a giggle rising. Closing the door on her, she thought: *I'm not angry. I won't cry.*

In the hall, she was surprised by laughter.

It was wonderful. She didn't even feel bad. Lavinia had done her worst and she couldn't even make Leslie feel bad.

"It doesn't matter, I have a secret," Leslie whispered, still laughing; it was true.

Nobody could make her feel bad because she had a secret now. It was like having a present that she could take out and open any time she wanted. Every time she did this, it was new.

In bed she debated telling Chad her secret just to see what he would do but he was tossing, restless and miserable. Had he guessed? Did he already know? She put her hand on his shoulder and tried to open the conversation. "What's eating you?"

He wouldn't answer; he just rolled against her and shook his head. She could tell he was straining against something, wrestling with it, pressed and anxious. If only he suspected, and *cared* . . .

"Is it about me?" she asked, and held her breath.

"No, babe, it isn't about you."

Her stomach clenched. "It's Lucky."

"Who?"

"The baby. Oh Chad. You've never forgiven him, have you?" What she meant was, he'd never forgiven her; Vassar girl, sort of, supposed to ride alongside him on the fast track and all she could think of to do with her life was get pregnant. So sad.

"It isn't either of you." he rubbed his chin in her hair. "It's just."

"Yes?" Yes, yes?

But when Chad answered it was from a million miles away. He could have been speaking from another planet, remote and faintly condescending. "If you'd ever had anything you really cared about, where your whole career was on the line . . ."

"Oh, that." Leslie let out all her breath at once. "You're worried about your goddam contract."

He leaned his head against her chest. He didn't have to answer.

She didn't have to tell him what she was doing, either, so she didn't. "You'll never guess what she had the nerve to say to me."

Right, she was pursuing something, repeating Lavinia: *You'll lose your looks and then you'll lose your man.* Was it really only his work that bothered Chad, or was he betraying her? Did he or did he not have somebody on the side?

She trailed this across his consciousness like a hook. "She says you'll leave me if I don't keep my looks, as if looks were all that mattered, you know? I love her, but I don't like her. She can be so *vicious* sometimes!"

"Small mind, stupid suspicions." He came back so quickly that she had to decide he was Not Guilty on that count, at least. "It's time you got even."

"Oh, Chad!" He didn't know she already had. Leslie, with her preemptive strike. A person has to live.

When he rolled over and went to sleep, she was relieved. Awake in the dense night, Leslie was excited, silent and listening: for the children to drop in their blankets as if poleaxed, for Frieda's Dave to bundle her on the motorcycle and take her off God knows where, from whence he would bring her back beaming; for the adults to fall silent and for her grandmother to make her last trip to the bathroom and the Petersons to make their peace with the hide-a-bed and flee into sleep.

She had to wait until she heard the footsteps. If anybody saw him heading outside, he was only going out to pee. Then she had to wait until the house was asleep, even though she was dying to run outside after him. First she had to wait for the last sounds to subside, after which she slipped away from sleeping Chad and threw on her robe. At the door she turned to make certain Chad was not awake and silently regarding her. As he groaned and rolled over in his sleep, she let herself out. Not even Lavinia heard. It was all right. She barely touched the stairs as she sneaked down, holding her breath as she crept past the living room where Zack and Polly slept and into the kitchen, grateful to the absent Frieda, and out the—yes, he'd left it unlatched for her—out the back door.

It was all right then for Leslie to step into her sandals and go down from the house, across the little clearing with the picnic tables and into the brush from which she had so carefully removed the poison ivy and up to the spare shed where, day-times, Zack attacked his screenplay without much success. They had chosen this shed because it was farthest from the house, beyond the big tree on the far side of the road—and he, never mind who; he was waiting for her as he had been every weekend since June.

Her secret lover had already gotten rid of his clothes; Leslie shucked hers and they were off.

She had a secret, yes, and they could judge her, they could think or say whatever they wanted because she had a secret, a present that was hers to hold close and keep for her private joy. She could take it out and examine it whenever she wanted, and it was brand new every time. Being there with him that night, with her two greatest critics nearby, lying with her secret lover with Chad and Lavinia sleeping right up there in the house, Leslie twisted against her lover in fierce enjoyment, thinking: So there!

When they were done with each other, she wriggled closer, put her face into his chest and murmured, "Darling, at the summer's end I'm going to run away with you."

Beneath her, she could feel her lover's belly get tight and tremble. "You are the most beautiful wonderful darling," he said.

9

Speedy

On the farm Speedy felt like an extra, fat brown hair, big feet, one of those people that didn't fit anywhere, grownups were always looking up at her, surprised: *Oh, it's you.* She was starting to get tall, which meant that nothing Roseann had packed for her for the summer still fit, and no matter how she tried to skin it back with rubber bands or hide it under a baseball cap her sandy hair kept getting loose. Speedy was the only one here without her folks, and it made her sick; she was the only one whose parents were breaking up. And—this was the worst. She was the only girl.

It was OK in the daytime, but she dreaded night. No matter how the day started out it ended in the shed chamber when they switched off the lights. In the dark nice guys she played with every day transformed into something else. They were like a single big animal, stirring in the dark. Gabe had this kid Kofi up for the weekend, some friend from his school, which made five against. Even Lucky ganged up. She gnawed the insides of her mouth, praying tonight it would be different, Dad would come and take her home or they'd let her stay up until it got light, but no matter how quiet Speedy was some grownup always noticed and sent her to bed.

So she was stuck in the dark in the shed chamber, this creepy gabled room above the shed. It opened on the upstairs hall but that didn't make any difference. If anything happened, who would hear? Who was Speedy supposed to tell? One girl alone in the jungle of boys. Her mom was six states away. She was scared to get out of her sleeping bag even to go pee. In the dark everything was sinister—sliding sounds, hysterical giggling.

"Oh, Hyacinth."

"Don't call me that."

She could hear them creeping closer. "Oh Hy-a-cinnth . . ."

They sounded like animals rustling in a nest, no, like snakes. Speedy dragged her mattress into the gable, where it was safe. She was always last to go to sleep because of the night noises, grownup laughter, dads crunching outside to pee, groanies coughing and never settling. When the house finally got quiet she lay there for a long time thinking of all the things that could happen to you out here in the country, in the shed chamber in the dark.

Then one night the monster slouched into the shed chamber and took up residence—huge and rotting, fierce. Where did it come from? Speedy didn't know.

Lucky just started. "Hey Speedy, I'd move my bed if I were you." It was like a werewolf movie. Her best friend was turning into something else. "That's the window the monster comes in."

"Monster!" She didn't know why she felt betrayed. "In hell."

Or why he sounded so miserable. "No kidding. He comes down from Scarth Cave."

"There isn't any monster." Then why was her voice wobbling?

"Yes there is." Lucky sounded like he had been dragged up from somewhere—hollow, strange. He was tense and concentrated, building something in the dark. "There was a farmer's kid, who used to live here? Ordinary kid, a lot like us. Except he had these evil brothers? They shut him up in Scarth Cave. They rolled a rock over the mouth and he was trapped in the dark forever." He rushed on. "Forever."

"That's a lie." She was aware of the others shifting and snick-ering; something was going on with Lucky that she didn't understand. "What's the matter with you?"

It was like he couldn't stop. "He lived on rats and bugs. They thought he was dead."

Speedy tried to write: *The end.* "So he died, right?"

"Not exactly." Lucky whispered unhappily, "He comes back."

"Lucky, don't!"

"He killed the evil brothers *right here in the shed chamber.* So watch out." Lucky's thin voice sounded like it was coming in on short wave. "He could come for me." That monster laugh! "Or you."

Speedy pulled herself into a knot, too late. The others stirred in the shadows: "Monster, wuoow." "The monster walks." Alfred snuffled, lurching along with one foot dragging. Kofi giggled hysterically, hee-hee-hee, and even Gabe was making monster noises.

Speedy rocked in the dark, hugging her knees. "Please shut up."

But he didn't. "Killed the bad guys *right here in the shed cham-ber.* About where your bed is."

"Bullshit," Speedy said bitterly. "I thought you were my friend."

"And now . . ." Lucky paused.

Before anybody could stop him Alfred rushed in. "Now he wants a *woman.*"

"Shut up."

He just kept on. "A girl. Like you."

Speedy was straight-arming shadows. "Just shut the fuck up."

Lucky said miserably, "Nooobody knows what the monster wants." She knew Lucky was messed up over something, she didn't know what, but it was Alfred who pushed it the rest of the way. "He wants girls." Alfred lunged at her in the dark. "Tag. You're it."

Don't!" But they were wild; Speedy couldn't tell where anybody *was.* There were sliding sounds, shuffling, yawns and hollow hoots, Kofi stifling that wild laugh—at least Speedy thought
it was Kofi. What were the boys doing, out there in the dark?
Were they about to gang up and pounce? "Just don't, OK?"

Fucking Alfred went, ". . . When he gets girls, he *does things
to them.*"

But it was Lucky who drove the arrow in. "Don't worry,
Speedy, he's rotting, so he glows in the dark? So at least you'll see
him coming."

"Don't. Just don't." It was terrible: the story, the way Lucky
sounded, telling it, the way the guys twisted and giggled because
it was girls who were the victims here. Weeping, Speedy exploded. "It isn't fair!"

Then she just lay there, waiting for it to get light.

Then it was Monday again and most of the kids were gone.
Thank God Mr. Darrow took the brothers; Speedy loved
Rocky but Alfred was like a hornet; you never knew when he
was going to whip around and sting. She needed to play outside
with no problems; she wanted to sit on a rock in the sunshine
and play checkers and talk about nothing with sunny, uncomplicated Gabe. But Mr. Peterson and Gabe had to drive Kofi to his
aunt's. Kofi's parents were taking the summer off to work something out, which made Speedy's heart give a hungry little leap:
maybe I'm not the only one.

So that week it was just Speedy and Lucky together at J.
Eden, no hurting, no making fun, two friends, and it didn't
matter that one friend was messed up over something and the
other was a girl. At night they went up to the shed chamber like
the peaceable kingdom, no problem, and rolled into their corners and slept safe.

Wednesday Speedy's dad popped into the living room, where
Speedy and Lucky were playing Clue. Stig looked completely
different; it was like seeing a sailor fresh in from a long voyage.
He looked like somebody else's dad with the blow-dried hair

and the khakis and polo shirt from Land's End. He was tanned and thinner, as if he'd gone out and rented a whole new body. She supposed he'd started working out. It was strange; in spite of the fact that he looked really good, something inside Speedy shrank the way it did when she saw a dog with a hurt paw.

"Pumpkin," he said with that dad grin. It was a joke.

"Stig!" She hugged him tight.

Turned out his eyes were wet. "I'm so glad to see you."

She wanted to hang on and tell him everything. "I'm so glad you came. Is Mom?"

"Not this time."

"Is she ever?" Coming.

"You know I'll always love her." His voice tore. "We'll get her back. We will."

She saw Lucky duck outside because he couldn't do this with her. Then her dad took her out to his rented Fiat. She thought they were going for a ride but he picked her up right there in the clearing and spun her around. He said he was going to take her to town for ice cream and presents, but first he had something to do. He left Speedy cooling like an abandoned prom date and went inside.

"Wait right here, you promise?"

"I promise."

He was inside talking. He was in there a long time. She wanted to go in after him. She didn't know why but she knew she couldn't. He was probably saying bad things about Roseann to the moms and Speedy didn't know whether to feel glad or guilty or what. She sighed because when you're waiting for something, no, somebody, you can't exactly start anything else. After a while it stopped being morning. After a while she stopped waiting for him.

Lucky came back. He was over by the big tree with his head down. He had a stick and he was messing with something in the sand. She went over. "What are you doing?"

"Nothing. Want to play?"

"I can't. I have to wait."

With a swift, merciless look Lucky said, "No you don't." It was true. He fell into a guerrilla crouch and Speedy dropped and followed; it was time to go. By the time her dad finally came outside looking for her she and Lucky were halfway up the hill. They settled behind a fallen tree and spied. Smoking Kofi's father's Gauloises, they watched Lucky's mom and Mrs. Darrow standing with Stig, hanging out in the clearing.

Then Lucky said, out of nowhere, "My mom says your mom is getting it from some body artist."

"Derek." Speedy's stomach shriveled. "Getting what?"

He didn't answer. Instead he said, thoughtfully, "My mom says it's no wonder she took off. She says your dad was asking for it."

Speedy fixed on the part of this that she understood. "Your mom thinks it's OK for mothers to run away?"

Lucky did not answer. "Maybe the monster will get this Derek."

"I wish you would quit it with the monster."

He squeezed out the words. "I can't."

"You're scaring me."

To her surprise Lucky said the next thing as if the monster was in charge. "If it wasn't for the monster, we'd be OK."

They were alone here on the hill; Speedy thought OK, time to get this over with. "There isn't any monster, so drop it. OK?"

He did not say OK. Instead he said in a funny voice, "My mom says your mom wants a divorce."

"Just say there isn't any monster."

"Did you hear me?"

She had. The word hit the fresh air with a thud. "Divorce."

Weird: divorce was something people did, but not people you knew. It happened on TV. It made Speedy feel strangely grown up. Now everything was important: the cigarettes, the best friend, the spot on the hill where she could look down and see people arranged in the clearing like figures in a movie. She was important. She and Lucky knew something her dad didn't know. It made them like God.

"Irretrievable breakdown," Lucky went on, as if from memory. "Irreconcilable differences."

"What's that?"

"What parents say when it's over."

"Right." From here on the hill, Speedy watched the moms and her dad. It was like one of those movies where the soldier is saying goodbye to his family before he leaves for battle: The Last Good Time. She remembered Daddy in the park last Easter. He took Speedy by the hands and they whirled like Pooh and Piglet in the tentative new grass without a rat's idea of what was going to happen to them.

"My mom says there's a problem about custody."

"That only happens on TV."

"That's what you think," Lucky said.

Speedy wondered if Roseann had told Daddy about the divorce. If she had, he wouldn't be down there laughing. She didn't know what to do about her mom. She didn't know what to do about her dad, either. It was terrible. She'd rather die than break the news.

Stig left for the city right after dinner which was just as well, because Speedy couldn't face him just then. That night she buried her face in the sleeping bag and cried.

Lucky probably heard her sniffling because the next day he was especially nice to her. He offered, "Want to see something?"

"I don't know. Do I?"

"Don't be scared. It's only Scarth Cave."

Suspicion made her cautious. "But what about the monster?"

He just grinned. "Forget the monster."

This was how she found herself crossing the main road with Lucky and climbing the steep path up the mountain on the far side.

Lucky was proud. "This is it. I bet you didn't even know this was here."

Speedy wasn't sure why they were here. She thought: OK, if he's really my friend he's trying to prove there isn't any monster. Still, it was scary. She didn't want to get close. Big, dark branches drooped over the cave mouth, which was boarded up and laced with vines—worse: it looked like one of the boards had been moved so somebody could get in. Or out.

There was a broken-down fence with a warning sign. Lucky turned. A strange grin pulled his face in opposing directions. "This is it," he said again. "Want to go in?"

"No!" It was an awful place. Inside Speedy knew there were littered tunnels and weird grottoes; it would be completely dark. Even at this distance it smelled of rotting leaves and dead animals. She thought she heard breathing inside: the farmer's son—no, monster—poor little kid! What if he was crouching just behind those boards? She was glad it was daytime, glad it was boarded up. She was scared. "So this is it. So big deal. Could we go now?"

"It's OK. He never comes out in the daytime," Lucky said.

She said shakily, "You know there aren't any monsters."

"That's what you think." He climbed over the chicken wire and knocked on the boards, yelling, "Come on out, asshole."

"I want to go back."

"Not yet." He yelled louder. "Watch out, I'm coming in."

"There's nobody here, OK?" More than anything, Speedy wanted Lucky to admit this. More than anything, she wanted him to get the monster out of their lives so things could go back to being the way they were. She wanted to stop being scared. "You're making it up."

He had a funny look. "What makes you think I'm making it up?"

"Come on, Lucky. Please?"

"If you think I made it up, why are you scared?"

So Speedy had to squirm under the chicken wire and go

right up to the cave just to prove there was no monster. She had to go up and bang on the sagging boards, yelling, "Come on out, asshole."

When nothing happened Lucky took out his recorder that he hid from the guys and they sat on a rock outside the boarded-up cave and wrote "The Ballad of Scarth Cave." They could have been anybody sitting there, Speedy thought; *The monster doesn't even know I'm a girl.* She wrote a verse about killing the monster. "Bye bye Monster, gone to hell."

She nudged Lucky until he sang too. "So he's dead, right?"

At least he didn't say no. What he did say was, "My dad says this would make one hell of a fallout shelter."

"When was your dad up here?"

"You could hole up in here for months. If they capture the farm this is where I'm hiding out."

"Hiding out from what?"

He did not answer. "You know. Anything could happen."

This made her shaky. *Anything.* "Oh shit, Lucky."

"If you want to, you can come too."

This should have made Speedy feel good but it scared her. Lucky didn't look so good himself. "I don't want to go in there."

He was drawn and thoughtful, dead serious. "It's the one safe place. Swear you won't tell."

"I swear."

He was looking at Speedy hard, as if deciding whether he trusted her. "Want to see something?" Then he showed her the cache. He had buried canned soup, canned tuna, for God's sake canned fruitcake under a pile of leaves not far from the cave.

"That's great," she said, confused.

His breath shivered. "So I'm ready."

"What do you think is going to happen?"

"You can never tell."

As they crossed the main road and came downhill through the woods, Lucky put out an arm like a traffic cop. Speedy ran up on his heels. "Shh. They're back." They were. The dads, with the other guys in the clearing in front of the house. Speedy was in no hurry to go down there; when she went down she'd be the outsider again, the only girl. She and Lucky lingered on the hillside one last time, watching people go back and forth. As long as you could stay up here watching, you didn't have to walk back into the frame.

Then Lucky said abruptly, "I am hanging on to mine."

This spun Speedy around. "What?"

"Mine. I wouldn't let mine do that." All this time being nice to her and now he was looking at Speedy like she had some kind of weird disease.

It was confusing. It made her feel awful. "Do what?"

"Run off with some guy," Lucky said.

"You mean your mom?"

He ducked his head and muttered, "The woman." It was as if he didn't want to name her because he was ashamed.

"Your mom would never do that," Speedy said quickly, because it was what Lucky wanted her to say. But she couldn't stop thinking about the monster. "If anybody did run off, what would you do?"

"Kill them," Lucky said so fast that he must have been thinking about it. "Go out with guns and ammo and bring her back. Moosh them together," his hands crashed, "like that. Like Siamese twins." Then he said this strange, unsettling, brute thing. "You've got to hang on. Tie it down. Lock her up."

"What are you talking about?"

"Don't tell anybody."

He was getting so weird that Speedy said, "Be cool. He's dead."

Lucky said blankly, "Who's dead?"

"The monster." She was sick of it—the fear and the responsibility; her face crumpled. "You promised."

"What?" Lucky blinked as if he didn't know what she was talking about. "Oh that. There isn't any monster," Lucky said.

He was OK now. He was her best friend. She was OK too. It was so bright in the daytime that she wanted to believe.

All right, he lied. When they got back downhill Lucky

dropped everything and ran off with the guys. It was like he could hardly wait to get away from her. And when the lights went out that night he started all over again. "The monster creeps. The monster walks." Her insides shrank. Lucky went hnyeh hnyeh hnyeh. "The monster grabs."

She was awake for hours. Next morning she overslept. Speedy dressed in a hurry, throwing on shorts and the only T-shirt she had that wasn't dirty, but when she came downstairs the guys were gone. She ran into the kitchen. "Where is every-body?"

"The boys are going to town with Calvin," nice Mrs. Darrow said. "If you hurry, you can catch them."

Sick to her stomach, Speedy ran out of the house. What if she missed them? They were slamming themselves into the car. "Hey wait," she yelled, but Mr. Darrow didn't hear. He gunned the motor. "Wait for me, I'm coming." By that time they were taking the curve by the big tree and heading uphill with Alfred and Kofi hanging out of the window like paired setters. Alfred looked back. Speedy knew he saw her. Kofi saw her too; he curled his mouth in a triumphant, tribal-looking grin. She hollered, "Wait up." But they rolled away.

The next thing Speedy knew, Alfred and Rocky's big old mom was behind her, pulling her against her strong belly and throwing her weight a little, so they swayed together. Speedy's heart did a double-stutter. *Mom.* Did Jane see how they ditched her? Did she know? Probably. She said what moms say. "Never mind the boys. Let's go make cookies."

Look, when the guys came back Speedy could buy them off with cookies. They'd scarf them up and let her play with them. "OK."

The women were all there that morning, all the moms of the summer except Speedy's mom. She was in the kitchen with Lucky's mother Leslie and this really nice Jane and Gabe Peterson's pretty mother Polly, who'd just come in with the grocery bags. It was just us girls. Even dumb Frieda drifted in, sitting on the high stool with eyes pink from crying, snarling up the string T-shirt she was knitting to keep her mind off it. Polly was unloading food while Leslie conned Frieda into folding the wash.

This Jane was your picture-book mother, nice big lady with big skirts. She knew how to make people feel better about being left out. Even girls. She said, "I can't do these cookies without your help." So she consoled Speedy with Mexican cookies which they were going to drop out of a pastry tube and deep-fry.

"Sweet," Leslie murmured, but the way she said it didn't sound sweet. She was always talking about things that gave you zits and things that made you fat but Mrs. Darrow didn't care and Speedy didn't care. It was nice having a mom, even somebody else's mom.

When Polly ran one of her ragged-looking fingers around the edge of the bowl and licked it, Jane batted her hand. "Stop that."

"You sound just like my mother."

"Mother! Try Lavinia if you want a mother." Leslie had been on edge ever since Lucky's great-grandmother left. Said she could hardly stand to think about her and all she could talk about was, did they think Lavinia had a good time, did they think she was impressed. "I've been mothered to death."

Polly said, "Mothers!" She made it sound like a swear.

"I know just how you feel," Jane said so fiercely that Speedy jumped.

Leslie groaned. "That's because you know Lavinia."

"Cheer up," Gabe's mother said, "she's gone. And mine is nowhere around."

Wait a minute, Speedy thought. *You're a mother too.*

"But I haven't stopped hearing about it." Lucky's mom looked less like a mother than an angry girl. "Why is everything I do wrong?"

"Because she's trying to be your mother." Jane's voice was so warm that Speedy thought: *I love you.* She did.

Leslie wailed. "Then how do I keep from turning into her?"

Speedy looked at her: the beautiful hair, the wild look. Who knew?

But Jane was reassuring her. "Believe me, you won't."

What if Speedy turned into Roseann, who ran away from people? *Not me,* she thought. *Not me.*

Polly Peterson sighed and pulled her cheeks back the way you do when you're playing face lift. "When did we start to cringe when we saw these women coming?"

"When did we not?" Then in this conversational tone, Leslie said this awful thing. "She never loved me."

"Not true. You had to learn love from somebody," Jane said.

Leslie's voice shuddered. "If she loved me, she would have stayed."

"I mean your grandmother. She loved you well enough to teach you how."

This was supposed to make her feel better. It should have made Speedy feel better too, but her stomach started sliding around. Instead Lucky's mom said the exact words that were forming inside Speedy's head. "I'll never be like that."

Polly shivered. "What if it sneaks up on you?"

"We won't be like them," Leslie said. She sounded so sure! "We aren't like them now."

Then Jane looked at the room full of women—Speedy too—with strange, clear eyes. "The older we get the more we become what we are."

Leslie covered her mouth. "Oh, Jane!"

Then Jane—Gabe's *mom* bit her knuckles. "God. What if we turn into them?"

Leslie said, "I'd rather die."

Then as Speedy moved closer, as if for warmth, Jane said with less certainty, "We're all too intelligent to be what they are."

Why couldn't they *stop?* Speedy didn't need to hear this. She didn't want to hear anything right now. Even if she gave hundreds of cookies to the guys and they let her play with them, they'd probably end up being shitty to her. They'd grab her and tie her to a tree somewhere. That's how things ended up. Her stomach hurt.

Leslie slapped the table so hard it made all the dishes jump. "I'm never getting old."

"Me either," Speedy cried so passionately that they were all surprised. Lucky was Speedy's best friend, and yet he invented the monster. She was as good as any guy and they wouldn't let her go with them. It wasn't fair. Her job was sugaring the cookies as they came out of the fat, but for reasons she wouldn't figure out, Speedy could not stop stuffing them in her mouth.

"That's enough for you, Speedy, OK?" Leslie said distractedly; then she went and looked out, as if from the mast of a ship. "There ought to be an island for mothers...surrounded by sharks."

"You're a mother." Speedy kept shoveling cookies in. "My mom is a mother." She couldn't swallow and she almost choked.

"Speedy, if you keep eating like that, you'll get zits."

She couldn't stop. She wanted to go to an island where there were no differences. "I don't care," she yelled, running out.

Thank God the guys came back. They had paper sacks filled with junk from Bradlee's and Caldor's, junk toys like the other junk the dads had been buying them all summer just to keep them occupied.

"I brought you a Spiderman." Lucky gave Speedy the comic to make up for leaving her behind.

So it would have been OK, she thought. If there hadn't been something the matter with her. It was Alfred who noticed. As she took the comic, stupid Alfred poked her right in the middle of her outgrown T-shirt. "Boop!" He pushed hard and said, like it was something to be ashamed of, "Hey, what's that on the front of you?"

She batted his hand away and raised the comic, trying to cover herself. "Nothing, asshole."

"Yes there is." Alfred poked again and his finger went in.

It was awful. "No!" Speedy looked down. Shit, he was right. It was humiliating. She was squashy in those places. She didn't know why, but it made her feel so guilty that she ducked her head and charged him, hammering. "There's nothing on my front. Nothing, OK?"

Jane came out with the cookies just then, like a saving grace. The guys rushed the bowl and everybody but Speedy forgot.

It was late by the time they went up to the shed chamber. In the dark it was like hanging on to the edge of a rats' nest, hearing slithering sounds and watching shadows move. The guys were whispering. Every once in a while somebody giggled. There was the deep silence you get in movies, right before the monster comes.

Speedy rucked the sleeping bag up under her chin. She felt sick. The guys were whispering: Alfred, Rocky, Kofi and Gabe, probably even Lucky, bsss bsss bsss, louder and louder until Speedy could make it out: "Boobies," Alfred giggling fiendishly, "Going to feel the boobies," laughing maniacally, all of them laughing and getting wilder and wilder until Speedy snapped into a coil like a snake.

Too late. In the dark Alfred howled and pounced; he pried away the sleeping bag and lunged for the front of her with his hands going rmmm, rmmmm, rmmm, grinding them like the knobs on a radio.

Speedy was shrieking, "Get off get off," crying hard, "Let go, let go," but he just kept on, "I'm only *feeling*"; everybody was vomiting laughter and Speedy could never account for the way this made her feel or why it made her howl with grief. She was crying so loud that it brought the groanies. By the time Calvin plunged in to separate them Speedy was hysterical because there were these squashy things growing on her front and she *would not have them*, shrieking, "There's nothing to feel."

None of the grownups knew what she meant but she could not control the weeping. "There's nothing to feel." Even though she *would* grow up as her mother had, as Lucky's mother had and all the mothers before them, Speedy kept denying it; she'd rather die than admit that it was true. Speedy, crying so loud that nobody could understand her, "There's nothing to feel!"

10

Polly

It was midmorning on the farm. Her friends were all deep in their projects while Polly Peterson lingered on the stone steps outside the front door and not for the first time found herself wondering what was the matter with her. If Zack was in the shed, he wasn't typing. Again. Brook Farm. Wasn't this what she'd been waiting for? She was supposed to be in her pottery shed but the clay was intransigent. The wheel was off kilter and her pots flew out of shape. Things cracked in the bisque firing. She hated going in.

Pressed as she'd been by keeping it together all these years, she was daunted by the responsibility of all this free time. Everybody was off somewhere. The boys and Speedy were inside badgering Frieda, whose job it was to produce food and settle fights and answer all their questions so the parents could, what, stretch and grow and OK, find themselves. It's what this summer was about.

She was supposed to find herself.

The trouble was, she'd forgotten who she was looking for. *I've been a mother too long.* Polly grew up believing she was destined to be *somebody,* but motherhood got in the way. Now that she was up against it, she could not remember who that person was. At twenty-two she was a studio potter headed for law school, but then she married Zack and had his kids and put the rest of her life on hold.

It's a long time since she's heard the recorded promise that one of our operators will get back to you.

Zack had a new Filofax and a cellular phone. Instead of walking places, he ran. He was, after all, a guy with a commitment to write a film. "I'm going to take you out of all this. We'll go to the Oscars in a white stretch."

Zack, she thought. *You're talking like a jerk.* But she never said so and she never even hinted it to the kids. Her problem was, she was terminally nice. Everybody expected it. What was it her mom used to say? "You're too pretty to make that face." It was a curse. Pretty was all people saw. They saw blonde hair and blue eyes and talked to her like a dull-normal—simple sentences, firm tones.

Look at Jane, she thought, grubbing away up there in the garden. She doesn't care what she looks like and look how far she's come, keynote speaker at some clinicians' meeting in September, when she gets up to read her paper nobody's going to care what she has on. Leslie's so chic and forceful that nobody forgets who *she* is, and Roseann . . . In a way, Polly envied Roseann. She was sick of being on hold. In another life she could have been attorney general. She could have been Henry Moore.

Biology might not be destiny but it was definitely a pain in the ass.

This was supposed to be her make-or-break summer. Her chance to turn herself around. She'd enrolled in classes to prepare for the LSATs. Nobody knew this, not even Zack, who thought she was taking English or history to upgrade her status at the grammar school. All these years she'd been waiting for her turn. Now she was going to make it with her bare hands. Enrolled in classes and set up her makeshift pottery studio. Hand-building a future.

She'd even cleared the decks by sending the two older boys away so she'd have only Gabe. Instead of the exchange program in France, she and Zack had to settle for a science camp in Ann Arbor. It was what they could afford. With the sublime, enfranchised indifference of the rich, Leslie asked, "What's the matter with France?"

Polly and Zack fought about it. She said, "If I was a lawyer we could afford France for them." She meant more than she was saying. "We could afford a lot of things."

And Zack in his own sublime indifference rubbed the sore spot raw. "You're so beautiful. Lawyers are so boring," he said.

This sent her to Bergdorf's with Leslie, who could buy anything. So Polly had to spend too much on power suits she'd never have anyplace to wear. Evening things. She did look good in them. But where would Zack ever be invited, that she could wear sequins?

Certainly not the farm. Nobody cared what you looked like here. Jane went around in loose shirts and painter's pants and she came down from the garden in rubber boots that she forgot to take off. Polly kept on the smeared, messy shirt she wore in the studio and let her nails stay dirty. It felt good. One steamy morning Leslie said, "It's so hot, let's take off our tops." Only Polly looked around to see whether the men were near enough to see. Leslie caught her hesitating and glared. Right, you weren't supposed to care who saw, or how you looked. Polly stopped shaving her legs and under her arms. Anything to escape the prison of her looks.

All her life she had fussed with her hair and done wardrobe when in fact she should have attended to the subtext: *It's not what you look like any more. It's what you do.* Well, she'd show them.

One night the parents all sneaked out on the kids and Frieda and went skinny-dipping in the reservoir, but they did it discreetly, dropping their clothes at the rim and slipping into the dizzyingly cold water naked in the dark.

Polly was the last. She hesitated on the bank. She undressed with an angry little flip because for her, at least, this was a political act. In the ideal world, bodies wouldn't matter, not in how they set you apart, not in how they made you alike. Even pretty women would be treated equally. Still it was exciting—Polly in the black water with Zack's arms around her, treading water not far from Jane and her Calvin, aware that poor Stig was all alone in the water, not all that far away. They could have been anybody, naked in the dark. They weren't. They were men and women, friends and lovers, successes and failures, no two alike. A shout split the night. In a swift, startling burst the water shattered and flew like chipped ice. Frieda's biker boyfriend Dave hurtled out of nowhere and came cannonballing into their midst just in time to remind them all that there was also a dichotomy between themselves and *young*. Then he hoisted himself up on the raft and stretched in the moonlight so they could all see.

Zack said through his teeth, "Goddammit, *I will break out.*"

It isn't what you look like, Polly reminded herself firmly, *it's what you are.*

Everybody had an agenda now. Zack couldn't see anything but this movie. The finished picture, not the script. He wanted so *much,* and the secret part of Polly that stood back and saw clearly wanted to warn him to watch out. Listen. Polly had arranged to get her pottery fired at the Eaglemont Art Institute, and the summer class in criminal justice? She was a grownup, she was organized. She was doing better than the undergraduates and she was going to make it if she could survive the professor. She tripped on the stairs and Professor Zayle put his hand under her elbow to steady her; to him she was only a pretty matron, which meant he condescended and never called on her in class. As she caught her balance he said a terrible thing: "Why waste your time on something you'll never use?"

She went white. Trembling, she turned on him and hissed in a hard, white voice, "I am not a dabbler."

Then goddammit she smiled and thanked him for helping her up.

The first time Polly tried to break out she got pregnant again—Zack's oversight? Hers? Just when their two big boys were in school all day, it happened and they had Gabe. It was important to Polly to believe the baby was a surprise. "I think it was an accident," she told Jane, "but maybe I just always wanted a lot of kids." Gabe. She loves him so much! When they went out the older two might slouch ahead, pretending to be no relation to that woman with the little boy, but Gabe laughed and told her funny things, ambling along with the sun shining on that chrysanthemum hair. *This,* she thought. *A mother. Maybe a mother is all I am.*

This June she'd shipped her big boys off to Ann Arbor so she'd have time to get in touch with herself. Then she and Zack ended up with three kids anyway—poor Speedy. Kofi, whose parents were running on empty: high-octane careers compounded by the pressure of expectations—supposed to be standard-bearers for African Americans everywhere. *Our best friends and they're breaking up.* Polly mourned. It was like a personal bereavement, friends splitting up. Zack saw it as a threat. "We have to be careful," he warned when they heard. "If it could happen to them, it could happen to us."

With a wild ambivalence, Polly said what was expected. "No it couldn't." She didn't know how she felt about the fact that this was true.

So when the Petersons came to the farm this summer Polly had Speedy and Kofi in tow along with wonderful, sunny Gabe. She had to admit she liked being important to these short people. *Maybe that's all I should be,* Polly thought with the sense that she might be busily writing her own excuses for the future: *Mrs. Mom.*

But on the farm they forgot about her and disappeared. She hardly saw Gabe except when Zack sent him up from the shed for new typewriter ribbons, fresh paper, his phone. She loved the freedom but in a funny way she missed having Gabe around. Maybe she did know what she was doing when she put the damn thing in backward. Making love with Zack, she felt her hands twitch; she felt like the unwilling serial killer who writes:

Stop me before I kill again. Look at it this way. When the Petersons went out they were something to be reckoned with. Together, they made a crowd. A part of Polly wished she had a dozen kids, so she'd never run out of sons.

She missed Gabe terribly. As late as this spring she'd been able to sneak up behind him and surround him with a hug. Here at the farm he was hard to catch. Call and he'd turn abruptly with that trapped honeybear look: "Who, me?"

Just when she was too depressed to move, much less stand up and go to her studio, the kids of the summer streamed out of the kitchen door, trailing ice cream wrappers and cookie crumbs, signs of Frieda's failed attempts to buy them off. Stumbling along wrangling, they made a ragtag procession, heading for the barn. "Gabe?"

My son the rat, she thought. There he goes, pretending not to hear. So she stood and called louder. "Gabe!"

Caught halfway across the circle, he turned.

Gotcha. "I need you."

"What, Mom?"

She couldn't bear to admit it was nothing. She felt her eyes fill. "I want to talk to you."

Dragging his feet, he came over. "What do you want?"

"I just wanted to talk to you is all. I wanted . . ." She didn't know. She wanted life to be simple, instead of hard. He stood looking at her out of eyes like hers, with wild hair and dirt like war paint on his tanned face. Her usually equable Gabe seemed different today, unsettled. He had this unaccustomed slouch. But she didn't ask. She wanted to grab him by the shoulders and pull him close and shake it out of him. Instead she tried: "Is something wrong?"

"You wouldn't understand."

When kids play together for too long, things always go sour. Mothers know. "Is somebody being pissy?"

He wasn't about to answer her.

From the barn Alfred shouted: "Gabe!"

"I just . . ." She wasn't sure how much longer she could keep him in place with her voice.

"Come on, asshole."

"Gabey?"

When he looked up she was surprised to see how black his eyebrows were. Thick, like Zack's. "No problem, Mom."

The other kids hung in the barn doorway, watching.

Embarrassed, Gabe said, "Can I go?"

Oh, Gabe. She might as well be standing on the shore watching him wave from the deck of a departing freighter. "Gabe, if there's anything you, ah, want to tell me . . ."

"Shouldn't you be making pots or something?"

Dismissed, she fell back. "I see." When she was with Zack and the boys they were a corporation. Standing out in the circle like this, she found that she lacked substance. One woman alone. Pretty soon he'll start pretending he doesn't have a mother. Who will I be then? "OK. I just love you, that's all."

"Me too." Gabe wanted to tell her something, he didn't want to tell her something.

"Please. If there's anything you have to say . . ."

"Ga-abe . . ."

"Not really, Mom. OK?"

The murderer tears out his mother's heart and is running to deliver it to the highest bidder when he trips and falls. The mother's heart goes tumbling in the dirt. As the villainous son scrambles to get up the heart cries, *Are you hurt, my son?* There was no way for Polly to explain what she wanted. "OK." Then she said, "Be good. Have fun."

Turning, she felt surprisingly light-handed, as if all her bones were hollow and her body could fly anywhere. *When Gabe goes I'll be left alone with Zack and whatever identity I've made to stand up in.* The question, the question. *Who will I be then?*

There was a stir in the kitchen—Frieda and her saturnine boyfriend and one of the men—Stig, she thought.

Stig came galumphing in last Sunday with a happy grin. "I've got the week off. Here I am!" Nobody had the heart to tell him he was in the way. Polly heard Calvin's thin greeting: "Oh, great." Another big kid on their plates this summer, unkempt and needy and importunate, tousling his hair with unsteady fingers and begging for attention. Polly could go into the kitchen and rescue him but she couldn't be sure whether that was Stig she heard arguing with Frieda and her boyfriend, or one of the other men. Calvin? Zack? She didn't want to just blunder in. It crossed Polly's mind that this Dave somebody, goes to U Mass, might take Frieda off to this commune or whatever it was where he hung out and keep her for good. Then she thought with a certain vindictive pleasure that instead of having kitchen help, privileged Leslie would have to fend for herself. Then they'd see who was who and what was what.

She could go up to her studio and try to work but to tell the truth her work wasn't going well. There was the arrogance of her teacher. It hung over her, like a curse.

"You can be good enough," she'd said, "but you'll never be great. It's like dancing or baseball or conceptual math. You have to start young and give your life to it." With the pity of a lifelong professional this studio potter in her early twenties nailed Polly's future, fixing her for all time: "It's too late for you."

Depressed, she went up to the garden to bother Jane. She took everything in her two hands, and held it out to her. "What if it's too late for me?"

And Jane? Polly's big confession and Jane just passed it off. Standing there in her rubber boots and her career like chain mail and her keynote speech for this shrinks' conference, Jane said, "It's not what happens to you that makes the difference, Polly." She pushed her damp hair back and under the Indian cotton shirt all the soft parts of her moved. God, the woman was trying to be kind; after a pause she finished, and this too nailed Polly in place, and forever. "It's how you handle it."

Polly sighed. "I suppose you're right."

Jane put down the hoe and straightened up with a grin. "Whether or not I am, it's a good tactic for making it through."

"Are what?"

Jane grinned. "Handling it." She was so damn *perfect*. It didn't matter that she had on that stained shirt and baggy painter's pants, she glowed. She was strong and in her own way handsome, capable and self-assured.

"You get all this support from Cal."

"Just lucky," Jane said, trying to keep that smile from getting too wide.

The miracle of sexual chemistry: sleek Calvin, comfortable Jane. Something made Polly think, *The woman has everything.* God she envied her. Adrift, Polly looked at the plants Jane was putting in and said, "Need help?"

Remember, they had set up this summer so the women would share the chores and have free time to do whatever they wanted. Which Polly was expected to do. This, then, is how Polly's friend reproached her. "I don't want to cut into your studio time." Then Jane turned back to her plants as if Polly had already accepted this gift of time she was giving and was already on her way back downhill.

Out of the tail of her eye Polly caught this kid Dave's motorcycle rolling out of the turnaround. He'd taken off his shirt and tied a strip around his head to keep all that hair from blowing in his eyes. As he kick-started the Harley poor Frieda came blundering out of the kitchen and ran across the circle, trying to find something to say in English that would make him stay. Somebody. One of the men? Somebody lingered in the kitchen. Polly could see his shadow just inside the door but she couldn't make out who. "Right," she said to Jane, "my work." Out of the tail of her eye she caught movement: Frieda, running after the Harley. By the time she turned, Dave had pulled Frieda onto the back and they were gone.

Polly decided to bag the studio, for today at least. No point in working when she was sour. With a resentful look at Jane's capa-

ble back, she headed back downhill to the house. By the time
she got there the kitchen was empty. Whoever had been in the
kitchen had gone—either upstairs or out the side door and
down into the fields. It was like walking into a still life, with
objects set up to represent—what? Dried herbs hung from the
exposed beams and on the butcher's block were tag-ends of
French bread. It was a perfect country kitchen except for the
table smeared with spilled chocolate milk and bowls of soggy
Cap'n Crunch. On an earlier summer Polly would have picked
up the dirty bowls and sponged the table and put the bread away.
Not my problem, she thought, and turned away.

Instead she went to the shelves and spent the rest of the
morning rearranging Jane's spices. It was an act of aggression
and she knew it.

11

Midsummer

One weekend Speedy's dad came out from the city in a new crumpled linen suit and a fresh haircut, with a big grin and a pump rifle water gun for her. We all went out to see. He always came with presents now because he had a new girlfriend in the city and he was tied up a lot. The gun was army-green plastic. It held about a gallon of water; it was such a neat toy that kids stood in line to take turns with it. It didn't take us long to figure out that one gun is never enough. You needed to be shooting at somebody who was shooting back. We started with the moms:

"You wanted us to go out and play, right Mom?"

"We just need something new to play with, OK?"

"So we can stay outside and get healthy, right Mom?"

"Can I, mom?"

"We promise not to use them inside."

"We'll never use them inside."

Monday the mothers gave us money just to get us off their backs. Then they stood by superintending to be certain Frieda got every last one of us shoveled into the car. When the gun-buying expedition left for Eaglemont the three mothers came out in the driveway to wave goodbye. If any of us thought about it as the car pulled away it was to imagine the moms all breathing a big sigh of relief. They probably opened the gallon of Ben and Jerry's and started to party as soon as the car was out of sight, the way grownups probably do every night. Why else would they be so crazy to get us to bed? The moms were preoccupied that week, laid back and so absent-minded that they would have said yes to anything. Nail guns? Sure. You want to shop for repeating rifles? OK, fine.

They waved goodbye with those sweet, distracted, mother smiles. "But be good," they said, it was the mother's litany. "And have fun."

That month the personnel at the farm were at the fine dead center of summer when kids can pretend it's going to last forever and just go coasting along. For us it was like being on a fun ride, at the pleasant high point that comes right before the slide down to the end. We thought: You never know if the downhill slide is going to be long or short, slow or fast. You don't even know whether you're going to land hard and get hurt but you'd better enjoy the middle for as long as you can string it out.

The fathers were all back in the city that week, which meant it was a quieter civilization, no great big ambitions crowding the soft twilight like shapeless large animals, no egos rubbing up against each other after dinner in front of the fire. The moms were cool, we kids were cool. For a change even dumb old Frieda was cool, even though she woke up with red rings around her eyes from crying in her sleep, and went for long walks and wouldn't let us go along and didn't want us to follow her even if we promised to stay out of her way.

We had to promise not to tell. Which meant that we had her in our power for today, at least. We could use her hard. So we made old Frieda take us to Bradlee's up by the Mass Pike and all the way to K-Mart and Caldor's and all the good places because everybody wanted a gun but nobody wanted the same one. No place in town had anything as good as the one Stig had brought Speedy so the object of the exercise was to find out which gun held the most water and shot the farthest, and if Frieda went a little crazy trying to keep the five of us happy, too bad.

Rocky and Gabe ended up with ray-guns, one red, one blue, and Alfred settled for a black plastic automatic, but it didn't hold much so he insisted on getting two. Then Lucky made Frieda take us to a hardware store and the rest of us freaked because we hadn't thought of it first and by that time we'd blown every dollar we had on junky plastic guns. Lucky, he bought a two-quart bug sprayer with a big pump and long hose and a humongous tank that you were supposed to wear on your back. Then we all went home and filled our weapons in the kitchen sink.

Alfred and Rocky's mom came downstairs in the middle of this and when Jane saw water in the sink and all over the counter and dripping on the floor and the five of us waving dripping weapons, she shooed us outside.

"You guys," she said, smacking Alfred on the butt to hurry him outside. "Look at all this water!" She gave Rocky a smack so he wouldn't feel left out; this was a mom who drove herself crazy, trying to be fair. "You guys!"

And didn't we just turn around and let her have it as soon as we cleared the kitchen door. In an ordinary world that would have been the end of it but it wasn't; Jane was still in the doorway gasping in the wet T-shirt, laughing and getting all red. Then she went inside and the next thing we knew she came running out with a huge, sloshing pan of dishwater. She came up behind Rocky and before he knew what she was doing she dumped it on his head. The other moms heard everybody laughing and they came out too with saucepans filled with water and let fly. Then Gabe's mom dropped her double boiler and went over to the spigot. The next thing we knew she'd taken aim and let Gabe have it with the hose.

Speedy's gun remained the best, like, *weapon*. It was big and accurate. For no reason, since it was Gabe who got squirted, she yelled, "Ow!" Then she pretended to bend over because she had something in her eye. So the biggest mother of them all came over to see was she all right and when Mrs. Darrow bent close enough, Speedy whirled out of the crouch and let her have it in the face. Then the rest of us let go with all pumps and barrels and we tangled with the mothers, who were punching and laughing like a bunch of great big huge girls.

We were in the middle when poor old Frieda came out of the kitchen door to see what was going on. For whatever reasons it was too much for her, seeing kids and grownups mixing it up like that, gargling laughter while we threw water and grappled and flailed. What may have been the worst part for Frieda was being from Finland and an outsider and seeing that in the new civilization out here in the country there was no authority she could tell her troubles to. Right then there were no responsible adults in this circle, at least not at this exact moment, there were only happy people laughing in the sunlight, exchanging insults as they tore around.

Then Speedy rolled over like a Marine with a Thompson gun and nailed the au pair and Alfred fired and Gabe and Rocky fired and even Lucky fired. So much for you, Frieda. Zot. Take that.

Frieda tried to cover all her private parts at once. "Oh please."

Gabe's mom raised a hand as if to stop them, but she was laughing too hard. "Stop it," she said weakly. Everybody was wet by then. It was plenty warm out and we thought, So what's the big deal?

Frieda was sobbing, "Please!"

Polly Peterson put on her own mom voice but absolutely without credibility because she was still holding the hose. "Come on, guys. Leave poor Frieda alone!"

"Poor Frieda, poor Frieda!"

"Please," Frieda said while everybody fired until their guns were dry. Then the au pair put together more words than we'd ever heard out of her. She must have been lying in there on the cot in her room behind the kitchen rehearsing; her pronunciation was perfect. "Can't you see I'm trying to sleep?"

So everybody had to let her have it at once.

Shrinking, she ducked back inside and we forgot. Everybody else wanted to play, even the moms. Kids ran around stalking and firing and then dodging behind trees. Speedy and Lucky took turns creating a diversion while we sneaked back to the faucet and reloaded our guns. We pretended not to see the moms sneaking up on us and the mothers pretended kids couldn't see them sneaking up because this was the best show the moms had put on all summer—kids and mothers alike, you know. Getting down.

Then the mothers huddled in the circle in front of the farmhouse, whispering, and after brief consultation they backed off and smoothed their hair and tucked in their shirts as though they were going back inside. The minute they turned their backs we crept down on them. The women waited until we were really close and turned on cue. "Gotcha!" They tackled Speedy and Gabe and brought them down as Jane lunged and grabbed Alfred and Rocky in one swoop while Lucky sprayed water that sparkled in the sunlight, dancing just out of everybody's reach. The mothers still outweighed us. They were giggling and tickling and Lucky and Alfred piled on and we all rolled around in a big tangle until everybody was completely wet, laughing and so plastered with grass and leaves and dirt that when we separated, kids and all the mothers had to take turns running under the hose to get cleaned off.

The weather was beautiful that day, air dry, sun bright, so Jane went back into the kitchen and brought out a fat plate of brownies she'd made while Frieda had us kids in town and we all sat on the grass and ate them in the sunshine while we dried out.

Of course Jane called Frieda to come outside with us but she didn't answer. Even after she sent Rocky in to deliver the invitation personally, Frieda sniffled and refused to come out of her room or even unlock the door.

We could hear Rocky in the kitchen calling to Frieda through the closed door. The mothers looked at each other over their knuckles apprehensively.

Leslie said, "Oh good grief, what have we done?"

Finally Rocky came out. "She won't let me in."

Leslie pounced. "Did you see her?"

"Not exactly."

"Is she packing?"

"She wouldn't open the door."

"What did she say?"

Rocky shrugged; after all, this was not his problem, it was Leslie's, right? He said to Mrs. Burgess, "She says she doesn't want to talk right now."

Leslie said, "Oh lord, we've hurt her feelings."

"We were just playing."

She groaned. "The girl is like a minefield. You don't know where to step to keep from setting her off."

Then Gabe's mom said, "Maybe she's just homesick."

"Homesick!" This sent Leslie up like a rocket. "Again. Do you realize what I've gone through to try to keep her happy here? That boyfriend. The stereo! Every first Friday I have to beg her not to go home all over again. I thought things would get better when this Dave started taking her out but they're only getting worse."

Polly said, "I can't be sure, but I think there's something else eating her."

When the mothers got talking, they forgot there was any-body else around, which meant that kids drifted closer, because this was how you found out things you wouldn't otherwise know.

Mrs. Darrow was saying, "You don't suppose she's pregnant."

"Oh God, Jane, spare me!"

We didn't think so. All the kids knew that pink plastic thing in the back of the top drawer in Frieda's dresser was her birth control pills and even though Alfred had the idea of taking them out and putting in something else we didn't, because we couldn't find any pills the right size that matched.

"Maybe not," Jane said, "but the girl's depressed. If you don't mind me getting clinical, I think there's something major going on."

"Maybe she's just homesick," Gabe's mother said again.

Jane shook her head. "She's clinically depressed. You need to convince her to get help."

Leslie was quick. "You don't think you could . . ."

From day to day kids forgot that people out in the world called Mrs. Darrow Doctor, even though she was just a mom, but the look she gave Lucky's mother was all doctor. "It's not that easy, Leslie. It isn't just me having a little talk. You need to get her lined up with a regular therapist. Somebody outside the situation."

"How would I explain to her parents?" Leslie was getting distraught. "How could I even admit there was anything to worry about? They'd drag her home on the next boat and then what would I do?"

"You'd manage," Jane said.

"That's easy for you to say."

Jane spoke deliberately, trying to be gentle. "She may need to go home to work it out."

"She can't leave." Leslie was looking at her hands; you'd think somebody had just handed her a little pink dishmop and three loads to take to the Laundromat. "If she leaves, my summer goes out the window. We'd end up stuck with everything."

But Jane kept on with it. "The girl doesn't have anybody to turn to."

Lucky's mom's voice went up in a little wail. "Everything."

"You're the responsible party, Les."

"Oh Jane, don't." Even kids could see Leslie scrambling around for some way out of this. "She talks to Speedy . . ."

This made Speedy duck behind the boys, trying to disappear.

". . . They sit in there and look at fashion magazines." She gave a funny little laugh. "The way I used to look at *Modern Bride*." This made her frown and she said, offhand, "Speedy, you go in and talk to her."

"The girl needs more than fashion magzines. She needs a professional who can help her open up." Jane said, "Speedy's just a kid."

But Leslie was determined to get on top of it. "The girls are *friends*. So. Speedy . . ." When Speedy backed away she said, louder, "Oh, Hyacinth."

Speedy put down the water gun. "Don't call me Hyacinth."

So they made Speedy go inside. She dragged her feet and tried to dig in. "Nobody calls me Hyacinth. Oh shit. I . . ." Her voice trailed off.

Jane said gently, "I guess it's your turn."

Oh shit, Speedy thought. Shit, shit. She scratched on the door trying to get Frieda to answer and when Frieda finally did answer in the thin voice that meant she was crying, Speedy had to beg her to open up. "Frieda, I brought you some brownies?"

The au pair's voice spun out like taffy. "Go away."

"It's OK, Frieda, we didn't mean anything."

"It isn't that." Her voice was all thin.

"We were only playing, OK?"

But Frieda was crying too hard to talk. "It isn't that!"

"It's OK, really." With Frieda sounding like that, Speedy didn't feel so good herself. "Everything's OK." When Frieda wouldn't answer she said, "Do you want to work on our special books?"

While the boys were off with the dads or ganging up against her, Speedy would go to Frieda's room and look at her snapshots of home. Finland. It looked like the moon. When Speedy got big she was going to visit Frieda there, and if she liked it, she would stay. On those deserted afternoons she and Frieda sat around on Frieda's bed cutting pictures out of fashion magazines. They glued them into composition books—pictures of everything they'd wear if they could be anybody they wanted. Princesses, movie stars, you know. They had photos of special dresses and great hair and spangled shoes and when she was pasting in the pictures Frieda would forget she was homesick and start laughing with Speedy, two girlfriends against the world. Speedy was only pasting in pictures because she needed the company, but Frieda called hers her fashion book. It was silly but it made her happy. Speedy liked hanging out, so she hung in. They could sit there and pretend.

Speedy cut out a lot of funky costumes with sequins and bangles, funny stuff. She thought it was a game, but Frieda was planning real outfits to wear to real places that she actually thought she was going to go to as soon as she figured out how to live in the United States. She had double pages for each outfit—perfect coat, perfect dress, perfect everything, right down to the shoes, and next to each item she wrote down the price. Like she was going to take all her money at the end of the summer and go out and buy everything in the book. Sometimes she talked about how they would look at her in downtown Helsinki in this outfit, and what her family would say when she walked in looking like a star.

But when Speedy brought out their paste-up books that day, Frieda just flopped on the bed and pushed her away. "Not now," she cried. There was a pattern on her face where she'd been lying on the towel she'd used to try and dry herself. She looked awful. She rolled over and put her head under her pillow. "Not now."

"Don't you at least want to look at your ballgown page?"

"Not now." The pillow was like a stopper shutting off Frieda's voice. She wheezed through three pounds of cotton, "Not now."

This left Speedy alone with the books. She opened Frieda's book to her all-time favorite, trying to think of something to say. Frieda had cut out and pasted in magazine pictures of silver shoes and a rhinestone comb and white gloves that went all the way up over the elbows. The long dress was white chiffon with floating sleeves and a big fat butterfly design in silver sequins on the front. This was supposed to be her dream outfit for the first big party she was invited to in America, and if the invitation hadn't come yet, well, it would. When it did she was going to add necklaces just like ones in the last picture she'd glued to the page—strings and strings of crystal beads. "Come on. It's your favorite," Speedy said.

Frieda still had her face in the pillow. Instead of cheering her up, Speedy wandered around the room looking at the things Frieda had marshalled to protect herself—two Hummel figurines, the girl with the birds and the boy with the balloons; pearl-handled hairbrush and comb set; the silver-framed picture of Frieda she had brought from home and propped up on the dresser like a charm that would keep her safe.

The moms were outside waiting for a communiqué; outside the other kids were reloading their water guns and Speedy knew Alfred had already appropriated hers, which meant she'd have to fight him to get it back. By the time she got back outside the brownies would be gone. Frieda just sobbed and wouldn't look at her. Speedy was marooned by the dresser, alone with the objects on the cross-stitched dresser scarf. Before she had time to wonder if Frieda would mind, she'd picked up the snapshot of Frieda in the little silver frame. It was of Frieda in a great big coat with a fur collar and a magnificent fur hat that looked like a black angora cat coiled around her head. She was standing in the middle of a snowscape with snow all around and fjords or something in the background, and rising behind them, what looked like mountains of ice. Even in the long shot Frieda's face was pink and sweet; she was happy there. Speedy could see she was smiling not just for the camera but for all time, and something about it—the distance between there and here, her home and the farm—tore Speedy apart. No. How young Frieda was, to be this far from home.

"Oh Frieda please talk to me."

If Frieda was still breathing, she made no sound.

"Come on, Frieda, OK?"

It was like being alone in the room.

In a silent movie Gabe's dad had shown on the old projector, a mountain climber finds the woman he loves trapped inside the ice at the bottom of a crevasse somewhere in the Alps. Even the name was sad. "The White Hell of Pitz-Palu." And his lost lover? Beautiful and perfect, frozen forever, preserved for eternity behind sheets of ice. Now Speedy saw Frieda frozen there. This scared her so much that she grabbed Frieda by the shoulder and shook hard. "Just say OK, OK?"

"Not now." Frieda sighed heavily. "Not now."

But instead of leaving, Speedy sat down on the bed. She stayed until Frieda knew she would never give up and go away. When Frieda's shoulders stopped shaking Speedy said, "I've got a new *Vogue.*"

Frieda rolled over so Speedy could see a corner of her face. "You do?"

"I'll go get it if you'll just talk to me."

What seemed like hours later, Speedy came out of the house.

The rest of us were sick of the water guns. The cookies were gone. We were more or less hanging out in the circle in front of the house while the moms sat on the stone front steps in the sunshine, talking and drying out.

Lucky's mother saw Speedy and pounced. "Well, where is she?"

"She doesn't want to come out right now."

Leslie got all anxious, rubbing her knuckles against her teeth. "Is it something we did?"

"Not exactly."

Mrs. Darrow said, "Is she all right?"

Speedy shrugged: your guess is as good as mine. In a way she felt like Frieda, stranded far away from home. "Friday's her birthday," she said finally.

We could see the light creeping across Leslie's face. It was like the sun coming out at the end of an eclipse. We didn't even have to stay around to know how the discussion would go. Everybody knew what Leslie was going to say. *Party.* She lit up. "Great!"

Speedy said under her breath, "But that isn't all she feels shit-ty about."

If Frieda had anything else on her mind, Lucky's mom didn't want to hear. "We'll give her a party," she said.

The moms all relaxed and smiled. "Of course."

It was her solution for everything.

Lucky said, "With lots of presents."

What surprised the guys was what Speedy said next, Speedy, who could care less what she was wearing from one day to the next. "I can tell you exactly what she wants."

It took ten phone calls, planning and collusion. We had to steal Frieda's fashion book. What we gave Frieda for her birth-day, no, what the mothers gave, was her dream outfit right out of her costume book. Mrs. Burgess was so fixed on making another perfect party that she took up a collection from the other moms and went down to the city overnight to get the dress and all the other stuff on a special shopping trip.

Instead of telling Frieda they had a surprise for her, on her birthday Leslie got everybody into the kitchen and then called Frieda out of her room, going, "Come on, Frieda, five o'clock." She said it was Friday and Frieda's turn to set the table, the fathers would be here any time so Frieda had better hurry up.

When she came out or her room the moms just hit her with massed shopping bags and a big Bergdorf's box, everything wrapped up in tissue paper with glitz-like confetti sprinkled on top. She looked so dumb, standing there blinking. "What?"

"Open it!"

She kept saying, "What, Mrs. What?"

Frieda wasn't excited or glad, she was poleaxed by this, like she'd just been hit by a truck. Instead of opening the things she took them from the moms as if she'd just been handed a bunch of ticking bombs: one false move and she'd set them off. "Thank you," she said. Her face was so stiff that there was no way to know what she was thinking as she piled the boxes and bags on top of each other and carried them back into her room.

Then she shut the door.

This left us and the moms standing around anxiously, like: What have we done? We all whispered and giggled nervously and the mothers exchanged looks and paced around the kitchen wringing their hands. The wait wasn't as long as it seemed. When Frieda came out she was holding her fashion book. She had it open to the page. And she had it on. She had put everything on. All the stuff she'd seen in the magazine and cut out and pasted in her fashion book.

She looked beautiful.

"Beautiful," Polly said, and Jane said, "Just beautiful!"

"Oh, Frieda," Leslie said, and us?

We were excited and jittery. When we thought about all the mean things we'd said to Frieda and the worse things we'd done, we were embarrassed. She looked so pretty that we were ashamed.

Everybody knew Frieda must have had some clue that something was up because her hair was freshly washed that day and for once she'd lost the braids. Instead her hair flew around her head in waves that were all crimpy from it being trapped in braids all the time. She had on lipstick and eye makeup for once and pearly nail polish on her fingernails and she'd painted her toenails too. Now that she had on the silver sandals the moms had given, it showed. The rhinestone comb looked perfect. So did the dress. The only thing missing was the crystal beads.

Frieda was so excited. She wanted to call up Finland and tell everyone. Instead the moms got her to pose while Leslie took gangs of snapshots to send her family and she was so tickled she forgot how homesick she was. She must have been thinking about her makeup too because even though she was happy, she didn't cry.

When the dads came they thought she looked beautiful too. Mr. Darrow had brought the crystal beads for Frieda's outfit and Japanese lanterns from Chinatown along with about eight dozen boxes of sparklers. Zack brought a rented projector and a sixteen-millimeter print of the old *American Werewolf in London* so we could have barn movies in Frieda's honor, something that had only happened once before. We knew Gabe's dad had to look at a string of monster movies that summer because he was writing this big movie that he wouldn't tell anybody what it was about. It was nice of him to lug a real live movie and a projector up here instead of just tapes.

The presents were over and kids were drifting away when we heard this voice. It was like the Ginsu Knife commercial. "But wait." Then Alfred and Rocky's father came front and center like a star, waiting until he had everybody's attention.

Calvin said, as if he'd arranged it specially for Frieda, "And in your honor tonight there's supposed to be a meteorite shower."

Meteorites! Alfred went, "Dad."

"Around midnight. Way after your bedtime, guys."

But we were all jumping up and yelling at him, with damn Alfred leaning on that shrill, high note: "Dad, *Dad.*"

So Lucky's mom said, "It's a special occasion, Cal. Right Jane? Right Polly?" and Frieda and the other moms backed her up.

So Calvin turned as if he personally had made the cake and planned all these surprise presents and conjured up this feat of nature in honor of the birthday, and said, "And in Frieda's honor, you guys can stay up for it."

We were psyched.

Then Speedy's father rolled in with a ruffly shirt for Speedy that was so fussy-looking somebody else must have picked it out, and when they told him it was Frieda's birthday Stig blinked and said Oh really, but he wished her happy birthday all the same and somehow she got the idea that the crystal beads were from him.

None of the kids were sure how Leslie had convinced Lucky's father to make it when he was busy in the city all the time, but even he was there, looking handsome and distracted with his indoor pallor where everybody else was tanned.

Chad came last. When he saw everybody assembled in the clearing he parked by the big tree and got out of the little MG he had bought so the family could keep the Mercedes at the farm. He had this serious look, like the mayor coming to crown the queen of some big city. "Well, Frieda."

She got all pink and glowed. "Oh, Mister," she said.

Then he bent over and pulled something out of the well behind the driver's seat and with an elegant flourish he handed her a box filled with two dozen white roses.

"Happy birthday, Frieda."

She was flushed and smiling hard. She looked as happy as she had been back there in Finland when somebody who loved her took her picture in that fur hat. "Oh thank you, Mister." She was so happy that she ran out of breath. "Oh Mister, thank you!"

Leslie moved in and took Chad's arm. "For you, Frieda. Happy birthday from all of us."

"Oh, Mrs!"

Success. Leslie turned with this triumphant look.

The mothers had gotten hold of this guy Dave that they thought Frieda was in love with and he came with a nice birthday present, earrings that dangled like Christmas-tree ornaments, touching her shoulders in little silver cascades. They didn't match the jewelry on her scrapbook page but she blushed and put them on. For the birthday Dave had shaved and pulled his hair back in a knot and dressed up in a black silk shirt and a white suit. He looked so fine that the groanies had to take pictures of Dave and Frieda standing together, and when everybody sat down to the birthday dinner they put Frieda and her boyfriend at the head of the table like a bride and groom.

We ended up sitting so Rocky was with Lucky at the end of the table like Batman and Robin, Tonto and the Lone Ranger, blood brothers, best friends, and for once Rocky lost that worried scowl. Even he could see Lucky was just being Lucky for once, happy and easy, so maybe the monster that had troubled us all summer had slouched back to Scarth Cave for the moment, leaving Lucky in peace. Gabe and Alfred lined up on either side of them. Speedy sat next to Gabe with her dad on the other side, and even though she knew she looked dumb in it, she was proud and uncomfortable in the frilly new shirt.

We had a special dinner, four courses, and after the cake Speedy brought in this thing she'd thought up. She had copied it from one of the hometown snapshots Frieda thumbed through with her on rainy afternoons. It was a wreath. The wreath was beautiful, ivy and evergreen twined into a circle with four candles set in the top of it. "Oh," Frieda said when she saw it. "Oh. Oh!" Her face got all happy and complicated, and as we watched she went back inside her head, looking for the right words. Jane saw something was going on and she moved in behind Speedy quickly, so she couldn't back off. After she thought about it, Frieda made a little speech. "So pretty. Yes! But St. Lucy's night is in the winter, you know?"

Speedy went, like, Oh shit, I should have looked it up. "Oh Frieda." She put her hand over her mouth.

"Come on," Jane said quickly, presenting both Speedy and the wreath. "You can't say no to a gift."

Reinforced, Speedy said, "I made it. It's for you."

"So nice. For me."

And Frieda took it and gave her a hug.

Then she put it on and Speedy smiled and smiled.

So when the kids and the groanies went outside for the barn movies Frieda was wearing the floaty white dress and all the other things the groanies had bought for her; she was carrying the roses and wearing the ivy wreath with four white candles set in the top. The little party could have been marching into a movie Frieda had written and directed for herself and was starring in, and if there was anything not like a movie it was the fact that the whole cast smelled of *Off*.

In spite of the bugs, barn movies were wonderful. The image flashed up there in front of you in the night and it was tremendous, bigger than any one of us, bigger than the dark that surrounded us, bigger than life. The grownups had brought out enough insect repellent and spray and citronella candles to keep the bugs away and they'd thrown piles of pillows on the blankets spread in the turnaround in front of the house. Zack ran a string of heavy-duty extension cords outside so he could aim the projector at the flat white wall of the barn. The picture was so big! You could see the werewolf big as *that*, his head was eight feet tall. The kids were clumped up in one place so there wasn't much wiggling and there was absolutely no punching, just people muttering as he went through the change, jaw snapping, snout poking out. The great thing about movies was that they couldn't hurt you, and one way or another, things came out all right in the end.

The moms and dads and Frieda and this Dave all curled up on blankets in pairs while we ate M&Ms and swilled Coke and Lucky lunged around with big bowls of popcorn and then threw himself down on the blanket with his mom and dad. We were all in the circle together, both generations, hanging close as though the moms and dads were the front ranks and between them they could hold off anything or anybody that came to threaten us. Between reels kids could lie on their backs and look up at the stars. It was like being on an island in the middle of the universe, everybody close and warm and mellow, it was fine!

"Oh, Mister," Frieda gurgled, excited and positively overwhelmed. "Oh, Mrs. Oh, kids." She didn't have the words to thank us.

Then it turned out she did.

Zack had the speakers aimed out the windows so they'd have stereo sound and in the big chase scene it all came together. We heard Frieda just as it ended and the projector went off. Her breath came out like the final chord.

"I wish this could go on forever," she said.

In that moment, everybody did.

When the boys had reeled up the wires and helped Zack take

down the projector, everybody carried drinks and birthday cake and all the blankets down into the field behind the house to wait for the meteorites. It was not our fault that nothing happened right away or that people were getting a little wild with waiting for it or that Alfred got bored. Alfred started trying make Lucky listen to this werewolf story. He said he'd made up all by himself. Then Gabe said no it was *his* story and Alfred hit him. They tangled and Zack had to wade in and pull them apart.

Gabe was furious. "I'm the story person, I'm the fucking story person."

"Enough," Zack shook Gabe. "Where is this coming from?"

"I am." He kept on with this even though his mom was shaking her head and going, *No no.* "I know beginnings, middles and ends!"

Zack yelled, "I said, that's enough!" Gabe didn't know why his father was so mad.

Then the groanies remembered the sparklers and Calvin went up and brought them down from the house along with a box of kitchen matches and before anybody saw what he was doing he'd stuck a bunch in the top of a rotting fence post and lighted them off. The mini-explosions made little rosettes of fire in the night. The next thing we knew every kid and grownup in the field was holding a bouquet of fizzing sparklers and somewhere in the middle of it Frieda had forgotten it wasn't either Finland or Christmas and let Dave light all the candles on the St. Lucy's wreath. This Dave was grinning and our Frieda was walking dreamily through all this celebration in a blaze of sparklers like the queen of Finland. No, the queen of the world, while the boys and Speedy zoomed around her in madly complicated patterns, lighting new sparklers off the last, waving so many at one time that the wires burned our hands. We were drunk on air and the night and so excited that we hardly felt the heat, all five of us swirling and dipping in the amazing night.

Then one of the dads went, "Oh, wow!"

And we looked up.

We had brought the meteorites.

So we were back in a circle again, moms and dads and kids all clumped, close in the dark, with Speedy snug between her father and the Petersons and Frieda hugging Dave, grownups craning and kids lying on our backs on the blankets with our eyes and mouths wide open, mesmerized.

There is no way to describe this.

We were in love with the sky.

Nobody wanted to admit it when the last meteorite had hurtled by and fizzled out. Finally the grownups began to stir.

Frieda murmured, "I wish it would never end."

Jane murmured, "I know."

Leslie said, "I'm so glad," and in the darkness chased with afterimages, the women's voices were sweet. The other groanies shifted in the dark, sighing and rolling apart.

"Well, I guess that's it," Chad said in a voice lighter than air. He was the first to get to his feet, standing, bemused, in the black night while at his feet Leslie hugged his ankles for a second before he dropped his hand to help her up.

Without noticing whether the children followed, the grownups got to their feet slowly like enchanted courtiers, and, colliding without impact, began drifting up the path to the house.

The kids were the last to move. When we finally stood up we were stiff and half blind with shooting afterimages, staggering around and bumping into each other in the dark.

Alfred shrieked and we all turned. "My God, it's the monster!"

"The monster!"

For the minute, we thought it was.

This rotting, glowing face hung in midair. It hung right in the middle of the path, terrible and luminous, bobbing up and down above our heads as if the body that we couldn't see was tremendous, huge and ready to devour us. The thing was between us and the house and we were terrified.

Then the grownups started laughing and we thought they were laughing at us.

"Don't," we screamed at them. "Help!"

"Don't be scared, it's nothing." They knew what it was. Nothing to be afraid of, kids. If we were afraid, it meant we were only children after all.

Alfred screamed, "Go away!"

Still it hung there, nothing we recognized.

But in the darkness ahead we heard the grownups jostling and laughing. Shaking, we figured it out. No way was the thing in the path the monster from Scarth Cave. It wasn't a monster from anywhere. It was . . .

Rocky yelled, "Watch out!" and lunged.

In the darkness we could hear our friend tangle with the monster. They wrestled. We stuck our fingers in our ears but there weren't any growls or screeches, nothing but hysterical giggling. We heard Rocky going, "Where did you get it, where did you *get* it?"

Then he and the monster separated and the monster came apart. The stick fell in one direction, Lucky in the other. He was laughing at us. Rocky danced away with the rotting, luminous face clapped on like a jockstrap and we all collapsed laughing because Lucky had sneaked out and bought this scary thing and he'd snuck it out here in his pants and while we were hung up on the meteors, giggling and fixed on the sky, he pulled it out and raised it on a pole. He'd moved so fast that he had us fooled. We almost believed that the monster from Scarth Cave had cracked out and come crashing down the mountain looking for us.

Right, we were supposed to know better. Even though we were pretty strung out on barn movies and too much sky, even though we were ripe with excitement and ready to swallow anything and be scared, we were reinforced by all those groanies, who were supposed to know better.

They knew better, so we knew better too.

Rocky swung the ghoulish face around his head in this luminous blur and then he stopped with a leap like a player making a free throw and whirled around and held it up. *Nothing to be afraid of.*

"See?"

It was only a rubber mask.

12

Gabe

If somebody dropped a stone into the web early that summer, the vibrations had reached the edges now. The whole thing was shivering. It was August. The summer was sliding downhill. There was something alien in the shed chamber. Someone stepped over Gabe in the night and he screamed. Gabe Peterson, who never screamed. He could not have said what twisted in his belly, or why he was so scared. "Leave me alone!"

Lucky growled, "Shut up."

"What are you *doing?*"

"Going out. It's no big deal."

Gabe choked with foreboding. "The Thing." He didn't know what was out there but they all knew there was something in the shadows that confused their days and troubled their nights. "Werewolves."

Lucky could not tell him there were no monsters. "It's cool."

"Oh man," Gabe said urgently, "at least keep the goddam charm on you." They all carried sharpened ten-penny nails. In case.

Lucky shrugged him off with this weird half-smile. "Werewolves aren't the worst thing that can happen to you."

Whether or not it had started with his dad's monster movie, Gabe and his friends had been stalking werewolves and vampires all summer, looking for telltale bite marks on the neck, black hairs sprouting on the backs of the hands. They said spells and went through doors backward. They improvised crosses, holding them up as if they really believed you could make evil forces cringe and back away. Only half fooling, they were giddy from keeping watch.

If his dad would only finish his script, they'd know how the movie came out. In a world filled with monsters, you need to know what kills these things.

So it was his father's fault for not doing what he said he was doing and finishing his damn script. Unfinished, it was scary. The monster that gets you by the throat and won't let go.

"The times," Zack had said *in their very own living room* last spring. He was so busy trying to impress his producers that he didn't care how scary it got or that Gabe was listening. "People get turned into something they hate, *against their will*," he said. He would have said anything. "When they get you, they turn you into monsters like themselves. Sink your fangs into somebody's throat. What a rush! Don't you see it? The vampire is the perfect emblem for the times."

They said vampires were over. They said show us something new and for a minute Gabe's dad looked like he was about to crumble. Then he straightened up.

"Werewolves," Zack said.

Now Gabe's father was like the werewolf caught in the middle—half professor, half something else. He said the script would be finished in March. He said it would be finished by June. Now it was August and he was still crumpling up paper and throwing it away, working on the electric typewriter out in the shed, hooked up to the house by a great big extension cord. It got hot and he went slouching through the days like a baggy monster in a maze.

He couldn't get it written and he couldn't stop writing it.

It was terrible. Like there was a hole in Zack's life and everything was slipping through. Gabe thought if he could just help his dad, he could make him smile. They would be partners.

The other kids thought he was really finishing his movie and it was cool. They dropped into slouches and bared their fangs and claws.

Their very first night up here, Dad told everybody about it at dinner. "When I finish, they're scouting locations up here."

"Up here!" They would all be in the movies for sure. "Oh, Dad. Can I be in it?"

Alfred pushed Gabe out of the way, yelling, "Can I be? Can I?"

Daddy laughed a big laugh and hugged Gabe. "Sure." Listen. It was possible. Dad was so happy. He couldn't stop laughing. "They've already given me money up front." Three thousand dollars, but Gabe wasn't allowed to tell; it seemed like a lot to him. That first night Zack was hopeful, expansive. "When they pay me the pickup, I'll buy you kids a car."

After dinner that night he went out in the long twilight with his notepad, picking out places for things to happen and writing it down. The kids followed in a flock. Zack had a Pentax and he went around looking at everything through it like a big director. To get his attention you had to walk right up to the camera and look at him through the lens.

"I love this place," he said. "Anything can happen here."

They were all bumping into each other in the dusk. The sky got light as their eyes got used to being in the dark. Carrying after-dinner drinks out the kitchen door, the groanies jostled and hummed. It was late spring. Daddy was right. Anything could.

"I love the farm," Zack said, while guys spread their arms and zoomed around him like biplanes. Even Speedy was going, rmm, rmm, rmm. "I love the idea that *those bats* . . ." Daddy's hand swept up and, lord, the fuckers began coming out of the attic and zooming around in the twilight. Bats!

What bats?

"Those bats . . ." As he spoke it became true. They filled the sky. It was like a sign. ". . . those *very bats* could be vampires."

Right.

"And werewolves lurking in those trees. One bite and you . . ." Dad's voice went out looking for something and did not come back.

"I know, Dad." Gabe couldn't help himself. He was gobbling with excitement. "Daddy, I know what happens to you."

"Shh, Gabe." Zack's voice created its own spooky hush. "Because in the country of the vampires, the werewolf walks. And then the werewolf bites, and then the werewolf . . . then the werewolf." It was where he always stopped. His voice trailed off because he didn't know what then.

That was in June. Here it was August and Daddy still hadn't figured it out. He was going around like that character in the comics that goes around with a cloud over its head.

Sometimes Gabe thought there was a cloud hanging over the whole farm. It moved in with the monster from Scarth Cave. Now they couldn't get it out.

It was OK in the daytime but as soon as the lights went out, Lucky would start. Some nights he said the farmer's son was still alive up there in Scarth Cave, under tons and tons of earth. Put your ear to the ground and you could hear his screams. On other nights he made the monster lurch downhill, making mouth noises until everybody could hear it snuffling and groaning right outside the door. Kofi shuddered in his sleeping bag. Speedy rolled up in hers and cried.

At least with werewolves, there were things you could do. Kids twisted fetishes in their hair and made secret designs on their hands with Magic Marker. Nobody knew which charms were supposed to do what. They weren't altogether certain what they were warding off, but at least they were doing something about it.

Kofi was there for the month. He was in his Afrocentric period. In the heritage he claimed were things Gabe could only guess about: dark magic and powerful spells. Together he and

Kofi thought up new charms; they walked ritual walks and spoke in code. The kids could not have told you what was going on but they knew there was something chained in the dark tower of the imagination, and it was getting huge.

Then Saturday Zack came out of the shed with three typed pages and Gabe thought, Finally. Everything will get better now. His dad was happy for the first time in weeks. He actually picked up Gabe and spun him around. "Progress," he said, hugging him. "I need you guys."

Gabe's belly went soft with pleasure.

"Tonight. After dinner." His beard was scraggly where he'd pulled it and his hair was wild. "Story conference, for Lucky's dad. I may need you guys to read lines so I can see how it plays."

It sounded so professional: *So I can see how it plays.*

Zack was counting on Mr. Burgess to put him in touch with the major players. It was like Chad was the only person that mattered here. It was weird, how Mr. Burgess was never around, but for all the other fathers, he was some kind of big deal. Like a train going somewhere, that they all wanted to get on.

It was late. Instead of sandals and pretty shirts Gabe's mom was clomping around in work shirts and Doc Martens most days, and instead of nice vases she was making humongous, angry shapes out of clay. Gabe was really glad his dad finally had some script to show. It might cheer her up. The trouble was when it came time, Dad didn't want her there. Leslie was trying to get everybody to go off to some bar halfway to the New York state line so they could go dancing, but when Mom asked Dad, Zack said, "Chad and I are talking. You go ahead."

Polly said, "We're not leaving yet. We can go when you're through."

"It's not that simple!" Then, boy, Zack did a dumb thing. He said, "Please, Polly, not now. I can't have interruptions when I lay this out for Chad." Gabe was embarrassed for both of them. With Mom around, it would be harder to act cool with Mr. Burgess, who was definitely cool in his expensive safari jacket, with the fold-up phone and pocket computer and three-hundred-dollar boots. So she gave him this look and made a lot of noise going back into the kitchen to wait for him.

Dad called all the kids into the living room.

Gabe didn't know whether to be proud or embarrassed. Some of the stuff sounded pretty good, but considering his father had been at it all summer, there wasn't very much.

It was definitely embarrassing, watching Lucky's father listening and being polite.

Zack started on strong but ended up waffling, as if he could get a running start and sneak up on his ending and pounce. It was like trying to catch a spool of thread that's rolling downhill; the longer it ran, the more it got away from him. He talked on and on.

The kids were beginning to squirm.

Maybe if Gabe gave him an ending Mr. Burgess would stop looking so bored and topping off his Jack Daniels. Right there in front of everybody, Dad would thank him for being such a big help. But Gabe was only a kid. He was not allowed to interrupt. Chad just slouched deeper in the chair while Zack rambled and Gabe sat with his insides itching, trying to tell himself it was OK, really, his father was not being a jerk.

Alfred was preening; you could almost see black hairs growing. Kofi kept drumming on the floor with his fingers. Speedy had her fist in her mouth; Rocky was weirded out and Lucky's eyes were fixed on something Gabe couldn't see.

Then Zack just stopped. He had absolutely run out. Gabe happened to know his dad was still having story problems. He wasn't supposed to know this, but he did. It explained why he got so pissed if you tripped on the extension cord, and why he couldn't do anything with you because he always had to work. Even Mom wasn't allowed to knock during working hours; She had to sit on the steps outside the shack like a kid, hoping he'd come out so she could talk to him. It was awful. But tonight he was smiling for Mr. Burgess, saying, "If I can just get a handle on this thing, I can break its back."

He still hadn't figured it out. Gabe was going to die if Dad didn't figure it out. Nights Gabe could go to bed in the shed chamber and see the whole ending—monsters. Werewolves, what they did to you, chapter and verse. And Zack. He didn't even know!

Gabe couldn't understand it. It was so easy! Ideas just came to him. It was like breathing. All you had to do was make it up. But you weren't supposed to say anything because it was your father's business and your father was talking to Mr. Burgess and you were only eleven years old. "Daddy," he said. "I know."

If his father heard him, it didn't show. He just said to Mr. Burgess, "You know what it's like. Right, Chad?"

"Old, Dad." Gabe said, louder, "In the end the werewolf bites you and you get old."

"Old," Zack said absently, "That's the last thing I need to hear."

"Old," Gabe said in case his father hadn't heard.

"Werewolves that transform you," Zack said dreamily. Three months and he didn't have a clue. He didn't have a clue as to what would come next. "What do you think? Chad?"

"I just told you, Dad." Gabe flexed his claws and made fangs. He bit his father's hand, worrying it like a wolf.

"Don't do that!"

"I fixed your story!"

"My story doesn't need fixing."

"That's not what you told Mom."

Dad freaked. "Not in front of Mr. Burgess. Please."

"Daddy, listen. Just *listen*." OK, maybe he did yell.

Zack gave him this look: *Chill out.* "I said, *not now.*" His voice got sharp. "I'm the writer here."

Lucky said kindly, "Want to play in the barn?"

He shrugged. "Not now. It's dark in there."

When he turned back to his father he was astounded. Right there in front of him, his father was telling Mr. Burgess, "The werewolf bites you and you get old."

Gabe said, "Dad."

Zack didn't hear! "You want to die. The worst part is, you can't."

"Dad, that was . . ."

"Old," he said anyway.

". . . my idea."

"Old for eternity, Chad."

Chad said dryly, "I can think of worse things than getting old."

Alfred roared in like a dive bomber, droning, "Oooold. I bite you and you get old." Something was wrong with Alfred this summer, Gabe thought bitterly. All the bad parts of him converged. The kids all hated him. The groanies thought he was cute. He roared into the middle of everything and swooped down on Gabe's father, baring his fangs and lurching and shriveling like a ham actor, which is what he was. "Old like this, right Zack?"

"Wait a minute, asshole."

"Gaby, that's enough!"

But Gabe said, "Bother your own damn father."

Then in this amazing act of betrayal, Zack grinned and ruffled fucking *Alfred's* hair. "Alfred, that's a wonderful idea."

"Daddy, it was my idea."

But Dad said to Alfred, "I think you're on to something. When I get this in shape I'll get a camcorder. We'll shoot a couple of scenes." He was only half fooling. "Stick with me, kid. I'll make you a star."

Alfred looked at Gabe from under Zack's elbow with this gratified smirk.

So Gabe hit him. "I said, it was my fucking idea!"

Know how you get upset and your hand flies out so you hit the wrong person? Dad swung. "Gaby, watch your damn lan-

guage!" This is how Zack dismissed him. "I'm the writer here."
Then with this helpless shrug he said to Mr. Burgess, "That's
what I have so far. Do you think it will play?"

Chad just made a Lucky face.

Dad was waiting. The only thing that mattered was what Mr.
Burgess thought and he couldn't get him to say anything.
"Werewolf and victim," he said, like a prompter. "Eternal. Un-
dead."

Lucky's dad just grinned a drunkish grin. "I'm already undead."

Then Zack changed. "Being undead isn't the worst thing that
can happen to you." He gave them *this scary look* and right there
in front of everybody his voice cracked in two. "The worst thing
is getting old."

Thank God Mom cut him off. Polly's voice was sharp and a
little stern; when had she come in? "Zack."

He could have been batting away a bumblebee. "Not now."

Polly leaned in the doorway, pretty and anxious with her hair
skinned back and her body hidden in a coverall that said *Sid's
Auto Body* above the pocket. "Zack, enough. It's time to go."

"I said, not now!" It was like he had slapped her in the face.
He didn't see; he just went on spinning Gabe's skein. "Ancient
werewolves, Chad. Ancient victims, and . . ." it just hung there.

This was it. It was now or never. Gabe spun a final twist. He
was yelling, "And only a kid can kill them, Dad." But probably
because he was the youngest and Dad was used to him, he didn't
hear.

Alfred did. He heard Gabe and picked it up and ran with it.
So it was Alfred who got Daddy's attention. Alfred, the idea
thief. He jumped up and lurched toward the dads, screaming in
that *stagey voice,* "Mr. Peterson, Mr. Peterson."

"All right, what!"

Sucking up to him like an A student. Call on me, call on me.
"It takes a kid to kill them, Mr. Peterson."

Gabe growled, "Wait a minute, asshole."

Zack hit his forehead: of course. "Kids!"

"A special kid. Like me."

Dad was like Edison discovering the light bulb. "Right."

"Wait a fucking minute," Gabe said, but it was too late.

"Hush, Gabe, I want to see this. Go, Alfred!"

"Shut up, shitass." Gabe hurled himself on Alfred, pounding hard and saying, bitterly, "Go bother your own damn father."

But Mom moved in from nowhere and stopped it. Polly put her arm around Gabe's shoulder and began shooing people off to bed. "OK, kids, time to break it up." She turned to Zack, trying to rout him out of his chair. "If we're going out, we'd better go." Before she let Gabe go she squeezed him hard.

"I told you, I don't have time."

Polly's voice was shaking. "Well I'm going and so is everybody else. Are you coming or not?"

Zack snapped, "Not tonight. This is a make-or-break situation, OK?"

She was madder than Gabe had ever seen her. Like everybody else, his mom was changing that summer; it showed in the way she acted and the things she wore, dumb disguises because no matter how tough she tried to look, she was going to be pretty Polly all her life. She smashed her hand-built pots back into raw clay while Zack sat out in the toolshed not writing anything. It all boiled up in her like a bad dinner. "This picture." Her face was set in a basilisk glare. "This picture. This picture."

He was cold, the way he was with a bad student. "Yes. This picture."

"*Men!* The only thing that's important to you is what's important to you." Then Mom slammed into the kitchen and kicked the door shut.

After everybody left to go dancing and the other kids went up to bed Gabe sat outside the living room, slumped at the bottom of the stairs. When Daddy got tired of talking and came up to bed, Gabe was going to stop him and tell about how Alfred stole his idea.

He and Mr. Burgess weren't talking business at all. From where Gabe sat, he could see into the living room. The dads were just sitting in front of the fireplace, having more drinks. Something had changed. Mr. Burgess was saying, "So when you think you're finally getting what you want you turn around and see that something else has slipped. Like, maybe you traded off part of your life in some unholy pact?"

"Chad, I would trade what I have for what you have in a minute," Gabe's father said.

Mr. Burgess said, "It's not a very big success."

"It's a success."

Mr. Burgess turned this sweet face to him. "But you have everything else."

And in one minute and with Gabe watching, his father turned their whole lives into nothing. "Well that's no big deal! I should have thought ahead," he said morosely. "A wife. Kids. How'm I going to get a chance when I have all these fucking responsibilities?"

Mr. Burgess was watching the fire like TV. "There's no law says you can't have both."

"Shit, Chad, I don't even have a script." Then Daddy said this heavy thing. "Do you know what I used to think? I used to think marriage was something you got out of the way so you could get on with your career. Big mistake."

Don't, dad, OK?

"All it does is tie you down."

Gabe groaned and hugged his knees. *Just don't.*

"Kids are like definitions, holding you back."

Mr. Burgess sounded fuzzy. "You can't blame Polly."

"Listen, Chad. I need this picture." *Daddy, shut up.* My God, Gabe's own father said, "I would die for it." And then he said the worst thing. "I would swap everything I have."

Gabe couldn't stand any more. He popped out and grabbed his father's dangling hand, shaking it and shouting, "Zack!"

"Not now, Gabe."

"Daddy, it's important!"

So he stood abruptly, Zack Peterson, who said he would never be strict and repressive like his own father, Zack Peterson, who said he was friends with his kids. His face was red and he shouted as if it was Gabe that had brought down all his troubles, Gabe that kept him from doing, or being whatever it was he wanted so bad. "Well goddammit, so is this!"

"I'm only trying to help!"

"If you want to help, get the fuck out of here!"

Gabe went back to the shed chamber and like an injured animal crawled back under one of the gables, dragging his sleeping bag. No wonder nights in the shed chamber were so creepy. *We are all in danger now.* Aching, Gabe lay in the dark waiting for the monster.

It didn't take long to come.

Alfred just started. "When his fangs sink in, you have this humongous gasm."

If not everybody knew what this meant exactly, nobody said so.

The others stirred to signal that they were still awake. Kofi went, "Yeah, man."

"What's he talking about."

Speedy said, "Don't talk dirty."

Alfred went on in a nasty voice. "But you wouldn't know, right Gabe?"

"Shut up, Alfred."

"You wouldn't have any idea what happens when people Do It, pussy."

He snarled, "That's what you think!"

"Well here's what happens."

This time it was Rocky who growled, "Shut up, asshole."

"You have this great big gasm."

"I said, shut up. You don't know anything."

"Well neither do you, Rocky fucking Darrow, you don't

know anything about sex." Alfred was getting louder and louder. "Well this is what it's like. When you get one, you shake and then you rattle all over. And sometimes you yell."

"Rattlegasm," Lucky said and then he pulled his head into his sleeping bag like a turtle and wouldn't talk to them.

Rocky groaned. "Orgasm."

"Big gasm," Alfred said.

Gabe wished Alfred would die.

"Now ask me how I know about the gasms," Alfred said. When nobody asked he answered anyway. "The only way you find out about the gasm is Doing It."

Rocky yawned the way dogs do when they want you to stop messing with them. "Oh shut up, Alfred."

There was a nasty little hush. Alfred waited until the air was completely still again and then he dropped the words in, like turds. "Or seeing two people Doing It."

"If you want my damn father so bad you can have him," Gabe said angrily.

But Alfred kept floating these things into the darkness. "I know a lot of things you assholes don't know."

"Well big deal," Rocky said, for all of them.

Inside the sleeping bag, Lucky's voice was muffled. "Shut your hole."

But Alfred wouldn't. "A lot of things."

OK, he can have my damn father, Gabe thought; he can have anything he wants if he will stop doing this. "Shut up."

Instead Alfred went on, miserably, "Now ask me how I know all about Doing It."

Then Lucky surprised them all. Their friend Timothy Burgess rose up in his sleeping bag like the monster and thumped two bumps across the shed chamber and fell on top of Alfred, punching, and because the groanies would raise hell if things got too loud, the two of them fought in more or less complete silence, all spit and hissing except at the end, when

SUMMER

Alfred wheezed, "OK, OK, I give, I give." Then Lucky got up off him and in these perfectly reasonable tones he said:

"So OK, Alfred goddamn fucking Darrow. Fuck you."

13

Roseann

Roseann was the only one Leslie told. Since all her good old friends had turned out to be holier than thou, it was ironic. Following some unwritten rule of the tribe, when she and Stig split the others took sides. Forget the women's revolution. Jane and Polly—Leslie, of all people, lined up behind the man.

Stig was living high off the hog that summer because everybody felt sorry for him. Without paying a penny for the privilege, he got custody of going to the farm while Roseann had to wait in Central Park like a panhandler just to get a few minutes with her darling girl, perched on a splintered bench like a squirrel begging for crumbs.

It all came down on her at the end of August, when she brought her boyfriend Derek up to New York. She had promised to take him around to galleries she knew to show his work. If he could just sell something, maybe they'd settle down. If he couldn't sell, he expected her to quit painting and get a job. She still liked art but living with an artist was something else. They only cared about their own work, not yours. They got all bent if you didn't love their work and said it wasn't the painting's fault, it was you. She and Derek were stuck on this lumpy sofa in his friends' loft while he went the rounds with his portfolio; every night he would slouch in like Willy Loman. Roseann would say, "You don't have to take this crap, let's go down to DC, where they appreciate you," and he would only sulk. She'd try to hug him, saying, "We don't have to do this." But rough Derek jerked away with this tight scowl that pulled his hair down to his eyebrows, saying, "Oh yes we do."

They couldn't make love at his friends' place because there were people sleeping in every corner, art school classmates who needed a place to crash. Derek didn't see what difference it made; kids don't mind these things, and if Roseann complained they got into a fight. The whole trip was bad for their relationship. She thought, OK, a little fresh air will fix me up. He needs space.

But when Roseann called the farm to tell them she was coming up to see her daughter, Jane got all weird. First Jane said they would love to see her and promised to meet the bus in Albany and then she said:

"You're not *bringing* him?"

"What if I am? Jane, we're in love!"

All Jane said was, "This is not the best time."

"Don't be crazy, it's time you got a look at him."

She sort of choked. "I think it would be very awkward, Roseann."

"No problem," Roseann explained. "Stig's staying in the city all week, so you don't have to worry about us bumping into each other at the farm." She kind of wished they would connect: she wanted Stig to see her. How good she looked with her new man, like a woman who was loved. She wanted to see how the summer had treated him; she missed him, weird as it seemed.

"It might be hard on Speedy," Jane said.

Stig gave her the nickname. He used it during those long silences when he wasn't speaking to her: Speedy, take this to your mother, speed it up. So she was a little cold when she corrected Jane. "You mean Hyacinth."

Instead of responding, Jane reproached her. "After all, you and Derek left without saying goodbye."

'Is that what Stig says?" She said, "Listen, Hyacinth loves

Derek. When we get married she's going to come and live with us." She said, "Why is this such a problem? Stig has girls. Nobody cares what he does on the side." Roseann personally knew the sainted Stig was boffing a lot more women than her so-called friends wanted to hear about, but as far as they were concerned she was the scarlet woman here, the bad mother who had to wait at the back door and beg. "I can't just leave Derek right now."

She could not understand what was Jane's problem, or what made her friend's voice so harsh when she said, "Are you afraid he'll step out behind your back?"

"I think you'd better let me talk to Leslie, Jane."

"If that's what you want you'll have to wait."

After a long pause she heard Leslie at the other end. "Leslie, thank God it's you."

Sexy Leslie, her best friend, what did Leslie say? "We'd *love* to see you, Roseann, but. Ah. It's a bad time. It's complicated here." She went on in an excited whisper that Roseann couldn't make out.

"What, Leslie. What?"

"Shh. Details when I see you, OK?"

"When you see me?"

"I need a favor," Leslie said.

So it turned out Leslie had errands in the city and she promised to bring Roseann's little girl down from the country with her so they could meet. Who knew she had ulterior motives? Roseann did, as soon as she saw what Leslie was wearing that day—Roseann, who had spent all summer bowing out of rooms backward in this eternal posture of apology because heaven forgive her, she got carried away. But Leslie, Leslie had secrets, which was how she ended up stuck on this park bench.

By the time she and Leslie sat down, Roseann was already pretty bummed; she was so excited that she said the wrong thing to her daughter first off. It was an accident; it had been two months and she was surprised. "Oh Hyacinth," she said when they hugged; lord forgive her, it just slipped out, "You're starting to grow boobies!" Mistake. The child clamped her arms across her front like a stone statue of Joan of Arc while Roseann rushed on. "Oh shit, sweetheart, that's not what I meant to say."

To make it worse, Leslie's kid Timothy corrected her. Like Hyacinth, this kid had another, kid name, what was it? Lucky? Why did these kids all hate their names? Lucky. He didn't look lucky. His face was squinched up as if it really mattered, when it was only a name. "She doesn't like being called Hyacinth, Mrs. Fenton. It's Speedy, OK?"

"Right." Oh, God. I shouldn't have left you behind for so long. She sighed. Children. *Step where I tell you. Say May I.* When she left with Derek she forfeited her rights.

Her daughter ducked her head and took off so Roseann had to call after her, "Speedy, I just meant I think you're beautiful," but Speedy was out of there. Probably Roseann should have run after her but the kids were so quick there was no catching up. Besides, she was too bummed. Kicked out of the farm like Philip Nolen, poor Mrs. Man Without a Country, and on top of that she'd hurt her little girl's feelings and made her run away. Even if Roseann caught up, there wasn't much she could do. She couldn't take Speedy back to the old apartment because Stig might have a girlfriend there. Derek and his friends were cool, but he woke up in a really bad mood today and he needed time to simmer down before she took these kids back to the loft. She couldn't focus on a plan because she was worried to death about Derek. Could she ever make him happy again?

Then out of a clear sky Leslie just began. "You're the only one I can tell," she said with a conspiratorial grimace. "You're the only one who can possibly understand."

Roseann said immediately, "You're cheating on Chad."

"Shh. The *kids.*" Leslie could hardly wait until they were out of earshot. She was so *pink.* "Oh Roseann, I'm in love."

It must be true. Leslie's hair was a new color. Instead of being that goddam genteel ash blonde, it was platinum. For the first time in her life it was out of control; tendrils kept curling in the heat, springing up as Leslie tried to mash them down. Roseann studied her. "Is he going to leave his wife?"

"How did you know he was married?"

Roseann just gave her a look.

They were on a bench at East 78th Street while her gorgeous little girl that she hadn't seen since early June and couldn't talk to played with Lucky right over there, near enough to see, but impossible to hug. She could be million miles away. Here it was, the day of Roseann's big reunion and Speedy and Leslie's untended-looking boy were grappling on the turf; all summer in that godforsaken patch in the boonies and they took on as if they'd never seen grass. Leslie had traded in her chic city clothes for this more or less transparent black thing that made her look like a dead princess; her black bikini underpants showed through the fabric, and the black bra.

Roseann couldn't handle it; she just snapped. "OK. Who is he?"

Leslie looked distracted. "I had to come down anyway, to get some stuff for Chad's birthday bash."

"Who is the guy?

"He's turning forty on Labor Day."

"I said, who is he, Leslie?"

Leslie didn't answer; she just went on. "So I made him promise to come up for his birthday. Forty. God. Poor Chad. Nobody wants to go through that alone. Besides, it's the last long weekend."

Roseann said, "You still haven't told me who he is."

"But don't say anything to anybody. It's supposed to be a big surprise." Leslie's voice dropped and she went on without missing a beat. "It's kind of awful, looking at your marriage and knowing that it's over, but you know how it is."

"You think I of all people know how it is."

Leslie said, "Something like that."

Roseann drew herself up. "We didn't mean to do it, Les. We were good people. We just got wrecked by something we didn't understand." It was part of the truth.

Who was Roseann to have to explain? With her, at least, Stig was almost impotent, blamed her, stopped talking to her. At least she had her reasons! Right, she thought, Stig smiles and laughs when he is out among the people, but in our house he turned to stone. You wake up one morning to discover that you are lying next to a statue and you know if you don't get out, you're going to turn to stone. She sat there looking at Leslie with tears in her eyes.

"Oh God," Leslie said gratefully, "I knew you'd understand. The thing is, I still love Chad. I do. I really love him and I think he's a wonderful person, but he just. It just." She started over. "Since this other thing got started . . . I can go through a whole week without ever giving him a thought. Chad's the sexiest, most wonderful husband anybody could hope for, and I hardly ever think about him when he's not around."

"All right, Leslie, who is it?"

The bitch. Here was Roseann on the line, naked and with her whole life hanging out, and Leslie wouldn't tell. Instead she went: I've Got a Secret. "I can't. If anybody knew, the world would blow apart. Listen, probably that's part of it, you know?"

Roseann did know: *the power.* "You get off on cheating."

"If you want to call it that." Leslie's eyes began to shine. "If you want to know, I get off on having something nobody knows I have. Having a lover . . . It's like having a jewel, a diamond, that I can take out and look at whenever I get low. Or a secret birthday present, that I can keep unwrapping, over and over, and every time it's a little bit better because I don't know what to expect." She made a fist. "For once I've got some power over my life!"

Just wait, Roseann thought sadly. Just wait.

"And to think you showed me the way." Leslie was radiant.

"It makes you feel so—I don't know. When Chad finally does turn up I look at him and I think, You think you are so superior, but now I am the one. I think, poor old Chad."

Why couldn't Roseann think anything except, Poor me?

Leslie was bearing down. "You want to know something? Something important. This has been good for our marriage. Sex is better. Chad's and mine."

Sure, Roseann thought with a twinge.

Leslie didn't seem to notice that she wasn't responding. "I think real love totally completes you. Don't you think love totally makes you who you are?"

Roseann thought: Love makes you anxious. "Amazing," she said.

"It makes me feel, I don't know. Generous. It makes me feel that much closer to Chad."

It tore her and Stig apart. At least Derek was single; Roseann wasn't the Other Woman, Derek was the Other Man. She wasn't trashing some unsuspecting wife. They were artists in love. OK, in its own way it was epic; when they rewrote art history, she and Derek would go down in the book. They mixed each other's sweat and hair in with the paints. Roseann was the one who got Derek the art dealer in Washington; in bed together they were tighter than *Laocoön;* hotter than the lovers in *The Kiss.* "But this guy is married," she said. "Right?"

Leslie glowed. "So I owe you a lot for going first."

This closed its teeth on Roseann's belly. "Don't lay that on me."

"Don't be sorry, be glad. Listen, it was inevitable. It's like a magnetic force. All we have to do is be in the same room. We don't know where, or how, but we know we'll be together when everybody else is sleeping, our secret, making fabulous love in the night." Leslie's face was alive; her eyes shone. "We're just terrible. I have to be so careful not to shout. It would bring the whole farm down on us."

Could Roseann help it if that morning she and Derek had a fight? Like a competitive teenager she had to say, "My Derek is amazing too."

"Have you ever had a lover before, Roseann?"

"Listen, what about his wife?"

"Oh, her." Leslie got that sober look The Other Woman always gets. "He just drifted into it. Tired of going home alone, she was sweet, it was time. Married too young."

My story exactly. Roseann sighed, "Not the best way to start." She did not say, "We all got married too young."

"He says they weren't really in love, it was What You Did. He says there's nothing between them now. He says she's frigid, she doesn't understand him. He says . . ." Leslie kept on saying what he said: too many reasons. She was doing what you do, piling up evidence, the new lover's wife charged and found guilty on too many counts. Leslie looked into her hat and pulled out the clincher, the rabbit Roseann was supposed to watch. "Besides, last April Chad had an affair."

Rock 'em Sock 'em Robots, Roseann thought. "Right." For God's sake, when she married Stig she was only a kid. How can you promise to do *anything* for life? She said sadly, "People can't expect you to be faithful if they aren't faithful to you."

Remember, Leslie was full of reasons. "He says his wife knows about us, and it's all right with her."

Just what I told Derek. How would she feel feel if Stig did that number on her? "Really."

"I'm certainly not going to ask her."

Roseann made a wry grin. "And I'm getting a hard time for running off with a single guy."

"That's different. You went public." Leslie gave one more reason. "He says there's nothing left between them but being parents."

"Girls or boys?"

"Oh no you don't," Leslie said.

"Kid, or kids?"

"Hey, I need a really big favor."

"I can't."

"It won't take long."

Leslie's favors! Roseann raised her hand as if she could prevent what was coming—demands from Leslie, who was wonderful at making you do what she needed and making you flattered that she'd asked. She shook her head. "I promised to meet Derek at five."

"I'll be back by four." Leslie was getting up. "I need you to watch the kids."

"You set this up and dragged those kids all the way down here for the day because you're meeting your new man?"

Leslie did not deny it. "I knew I could count on you."

"Leslie, for Pete's sake!"

"This is really it, Roseann." Her eyes were shining like a bride's. "The first time we don't have to sneak around. The first time we can really be alone." She handed over her big canvas shoulder bag. "I bought some things for you guys to have for lunch."

Roseann looked into the bag, which was filled with God's bounty: fresh peaches and Italian bread and French cheeses; cakes and chocolates. Leslie must have left the farm at dawn so she'd have time to do her shopping at the little stores on Madison. "You planned this!"

"I knew you were dying to see Speedy."

"How did you know I'd say yes."

That smile almost redeemed it. She could light up a coal chute. "Because you're my friend!"

"We're all your fucking pawns. Oh, Les." Here was Roseann, banished like the scarlet woman, found guilty and not wanted on the voyage, and here was Leslie Austin Burgess buying her off with her expensive-looking bakery cartons and her crunkly little East Side deli bags. "You're making me the beard."

"Shh. I can't thank you enough." Anything Leslie starts must run smoothly. She went along as if Roseann was fine with this.

"This is wonderful of you. I got sourballs, for later. You can bring out the Frisbee when the kids get bored. Wash'n Dris. The only thing I forgot to get is drinks."

"You set me up." Roseann half-expected her to hand her exact change for some Coke machine. "It isn't fair!" But Leslie was patting her hair, so those bangles clashed.

"Oh, Roseann, thanks so much! I knew you'd understand. Oh, kids . . ."

The least Leslie could do was tell her who he was. "Say hello to . . ." she tried.

"It's not who you think."

Roseann's heart clanked. "Oh my God, it isn't Stig."

But Leslie's face was perfectly smooth. "If they get bored, you can take them to the movies, OK?"

"Listen, I have to get back downtown to meet Derek at five." If she didn't, he might take off for the weekend without her, and then what was she going to do? "We have a ride out to East-hampton to go around to galleries, and Derek doesn't . . ."

"I promise, I'll be back by four. Shh. Here come the kids. Look, they've found some flowers. Hey, kids."

Roseann said resentfully, "If I'm late it'll ruin everything."

"Oh aren't those pretty. Speedy, your mom wants to be alone with you guys, the rest of the afternoon is her treat."

"Leslie, listen."

("You wanted to see Speedy, didn't you? Oh, Rose, enjoy!") Leslie raised her voice. "Kids, this nice mom is all yours. Be nice!"

Timmy threw his mother a tight little squint like a cartoon mouse watching the cat. He was a strange kid anyway, with those pale eyes—too smart, Roseann thought, although he hardly ever said anything; he would just look at you and judge.

For thirty seconds, maybe, Leslie wavered. Then she moved to the curb and put out her arm. Over her shoulder she repeated, "OK?"

"OK." Roseann shot a quick look at her daughter, but

Speedy was neither here nor there. If it was Stig that Leslie was seeing, it was clear her baby didn't have a clue.

Leslie opened the cab door but she didn't get in. She could have been waiting for the Good Housekeeping Seal of Approval.

"And when I get back we'll go to the Plaza for early dinner, like I promised." Timothy was supposed to say, OK.

Instead he shrugged and so Speedy shrugged. Leslie took this for a yes and got in the cab and rode away. She probably thought it was just fine with her little boy, but Roseann saw his face.

"OK, kids." Roseann was doing her best to sound, you know, up, but it was hard. For the first time all summer responsibility descended, like a harness. Back in the city three days and she was stuck again, taking care of kids. She loved Speedy, she was really glad to see her, but getting stuck had always been hard for her. The two kids were looking at her suspiciously, like pigeons waiting to be fed; one false move and they would fly away. This was her daughter that she'd known all her life and Roseann needed to win her with Leslie's fruits and Leslie's chocolates and Leslie's fucking Frisbee with the Save the Whales sticker. She began bravely.

"First, let's see what we have here for lunch."

What did they do? She took them to the Petting Zoo. They had too much time left over so they walked across the park to Central Park West. Who knew the cross street would come out a hop, skip and a jump away from Roseann's old apartment? She did. What did she think she was going to do, going up there? Catch Leslie with Stig?

The doorman gave Roseann a big smile and asked where they'd been all summer. She told him they were staying in the country. He didn't have to know that Speedy was in Eaglemont while she herself was camping in the mud in Virginia with Derek in the Tidewater Artists' Colony. Upstairs, she didn't try her key because she was afraid Stig really would be in there with

Leslie, afraid he wouldn't be in there at all; she rang the bell. She thought the bell must be broken and she knocked. Nothing happened. It was bad. Speedy just stood there in the empty hall with a smug look and when Stig didn't answer and *didn't* answer, she stood there a little longer, watching while Roseann decided the place was empty and it was OK to go on in. She was watching Roseann poke at the lock. Her key didn't even go in right, much less turn, after which Speedy finally said practically the only thing she had said directly to Roseann all day. "It's OK, Mom, you can use my key. Daddy changed the locks."

When they got inside Roseann called, "Stig?" Accidentally, she tried, "Leslie?"

Behind her the boy squiffled like a speared rabbit. "Ooof."

The kids split as soon as it was clear nobody was there. The place was completely quiet. If it was Stig who was seeing Leslie, he wasn't doing it here. Roseann murmured, "It looks so *different*." The whole place said, *See how much better I do without you.* He had gotten somebody in to clean until it looked like somebody else lived here, not the Fenton family. He had bought designer hangers for the flower pots. The son of a bitch had started watering the plants. Everything was in its place, wherever that was, and there was a new TV-VCR cabinet and a new magazine rack. Even today's paper had been thrown out.

OK, Roseann thought. Who is she?

She felt like Nancy Drew, going into the empty kitchen. If it wasn't Leslie, who? Would she find the napkin with telltale lipstick, or the two champagne glasses in the sink? When she came back into the empty hall she almost had a heart attack. Stig was standing there. He was thinner. He was wearing a summer suit she had never seen before. His hair was different.

Startled, she fell back."Stig!"

When she thought about it later, she would always remember thinking: *This is not the man I married, this is the man I wish I'd married.* Stung, she would have to wonder if it was too late.

He said, "What are you doing here?"

She didn't have an answer. She looked into her open hands. "My own house, and our daughter had to use her key to let me in."

"Sorry about that." He blushed. "Lawyer's advice."

"I knocked and knocked."

"I know."

It was just too much. "Why didn't you answer the door?"

He got red in the face. "I knew it was you."

"Then why in hell didn't you let me in?"

"I was afraid of seeing you," he said.

In all the times Roseann thought about meeting Stig again she never expected it to be this painful. "All I wanted was to come in."

"It's a bad time," Stig said. Jane's words. Leslie's words.

"Oh shit, do you have somebody here?" If he did, it would make things either easier or harder, Roseann was not sure which.

"I would never bring anybody here."

But Roseann had. For all those weeks when Stig was sleeping on other people's sofas, she and Derek were in the king-sized bed. "Oh, Stig." It all came back on her then, all the missed chances and betrayals. If Roseann had blown this marriage, she hadn't done it single-handed. Her voice shook. "How are you?"

He said, "You look terrific."

"Do I?" Maybe she did. After that morning's fight with Derek she just took off without even looking in the mirror. She was thinner, she knew; her body was taut from working out in the community fields and swimming in the pond. She had an all-over tan.

Stig said, "Something in your face. You look wonderful."

And all at once she was homesick as hell. She could hear kids' voices from the back of the apartment; she could imagine her and Stig together in good times; her hands were twitching; they wanted to fly up and touch his face; she hung tight to the pockets of her jeans to keep them where they were. "You too."

He said, "Did you know I've quit the brokerage?"

"You're kidding."

"Time to start over, you know? You taught me that."

"Oh my God." First Leslie and now Stig. Then her legs got weak—everything: ankles, knees, thighs, snatch—because when she first saw him standing in the hall it washed over her that instead of starting over she wanted to go back. But she had cut him off, it was not the other way around. If she went back on her decisions now it would make her look like a jerk. Her heart broke. "Oh, Stig."

"Do you want this place in the fall? You and Derek, I mean."

They were negotiating a deal. "And Speedy?"

"I'm going to be in Rutgers," he said. "Graduate school. I won't have the kind of time she needs."

"And Speedy . . ." She didn't know how Derek was going to take this, but she made the offer anyway. "How. Ah. How long are you going to be gone?"

Stig's hands were twitching just like hers, trying to fly up, as if he wanted them to touch. He said, "As long as it takes."

What was she supposed to do then, plead and apologize? It might be what they both wanted but Roseann was prevented by the cold thought: what if I get back into it and it's not what I wanted after all? "At least we had a dozen good years."

"I'm going to miss you, Roseann."

"Me too." So for a second there she and Stig were regarding it—what was irremediable, what they might have had, that they had lost. Then the kids came out of Speedy's room with a bag of toys and so Roseann had to ask him quickly, before they swept her away. "Is there somebody in particular?"

"It's never going to be like the first time, but yes."

"Is it Leslie?"

His eyes didn't even register this. They were fixed on the next point. "If you and Derek aren't planning to get married in the next two years, I thought the standard separation agreement might be best. Everybody comes out clean and at the end you have your divorce."

Clean, she thought, and nodded. There was nothing else to say. "Goodbye, Stig," she said, and ran away. At least Leslie wasn't there with him.

She had to take the kids downtown and talk to Derek. She'd left this morning before they made up. Besides, she had these kids to entertain and too much afternoon left to kill; being on the subway going and coming would use up a little of the left-over time.

Her lover was there, slouched on the batik-draped sofa where the two of them had spent so many miserable nights. Without the kids, Roseann could have slumped down next to him and made up without having to say anything. Derek did not get up. She stood in the middle of the distressed Oriental carpet watching Derek, watching the kids, not knowing who to please.

Speedy didn't say anything. Lucky looked around at the furniture washed up on heavy litter night, the graffiti mural, the junk sculpture, the empty six-pack and the smoking joint. "Wuoow."

It was clear Derek had not been out of the house today—no flogging the portfolio, no interviewing at art colleges, no trying to make a better life for him and Roseann. How was she going to break the news to him that they had a place to live for the fall, rent-free, but it came complete with a little girl?

"Honey, you remember Derek."

"Hello, Derek," Speedy said.

He raised himself on one elbow, rumpled Derek with the beautiful body. He yawned. "Hi kids." He had forgotten who the child was.

This was a bad scene. Roseann said, "We just came here to pick up a present I got for Speedy. Look, baby." Quickly she pulled off her jade bracelet and gave it to her. Even though it was barely three o'clock she said, "OK, kids, we've got to hurry. It's time to meet Timothy's mother in the park. Now you guys tell Derek goodbye."

"Bye Derek."

There were a lot of things Roseann wanted to say to Derek,

things she knew she ought to do to him in order to make things right, but the kids were there and when she split all she could think of to say to her lover was, "Back by five."

At least he waved.

They got a cab uptown. The kids were busy with Speedy's books and her little tape recorder that she'd picked up in her room back at the apartment, so at least Roseann didn't have to talk.

As they got out of the cab Leslie's boy looked at Roseann out of an old man's eyes. "We're here too soon. My mother is always at least a half an hour late."

Then Roseann did something weird: she hugged him, surprised at the last minute by how tall he was, and she said in the lightest voice you could imagine, "She was going to the dermatologist, and you know how doctors are." It was funny. They both knew she was lying, but the boy hugged her back.

By the time Leslie came it was almost six. Roseann was pissed and desperate, feeling bummed out and strangely unshelled, the product of being cut loose in Manhattan with no home, no place to go except hotel lobbies or park benches where sooner or later some police person would poke her with a night stick, moving her along. The children had given up on playing a long time before and were sitting with their backs against opposing trees, reading Speedy's Narnia books from the house. It wasn't as if they hadn't read them a dozen times, but they didn't even look up when Leslie spoke. Naturally her face was pink and her mouth smirched, her throat marked with love bites and her cheek bright with whisker burn. She smelled of sex and champagne and she could barely get her act together to apologize.

"I'm really sorry, we got held up, I can't thank you enough!"

"It was nothing," Roseann said. By five-thirty she knew Derek would have quit waiting and left for Easthampton without her. As a couple they made a big thing of being independent, right?

"I'm just so terribly sorry." Leslie had changed clothes. The bitch had met her lover and then gone back to her own apartment for a bath. Her voice dropped; she cut her eyes at the children, who could have cared less that she was there. "Look what he gave me!"

It was a turquoise ring. Because of Leslie, Derek had taken off for the entire weekend without Roseann. She was faced with two nights alone on the sofa in someone else's house or a miserable ride on the Long Island Railroad, followed by a fight. "Nice," she said.

"Oh Roseann, thank you, thanks a million."

"It was nothing," Roseann said bitterly. Talk about depressed!

But Leslie didn't notice; she was rushed. "You know how much I appreciate this, and you must know how much I trust you. After all," she said, scooping up the kids before Roseann could say a real goodbye to her daughter or even hug her close and take in the smell of her, and then she finished, astonishing them both, "You're my best friend."

14

Rocky

Rocky was older by six months, so he was a grade ahead. In another three weeks he would be twelve. Compared to Alfred he was practically a grownup; Dad punched him on the shoulder, grinning. "Good man!" But when Calvin got pissed he'd go, "You're old enough to know better," even when it was Alfred who started it. The groanies expected Rocky to keep order, get kids places on time, break up fights. It was both terrible and kind of cool.

They were sick of the farm. Totally burned out on it. You get too much of anything good, even chocolate, and you burn out on it. They were bored of everything.

By the time August drained out, nothing was right. Rocky's mouth was dry all the time now and his neck was stiff from holding his shoulders so high. At any moment something awful could come down on them and rip out their throats. What was the matter with everyone?

At first he thought it was the weather. The air was steamy, filled with clouds that never broke in rain. Hot. Wet. Close. Even the grownups were fighting; they were tense and distracted. Frieda's eyes took on a frantic glaze and all her bodily hair stood on end. The still air had things swimming in it: plant stuff, bugs. Kids. They rattled around the woods like pinballs, ricocheting off trees. Inside, they bumped into things. They went to sleep hot and woke up sweating. Rocky was sick of Alfred. Gabe and Kofi fought all the time. Everybody ganged up and to Rocky's grim pleasure, they made Alfred cry. Speedy had gnawed the ends of her hair until they frayed like rope. She used to be tough but these days all you had to do was look at her and she'd cry. Lucky slept and played in the same T-shirt and shorts for three weeks. Rocky was worried about him.

Kids kept falling and hurting themselves and breaking things and getting into fights. Frieda cried all the time and wouldn't say why. Bug bites festered. Gabe's nose was sunburned practically to the bone. One night everybody threw up. Rocky broke his pointer sliding into home plate and Lucky had his wrist in an ace bandage because the night he and Rocky tried to sleep on the side of the mountain he wrenched it coming down. Speedy's fingers were disgusting; she'd run out of nails to bite and gnawed the skin. Kofi came home from backpacking camp with head lice. The moms washed everybody's hair in awful stuff and tortured them with metal combs. Kids could freak out any mom just by pretending to scratch.

They had been living together for so long that they knew who was allergic and who cried in their sleep and which ones farted secretly. Kids got in fights over the stupidest things. They were like the prisoners with the joke book, all you had to do was say the page number and everybody would laugh.

There was nothing to do. The only books left unread were the ones you wouldn't touch. They were sick of Frieda and sick of the grainy one channel on the black-and-white TV. There were no new movies in Eaglemont and nobody would drive a carful of kids to the next big town, probably because the groanies were sick of them. They could either hang out in the barn where it was hot and buggy or hang out in the house until some grownup said for God's sake, go play. They were sick of bike riding and sitting in the reservoir until their fingers looked like white prunes. They had been to Bradlee's a hundred dozen times and once they sneaked over to the next farm to tip cows, but the farmer called the state police.

All their things broke. What did the kids have left over, from all the games and junk toys the groanies had bought to provision their summer? Alfred trashed the *Risk* set because Rocky always won. Somebody left *Monopoly* out in the rain and the board warped; if you built on Park Place the houses would slide into Boardwalk. The water pistols leaked. The balsa wood gliders were splintered, all the marbles had rolled under furniture and the last surviving Slinky was rusted and bent. The moms threw out the green goo and Silly Putty because kids got them in the living room rug. The Frisbees faded and cracked and Speedy's Dawn doll had bubble gum in its hair. The best things were either lost or wrecked. Nobody wanted to buy new things for them because the summer was practically over and besides, the grownups said, you kids never take care of anything.

They weren't the only ones.

The house was a wreck because the compulsive moms were sick of cleaning up after the messy ones. The food was going downhill. They had Cap'n Crunch a lot, and instead of Pop Tarts or Eggos, they got wheat bread, tough rocks. When they remembered to eat, kids got their own lunch. Except for weekends, when the parents still showed off for each other, they had hamburgers or hot dogs for dinner, plus stuff from the garden that the moms said was good for you but nobody liked. One night they came down for supper and all there was, was corn and dessert.

The nights were the worst. They got sent to bed way early all the time because they were getting on the groanies' nerves. Everybody knew how to stay out of the parents' way, but they were too deep in the summer to give a shit. They ended up stuck in their sleeping bags with their fingers clamped on the edges and their eyes popped wide because they were too bored to sleep and it was still light. The monster set up housekeeping in the shed chamber and would not move out.

Lucky was wired. All he wanted to do was talk. It was like he never slept. Even after the sun finally went down and people slid into sleep, he jabbered, keeping them up. In a way it was a good thing, because in the dark he sounded more like Lucky, you know? But it was also a bad thing because all he could talk about was the monster. He couldn't quit.

It didn't matter. They were awake anyway.

The monster filled the shed chamber. It moved in close and sat down on their chests.

"Think about it," Lucky said for the hundred-fifteenth time and Rocky thought, Oh shit. "Trapped in Scarth cave. In the dark. In the middle of the night. Creepy, right? It could happen to anybody. Could be anybody."

Alfred was getting all bent; he was shifting around like a trapped hamster, yipping, "Bullshit."

Lucky's voice dropped to a gutty whisper: "Could be you . . ."

Alfred squeaked, "That's crap."

". . . could be me."

Rocky hated the job of big brother, but he did it. "Chill, Alfred. It's only a story," he said. "C'mon, Lucky."

"No," Lucky said. "You come on. He's alive. He's here," he said, in a chillingly matter-of-fact tone.

"Enough."

"Nobody knows who the monster is." Lucky got up and hunched into the monster slouch. He was shagging around with his sleeping bag dragging around his ankles. "Whooo knows."

"I said, that's enough." Rocky grabbed his knees and pulled him down.

But Lucky just went on. "So OK, who is it? Listen, the monster could be Alfred."

"Shut up, OK?" Alfred was getting shrill; he was flailing at the shadows. "Shut up."

But the rest of the kids heard Lucky repeat in this soft, miserable voice: "Could be me."

There was no stopping him.

"When the first rays of the full moon hit you, you can see the signs," he said. His voice hit a fine, tight hush that made their back hairs rise. "The beginning of the change."

Rocky said, "Don't," but Lucky didn't hear.

"Watch out for it," he rasped. "The thing you're turning into. You are turning into something terrible."

"Come *on.*"

His voice got all furry and sinister. "So watch out for the signs. First you feel bumps in your mouth where the fangs are going to pop. Then you find black hairs sprouting on the backs of your hands. Next the green rot starts on your face and you catch it crawling up your legs and you go, Oh God help, no, because you know what's coming. You're turning into something you don't want to be and you go, *Lash me to the bed.*"

There was a vibration in the shed chamber; everybody getting uncomfortable all at once, but nobody could stop Lucky once he got started, even though they had to try.

"But it's already too late. You can run into Scarth Cave and try to hide from the rising moon, you can go as deep as hell and it's still going to get you."

Alfred was shrill. "What is? What is?"

Then Lucky let him have it in an angry hiss. "What you're going to become."

"Come on," Rocky said. "Just don't."

"You're turning into the monster and there's no stopping it. The worst part comes after the change . . ."

It was bad. "Shut up!"

"One day you're you, and the next day you're *something worse.*"

The kids lay there in the dark with their bellies shaking: *Not me, not me.*

"And you will do anything." He went on in this helpless tone. "Anything."

Even Rocky squirmed, thinking dark, unhappy thoughts. What he said was, "Quit being an asshole and shut up."

By the end of August, he had it by heart. "Sometimes you get caught in the middle," Lucky said, "Not one thing or the other. You don't know the *pain*." He sounded like it was him, Lucky, caught in the middle of the change. His voice cracked open, changing until Lucky and the story were all one thing that went on and on, snowballing because it was too big to stop.

Desperate, Rocky pounced and grabbed him by the shoulders, barking like a drill sergeant, "Just cut it out!"

Lucky's voice was small, but very clear: "I can't."

No wonder Mrs. Burgess decided they needed a party. After all this sameold sameold, it was a relief. Either because or in spite of the weather, Lucky's mom was throwing another of her big weekends. Leslie was giving a surprise birthday bash for Mr. Burgess, over Labor Day.

"Jane," she said, and Rocky thought, Oh shit, without knowing why. "This party is going to change everything."

And his mom got all pink and said, "I'm so glad."

What bothered Rocky was, why was his mom killing herself to make somebody else's party a success. She went nuts combing her cookbooks for some dish that would make her the hit of the birthday dinner. She spent days in town shopping for the right thing to wear. Rocky's dad tried to cheer her up and only made it worse. Calvin said, "It doesn't matter what you put on, you're always beautiful to me," but all it did was make her cry.

Jane kept obsessing over whether she should dye her hair. Gabe's mom offered her lavender silk blouse. "Polly, what's the point? You're naturally gorgeous. All I'll ever look like is me," she said, and would not be consoled. If she was going to knock 'em dead, it would have to be with food.

Thursday she made Rocky stay in the kitchen and help her bake. Nine a.m. and it was already like a boiler in there. The only good thing was getting custody of Mom—no Alfred hanging around getting in the way.

The trouble was everybody else was getting cool in the reservoir and Rocky's mom was melting chocolate with sweat running down her face, unless it was tears. Rocky was stuck in the corner whipping sugar and butter for Jane Darrow's death-dealing Black Forest Cake. That's what she called it: Jane Darrow's death-dealing Black Forest Cake. This wasn't even the real cake. It was a tryout cake. When they ate it that night she was going to win hands down over all the battling baking moms and the Balducci's-shopping-bag moms. Friday she'd make another cake, for real. She might not have the best clothes or hair but Rocky's mom could still star. On the big night, she'd bring in the birthday cake, with the forty candles lighting up her face. When Mr. Burgess blew out the candles and cut the first piece, Jane would shine.

Rocky didn't know why this made him feel so bad. There was something in the air—trouble, a thunderstorm, the monster moving way off somewhere, sloshing up out of the reservoir or stirring deep in the cave. He didn't know; he just knew anxiety gnawed at his toes and made him wish this summer was over and they were back in the city where it was safe.

Then out of nowhere his mom said in this soft voice, "I knew I could count on you, Rocky. And I always can." It was so hot that when he raised his hand the melting butter ran along the whisk and started sliding down his arm. Her tone made his stomach clench. *If I'm cut, she bleeds. When she sneezes, I wipe my nose.* Poor Mom. Something was the matter. No wonder he felt bad.

To take her mind off it he said, "Mo-om. Are you going to use all that chocolate?"

But she went on sadly. "You're going to make a wonderful husband some day."

"I mean, that's an awful lot of chocolate."

"Don't get too busy, like your father," she said.

"I mean, in view of that I'm starving?" He had to turn her around, make her sound more like herself, make her play Mom and Rocky instead of talking on in this sad, sad voice. He made a grab for the spoon. "Food. Godzilla needs food!"

Her mouth looked smeared. Her eyes weren't exactly watery; it could have been sweat. "Don't ever hurt somebody you love."

"Foooood . . ." Rocky started making strangling noises and lurching in his chair; he made his eyes pop. Come on, lady, OK? This is supposed to be funny, OK? Could you please smile please?

"Oh Rocky."

One more try, he thought; one more beat and he could turn her around. He put both hands around his neck, pretending to strangle. "Fooood . . ."

"Oh shut up." Smiling, she gave him chocolate on the long-handled spoon and melted extra to cover her losses. "Oh here."

Which Rocky took with one of those smiles that always made her smile. He had always been able to get her to do anything he wanted. "Then can I go swimming too?"

But she was still the mom. "Not yet. I need you to whip in the egg yolks. Not like that! One at a time."

It was OK, Rocky thought, sitting with his mom in that messy kitchen; she had mellowed out enough to let things go instead of cleaning up after everybody else the way she used to. She'd cleared enough space to work in and left the rest the way it was: dried egg on Mr. Peterson's frying pan sitting on the front burner, kids' Count Chocula sogging up the sink. She seemed to be feeling better too. At the end she would let him have the bowl.

"It would have been buggy at the reservoir anyway," she said. "And when this cake is done, you're going to get the first and biggest piece. If you think it's OK, then we'll go upstairs and I'll show you my surprise." She was saying all the right things but there was definitely something different about his mom today, an edge that made her hands shaky and her voice sharp. "It's important, Rocky. But first you have to tell me how is the cake."

Her tone was off; he should have known! "You're not having any?"

To his chagrin she snapped at him. "Can't you even tell I've been on a diet for three weeks? Don't I look thinner?"

Bemused, he looked at her. "Huh?"

"Don't I? Look at me." She turned sideways so Rocky could see, but in the big shirt, it was hard to tell. "Am I thinner?" *Am I?*

What was he supposed to say? He did what Dad would do; it was the only thing he knew, that same there-there tone. "You look fine to me."

But she said, "Oh shit!"

This hurt his feelings. "If you wanted a better helper you should have asked Alfred."

"Oh, Alfred. Nobody wants Alfred, Alfred's a pain in the ass." She said, "I don't know what's the matter with him this summer. The way he fights with your father. It's terrible."

"He fights with everybody," Rocky said. Take that, bung-hole. Mr. Show-and-Tell, Daddy's favorite.

By August Alfred had a bumble bee up his ass, or an entire fleet of wasps. He went around with this know-it-all look. So, what? Had he gotten some prize they both wanted that Rocky didn't know about? Pushy Alfred, Mr. Me-First. I don't care, Rocky thought, whisking the cake batter. I come first with Mom. So he was more or less happy in that sunny kitchen until something strange happened and the light changed.

Rocky didn't see it, exactly. He felt it in his stomach, like something cold.

The air shuddered. Something changed. He flinched; it hurt! OK, Alfred. You made me flinch.

"Are you all right?"

All that stuff about people Doing It. *He knows something I don't know.* "I hate Alfred," he said.

"Cain and Abel." At least his mom was smiling, drizzling in melted chocolate while he whisked. "He's a lot like your father."

"Well Alfred sucks."

"Don't talk that way about your father," she said.

His father. As far as Dad was concerned Rocky could be at
the north pole, or on the moon. "He likes Alfred best."

"But you *are* best." Somehow she had her arms around him.
Right. The two of them were linked. His father had already
voted Alfred Most Likely to Succeed, but one night Rocky
overheard his mom saying to Calvin, "Alfred is flashy, but
Rocky is deep."

When they were little, in the way of brothers they lived on a
seesaw. When Rocky was good, Alfred was bad. Remembering
that day, Rocky thought that what his mom said when she
hugged him close was actually, "You. You are my rock," but she
was tired, OK? If he was in here in the kitchen being good, he
thought, fucking Alfred must be off somewhere being bad.

It was OK; if Gabe and Kofi and all wanted to hang out with
goddam Alfred, fine. But he couldn't quite let it go. "Everybody's at the reservoir. Mr. Peterson is stringing a rubber tire
over the water so we can swing and jump."

"I'll let you lick the beaters," she said.

So Rocky sat there stirring, watching ants go in and out from
under the fridge. After Jane got cake layers into the oven, she let
him scrape the bowl while she boiled down cherries with nuts
and sugar to put between the layers, and at the end—his payback
for hanging in here with her—she cut him a humongous piece.

Rocky was finishing his piece of cake when he heard voices;
everybody else coming back from the reservoir, kids and
grownups in suits and T-shirts except for Lucky's mom, who
was in her bikini with the see-through cover-up that showed
most of her tanned legs. Even when they were out mucking in
the garden Leslie managed to look like something out of a magazine. They blew into the kitchen like a cool wind, dragging
wet towels and scattering water.

It was like seeing them for the first time: sexy Mrs. Burgess
and skinny Frieda with her legs blue-white from cold and, right!
Mrs. Peterson, who looked like a model even though she'd
stopped shaving her legs. So even though he didn't want to,

Rocky had to see that his mom did look different, and if they all treated Jane like their mother it was for a reason. She just plain looked like the one, belongs in the kitchen, takes care of everyone. He could see it in the way the other women said hello to her, even though they made a big fuss over her masterpiece, the Black Forest cake. This made him proud and angry at the same time—his mom!

"Oh Jane," Leslie said, "you're brilliant, and it's beautiful." She could have been talking to the maid.

But Jane was making up to her, that sweet voice! "I was thinking, if you like it, I'll make it for Chad's birthday . . ."

Leslie Burgess bent over her, tan and limber under the cover-up, and in spite of her slithery wetness and the chocolate smudges on Jane, they hugged. "Oh would you? I'd be thrilled."

You would have thought they had given his mom the Nobel Prize. She was like a Miss America on the runway, trying not to cry. "I'll do anything if you help me figure out what to wear!"

Leslie hugged her with a compliment that made her face crumple. "Oh Jane, you're wonderful. It doesn't matter a bit *what* you wear!"

So Rocky was standing there trying to figure out how this whole thing could get better, or at least different, when Alfred clumped in the way he always did, getting in the way. It killed him to see Rocky eating the cake. He began jerking on Jane's elbow, going, "Now, I want my cake now."

Mom snapped at him! "Stop that, you sound just like your father."

Dumb Alfred didn't take the warning. "You gave Rocky some."

"Well Rocky stayed here and helped." She covered the cake and shot him a stern look. "Everybody else has to wait."

Alfred was bobbing like a balloon. "Mo-om."

Then *for no reason* Jane lashed out. "I said, not now!" Then she murmured, "Come on upstairs, Rocky. There's something I want you to see."

So he'd beaten Alfred this time, and with his breath fluttering for no real reason, Rocky followed his mom out of the room. Behind them the moms were beginning to pull out bread and salami for sandwiches for the mass feeding, and Alfred stood with his hands out like a plastic Mickey, fixed in a position with no real function and smiling a silly smile. At the last second, he stabbed with his hand and grabbed an ugly handful right out of the center of the cake.

He followed her upstairs. In spite of the voices drifting up through cracks in the floorboards it was quiet in their bedroom. In the silence, even in the absence of his father, Rocky could smell him: Calvin's aftershave, 4711; he could see the set of brushes he kept on the dresser, awaiting the weekend. Startled, he almost spoke to Calvin's chinos and polo shirt, which still held his father's shape. They were hanging on one of those arrangements with the wooden shoe rack and shirt and pant hangers, the EZ Boy Valet that looks kind of like a person, with Dad's Reeboks resting on the kneeler. It was like having him in the room.

But Mom was already in the closet changing. She came out in a flurry of orange silky stuff. It was supposed to be special, but all it was, was, one of those dumb Indian tops with the big skirt ladies wear because they think it hides their butt. Rocky's heart sagged. "Is that it?"

"What do you think?"

"Is this the surprise?"

Jane looked upset. "Maybe not."

What was it you were supposed to say? Rocky would do anything to make her smile. "I love it."

But it wasn't enough. She sighed. "I have some other things."

"This is great."

"If this isn't right, I have to get something else."

"Really. It's fine."

"Listen, if it takes all day I'm going to get it right."

"Mom, wait!"

But it was too late. Her voice zig-zagged. "I have to get it right." Before Rocky could say anything to make her feel better Jane was back in the closet, thumping, and she came out even faster than she had the first time in a new costume, with her eyes wild and her hair askew. This one was blue and looked too woolly for August. She said, "It's a little heavy for the summer, but what do you think?"

"It's good. Really. When did you go to the store?"

"All summer," she said.

He choked. "It's *great*."

"If you don't like it, say so."

If she didn't quit they were going to both cry. "It's fine."

"No it isn't." She went back in the closet and when she came out, oh wow she had on a third dress that looked like dragonfly's wings or the pond when the algae get too thick, a kind of iridescent green. Rocky was relieved. This one looked wonderful and this time so did she. "What about this?"

"Oh, *wow*."

She should have calmed down and started to smile but instead she was getting frantic. "Just, *oh wow*?"

"I mean it's great, mom, oh please. Really." Nothing he did now would slow her down; she was beside herself, no, Jane was more like three people—her old self plus two others, that Rocky didn't recognize.

"Wait a minute. What do you think of this?" She was a storm in the room, picking up jewelry and throwing it down. "Or this? How would it go with this?"

"It's fine. Please don't!"

"Wait. Just wait a minute. Let's just try it with this."

She was rummaging in the dresser for scarves, rattling beads, waving earrings, everything, checking things out in the mirror and throwing them on the bed. His strong mother that Rocky counted on was wild, anxious; she was looking different, all right, he did see one thing now; she was really thinner, not a lot, but enough so Rocky could see that all that time everybody else was having fun his mother was brooding and starving her-self.

"You look great," he yelled, "Mom, you look a lot thinner. Really." At the top of his voice he was going, "THINNER," and all she did was tear this rhinestone butterfly out of her hair.

"It's this goddam hair. It doesn't matter what I do, I look the same."

"You look wonderful."

"No I don't. I look exactly the same." She sounded raw and unhappy, going, "Same Jane."

She was desperate, whirling until she had Rocky revolving too, trying to snag her and yelling miserably, "Oh Mom, please don't."

She raked her fingers down her face so hard it hurt, grinding it out through clenched teeth, "I have to. I have to change."

By that time he was bawling like a little kid, Rocky in tears and begging her, "Oh Mom, please don't change."

Trust Alfred to catch them like that. How did he get in? There was his hateful, relentless brother standing in the open door watching Mom crying over a stupid dress. Rocky hated him for seeing her like that. It was like spying on God. The next thing he knew, Alfred had grabbed their mom's pretty orange top off the floor. He twisted the cloth and draped it over his head, shagging the whole thing down until it flapped around him like a dress. Then he made a mouth like a stripper; what was he trying to get even for, the cake? Something worse? Rocky didn't know. All he knew was that fucking Alfred was flouncing around in his mom's dress like Marilyn Monroe or their father in drag, looking back at them over his shoulder as he said in a big loud voice, "Hey girls, how do I look?"

"Stop it, Alfred. Cut it out!"

Alfred just threw a scarf around his neck and put his hands on his hips. "If you don't like that one, how about this?"

Rocky was grinding the tears out of his eyes so Alfred wouldn't see him cry. His mom had her hands out and her face just disassembled. She was beyond tears and begging. "Oh Alfred, please!"

He screamed so the monster in Scarth Cave could hear: "Do you like my dress?" Then he started swaying so her best fake pearls swung in a loop. "Ba dum ba da da, ba da da da bump . . ."

Didn't he see how sad Mom was? Rocky gave him fair warning. He growled, "Stop it!"

But Alfred was smashing powder on his face and making his mouth purple with her lipstick. "Or this?"

This made Rocky furious, desperate. He hurled himself at Alfred and fell on top of him, clawing and screaming, "Faggot, faggot," he would do anything to get him to stop. And Alfred? He heard, but he didn't understand; instead he squirmed and giggled wildly, hee-hee-hee, as Rocky pinned him and sat on his chest.

"I'm not the faggot," he said, just like that. Alfred didn't even fight. He just kept on giggling and looked up at Rocky with this shitty grin. He thought it was a game, right up until Rocky punched him in the face.

Funny, in the seconds before Alfred started fighting back and the brothers went at it, fangs and gouging fingers, elbows and knees, Mrs. Peterson came in, sleek as a seal and still damp from the reservoir. She was cool; in spite of the carnage she sounded easy with their mom, so that as Alfred and Rocky tangled she asked in a perfectly everyday voice, "Jane, is everything all right?"

So this is how bad Mom was. She turned away and began to sob. When she could talk again Jane did not say anything about the fight. She cried, "Oh Polly, what am I going to do about myself?"

"Jane, what's the matter?"

"It's me. Look at me!"

To which Mrs. Peterson said, "You look wonderful. That dress!"

"No I don't."

"You're fine. You're a wonderful woman, now shhh."

On his back, with Rocky's knees in his chest, Alfred pulled the veil off his face and glared into his big brother's eyes.

"Faggot," Rocky said and punched him in the nose.

But by that time Jane was inconsolable; he heard his strong mom, that people got advice from, sounding shaky as a kid, "I mean, what am I going to *do* about this party?"

"Oh Jane, your cake is wonderful. *You're* wonderful."

So that as Rocky bit into his little brother's shoulder, growling, "Faggot, faggot," and Alfred yelled, he heard his mother's voice, still rising.

Jane, beyond tears: "What am I going to do about my life?"

In the still moment before they began to tangle for real Rocky heard Polly Peterson in the background, sounding friendly and so matter-of-fact that she and not his mom could have been the trained psychologist, trying to start with something the patient could handle; she said, "I'd start by losing the hair ribbon, Jane."

After which Alfred quit simpering and hit Rocky in the ear so Rocky could go ahead and beat the shit out of him.

They were on top of the barn. Thank God the day was almost over. They were sitting like owls on the rooftree: Rocky, Lucky, Speedy, Gabe. Alfred and Kofi were down below, running in circles and screaming somewhere just out of sight. It was getting late. In another couple of minutes it was going to be too dark to get down.

"When I grow up I'm going to kill Alfred," Rocky said. Mom had freaked and there was Alfred zooming around in the twilight like the Invulnerable Man.

Gabe said, "I thought you were growing up to be an astronaut."

"After I kill Alfred," Rocky said.

"Alfred's going to grow up to be an actor," Lucky said.

It was weird up here in the dusk, the air was almost cool for once. They were weird. Exposed. Downstairs, Mom was still changing dresses. That is, unless she was making another cake, sobbing while she ate it all herself, and fucking Alfred didn't care. He just zoomed around. Rocky growled, "If he lives."

When it's just getting dark you can say anything you want because nobody sees you. Gabe's voice rasped like a metal file. "When I grow up I'm going to do nothing. Nothing at all."

"I'm never growing up," Lucky said.

This made Rocky stand so quickly the others flinched, but his balance was perfect, perfect. "The fuck you're not. That's bull-shit. Bullshit!" He meant: Please stop. At full height he pointed a hand like a wand, drawing Lucky to his feet.

Lucky unfolded as if hypnotized, moving fluidly and with great care until he too was standing. "Or not."

"Cut it out, Lucky." Against all logic, even though it was too dark to do this, Rocky started out like a ropewalker. "Let's go."

Lucky followed. They made a careful progress along the rooftree to the far end of the barn, where Rocky got to his knees and lowered himself until he hung by his fingers. Then Rocky swung through the opening into the hayloft.

"Come on!"

When Lucky didn't follow he leaned back out, looking up. Lucky was still flat on his belly on the ridgepole with only the top part of his face showing over the edge of the roof.

"What's the matter?"

"Nothing." Lucky didn't move.

"Come on in."

Lucky whispered, "I can't." Something was shaking him apart.

"Come on! you can do this, you can do anything!" He was begging Lucky to be OK.

It was terrible. Lucky was plastered to the rooftree, agonized. Lucky, who would retreat in another minute, humiliated and wriggling backward to safety. Stuck, framed against the pale sky

like that, he was an unreadable silhouette. Like a cardboard person. Helpless. Miserable. "I can't."

Rocky tried to give him everything he had. "All you have to
do is let go."

"Well I can't do it, OK?"

LABOR DAY
WEEKEND

15

Friday

We could hardly wait for the party. We were going to turn into werewolves for Mr. Peterson and when the cameras started rolling, we would slaver and growl. It was about time. All summer we'd been rolling toward this weekend without knowing where we were heading.

We were supposed to be practicing for the big show. Mr. Peterson was renting camcorders and lights so he could shoot werewolf scenes right out of his script. He was in town getting this *professional equipment;* it was supposed to be a very big deal, but so far nobody had bothered to learn their lines.

We didn't feel like it.

Gabe went bike-riding with Kofi and wouldn't let Alfred go. Rocky went around with his jaw clenched and his shoulders set like he had his mind on something, and if you talked to him he barked. The rest of the time he hung out in the shed chamber, helping Lucky wait for his skeleton shirt to dry. When they came out they didn't want Alfred along either. If he asked Speedy to play, she just shrugged. She hung out in Frieda's room looking at her *Vogue*s and asking her about sex. She cut out thousands of pictures of clothes she'd like to have. Lives she wanted to go to live in. Everybody had somebody except Alfred.

By that time Alfred was so pissy that nobody wanted him around.

Something was eating Lucky, but nobody knew what. He was never around so you couldn't ask. While we weren't looking, he had shot up to be the tallest, and after all his mom's expensive haircuts, he was shaggier than us, going along with his head down and that hair flopping. You could yell and he wouldn't hear. He had to concentrate. He was drawing this monster from Scarth Cave comic for his father's birthday? Better than *Watchman, Tank Girl,* everything put together. It was all he could think about. It was going to be great, he said, it had to. The present that was going to kill the world. Which would have been OK, except he got all weird if you asked to look at it.

There was another strange thing. Lucky had started hanging out with his mom. He ran along beside Mrs. Burgess like a sheep dog with his mouth cracked wide and his tongue hanging out, and we couldn't tell if it was because he was dying to be petted or he was, like, herding her, like a stupid sheep that you have to steer out of trouble so it won't hurt itself.

He had gotten thin. He only wore this one black T-shirt. It had the name of some hospital for joint diseases across the back but that wasn't why he liked it. It was the design on the front. He felt like the Visible Man, like all the parts of Lucky's skeleton were printed on the outside of him. You could see him: clavicle, ribcage, the spine, femurs, all the parts of the skeleton inside the body inside the shirt.

If a mom tried to sneak it away to put it in the wash, he stayed in bed until she brought it back. He couldn't go out. Instead he waited in his sleeping bag until it got almost dry enough. Rocky would sit in the shed chamber and talk to him. The mothers couldn't let it go. Gabe's mom even made a special trip to the hospital one week to get him a second shirt. It looked just like the first, but even we could see it was not the same. He put it on and Mrs. Peterson hugged him hard. "Oh Lucky, here's your backup shirt, OK? Now you can go out whenever you want."

He wore it once, but it didn't take. He just sighed and put it away. There was only one shirt.

He went a little crazy trying to keep it clean for the Labor Day weekend. Then Thursday night Alfred accidentally hit his arm and he got chocolate all down the front of it. They made him put it in the wash and he let them. To look good for his dad on the big day. It was that important. Which was how he and Rocky got stuck up in the shed chamber in the middle of Friday of Labor Day Weekend, waiting while Mrs. Darrow ran a special load of wash. Rocky was the only one Lucky let into the shed chamber, because Rocky was the only one he could trust to sit there and not say something dumb. He was the only person Lucky could stand to have around.

Rocky sat on his sleeping bag with his knees up and his fingers stuffed in the tops of his black hightops, keeping him company, unless he was looking after him. At first they tried to pretend they were doing something else: planning a House of Horrors for Saturday, or figuring out costumes for Mr. Peterson's big production up at Scarth Cave, but they weren't. Lucky was just waiting for the shirt to come back and Rocky was waiting for him to come out with what was his problem or else for the shirt to dry, so they could go outside.

Without the shirt, Lucky couldn't even draw. He sat there with the comic on his knees and when the silence stretched too thin even for him he said, "I don't even know if my dad likes comic books."

He looked so bad that Rocky said, "He loves them, OK?"

"He doesn't love anything." Lucky was screwed up tight—eyes, face, everything. "All he wants is a kid that throws the ball around with him. He hates that I'm not that kind of kid."

Rocky said, "That's shit." He threw the ball around with his own dad and it was nothing.

"He thinks I'm a baby."

"You're already taller," Rocky said.

Lucky was depressed. "Or something worse."

"He doesn't care about you drawing?"

"He says I run like a girl."

"That's crap."

"He says I might end up being a faggot," Lucky said. From the way the groanies talked about it, the fond way they laughed about their faggot friends, he and Rocky guessed this was a bad thing.

Rocky considered. "Because he thinks you run like a girl?"

"Because I can't throw the ball."

Rocky shrugged. He couldn't help it if Lucky got picked last for teams. What difference did it make? It was no big deal. Tough Rocky always got chosen first; he was usually captain, and that was no big deal either. He said, "That doesn't make you a faggot."

"He says you're a faggot if you run like a girl." Lucky was, like, turning into the monster? Looking into his palms for the green rot to show up. "Do you think I'm a faggot?"

Rocky laughed and poked him with his toe. "I think you're a pussy faggot," he said in a voice pushed up a notch to let Lucky know he was definitely not.

"OK, so I'm not, but I think I am getting weird."

Rocky wanted to deny this too, but he couldn't say Lucky wasn't weird.

"You want to know something awful?" Lucky's voice shuddered. His voice got small and scared. "I can't live without the shirt."

So Rocky was forced to say, offhand, "That's OK."

It wasn't enough. He grabbed Rocky's arm and said something worse. "What if I really am turning into something else?"

Rocky jumped away. Lucky looked bad, lying there in the sleeping bag, waiting for his shirt to dry—maybe he *was* turning into something else: the monster? What? "Don't talk like that or you *will* turn into something."

Lucky's voice got small. "What do you think it is?"

"Could be a turnip, asshole."

At least Lucky was OK enough to laugh.

Rocky pushed harder, trying to force Lucky to deny it. "So

you're growing black hairs on the backs of your hands, and fangs."

Lucky didn't deny it. He only blinked.

Rocky hated him for acting sick, for lying there. He started yelling. "OK, you could be turning into some kind of fucking nut case. That shirt is nothing, OK? Nothing. It's only a shirt."

"I know."

"So why don't you get out of the stupid sack and put on some other stupid shirt?"

After a long time Lucky squeezed it out. "I can't."

Rocky didn't know why this made him so mad, or whether he was talking about the clean shirt or the beginning of the telltale rot, you know, the Change. He yelled, "Then shut up and wait for it."

Lucky just lay there staring into his hands while Rocky stared at the tops of his socks—nothing unusual. Rocky hated colored socks but they were at the ass-end of the summer. One was green and one was brown. Then after a long time, Lucky said, "Rocks, do you ever think something is happening to you that you can't help it?"

Thud.

This was precisely when Rocky's guts began to twitch. It got hard to talk. Yes there was something happening to him. Or something about him. He could never tell Lucky; he couldn't tell anyone. He said, "Not really," but he could hear his voice crack.

But Lucky was too hung up on his own sharp, private hook to see what made his best friend's voice crack and his head jerk. Brooding, he said, "What if my father is right?"

So Rocky had to look right at Lucky and say in a strong voice, "I don't know what you're turning into, but I don't think it's a faggot."

After another long time Lucky said, "I'm glad."

Lucky was afraid of turning into . . . Rocky was afraid of . . . He did not know what just yet, any more than he knew exactly who he was, or who he was going to be, maybe, did not yet know but would go forward to meet it anyway blundering on in a troubled, sweet confusion, going—he was not sure where.

When Lucky got back his shirt and they went outside they stumbled, blinking like two bats surprised by daylight. If the rest of us noticed, we were too hung up on the birthday bash to pick up on it. The equipment was here. We were into the werewolf thing.

The dads had rolled in with carloads of food and beer and wine. Everybody was slipping into the party mode. Mr. Peterson was back from the city with his outdoor lights and a little generator and more instructions than any twelve kids could carry out. The birthday was today!

We were all dressing for the party except for Lucky—guys in whatever shirts or coats or funky coveralls we thought were-wolves would wear because Mr. Peterson was casting that afternoon. We were making a professional-quality video up there at Scarth Cave, according to Mr. Peterson. Everybody wanted to be a star. Gabe and Kofi were busy in the barn building special things Zack said he needed for the set. Gabe wouldn't let any-body help. Alfred was bent on being the star. Total Alfred. He had to look the *most*. He was emptying trunks in the attic. Every few minutes he came down in a new combination—tail coat and jeans, coverall and top hat.

Speedy and Frieda didn't get costumes. Mrs. Burgess had bought dresses for them, for God's sake, *dresses*. They looked like angel robes, long and white, and in spite of what Speedy said, she made them put them on. She had this idea the girls ought to gather at the mailbox like medieval minstrels or some-thing.

"Beautiful," Leslie said with a feverish little gesture that made them know it wasn't true. "You look beautiful. This is going to be great."

When Mr. Burgess came in the Mercedes, Frieda was supposed to start playing "Greensleeves" on the recorder and she and Speedy were supposed to sing.

For whatever reasons, even though it wasn't Speedy's father's birthday, she got all bent about how she was going to look. She'd washed her hair in Ivory liquid and rinsed it in vinegar and rinsed it again in beer. Then she'd gone out into the sunshine and brushed and brushed so it would dry in waves. She had to look good because her dad was coming, and he hadn't been up to the farm in weeks.

While Alfred flounced in and out in a string of new costumes, Speedy ran back and forth with her fresh hair flying, excited and pretty and tense. She was glad Stig was coming, but she was scared. There was something very special that she had to ask.

When she asked him, she wanted to be beautiful.

She was supposed to be rehearsing with Frieda and her recorder but at the moment Speedy was hung up in front of Leslie's bedroom mirror, messing with her dress. She faced the mirror in this dead white thing Mrs. Burgess had bought for her, and decided it was so white that it made her disappear. Then there was her hair. She was going nuts trying to make it stop curling so she could pin it up. In another couple of hours the last two dads would be here.

Instead of hanging around here messing with flowers and Kofi's Afro comb, Speedy was supposed to be rehearsing and she knew it; she could hear Frieda outside in the circle, calling in her piping, helpless-foreigner's voice. But she couldn't go yet. She had to look her best for Stig! If she could just make herself pretty enough, he would hug her and tell her things were going to happen exactly the way she wanted without her having to ask.

The moms had done a number on Speedy's dad. They told him this birthday weekend was a big deal and Stig had to come no matter what. They needed him to get Lucky's father here without blowing the surprise. Because of the moms, Stig was coming up without this Virginia he'd started going out with, so there was that, at least. This Virginia was skinny and neat where Speedy's mom was skinny but big up top and messy. Roseann wore body suits and chiffon scarves that matched her skirts while uptight Virginia was into Peter Pan collars and stupid little suits with matching high-heeled shoes. Speedy's dad had met Virginia while he was at Rutgers, deciding whether to apply. Now he hardly ever came up to the farm. Maybe he felt guilty, he called Speedy every Sunday and told her all these things about his new and different life.

He said she would love Virginia. Virginia sent Speedy nice presents, pearl drop earrings and a five-year diary, but the one time she and Daddy were together with Virginia, this Virginia got in the middle of everything, clunk clunk clunk. How could Speedy ask Stig the big question with this Virginia around? How could she even talk to him? She was supposed to like Virginia, but Virginia was not her mom.

Right then she didn't even like her mom, but hey, she was her mom.

The trouble was, Roseann said she had to run away from the family to save her life, but when Speedy saw her again, she didn't look happy, she looked terrible. The day they went to the city, Speedy took one look at Roseann and her heart got hung up. Maybe she really did run away from them to save herself, but instead of making her young, being with Derek gave Roseann zits on her nice face and great big dark circles under the eyes, and—weird. After all those years of worrying about her weight, she was too thin.

Speedy could hear Frieda outside, getting plaintive, but she was hung up on this. If she looked nice enough, could she just ask Daddy the big question and settle it first thing?

Could she ask him at all?

The thing was, Speedy couldn't go to live with Mom and Derek—one look at Derek and she knew. Her mom was too distracted and unhappy, and Derek? In between times, Derek forgot who she was.

She stared hard into the mirror one more time, trying to see what Stig was going to see, when it smacked her in the face . . . My God, it must have been the light; looking in the mirror, Speedy saw her mother standing there. She hated it. She had to get away.

But she ended up stalled on the stairs. Lucky was in the way. He had his junk spread all over the steps, eight inks and a gang of pens and brushes laid out in a row along the next-to-bottom step. When she spoke, he didn't even hear. He was obsessing over this comic, trying to finish it by tonight. He wanted to have it ready so he could take it up to the road and give it to his dad before the party began. He was going to do it right after she and Frieda sang.

Speedy said, "Hey?"

It was as if she'd waked him up. "Oh, Speedy. Hi."

"Are you OK?"

"Look. I'm almost finished. Better than Batman."

"You know it." She looked. It wasn't anything like *Batman*. It was more like those big, confusing, violent Bosch pictures Roseann dragged her around to on all those afternoons last year during her Art History period, sticking Speedy on benches in big, boring galleries while she and Derek talked. She couldn't help what came out of her. "God. Is this it?"

"This is it," Lucky said. "What do you think?"

The drawings were weird, these careful, careful pen lines and different-colored shadows that must have taken days to make, all in Day-Glo colors. It was like seeing inside the monster. It was beautiful, scary. Odd. There were ugly things hanging upside down in Scarth Cave like knotted ganglia, and along with the words in the monster's talk balloons, there were terrible rosettes studding every line. Another problem was Lucky's printing. It was dense and tiny as bug tracks. He was trying to tell everything, but the writing was so crabbed only Lucky could make it out. How was Mr. Burgess going to know? She said, "It's great."

"Do you think he'll like it?"

"He has to like it. It's from you."

Lucky just gave her this look. "What do you really think?"

It was the last minute. The dads would be here before they knew it. Mr. Burgess was driving Speedy's dad up from the city. What would Stig think when he saw her and Frieda by candlelight, singing "Greensleeves" at the top of the drive?

Would he think Speedy was pretty? Would he like her dress?

In another hour the party would begin. The presents would come out. Lucky was red around the eyes and his hand was so jittery that he could hardly finish the last drawing. It was practically time, and Speedy was supposed to tell him the lettering was too squirrely to read?

No way. She didn't know how Lucky's dad was going to make out even one word, but the colors were gorgeous. Maybe he wouldn't mind. Maybe Chad Burgess would actually love it. Lucky cared so much! If he didn't love it, Speedy was going to murder him. She gulped. "It's wonderful."

Lucky was edgy. He was waiting for her to say something in particular. But what? He prompted. "So, ah. He'll get the point?" "The point. Ah . . ."

Lucky nailed her with an angry look. "You know, the point! The whole point of the whole thing."

"The point? Oh, right. The point." It was one of those times, you know—like when you are stuck in school, thinking about one thing while the teacher's talking about another and then they call on you? You go, *Ah, uh. What was the question?* Speedy was afraid to sound dumb so she said, "Sure he'll get it. He's your dad."

This made him bleak. "That doesn't mean anything."

The two of them stood there on the next-to-bottom step without talking for a long minute.

The silence made Speedy afraid. She touched his arm. "Lucky?"

He came back from wherever he had been wandering. He

blinked. As if entranced, he said, "The story's changed. It's. Ah. Gotten different."

Speedy looked in the hall mirror. She had gotten different— bigger since the beginning of the summer. Scabs ringed the beds of her fingernails. There were these *things* growing on the front of her. She had been out in the sun so much her hair looked white, but in spite of the beer and the vinegar and all her hours of brushing it was dried out and seedy-looking too. Would Daddy mind? What would he think of her?

Lucky said, for both of them, "I just hope he gets it."

And her mouth dried out and her belly trembled. "He has to," she said.

16

Friday Night

By the time the party started we were all excited, even Alfred, who'd been sulking because nobody would mess with him. Everything was going to be so *pretty*. Speedy too: there was something *different* about being in a dress. Her dad was special too because he was in on the surprise. Stig was the one who had to convince Mr. Burgess to drive up from the city when he didn't want to. What's more, he'd done it without giving anything away.

Going up the road to the mailbox with Frieda, Speedy felt the filmy white cloth against her bare legs and thought: *When he sees me in this, he'll take me home with him for sure.*

We had spent all day on the party, blowing up balloons and stringing crepe paper in the house and making outdoor wind chimes out of tin cans to make everything look not necessarily better, but *different*, like an enchanted forest or some part of Oz.

Now Gabe's father had finished putting the last things in place for what he thought of as the main event, and if Gabe was a little pissed and not as excited as he should have been, it was because when push came to shove over the script, his father had given stupid Alfred the big part, even though we kids had all had the pages since Monday and nobody had bothered to learn the lines. As soon as they got Lucky's dad into the clearing and shouted, "Surprise," the birthday party would form a procession, with handmade banners and before-dinner drinks. Then Zack Peterson would lead the progress up the driveway and across the road to Scarth Cave for the big birthday show.

We were doing a scene from Professor Peterson's movie up there, the first big birthday event. The trouble was, only boys were in it. They were at Scarth Cave all day rehearsing, while Speedy and Frieda got stuck cleaning and fixing up the house. The girls put colored lampshades in the living room and new purple plates on the table, along with snowballs Leslie had dyed purple by putting the stems in ink. The cloth was lavender, and Leslie stuck matching napkins folded like flowers into the new champagne glasses. We were having champagne and Mrs. Peterson's chicken velvet for supper, followed by Mrs. Darrow's death-dealing Black Forest Cake.

At five o'clock the girls rehearsed one last time. Frieda played her recorder and Speedy hit her tambourine and they sang "Greensleeves." When Dad got here with Mr. Burgess, the girls would be stationed at the top of the drive, waiting by the RFD mailbox surrounded by lighted candles in paper sacks. They'd start singing as soon as the Mercedes came in sight, and if their voices sounded thin and weak in all that fresh air, what difference did it make?

Naturally Mr. Burgess would stop to find out what was up.

Speedy would curtsy and say, "Welcome to the mysteries."

Frieda's line was, "Let the revels begin."

As Lucky's father got out of the car the girls were supposed to put the daisy wreath around his neck and lead him down the driveway to the little clearing in front of the farmhouse.

"Candlelight. Girls in pretty dresses," Leslie said. "How could he not be charmed?"

Speedy was tickled because her dad was in on it: Stig was supposed to say, "Why Chad, what's this?" At the bottom of the driveway, Rocky and Lucky were supposed to be waiting. They would hand Chad the silver birthday goblet and the hand-lettered birthday scroll. When the girls led Mr. Burgess into the clearing he would see all the other parents waiting at the punch table, done up in party drag, yelling, "Surprise."

Chad would be so pleased! After he got over being surprised, the dads would give him rum drinks in frosted glasses and Mrs. Burgess would lay out hors d'oeuvres. She'd bought crusty French loaves and smoked salmon and caviar for the grownups to take with them on the safari to Scarth Cave.

Zack had rigged lights with a rented generator up there, and set up a ring of chairs. Gabe and Kofi and Alfred were waiting to act out the best parts of his werewolf script. Rocky and Lucky were supposed to lead the groanies up the hill with torches, crossing the road with the singers following and parents coming last. Speedy thought, *Daddy will see me in this dress and everything will change.* She thought her father was going to need somebody, now that her mom was gone. When we came back downhill from the show and sat down to the birthday dinner at the big trestle table, Speedy's life was going to change. When the cake came in Stig was going to hug her and when the party was over, he'd take her home with him.

Leslie was right. It was going to be beautiful! Standing up there in the dusk next to the mailbox, Speedy felt beautiful in the gauzy dress, and Frieda? She supposed Frieda felt beautiful too; the au pair kept touching her loose, freshly unbraided hair with her fingers and Speedy could hear her breath coming and going in a ragged little flutter: huh-ah, huh-aaaah. Love, maybe, but it had been a while since they'd seen anything of Dave. Had they broken up? Speedy didn't know. What she did know was that she could hardly wait for her father to come.

Nothing worked out the way we thought it would. By the time the party finally did start it was too dark to see anything and so late everybody was too pissed to care.

This is how it went wrong.

It was Labor Day Weekend and up on the Mass Pike, everything was hung up because of a four-way crash.

The girls stayed by the mailbox striking poses, but Mr. Burgess didn't come and he *didn't* come. It took so long that the candles began to gutter out. One fell over and set fire to the paper sack and Frieda was so jittery that she started sobbing when she stamped it out, and when Speedy asked her what was the matter, she just swallowed hard and wouldn't say. Still Speedy and Frieda waited, slapping mosquitoes and scratching, watching the road and striking their pose whenever they heard the sound of a motor, but none of the cars was the Mercedes, and none of the drivers was Chad.

Lucky kept running up from the house to ask Is Dad here yet, where are they, which is how there turned out to be three people waiting by the mailbox when his father's big old Mercedes finally did nose around the last curve, after the sun went down. The girls had been waiting for so long that they were caught off guard. It was so late that they sang raggedly and they completely forgot their lines. Lucky flinched and tried to hide behind Frieda. It would have been OK if anything else had gone right.

Chad was strung out from being stuck in traffic for hours. He might not have gotten so pissed at things if it hadn't been practically dark by the time he got here, or if there hadn't been any fortieth-birthday party, or if the party hadn't been a surprise.

He was ready to zoom past the little pageant when Lucky hurled himself into the middle of the road, fanning his arms like a flagman trying to stop a runaway train.

Chad jerked to a stop. He'd been stuck in traffic for so long that everything made him mad. "What's this," he said, without getting out of the car.

Lucky ran around to the window. "It's for you."

Chad looked pale and rumpled, the way fathers do after hours of heavy traffic, and he was pissed. "What's going on?"

Lucky was trying to tell him, "Dad, it's a."

But his father just said, "For Pete's *sake*."

Then Speedy closed in, trying to get the birthday daisy wreath on his head so she could say "Happy birthday," which would at least give him a clue. The trouble was, Chad couldn't see it was only flowers, so he yelped and ducked away with the wreath halfway on. It was sliding down over his ear. He tried to bat it away.

"What *is* this?"

On his other side Stig was explaining, but Chad was too pissed to listen. Frieda started to cry.

"What's this *thing?*"

"Oh shit," Lucky said, and handed him the scroll. "It's your birthday, Dad."

"My fucking birthday again."

"I'm sorry," Lucky said.

"Ow! Would you cut it out!" Chad was grappling with the ring of daisies; he accidentally hit Lucky's arm so the scroll flew and Lucky's torch flew into the bushes and went out.

Lucky had his arms out: Oh, no! and in the flare before the light died you could see right through him. In the skeleton shirt he looked like the Visible Man.

"Oh Lucky, oh shit, I'm sorry," Mr. Burgess said right away. "It isn't your fault."

Lucky just said glumly, "Happy birthday anyway."

"Leslie!" Mr. Burgess was reaching for Lucky to make it up, but he was upset and scrambling away. Chad's voice quieted down and he asked tiredly, "Lucky, is this your mother's idea?"

Lucky's face went askew. "She just thought . . ."

But his dad groaned and said, "Yeah. Right. Goddammit." He sighed. "OK, climb in kids, and let's go down and face the music." He had Speedy's dad open the back door so they could pile in.

"Anyway," Lucky said. He knew his dad was pissed but he'd been waiting on this for so long he couldn't help it! "I have a present for you, dad."

Frieda wouldn't get in the car. She hung by the mailbox, fretting. "But the procession!"

"What procession?"

"Mrs. Burgess intends for us to march."

"I'm tired," Chad said. "It's late. Let's just fuck the procession, OK?"

Speedy looked at Lucky, secure in the back of his father's car. In spite of everything, his face was glad. And her. That was her dad in the front seat, half-turning to wink at her. *Oh, Daddy.* She knew just how Lucky felt. But Mr. Burgess? That was another thing. "Come on, Frieda. Get in."

When they got to the bottom of the hill the groanies started singing as planned but it was late and half the food and most of the punch was gone so if their voices were a little fuzzy, too bad.

Chad came out fighting. "OK, Leslie, what's going on."

She didn't even care whether he liked the party. "Darling," she said, "Chad. Happy birthday. Isn't it wonderful?"

He wasn't too pleased. In spite of everything he tried to act pleased, hugging Lucky, who leaned against him looking somehow at *rest*, for the time being, at least.

Then Leslie said brightly, "OK, time for Scarth Cave."

This is when he dug in his heels. "Scarth Cave!"

"Something special," she said with look that let everybody knew she was tired from smiling for so long.

"For God's sake, Leslie, we just got here."

She said, "Come on. It's the next surprise."

But Mr. Burgess grumbled that he'd had enough surprises, thank you, and he sank into the throne that Rocky and Lucky had fixed for him and said he had moved three miles in the last hour he was on the Mass Pike, and he was too beat to move again.

Her voice got steely. "Chad, this whole thing is *planned*."

Lucky saw what was coming and he got up, bent on creating a diversion. "Dad."

But Chad went on as if he hadn't heard. "Well I'm sick of your plans."

This was how Lucky put himself between them. "Daddy, I made you a present."

There was no telling whether Chad even heard; he and Mrs. Burgess were having the fight.

"Wait, I'll show you." Lucky peeled off and ran into the house to get his comic anyway; he had that look he got when he was just about to launch one of his models to see if it would fly. We didn't hear what Lucky's mom and dad said to each other, but we saw from her face in the lamplight that it was bad.

Rocky and Speedy and the other groanies were standing around awkwardly: should we stay here waiting or should we head up to Scarth Cave for the werewolf show? Was this still a party or what?

Then Lucky got between his folks, pushing Leslie out of the way so he could give his father the present. His dad did stop and smooth his hair nicely and say, Thank you very much he didn't have time to look at it just now so would Lucky take care of it for him?

Lucky's *face*! It was too dark to go to the cave, but Speedy wasn't disappointed. It gave her a chance to step in next to her father and hold on.

After a couple of minutes Chad and Leslie quit fighting and Mrs. Burgess turned around with that fake smile she set so much store by, The Perfect Hostess, and she went: "OK, fine. No safari to Scarth Cave," so, tough about all the boys' efforts, smashing wood together to make the werewolf funeral pyre and getting scratched and banged up hanging the lights.

Everything went for nothing then, with Leslie waving at nobody in particular, "Go tell the kids the whole thing is off. After cocktails we'll just move on to Phase Two."

What were we doing up there all that time, hanging upside down in the cave? What were our hopes? What did we think we were waiting for?

Scarth Cave was creepy even though it was boarded up. We were not precisely what you would call hanging upside down. It only felt like it.

Instead we were waiting. We were waiting so hard that we were turning blue. Hanging in territory halfway between pretend and actual. Alfred, Gabe and Kofi, and not one of us could have said whether what we were doing that night up there at the batcave was pretend or for real. We and the groanies had been together for so long that our lives had overlapped. Stuff had begun to mingle—what the parents did was inextricably tied into what we played.

We couldn't be sure which things happened for what causes, which was real and which was made up.

If the whole monster-werewolf thing was imagined, kids didn't know where it had come from; had we made it up, or was it really this movie that Gabe's dad couldn't stop working on and couldn't get right? Were we really going to get into the movies, or did Mr. Peterson just tell us that so we'd stay up there at the cave until the groanies came? Did Zack believe in his movie, or not? We didn't know. We thought it was real.

We would have done anything.

We were waiting for everybody to come uphill so we could go into our act. Gabe couldn't hit the lights until he heard them coming or it would ruin the surprise. It was getting cold. He and Alfred and Kofi were about to starve. We were bored of waiting and the bugs had moved on us. Alfred was getting on our nerves. Kofi was bitching and Gabe was going crazy, trying to keep us quiet so we wouldn't give away the secret and make his father mad at him.

Gabe's dad had given all three of us marks to stand on. We couldn't stray far because at the first sound of Frieda's recorder, Gabe was supposed to hit the lights and all three of us would leap into our places and begin the show.

Gabe played Tic-Tac-Toe in the dirt with Kofi to take his mind off it while Alfred lunged in and out of the bushes in his werewolf suit, which turned out to be baggy pants and a jacket big enough for Young Frankenstein. Down at the farmhouse he was a pain in the ass, which is how everybody treated him, but up here in the dark like this, he thought he was a star. Last summer the Darrows had sent him to acting camp and by this time he'd bored us with every attitude he'd learned. He had the idea if he was good enough, when the werewolf movie got made, he, Alfred, would be a star.

Kofi was in what he called one of his black rages: why for you persecute me, white man, two hundred years of slavery and now this, etc. etc. Gabe had to beg him to stay; he'd promised his dad to make this scene good because—it was strange—Zack had the idea that if this worked, the whole movie would work. His dad was counting on Gabe. Kofi's folks were getting divorced so they wouldn't even be here for the show, so unlike Gabe and Alfred, he had no stake in this. This meant he was doing Gabe a tremendous favor, which got bigger and bigger the later it got.

Plus, Kofi kept hearing things moving deep inside the cave. Stirrings. Weird little cries. Alfred said it was rats. Gabe would have told us it was the Easter Bunny if it would keep us there.

Alfred the star. It was enough to make you puke. He didn't care how late it got or how creepy it was. All he cared about was lurching around in the big black coat, showing off under the lights. Alfred got to drop out of the trees with a howl while Gabe and Kofi sprang out at him with silver stakes.

It was dark. The black cracks between the boards across the cave mouth had gotten wider. Alfred kept forgetting his lines. Kofi had lost his silver stake while we were fooling around getting ready, and the paint was peeling off of Gabe's so it looked like what it was, a piece of kindling with aluminum paint.

Plus damn Alfred wouldn't go up the damn tree when Gabe told him to. He wouldn't even stay near it so he could climb up fast when they came. Instead he hung around bothering us while Gabe worried because it was so late. It sucked, but he couldn't quit. Dad was counting on him.

So what if Alfred messed up?

It would serve Alfred right if the grownups all came up here in a good mood and excited about the party, and the show started and he missed his cue. Gabe would like to see Alfred the showoff embarrassed for once. The trouble was, if we fucked this up, his father would blame Gabe.

Alfred kept running to the crest of the hill. "Are they here yet? "

Kofi said, "Man, we don't need this."

"Be cool," Gabe would do anything to keep him. "They're on their way. It's so late that they've gotta be on their way."

Alfred whined. "They said they were coming before dark."

"Come on, man, how long we're going to hang around here for nothing?" When Kofi started what was it, *getting down* with black talk, Gabe knew he was in trouble.

What should he do? It was dark. Late. He had to make stepping stones out of words and lay them out so the three of us could walk away. His voice spiked. "Maybe something's happened to them."

As soon as he put the words in the air, Gabe sniffed disaster: the entire birthday party massacred around the campfire without his knowing it, bikers or terrorists roaring away. He gulped and thought of something less scary to say. "Hey, what if they really aren't coming?"

On one side Alfred punched Gabe's arm. "You son of a bitch, of course they're coming . . ."

On the other, Kofi grumbled. "You promised this would be over before supper, white man . . ."

". . . You think they wouldn't tell us they weren't coming? After your father made us promise?" Alfred hit him on the arm.

Kofi growled, "You said we'd do this show and be out of here in time to eat."

"They're coming, asshole," Alfred said.

Kofi said, "If they're coming, they'd be here by now."

"I promised Dad." What if this messed up because Gabe crapped out? The whole thing was so mixed up in Gabe's mind that he got the idea Zack was right, tonight would make or break his film career. If they left and Zack didn't get his pickup money, it would be Gabe's fault. He hated Alfred. "I don't know what to do."

"It's our big chance, asshole. We have to hang in."

"And fucking starve to death," Kofi went on, as if he hadn't heard.

"Shut up, Alfred. If you're so damn sure they're coming, get up in your goddam tree and take a look." Gabe's anxieties were running along ahead. What if nobody was coming because something had happened to Dad? A heart attack from stressing? Some kind of wreck? What if something had happened to Mom too, and Gabe was an orphan? Awful things happened to other people's parents all the time. One minute they were there, the next, they weren't.

Alfred said, "You want somebody to look, you go look."

He didn't know. "If they don't come soon, we'll split."

Kofi rumbled nonstop now. "Well it's stone dark, man, and the natives are getting restless."

Alfred whined, "You're jealous, so you're trying to wreck the show."

"There may not be any show." Unsettled, Gabe strained at the approaching night. Did he hear the faint sound of Frieda's recorder, tweeting far away? Did he see distant torches bobbing between the trees or were those only lightning bugs? If it was the recorder, his folks were all right and Gabe was all right.

"There is so a show. *I'm* the show."

Listen. Parents could drop right out of your life. They could disappear without a trace; he was so *scared*. But Gabe had to put Alfred down. "I don't care who's the star, I'm running the show."

"If you running it, man, let's us get out of here." Kofi was growling. "Are we going or what?"

Gabe was scared. Something was wrong. If only they'd come up the path. He wanted to know for sure they were all right. "Please wait. Ten minutes, OK?"

Kofi sighed. He was Gabe's best friend. "OK, man. Ten more minutes. Ten minutes, tops."

Gabe died, looking at his watch. At the end of the ten minutes he got up stiffly and said, "Well."

Kofi got up and stretched, saying, "Well." Then Gabe said OK and Kofi said OK and that should have been it. Would have, too, except for Alfred. "Come on, Alfred. It's over."

"Wait a minute." Alfred threw himself at Gabe, grappling in the cape. "Let's fucking wait just another fucking minute."

Gabe shook him off. "We can't wait, Alfred, it's too dark."

Alfred's voice cracked. "Then hit the lights."

"Can't." Reliable Gabe: father's orders. "If we hit the lights, we'll wreck the secret."

Alfred pounced like a cat. "See? There still *is* a secret. You don't want to give it away because you still think they're coming."

"We can't give it away because we might have it tomorrow," Gabe said.

It was hard to explain but Kofi just started getting blacker—the way he stood with his fist on his hip and his butt lifted, the way he talked. Gabe thought he had actually curled his lip and flashed the whites of his eyes. He looked like a tribal prince. He did this thing he did when he was really pissed at you; he got down. "I don't be studying no tomorrow. I'm out of here. Aaite?"

Gabe turned his back on Alfred. "All right."

"That's more like it," Kofi said in a cool, civilized tone, and he turned back into Gabe's friend that he knew.

So they left Alfred on the hill in front of Scarth Cave cursing and breaking things: the silver stakes, Gabe's father's reflectors, dead branches—anything. Gabe knew it would only be a minute before Alfred threw away the pieces and followed.

"Listen, it's only put off until tomorrow," he said, more for himself than anybody else. Everybody had practiced all day; there was no way his father was going to miss shooting this big scene. Then it hit him in the belly like a boulder. *Unless something awful really has happened to them.* Gabe was sick to his stomach not knowing, rushing through the dark bushes, stumbling, tearing his jeans on barbed wire. The devil was on his heels; he had to get back to the farm and find out what had happened to them.

By the time he hit the road and started down the driveway Gabe was running flat out, choking on his own breath and imagining some terrible disaster had befallen his parents, imagining the worst in the second before he cleared the last big curve in the driveway that showed him the circle in the clearing, everything.

Then he saw them. Gabe came out into the open; he didn't even know he was screaming, "Mommy." His voice sounded weedy and thin, just the way it did when he was little, and scared in the night.

"It's Gabe." Polly called. "Gabe!"

"Mommy, *Dad!*"

"Zack, it's the kids!" Polly saw and raised her hands. "Oh, poor Gabe!"

"Oh," his father said, suddenly embarrassed. "You guys."

Gabe swallowed air. Surprised. Zack was surprised. His father had forgotten them!

"Oh, wow. Gabe! Where were you?" He ran all his fingers through his hair so it stood straight up. "We've been waiting and waiting for you."

In all his fearful imaginings, Gabe had thought this, thought that, thought terrible things but in no way imagined they had forgotten him.

They had forgotten all three of them.

They'd just plain forgotten there were people stuck up there at Scarth Cave waiting under instructions. The grownups had just rolled right over that part as if it had never been part of the plan and now they were sitting in lawn chairs around the fire having rum drinks. The grownups were lounging there pigging out on smoked salmon and caviar under a couple of dozen bug lights, carelessly eating and laughing among themselves.

Enraged, Gabe ran faster; he heard himself, "Aarrgh," heard Kofi roaring, Alfred howling as we tore into the clearing. Swelling with rage and frustration, Alfred was faster and louder than anybody, with this roar ripping his throat. Like the monster. Breaking out.

Zack came uphill to meet us. "Where've you guys been?"

"Where the fuck do you think we've been?" It was hard, needing for his father to know how mad Gabe was and at the same time being so glad he wasn't dead. Gabe barreled into him. "Where were you?"

"Didn't you get the word?"

"We were waiting," Gabe yelled.

"We sent a kid to tell you," Zack said, shaking his head.

"We waited forever. Where were you anyway?"

"I'm so sorry. I thought they told you. It's off for tonight." He was all rumpled and upset. "It may be off for good."

"Somebody was supposed to tell us?" Alfred came screeching to a stop in the gravel.

"Didn't they come and let you know?"

Next to Gabe, Alfred barked, "Didn't who come?"

"I thought somebody went up to get you," Gabe's dad said vaguely. "One of the kids."

"Who?" Alfred was all teeth. "Come on, who?"

"What does it matter, now that it's all over?" Zack said and absent-mindedly, he gave up the perp. "Lucky, I think."

"Lucky?" Alfred swung around like an infernal machine. "Lucky!"

"Whoever," Zack said, but you should have seen Alfred's face. "It's OK. You're going to be a star, Alfred, just not tonight."

But rage roared over Alfred like a flash-fire. He was burning and he never heard.

Dad grabbed Gabe and hugged him hard, going, "Oh shit, Gaby, I'm sorry we messed up. Gabe. Kofi. Guys. Come and have something to eat."

Kofi was grrr-ing like a police dog and for a minute Gabe stiffened resentfully, but this was his father, so he let Dad pull them both around to where Mom was talking to Speedy and her dad. He could feel Alfred sweeping the place like a flamethrower.

Then Alfred plowed past and hurtled into the middle of the circle, swinging his fists. Gabe thought Alfred was looking for *his* mom and dad, but no.

Nobody was sure what set Alfred off, whether it was all that waiting for no reason, or if it was finding out he'd been forgotten or if it was something about the way his father looked, standing with Mrs. Burgess by the drinks table in his new pink striped shirt. Maybe it was seeing Rocky scarfing potato chips as if nothing had happened while grinning Kofi gave Alfred the finger or maybe it was how fat his mom looked next to the other moms in her big silk smock.

He went off like a fucking bomb. "Son of a bitch!"

He wheeled, raking all the objects of his rage with this great revolving glare. Then he zoned in on Lucky. Locked on. We heard the click.

Lucky was just sitting there on the ground next to his dad, so deep into his comic that when Alfred yelled he didn't even look up.

Alfred stood over him with this ugly glare. "You were supposed to come get us!"

Then Lucky looked up. He could hardly see Alfred for the wild afterimages of the drawing he had been staring at. "Oh, was I? I'm sorry, I forgot."

Our fifth-grade teacher had showed us chain reaction by throwing a ping-pong ball in the middle of a gang of set mousetraps; they all went *snap* one after another as the ball kept bouncing around; it was something like that: sprong, sprong, sprong, all that waiting setting off Alfred, Sprong! Sprong!

Sometimes you accidentally start something you don't even know about.

That's what Alfred did. He was snarling like a werewolf,

spraying spit. "You fucking *forgot?* He picked up a rock. He was about to smash it down on Lucky's head.

Gabe brought him down before Lucky even saw.

He and Alfred locked and wrestled until Mr. Fenton separated them. When they got up, Lucky was still bent over his comic in the light from the fire and the bug candles. Whatever was going on, he had already forgotten it. He was so far into what he was doing that he never saw Alfred, or what was boiling in his eyes.

"Nobody forgets me," Alfred howled.

Chain reaction. Sprong.

"I'll get even, you just wait."

We didn't know yet, but it had begun.

Then Mrs. Burgess looked up from her conversation with Alfred's father and said, "Oh, everybody here now? OK, let's go inside for dinner and the cake."

So after being separated all night the five of us were back together, kind of, sitting down for one more meal at the long table, but we didn't talk much because in one way or another all five of us were all turned in on ourselves—what we had hoped for with this big party, what had come of it.

In spite of everything it felt good, sitting inside at the long table like the Waltons with our heads bent in the candlelight, eating pretty food and knowing there was going to be cake. Frieda was out with this guy Dave, he just came in on his bike right before dinner and said they had to talk. Frieda said stuff to him in Finnish that he ignored. We saw him jerk her up on the back of his motorcycle like a runaway prince and they roared away. So it was all families that night except for Kofi, even Speedy and her dad. She didn't need to ask Stig what was going to happen to her in the fall. They were so close right then that Speedy just knew it was going to be fine—her and Daddy living somewhere in a nice new apartment, Daddy and her.

Everything looked so *pretty,* all of us mostly in a good mood and wearing party clothes. Leslie and Chad were sitting up at the head of the table, Chad lounging, with his black eyes and the shelf of dark hair, looking handsome and reckless where Speedy's father only tried, with Leslie looking like a magazine model, sleek and silky at his side. They were king and queen of the summer, with the rest of us sitting across from each other along the sides—the Darrows, the Petersons, Stig and Speedy and the other kids, arranged in descending order like the royal court.

In the white dress Speedy thought she looked almost as good as Mrs. Burgess; something had happened to her over the summer so she had ended up almost as tall as the moms. If it came to that, Speedy thought, she could be the lady of the house for her dad. Who needed Roseann? Mrs. Darrow had taught Speedy to cook over the summer and she could make nice curtains, even if she had to do it by hand. Maybe Stig would send his shirts out to the laundry, which would take care of that. Speedy was feeling warm and full; there was rum in the fruit dessert and she had sneaked most of the juice and when nobody was looking she got up and poured more rum on it, so Speedy had a little buzz on.

It was the kind of buzz she would go out looking for as she got older and things turned out wrong, but at the time she just felt warm and well—so fine.

Then Rocky turned the lights out and Mrs. Darrow came in with the cake, all forty candles making her face glow, so she was pretty for once. Everybody stopped what they were doing, underscoring the moment with a little hush.

"This is the last one of these," Mr. Burgess said.

Mr. Darrow said, "You'll live to be a hundred."

"I'm never having another birthday," Mr. Burgess said. Then he cut into it and everybody went, ooohh.

Everything was sweet—the cake, the filling, the chocolates Mrs. Peterson passed around at the end. For the first time all summer Speedy was happy because she truly thought she and her dad were going to make out all right.

Even though he was cross when he first stopped the Mercedes up there by the mailbox where we were waiting to sing for him, Mr. Burgess had gotten into having the party. He was wearing the silk shirt Mrs. Burgess had bought him for his birthday and by the time the kids and adults went into the living room to sit around the fire he had mellowed out so much that he pulled Lucky in to sit next to him and tousled his hair. It was getting cool outside so Leslie scratched the plans for dancing outside in the clearing. The groanies stayed by the fire instead, and when somebody opened the back door to bring in more wine or more firewood, you could feel the end of summer coming in.

17

Saturday

You'd think that after the mess last night, the missed show and the anger and confusion, somebody up there had decided to make it up to us.

Saturday was kids' day, the grownups would do anything we wanted. It was nice out, so when two of the dads headed up the road in the sunshine, Rocky and Lucky peeled off and went after them. Rocky went because, well, why not?

And Lucky? He went because it was his dad. Chad and Calvin were so mellowed out that they didn't mind being followed, even when Alfred crashed out of Zack Peterson's studio shack where no kids were supposed to go and came running after them. To Rocky, it was close to perfect—he and his friend Lucky together in the sunshine, hanging out with their dads. For once, Chad and Calvin were like two extra kids, content to bop around on the hillside, noplace to go, nothing they had to do.

The only problem was Alfred. That day he was like a little time bomb; Rocky could hear him tick.

He and Lucky took the dads skinny-dipping in the reservoir and then they drifted up to Scarth Cave with Alfred lunging back and forth in the path ahead. The lights and the werewolf funeral pyre were still in place and Rocky thought: oh, shit. If anybody mentioned the show that they never had last night, Alfred would go up like a Roman candle. The little jerk was still pissed at Lucky for leaving him stuck up there at the cave with his jaw flapping and his thumb up his ass. But the sun was bright and somehow it never came up. You'd think neither of the dads had ever seen the cave before, even though they probably had. Lucky's father was politely surprised, like: hey, this is interesting, and Rocky's dad talked too much. Big Cal was bluff and distracted, pretending to look around without really looking around.

It was funny, going back downhill with the fathers, who talked their own talk. Rocky and Lucky didn't talk much because what one knew, the other understood. Alfred was the leftover, dancing backward in the path ahead. Rocky was sorry Alfred had ever gone to acting camp. It was like, if they didn't like Alfred one way, he would try a different part? *So, you don't like me? Surprise. That's not me.* He'd put on a new face, like: *Guess who?* As if they didn't know it was only Alfred underneath, and Alfred was all this person was ever going to be. That day he was pissed at Lucky and hiding it, playing Charming, like it was the name of a person you could be. It made Rocky sick.

Alfred was right out of some old Errol Flynn movie on TV. He kept darting away from his shadow, fencing with sticks, showing the dads pieces of glass and junk that he had found in the road, holding all these things up to them with this revolting cute grin. Rocky thought Mr. Burgess was treating Alfred like a big showoff, which is what he was.

But Dad didn't notice. Calvin had his mind on being nice to Lucky. You'd think he had set out to show Mr. Burgess how dads were supposed to act. He brought Lucky on with in-jokes, bizarre facts; anything that would make him shine. Rocky imagined his dad was doing this for his sake, because of Lucky being Rocky's best friend.

In the sunlight Mr. Burgess forgot all about last night.

If Chad got pissed and yelled at everybody Friday night, Saturday morning it was like it never happened. He and Calvin were punching each other and kidding around, like they'd never left fifth grade, and they pulled the kids in too. They could have been playmates instead of fathers and sons. Calvin punched Lucky in the arm and it made Rocky feel good. He could see Lucky was tickled. He blushed and grinned: *Just one of the guys.*

So Rocky thought, Great. Mr. Burgess will leave off telling Lucky he's going to grow up to be a faggot. Then Lucky can quit it with the monster. He can be glad.

We hunkered on the hillside with the dads, spying on the farmhouse, with the sunlight hitting our heads in patches between the shadows of moving leaves. Anybody who didn't know would think it was boring, sitting up there on the rocks without talking, but there was something about it—guys with their fathers, just *being* there. The sun made us so sleepy that we hummed along, burble, mmmmzzz. Feeling good, Rocky sat on one side of Calvin with Lucky on the other and Lucky's father on the other side, a family sandwich. Except we had one extra. In the shakedown of dads and kids, Lucky was sitting on Calvin's other side, so Alfred was out.

It would have been a perfect day except for the kid brother dancing and jiggling; he dangled in front of us like a black rubber spider on a string.

Fathers and sons sat on the log watching the moms go back and forth in the clearing like mechanical toys wound up just to amuse them; it was kind of like being God. The women looked like dolls, going in and out of the house, Rocky and Alfred's mom and Lucky's and Gabe's, along with Speedy and Frieda, laying out lunch on the picnic table. There were the women down there at the bottom of the hill doing nice things for us while guys hung out up here on the hill dreaming; you could almost forget Alfred. Mistake.

Rocky never found out what there was about the scene below, what Alfred thought he saw or what one of the kids or fathers did that set fire to his ass. Whatever it was that got to him, it made Alfred wild. He started whirring around the log in a big figure eight, whizzing on a loop like a wasp getting ready to sting.

He kept darting closer, until on the last zoom he came too close and clipped Lucky hard on the side of the head. Could have been an accident. Not. You could hear the *crack*.

Lucky didn't hit back. He just ducked. "Quit!"

Down there in front of the farmhouse Mom was talking to Lucky's mother, who looked glamorous, not like a mom at all. What Leslie looked like was a model, whereas nice old Mom didn't even know enough to fix her hair right or pull the denim shirt down over her humongous butt. Rocky loved her, but in a way he was embarrassed for her. Rocky was OK with this, but it left Alfred pissed and whirring—like whatever moms looked like when you compared them, and whatever else he knew that he wasn't telling, the whole thing was Lucky's fault.

He was like the Toxic Avenger, fixing to poison everything.

Rocky saw it coming. He yelled, "Lucky, watch out!"

Too late. Alfred zoomed in and smacked Lucky's head so hard he rocked. Alfred grinned as if it was all worth it, no matter what happened to him.

Mr. Burgess stiffened. His head came up. He could have been coming awake after a long night. "Lucky!"

Lucky was trying not to cry.

It was amazing. Lucky was hurting and his dad wheeled on him and blamed the wrong person. "Lucky! Are you going to put up with that?"

All Lucky did was shrug.

This made Mr. Burgess furious: Lucky's own father! It was weird. Chad barked like an angry general. "Come on, Lucky. Aren't you going to fight?"

If it had been Rocky's dad, he would have yelled at him and made him understand but Lucky just said mildly, "Alfred, I told you to quit."

So Alfred had to bop him again.

Chad snapped, "Are you going to stand for this? Are you? Going to stand for this?"

Lucky just dropped his head.

"When bad things happen to you, you have to fight them, OK?" His father sounded so upset it could have been him Alfred was hitting. "You can't just lie down and let him roll over you."

Lucky looked at Chad with water standing in his eyes. He wouldn't do anything, but he would die before he let his father see him cry.

"For God's sake!" His dad got this uncomfortable scowl, as if last night had come up in his throat like rancid food. "OK, Alfred. Go ahead. He's all yours."

This caught Alfred in midair. His arms jerked out like broken springs and he landed with this ooooff, as if somebody had gored him with a stake. It was not what he expected. He blinked. "What?"

"I said go ahead and hit him. Hit him hard."

For the moment, even Alfred was stopped.

Something was eating Chad, and Rocky got the idea that whatever it was, it wasn't really Lucky's fault. He was practically begging Lucky, "Son, aren't you going to stand up for yourself?"

And Rocky's best friend, whom he loved *but would never understand,* gave his father a stone blank look that made him shout.

They must have heard Chad shouting down below. "You can't let people get away with anything or they'll get away with everything!"

Lucky just shook his head and wouldn't move.

"I said go ahead and hit him, Alfred. Serves him right."

So Alfred made a feint at Lucky. It wasn't much; maybe it wasn't anything, but it brought his own father to his feet. Calvin glared. Then out of nowhere, he turned around and whacked Alfred so hard his head rocked.

Even Rocky gasped.

Then Calvin said, "OK, asshole, how did that feel? Didn't you hear Lucky? He told you to quit!"

And Lucky? Rocky saw Lucky curl in on himself, miserable. Like he wanted to disappear. Or die.

By that time Alfred was inflating like a parade balloon, huge and purple with rage. He bloated until he couldn't contain it and then he let it out. He shrieked, whether at his father or Lucky, Rocky couldn't say. "Son of a bitch!"

The rest of the air went out of him like a gigantic fart, blowing Alfred backward down the hill. That should have been the end of it, but it was not. What was it, anyway? Just two kids mad at each other—it should have been a little thing.

But it got big.

Imagine pushing something huge off a building and waiting to hear the crash. Feel the moment of suspension: the breath taken in and not released.

Rocky and Lucky went back to the house, trying to pretend it was OK, even though it was not. They were waiting for the rest: suspense broken, the breath released.

The chain reaction, remember? Sprong. Sprong. Fucking sprong.

My best friend Lucky, and I hit him, Alfred thought. *My best friend and I hit him and after that I did something even worse, so if you want to know who is the Judas here, it's me. I don't think I meant for it to happen, but who knows?*

I wanted to get even so I told.

In Sunday School they had all about Jesus and the apostles and this Judas that turned Him in and afterward the guilt was so bad he had to go and hang himself. Well that is just how Alfred felt. *So it was me,* Alfred thought. *I was the one who told, and brought everything down that night.*

He didn't even know why he did it. Dad never should have smacked him, that was one thing. But that wasn't the real reason. It was the other thing.

The thing that Alfred saw in the middle of one night at the top of the summer, and could not stop seeing. Knowledge that he fell into like a pit. He fell into it when he least expected it. All he was doing was going outside in the dark to pee, just like the fathers did. So Alfred accidentally heard: crazy rolling and yelling out there somewhere. Shit, he thought two groanies had been poisoned, or were having a fight. They were thrashing in one of the sheds. He had to look. How do you know what these things are? You just know whatever they are doing is making your mother cry. The—they didn't see him, but he saw it, it was revolting. God!

Afterward, he had to go around *knowing* when nobody else did. It was terrible. Knowing started a buzz in his head that would not quit. He would have done anything to make it go away.

It filled him up—the noise! By late August Alfred was drowning in sound. By the Labor Day weekend he was choking on it. The knowledge got so big that on that Saturday when Calvin turned around and smacked Alfred, all Alfred wanted to do was hit back.

When they got down off the hillside, he couldn't leave Lucky alone. No. He couldn't quit.

The dads went inside and left us standing in the grass in front of the house. Alfred went, "So, what, asshole. Had enough?"

"Don't." Rocky had his hands raised; he was trying to think of some way to make it better, but when Alfred feinted, Lucky ducked his head and ran into the barn.

"Even your father thinks you're an asshole," Alfred said.

Rocky called after Lucky, but Lucky didn't stop. Instead he looked back like a hurt animal: *Leave me alone.* Rocky wheeled and smacked Alfred. He was only a year older but sometimes he acted like God. "Enough. Leave him alone."

How was Alfred supposed to explain that he couldn't? He couldn't leave it alone. Could. Not. Against all the rules, he followed. He just followed Lucky into the barn. Maybe it was, like, preordained. Maybe they had to go in there so it could come down. Alfred thought the Judas thing was a cheat: setting him up. Turning some poor jerk into a villain just so the Bible can happen as planned.

Or else he followed Lucky because he was sorry and wanted to make up. Here was the best friend he had and Alfred had been shitty to him without really even meaning to.

The whole thing made him so miserable and driven that he barged into the barn where Lucky was hiding and instead of making it up he ended up getting into a great big fight. He told. He vomited it right in Lucky's face. Look, it was an accident. The minute it fell out of his mouth he was scared. He would always remember yelling, "I'm *sorry.*"

Sorry is never enough.

He never would have told if Lucky hadn't finally hit back. This fight wasn't to impress the dads. It was private, filled with hate. When Lucky finally tangled with Alfred it was fierce and almost silent, they grappled on the barn floor where nobody could see, a fight to the death. It had been building since Alfred got stuck waiting at Scarth Cave last night, just hanging there, duh-duh, duh-dumb, because stupid Lucky was supposed to come and get them and he forgot. It had been building since Calvin smacked him for no reason. Shit no. It had been building since June.

And it was Lucky's fault. All of it.

When Alfred charged in, Lucky was at the bottom of the ladder to the hayloft, brooding. The barn was so dark after all that sunlight that Alfred ran right into him, *smash.* Maybe Alfred was, like, trying to find him so he could make up? But accidentally he crowded Lucky, smashing into him by mistake.

Out of nowhere, Lucky turned on him and shrieked, "Goddammit, Alfred. Quit!"

Blood exploded in Alfred's head. Rage, webbing his eyes.

"Quit what?"

A bubble of spit sealed Lucky's open mouth. Words broke out. "You know goddam well what."

"I didn't do anything."

Lucky grabbed Alfred's arm and pushed. "The hell you didn't!"

"The hell I did!" Alfred smacked him.

"Liar!" Lucky smacked him back.

They grappled and locked. Lucky threw all his weight against Alfred, smashing him into the ladder so wildly that they both fell. Snarling, they rolled and thrashed, sobbing and cursing, but Lucky was never a fighter so it was only a matter of time before Alfred had him pinned. But if he was the winner, why was Alfred sobbing helplessly? He didn't know. After he got Lucky down and sat on his chest, Alfred glared into Lucky's face, gargling tears of rage, and it all came down in on him, how all he'd ever wanted was to be best friends with this person, and all Lucky ever did was shut him out. It was too much!

It piled up inside him along with everything else, until something snapped. The truth poured out of Alfred like boiling vomit. "Smartass, you think you're so goddam fucking smart."

Lucky foresaw it and fell back. "I don't think I'm smart, I just."

"If you're so goddam fucking smart how come you don't know about your goddam fucking mother." Oh my God. It was an accident! Alfred shoved his fist in his mouth because now that he'd said it, he was scared.

All the air just went right out of Lucky, Whoof. He went cold as death. There was a terrible pause. When he finally spoke it was in a dreadful, still voice, "Don't you think I know?"

It was awful. *I didn't mean it.*

Too late. With nobody mentioning it, they could both pretend nothing bad was happening, but now?

Now Lucky knew he wasn't the only one who knew.

But that wasn't the worst thing. Before he even started,

Alfred knew these things. That silence was a pact you had to keep. But he went on yorking it up just to see the look on Lucky's face.

So it was this that Alfred was most ashamed of.

Rubbing Lucky's face in it.

They still could have redeemed it, but in his guilty shame Alfred kept on until he said something even worse. The trouble was, he had to stop the furious buzzing that had started inside his head when he first caught the groanies together, he'd do anything to silence the noise that had tortured him all summer, growing until now it was so huge that he couldn't stand it any more. So he knew it was terrible and he said it anyway. And it was this that brought the inner, hidden Lucky out front and brought everything else down on them.

"Then why the fuck why don't you do something about it!" The minute he said it, Alfred was crazy with grief.

Lucky didn't move. He didn't speak. He made a noise Alfred had never heard before. That was all.

"Oh fuck." The silence got huge. "Oh shit, Lucky, I'm sorry. I take it back!"

Lucky was so quiet that Alfred thought he would die of it.

"Lucky. Man?"

He didn't move. He wouldn't speak. His face was so terrible that Alfred just climbed off his chest and left.

18

Saturday Night

Saturday we ate too much of Mrs. Darrow's fancy curry and too much ice cream because there wasn't enough of that French-name dessert she made, and after dinner Speedy burst into tears for no reason and Lucky disappeared. When he finally drifted back into the living room he dug his chin into his collarbone and wouldn't talk to us. Gabe popped a rash and Kofi threw up. Alfred was mad at everyone. The birthday had just gone on too long. When you were over at somebody's house in the city and things went sour, at least you could go home, or the other person's mom would send you home, but we were stuck in this place, with nobody to break it up and noplace to go. The groanies were all dressed up and talking a lot and laughing in the wrong places, and by suppertime Mr. Burgess was drunk. On the farm when we got stuck with each other we usually took off before we started to fight, but grownups don't have the same protocol. They get hung up on, like, events. They will go through with anything just because it's planned.

Mrs. Burgess kept looking over at us with this weirdly sweet grin, like—*aren't you having fun?*

Huh, huh?

I mean, aren't you?

She was so desperate that she threw a TV party for us with Jolt Cola and Scooter Pies so she wouldn't feel guilty about going out and then she got all the groanies into cars and headed for a roadhouse just to get away from us. We were sick of eating and sick of each other and sick of ourselves, so after the groanies left we zoned out in front of the TV. We were going to sit there eating and not talking much until we got sick of having fun and straggled up to bed. God, all right, we should have taken care of Lucky, we should have dragged him into the shed chamber and made a fuss over him, but nobody knew anything was wrong except Alfred, and only Alfred knew what was wrong.

We should have hung on to him. We should have lashed him to the bed, because right there in the light from the TV he started morphing into something else. Turn his hands over and you might see black hairs growing on the backs and rot spreading in the palms. If you felt his gums you'd find bumps from the beginning fangs. Right, Lucky was changing, but we were too stuffed and tired to see. Then while we weren't looking, he slipped out.

We would have done anything to keep the rest of the night from unfolding, to stop whatever happened between Lucky and his dad that blew the place apart, but by that time we were sick and tired, it was confused out, it was late.

We were in our sleeping bags when the groanies came back from dancing. We half-heard our parents lurching in, laughing in that stagey way you do at the end of parties when you haven't had as much fun as you thought. Then we heard them creaking around getting ready for bed.

Hours later, Rocky saw Lucky drag himself in from somewhere and roll into a ball in a corner like a porcupine warding off an attack dog. At least the kids were all accounted for; he could quit watching for the night.

After a while even Lucky went to sleep.

The crash woke us up.

The noise. It was like the earth cracking. Something broke in two.

It was one of those cold, completely silent country summer nights torn to shreds by the terrible, screeching roar. We undestood later, when we were out in the open, that what we'd heard was the sound of Mr. Burgess's old Mercedes, bombing down the dirt driveway at top speed, going nonstop until it smashed into something hard, hitting it with a terrible crack.

Nobody was sure what Lucky's father intended. Chad was going so fast the car either overshot or failed to take the curve at the end of the drive and instead of rolling into the circle or wiping out on the big tree Mr. Burgess and the Mercedes barreled into the rickety shack where Mr. Peterson had been holed up all summer, trying to write. It probably saved his life. The crash wrecked the shack and set fire to the dried-out wood; we saw the glow in the square framed by the shed chamber window. The night was turning a color no ordinary night had ever been. We jumped up and ran outside. The trees seemed to be changing shape and turning orange in the light from the flames.

Everybody screamed and came running out. Or almost everybody. Grownups came out of strange places, like surprised rats.

The first thing we saw was the Mercedes. It had nosed into the near shack, which was burning fast. At first we thought Lucky's dad was inside the car, but it turned out Mr. Burgess had been thrown clear. He'd landed in the bushes. We could see him thrashing and just beginning to try to sit up.

So it was the fire, really, that ended the summer—the fire and everything it brought out—people, truths. It burned out the shack and some of the woods and it exposed what we all secretly suspected but did not want to see. It brought out something we couldn't name but were most afraid of.

Things changed. In the orange light we saw Gabe's dad pulling Mr. Burgess out of the bushes, going, *Chad, Chad.* Zack peeled back Chad's eyelids to see if he was all right and then rushed him away from the burning wreck in case the car blew up.

Mrs. Darrow came stumbling out of the kitchen in her fat flowered nightshirt, holding a platter and a dishtowel even though it was about three in the morning and too late to be still cleaning up. Right behind her came dumb old Frieda's boyfriend, surprise. This Dave had been in the kitchen talking to Mrs. Darrow, who knows why. He'd been crying. Weird. She had too. So we knew that this Dave, who was supposed to be Frieda's boyfriend, had been sleeping over with Frieda all those times the groanies pretended he was not. So, what about Frieda, like, where was she? We were too crazy with revelations to care.

Revelations. They kept coming. Understand, it all happened at once.

Gabe's dad was dosing Mr. Burgess with Jack Daniels, when instead of coming down from their bedroom, Gabe's blue-eyed mom came rushing out of, no, *up* from. Rushing up from the field in her little slippers that she wore only to go to the bathroom in the night. Gabe's father said, "Polly!" That was all. So Gabe's pretty mom came running up from the field behind the house with her shirt tails flapping and her long curly hair pushed back. Gabe's mom and—oh wow!—Speedy's father. Stig.

Stig Fenton followed Mrs. Peterson up from the stone wall in the field where they had been—what? Polly's shirt was open at the throat and her face was pink but it could have been the fire. What was it they had been doing? What? Maybe Polly and Stig were only sitting together in the moonlight sharing tribulations, like kids, or maybe it was something else. We were never going to find out if they were just talking or actually making out or what, but when Speedy saw her dad with Gabe's mother like that, she made a noise like she'd been smashed in the gut. All the air came out of her: *Oooof.*

This was by no means the worst thing that happened that night. By that time this Dave that Frieda went with was a little crazy. He couldn't find Frieda. "The fire. My God, she's in the fire."

The fathers had to keep him from rushing into the burning shed to look for her. When the flaming sides fell out and it was clear the shed had always been empty, Dave started running here, there, until we lost track of him.

And us? We were looking at something else.

We never found out whether Mr. Burgess wrecked his car by accident because he was drunk that night or if he got drunk so he could wreck it on purpose. We didn't even know whether he ran the big Mercedes downhill with something specific in mind and accidentally hit the wrong shack, but either way, Chad Burgess brought us all out where everyone could see.

Which changed everything.

This, then, is what the kids of that summer saw. This is what we were looking at, and this is what made all the difference. See!

Out of the utility shed on the hill the last two grownups came running, Alfred and Rocky's father in nothing but a T-shirt, with his face stretched in fear and his privates flapping. And her.

Her! For the first time we saw it clear:

Mr. Darrow is doing it with oh my God, Mrs. Burgess is doing it with . . .

And the whole time this guy Dave was going, "Frieda?" in a voice stretched thin with anxiety, but we didn't even hear.

Instead we fell back with our mouths open and looked.

Mr. Calvin G. Darrow, father of Alfred and Rocky and husband to the best of all mothers, nice Jane, Calvin the slick dresser, the sneaks-around, never-quite-looks-at-you Calvin Darrow the big ad man was out here in the open in his nakeds, right here in front of everyone. Out in the open. God! Calvin was running toward us with his face red and his big raw dick hanging down, flapping against his legs. "What's the matter?" he screamed. "What in God's name is the matter," with the dick bouncing because in his alarm he'd forgotten who we were.

So we saw him and Mrs. "You-guys-can-call-me-Leslie" Burgess, our best friend's mom, Lucky's pink-and-white mother holding up a towel trying to cover *her* nakeds, because she was so scared she'd come running out without any clothes. The last two groanies had come spilling out of the utility shed in their anxiety and confusion and the rest of us, kids and adults, were standing there, all rubbing our eyes in this confusion of flashing pink tits and white flanks, everyone exposed. A major first. It was a major first for us, my God!

The Darrows' dad is fucking Lucky's mom.

So we hardly heard this Dave going, "Has anybody seen Frieda?" The guy was wrecked over something but by that time we were too crazy with excitement to care. The car was totaled. The place was filled with naked people that we used to think we knew. The shed was on fire.

Everything was fucked.

So that was it, OK? That was it, everybody turned out in the firelight—the end of summer, with everything revealed. Unless it was not just the end of summer that we saw, but the end of everything the way we thought it was. The web that held us all in place had been vibrating all summer. Now something had crashed through it, ripping a huge, unmendable hole.

Listen: it was not what the Darrows' dad and Lucky's mom were doing up there together that was so bad, or that they'd cheated and lied to everyone. We'd seen that stuff in movies and magazines. Other people's parents cheated all the time, but it was something that happened to other people, never to you.

Until suddenly, it did.

It was happening to us. And it was raw and new because when you're little, understanding hits with the fresh impact of first times.

The effect was astounding. Seismic. Everything underneath the surface slid and cracked that night, opening a chasm between the future and the past.

So what blew the kids of that summer apart, what disrupted and almost overturned us was the sudden, breathtaking *shift* that comes with learning that whatever you thought was the case was never the case.

Nothing that went before was what we thought it was, and nothing that comes after will be what it seems.

And nothing will ever be the same.

You go along thinking the world is one way, flat and safe, and then the air shakes and you discover that all along you've been in mortal danger, bladerunning the edge of the crack. It changes the way you look at everything that came before. And everything that is to come.

If this can happen to the groanies, our parents, in spite of all their promises to take care of us, what's going to happen to us? Anything can happen to us.

Anything.

Maybe the earth does heal and grass and trees grow again after these seismic changes. Buildings rise, everybody running around as before, but it's not the same. Nothing is ever the same. The world under your feet has shifted. It will again. Again. Take care!

So everything was overturned at once, the assumptions of our short past, our expectations, everything. Even the moment was changed because as we stood there, Dave came running out of the barn. He was white and terrified, yelling, "Come here!"

And at the same time, we saw Alfred and Rocky's mother turning into something else. Of all of the people of that summer, Jane Darrow was the most damaged. She was enormous with it, grim and weeping. Her mouth stretched large and square with rage and she roared like something even her own kids didn't recognize and could not identify.

Her voice was huge. "Calvin. Leslie. God damn you, there are children here."

At least the car didn't explode.

By the time the ambulance and the police and the fire department left, the sun was up.

We couldn't find Lucky anywhere.

FALL

19

Chad

The lease on the farm ran until the first day of autumn, but after Labor Day nobody really wanted to go back to Eaglemont, not after everything. The crash and the fire. Leslie's and my own personal tragedy. And the suicide. The suicide.

I felt responsible. If only I'd kept track! If only I'd been there to listen, said the right thing, but I was running flatout and so was Leslie. When you're as disrupted as we were, crazy and fixed on your own desires, things get lost: people, entire worlds. Missed moments like so many lost cities, submerged under tons of black ocean, gone for good. Didn't see what was going on with Frieda, didn't hear.

God we're careless with lives.

We were so preoccupied with our own miseries that we never even saw what was happening to our au pair, who was the last in a string; she was, forgive us, peripheral, the supporting player who stays in the wings so you can play your own terrible scenes. I'm so sorry, Frieda. We assumed.

The person you leave your kid with has got to be able to take care of him so you can go and *do,* or *be.* This is what you have to assume or you can't leave him at all. It's a self-fulfilling prophecy parents make every time they hand their children over to a care-taker in hopes, in hopes. We didn't see what was happening to Frieda. Her death was our fault. We launched her in the new world without knowing for certain whether she was sound enough to float.

Dave blamed himself. The poor guy was in love with her. He was the one who dropped Frieda because she was boffing another guy, and wouldn't tell him who. He was so mad that he turned his back when she broke down and sobbed that she couldn't help it, she had to, it . . . My God, one of *our friends* had told her it was part of her job. Dave thinks he said he didn't care if she lived or died. He was explaining all this to Jane in the kitchen the night of the crash, while Jane paced and growled because she could not know—we—do—not—know—to this day whether Calvin was involved. Dave talked his heart out, staring mournfully at Frieda's locked bedroom door, waiting for her to come out so he could apologize and they could make up.

Dave refused to tell us more. A gentleman to the last, but who was he protecting? Her, or the other guy? "It wasn't anything Frieda did," he said at the coroner's hearing, and he was sobbing with regret. "It was the way I handled it."

We told him it was our fault. Didn't we bring the child halfway around the world and turn her loose in America, sink or swim? After everything Leslie and I were barely speaking but we did talk about this. It was more bearable than talking about Lucky, you know?

"It wasn't Dave's fault," I said, "it was mine. If I hadn't trashed the car we might have found her in time."

Leslie said drily, "If you hadn't trashed the car, we wouldn't have found her at all."

This was not precisely true. It would have been morning before anybody came out and even later before anybody noticed she was missing. At least the body would have cooled.

"We were supposed to be *in loco parentis,* Chad." Her sigh was for all of us. "She thought she was getting a nice American family, and all we were was us. Poor lonely, homesick thing."

What I said next surprised both of us. "That was only part of it."

"A world away from home. We should have *talked* to her." In her own way, my Leslie was grieving. "I gave her my flowered chiffon dress. I let her wear my pearls."

"Who was she sleeping with?"

Leslie went on as if she hadn't heard. "I guess the birthday party wasn't enough."

"Was it Stig or Calvin or Zack?"

This made her whip her head around. "What?"

"That miserable bed in the cave."

"What bed?"

"Mattress I found. Blankets. The works. When I." Memory sawed my heart in pieces. "Never mind."

"Is this something about Lucky?"

I didn't answer. We still couldn't talk about it. "Who was it that fucked her and broke them up? Who broke up poor Frieda and Dave?"

"Oh Chad, what does it matter, now that she's dead?"

It mattered to me. At Frieda's memorial I would look into the other faces: Calvin's, Zack's, Stig's. Is it you? We would gather to pray for Frieda, who was being buried under Finnish earth halfway around the world. Nobody would meet my eyes. *Is it you?* I needed to know which of my friends was hitting on this poor foreign schoolgirl, flirting, badgering, then ordering her to sneak away with him. They did it in the cave. I found their pitiful secret love nest when—

Not yet. I can't talk about the cave.

Leslie said unexpectedly, "I know it wasn't Zack."

Friends, who become lovers. I groaned. "Right. He was in love with his script. And Stig was in love with long distance, and . . ."

She was looking at me through slitted eyes. "So, who?"

But I couldn't give Leslie the pretext she needed to file for divorce and come out the noble victim instead of the perp. "You know it wasn't me."

I wanted the culprit to be Calvin so I could dump the whole

terrible summer on his back and walk away. I wanted to put it all into one package—Frieda too. Funny, instead of mourning for the marriage I was in mourning for the friendship. It had to be Cal who did Frieda, on top of what he and Leslie were doing. Then, at least the parts would match up. I couldn't bear to lose any more friends.

We never did find out which of the fathers was sleeping with our au pair, but I know Frieda never wanted it. She had to go along, and Les and I—we were the grownups in that situation, U.S. citizens and leaseholders, and she was the alien and beholden to us. Worse. *In loco parentis.* We were supposed to be the parents in residence and she was only a girl, and I was off in the city and Leslie was off in love. Poor Frieda did what adults told her, when they remembered to tell her anything. It was so sad.

After the fight with Dave, Frieda took pills and hid in the barn. By the time he came back to apologize, it was too late. Counselling reconciliation, Jane was probably glad to have something to take her mind off the party rubble in a house that wouldn't go to sleep. She kept Dave talking so she wouldn't have to go back upstairs to her empty bed. That night she thought Frieda was sleeping behind her locked bedroom door. Nobody knew she was lying out there in the straw, waiting to go to sleep for good. Poor, pretty kid.

At first nobody knew. Wading around in the mess I had created, I was too battered and humiliated and miserable to understand. When I followed Dave into the barn in the waning light from the fire, it was partly to get away from the scene of the crime. It was easier for Les and me to look at poor Frieda than at each other. I was half-drunk, so stupid with grief that I thought she was only asleep. We all did. When the worst is happening, you can't comprehend at first. I blessed her for having the grace to spare herself the ugly scene I had, what, ignited. She looked so pretty sleeping in the straw in a strange barn light-years from home. My heart fell down. *At least you are safe.*

Someone said, "Oh my God."

Then Zack knelt and told us she was dead.

When we finally cleared the farm and got back to the city, Leslie turned in on herself. I could have been dead too. All she could think about was Lucky. She wouldn't talk to me and she wouldn't talk about what had happened to him. She thought if only she could fix Lucky, everything would be right. She told me it was all my fault and I let her. If fixing blame would bring Lucky back, then why shouldn't I take the blame? After the horror, Lucky and I reached our own accommodation. It was the least I could do for her. Leslie was like a tigress, brooding over him. We had to let her work it out.

This meant that when it came time to clean up the place at Eaglemont and hand it back to the realtor, it fell to me. "After all," Leslie said gravely, "after what you did."

"After what *I* did."

"You trashed the place." The hell of it is, she was right. I was the asshole, so intent on confrontation that I didn't care who got hurt. Selfish of me to crash the car and flush her and Calvin out in the open, in front of Lucky and God. "The farm." Tears stood in her eyes. "You have to go because I can't. I just can't."

"OK," I said. I did it to make it all up to her. "OK."

It was my job to clean out last things and turn in the keys. I was supposed to sweep all the rooms and check for small objects our friends had left behind and then I was supposed to put the place to bed for the winter, part of the deal Leslie had made with the absent J. Eden, whoever he was. I had to contract for the removal of the wrecked Benz.

I couldn't bear to go alone.

Everybody was somewhere else. Roseann Fenton was in Virginia with this kid Derek; Stig had met somebody. He was in Haiti, getting a weekend divorce. Leslie was folded in on Lucky, obsessing as if the right school and the right psychiatrist would cancel the summer and make him forget. Calvin was in a paroxysm of Doing All the Right Things: seeing his lawyer, going with Jane for marriage counseling as if he could get the right counselor to convince her he hadn't done anything wrong. They would learn to be happily married by the numbers: gifts, caresses, conversation. One. Two. Three.

It was like having a fight at a party and looking up to discover all the other guests had evaporated out of tact or embarrassment, I can't say which.

In the end I made Zack and Polly follow me up to the farm in their big, square Volvo wagon. Listen, they were generous. They loved each other and whatever was going on between them that summer, they'd made it up.

Polly asked Jane. Bundled together in that safe marriage like two kids in a blanket, she and Zack decided that Jane needed us. *Largesse.* Listen, every banquet needs its Lazarus. It's about contrasts. How else are you going to know you have everything you want? OK, I suppose they thought I needed them. God knows I needed something. The four of us could sit together in front of the fire while tears ran down all the walls inside me like condensation in a wet climate, and Polly and Zack would help me pretend I was OK. On those cold nights in early fall we could circle the wagons and let Jane talk it out.

At first she refused. "I can't come. Cal needs me right now."

We all knew Calvin could hardly stand the sight of her. No. He could hardly bear to have her look at him.

When Polly made me call to reinforce the offer, Jane confessed. "I can't go back. It's just too much to bear."

"Neither can I." I cleared my throat. "Somebody has to do it."

She said, "I can't."

I don't know if it was to get back at Calvin or get away from him, but at the last minute she changed her mind. It would become clear that what she thought she was doing was at odds with what she actually did: Jane, who came out of the elevator in full makeup and silver necklaces, trying to look like somebody else.

We all stood in the lobby of the Darrows' good old building, not knowing what to say. Jane was plump as ever, sweet and tremulous, but done up for the trip in new cowboy boots, new color in her hair, a flowered silk shirt with the price tag still hanging. She was nerved up for an excursion, when what the Petersons and I were doing was, essentially, holding another wake. Jane's smile was off-center, as if it had been smeared by an unexpected blow. "How do I look?"

Polly hugged her. "Terrific."

Zack said, "You look great."

I looked at Jane. "You look fine."

It was confusing. Jane looked back with this significant, off-center smile. "I just had to get out of the house."

I couldn't stand being close to that much unhappiness; all my antibodies for that were more or less used up. I put Jane into the Petersons' wagon and followed in my little MG, feeling, I don't know, like an egg that's just been shelled. So four of us went up to Eaglemont over that last September weekend to clean house and close out the farm.

We could have used a few kids. There was plenty of room. Having the kids along would have cheered things up a little, but Jane wouldn't let her boys near the place and: this is interesting. The Petersons found it necessary to leave Gabe and their older two behind, like we had done something at J. Eden that had spoiled the earth forever and they didn't want any children of theirs inhaling the fumes. Zack made a special trip to leave the boys with an aunt in Westchester. They didn't want Gabe going back. You'd think we were revisiting the scene of a murder and they were afraid of tripping over taped outlines of the victim's body in the living room or finding dried blood blotching the carpet. Jane was quiet. The Petersons were polite but withdrawn; you could see them pulling their marriage around them, as if it could keep them safe.

I was ashamed, seeing the gash where my car had ricocheted off the tree. Like looking into your own appendix scar.

Jane had told her story more than once. That weekend we heard it again after we'd finished eating and were sitting around the abandoned-looking living room. Without Polly's pottery and Leslie's Haitian primitives and the plastic rubble of a dozen pieces of the kids' games and construction sets, it was desolate. The house looked dead empty. All we could see were the stains in the wallpaper and the threadbare upholstery. It was dreary, like a set for *Ethan Frome*. Outside, everything had died in an early frost including Jane's garden. It was as if we'd never been there, much less had any pleasure in it.

At least Jane's recital gave us continuity. In a strange way, it reminded us that there really had been a summer. Jane probably didn't realize she was repeating herself. Each time she told her story she presented it like a fresh discovery. After everything, it seemed appropriate to let her work it through. By Sunday night we knew it by heart, and if Polly and Zack sat together on the sofa, listening with fingers linked, and if they went to bed early, leaving Jane and me to drink by the fire; if in the absence of their kids they screwed every night with the savage joy of the survivor, then that too was appropriate.

But that left Jane and me. With Zack and Polly gone, we moved to the sofa. Jane said it was so we could look into the fire, which we did. In the absence of TV, it would have to do.

Jane said in a low voice, "I'm so sorry about Lucky."

I was not ready to talk about Lucky. "I'm sorry about Cal and you."

Jane was over-liquored: not like her. "You can't know what a tremendous blow it is to your pride."

I did. It's like being smacked in the crotch with a bat.

"And Calvin?" Her voice got small. "The worst part was his *reason*."

I didn't really want to know. "Maybe you shouldn't . . ."

But she did. "He said it wasn't love, it was despair. Oh God, Chad, can you imagine?" I wanted her to stop but she just kept going. "He said there are a limited number of seats at the top of the world and he didn't see his name on any of the place cards."

She looked up. "You know he thought you won every game."

Oh shit, I thought. So what he did is kind of my fault. "You mean that was it?" I meant, *I did this to us?*

"That's what I said to him. I said, 'That's it? You mean that's all?'" She was shivering.

"I will never forget the way Calvin looked at me. He said, 'Sometimes you just get depressed.'"

"He fucked my wife because he got depressed?"

She made a face. "'You don't have any idea what it's like' he said. Words of one syllable. He could have been talking to one of the kids instead of . . . instead of . . ."

I was feeling all my own bruises, so I helped her finish. "The person he had just run over with a truck."

Then Jane said a thing only a woman would say. "And when I asked him how he could do it to us . . ."

Didn't she mean *me?* I said, "Us?"

She wrapped the flag around herself, like Mother Courage. The family. "Me and the boys. When I asked him how he could do it to us, Calvin started crying. You can't imagine what he said to me."

But I could imagine. My lips were already moving in synch.

Grieving, she presented it like a fresh surprise. "Calvin said, 'I wasn't doing it to you, I was doing it for me.'"

I sighed. Of course I knew. In some ways Calvin and I were the same person. It made me ashamed.

"I couldn't stand it any more, I begged him to stop explaining, but you'd think he was trying to convert me. 'Oh Jane, what are we trying to teach our kids, really? That all their efforts are doomed? That their yellow pony died en route?'"

"The yellow pony," I said to Jane, who was crying. Probably I was more than a little drunk; by that time even I was crying.

She gave me this soft look, full of lost moments, and said, "The yellow pony."

It was like looking at a polaroid from a time when we were still happy.

One day in the park my friend Calvin and I invented the yellow pony. We made it up. Then we watched it pass into the language of families, the lexicon of tag words and private codes that make every family different from every other family. When two families have some of the same words in common, it means they are singularly close friends.

The yellow pony just came up one brilliant Saturday, when Cal and I and our boys were hanging out together in the park. He came up in conversation, he trotted into our lives and took up residence.

Lucky was four; he was chubby as any ordinary kid and he still smiled at everybody, big blue eyes like gilliflowers and that *grin*. It was before our family took sides. It was before Leslie managed to pull him into her corner and rope him off from me. The women had gone shopping and Cal and I were babysitting. At the time he and I were boon buddies, so close that we looked for reasons to hang out together in all the same places. Even if it meant taking care of the kids on a Saturday afternoon. We were in the park, playing: the kids, us, laughing and rolling in the grass. Imagine me and my friend Calvin wrestling with our little boys on a pale green and golden afternoon at the beginning of some lost summer while we were still beginning and everything was ahead. Were we ever that young? I wonder. In the snapshot, it's always sunny. The air is humming with laughter and Cal and I are high on invention.

The kids were getting restless and loud. The mothers were late coming back and we had to keep them from getting bored. We had to think fast or somebody would start crying and we'd be blamed. Who started it? I don't even remember. Yes I do, it was me, lying on my back jiggling Lucky in the air until he giggled and then setting him down and rolling over to look at the three of them—my boy, Calvin's two. My beautiful son Lucky and curly Alfred and stolid little Rocky sitting on the grass like garden trolls, regarding me.

"We're bored."

"You'd better be good, OK?"

They were pushing and scratching. You knew that any minute one of them was going to cry. "When's Mom going to come? We're bored."

"Do you hear me?"

"But there's nothing to do."

"There'll be plenty to do when the yellow pony comes." This perked them up. I liked the ring of it. "If you're good guys and you entertain yourselves, maybe your yellow pony will come."

This brought them around. "Pony?"

"Pony!"

"What pony?"

I said, as if it was obvious. "The yellow pony big boys get for being good."

Over the kids' heads Calvin grinned at me. He said, "If you're really good, some day you're going to look out your front window and see a nice man bringing you a *yellow pony*."

"And it will have a red bridle and a red patent-leather saddle with golden stirrups."

Then little Lucky, my boy *Lucky* giggled and rolled. "And bright red cowboy boots for us."

I loved him! "And it will be all yours and follow you forever."

And Lucky said, "And I can get on it and ride away."

Calvin said, "If you're good guys."

I gave Lucky a hug. "And you can ride anywhere you want."

My friend Cal had a strange look I should have paid more attention to. He finished, "And always get everything you want."

They were wild with it. "And we'll get everything we want!"

Everybody but Calvin knew it was a joke. I was the one who told Calvin the story about Cecil B. De Mille. When the old director was little, this entrepreneur named Belasco made him a promise that taught him everything about desire and ambition and the way of the world. Later, whenever we were together and drunk, ambitious Calvin would fan his hopes like a winning hand and number the cards. Then he'd ask me whether I thought his yellow pony was still coming or if it had died en route, but that day everything was still in front of us. You could almost hear the jingle of bridle brasses and the clop of varnished hooves.

Even Alfred, who couldn't have been more than four, knew it was only a game, and yet, the possibility. The *possibility*. It was amazing. We were talking about something precious, elusive, wild. And I did the kids the favor of not telling them the rest.

When De Mille was five, Belasco promised him a yellow pony for his sixth birthday. The night before his birthday he was so excited he could hardly sleep. At dawn he ran to the window, but the pony wasn't there. He waited, but it didn't come. He wouldn't leave the window because he was sure in just another minute a man would come around the corner leading the yellow pony, and it would have a red bridle and a red patent leather saddle with red cowboy boots turned backwards in the stirrups just like Belasco said. He waited all day. When it got dark and the pony still hadn't come, De Mille the kid knew something that made him strong.

He learned that what you expect isn't necessarily delivered. And he learned what to do. He knows what you do when promises aren't kept and all you have left are promises.

Which is, you just go on.

You spend your life hoping for your yellow pony and figuring out how to handle it when the sun sets and it still hasn't come. You learn that it isn't getting things that makes the difference, it's not getting them and knowing how to handle it that makes you strong.

Why couldn't Calvin see?

"I hated the yellow pony," Jane said. It was late. Brooding, she and I sat shoulder to shoulder on the farmer's lumpy sofa. I wanted us to just be quiet and watch the fire, but Jane kept on telling me things I didn't want to hear.

See, in the car going home from Eaglemont after Labor Day, when life as Jane knew it was coming to an end, her unfaithful

Calvin in his folly heard his sons squabbling out of sheer nervousness. He made a terrible mistake.

He tried to pretend nothing had changed.

"Look," Cal said, trying for the old tone as if that would make the family whole again, "if you boys don't stop fighting, you're never going to get your yellow pony."

As late as that summer the old joke still brought a chorus of promises, the litany—red bridle, red patent-leather saddle with golden stirrups, and bright red cowboy boots . . .

But summer was over. His boys were riding along in the car with his guilt and they knew everything. Nobody spoke.

Calvin said uneasily, "Guys?"

The kids' sudden silence was so stony that Jane was afraid.

Cal leaned on them "Did you guys hear me?"

"And a red bridle," Jane said. Despising it, she lied to herself: *I am doing this for the children.* So in spite of everything Calvin had done to her, she offered her whole person, turning herself inside out in a show of forgiveness. No. Of love. She tried to spin out the old litany. "And a red patent-leather saddle."

"And you'll ride away and be happy forever," Calvin said. "Right, guys?" His sons were supposed to pick up on it. Jane was waiting. Calvin was waiting. Although they'd never agreed on anything, Alfred and Rocky stonewalled Calvin, thus forcing Jane into the role she's going to play for the rest of her life.

Jane swallowed her sobs so she could finish in that bright, mom voice, "And red patent-leather cowboy boots . . . Come on, guys . . ." When she turned to her sons her voice shook. "He's still your father." Bereft and furious as she was at Cal, Jane Darrow was going to use everything she had to keep her own small constellation of souls in place. She dropped the next words on top of them like stones. *"And he always will be."*

Telling me this, Jane could not stop crying, so it was natural for me to hug her and give her as much there-there as I could manage just then because she was bent on saving her marriage and I already had one foot out of mine.

"Oh Jane," I said. "Oh, Jane."

And to my astonishment I felt her stir and lean closer so that all the soft parts of Jane Darrow were squashing against me, T. Chadbourne Burgess, the other wronged party, and I did what you do when you are stirred by creature comfort; she was leaning on me and, grieving, I leaned back. Then I looked down and discovered that her lips were open and her eyes half closed. She was . . .

She was coming on to me. It was so sad.

I moved away and my arms dropped. "I am so sorry, Jane." It was just too sad.

She flashed her teeth in rage. "What's the matter?"

"Oh Jane, you don't want to do this."

"It's because I'm fat."

"No!"

I hope she was drunk; she said, "I'm too fat. Calvin thinks so. You think so."

"I don't think you're fat, Jane, I think you're wonderful." I kissed her just to prove it; I kissed her to let her know we would always be friends. "Wonderful. You are. I just don't think I can do this."

We managed to make it seem as if none of this had ever happened, but I saw the look on Jane's face when I set her back in place on her half of the sofa and patted her like a toy I'd put on the shelf. *Oh, there. Please stay there.*

She said, "I would do anything to get him back."

I said, "Oh Jane, I'm so sorry."

"Well don't be," she said. "I can do it."

We didn't know that within the year she'd have Calvin back. I have watched them since, Jane and Calvin. They've been going through the motions of happy marriage for so long that they almost believe in it. It became important for the Darrows to do a lot of public stroking, talking and dancing together with the mechanical precision of people painting by the numbers, calling attention to how pretty the picture, how sure their touch. They would recite names of restaurants they'd found together; they showed off the pieces of jewelry Calvin had bought for Jane and named the gifts she'd bought for him, as if all they had to do was get the details right and make the right moves to make their story sound. They practiced, *practiced*. Now they have the myth by heart: Calvin and Jane Darrow, happily married, and for life.

And I? I still see the yellow pony dancing at the periphery of my vision, a sweet, receding figure on the horizon; a part of me will always mourn for the days when love was unselfconscious and everything was possible.

It was sad, plowing under the last bits of the abandoned garden, remembering how carefully Leslie had designed the plantings and how lovingly Jane put them in. I could hear kids shouting, Zack and Calvin wrangling over how to lay out the paths between the beds. That last weekend I spent at the farm, the dirt kept yielding up kids' plastic toys and rusting Matchbox cars like fossils of once-living things that were now extinct. Rolling up abandoned sleeping bags and collecting pillows in the shed chamber, Jane began to cry; she was looking at some funny, senseless verse Alfred had embellished after Rocky and Lucky wrote it on the walls. It was only a cartoon but it almost overturned her, so Polly had to hold her and keep holding her until she settled and was quiet.

Then I went into the au pair's room to get Leslie's little dresser lamp and my breath caught up with me. The place was worse than empty. The stains on the bed could have been left by the characters out of *Sanctuary* and the windowpanes were warped, as if still fogged by homesick Frieda's breath as she watched for somebody she cared about to come and rescue her. Dave? One of us? No matter. Too late. The wallpaper was blurred, as if by Frieda's tears, and caught in the corner of the old mirror frame there was a snapshot of Frieda rosy and smiling in the Finnish snow. That poor sad lonely girl, I thought, but that wasn't it.

Poor Jane, I thought, but that wasn't it. Poor me, I thought, but that wasn't it either.

It was Lucky. What had we done to him?

"What did we think we were doing," Jane said on that last afternoon at the farm. We sat in the kitchen with our legs stretched in front of us, drinking Zack's homemade wine and studying our feet while Jane scrubbed invisible dirt from the wooden kitchen table.

"Trying to be happy," Zack said. "Which was what we were."

Jane said, "Sometimes."

Polly said, "Mostly."

I said, "Not at all."

Polly said gently, "We were making a perfect summer for the kids. We tried so hard!"

Jane rested her fists on the rag and looked up at us. "Why did we imagine we could keep them safe?"

"It was our mistake," I said. *My mistake.* Oh, Lucky. Son. "Nobody's safe," I said.

"Shh," Polly said on that quiet, golden, late-September afternoon. "We had to try."

Agonized, Jane looked up at us. "Why didn't anybody warn us?"

But Polly pointed to a flash of red outside the kitchen door: a cardinal flying past: "Oh, look!"

It was two in the afternoon; we were sitting in the farmhouse kitchen having a drink before we put the last things in the car and started home. The kitchen was cleaner than it had ever been, all traces of four-alarm chilis and death-dealing cakes erased. Sunlight struck the raw surface of the table, which had been scrubbed, as everything had been scrubbed, Polly and Jane working as if cleanliness did indeed have something to do with virtue, and mistakes could be erased. Through the wavy panes in the clean kitchen window, we saw the leaves catch sunlight and move it, so that masses of light and shadow flickered in the breeze. The back door stood open and we could see the path down to the neatly raked turnaround, the remaining sheds, leaves on the hillside beyond already turning color. Getting up, Zack touched Polly and she lifted her head so that his hand swept along her cheek. Then he went out to check the bolts on the shed doors and as he left I was surprised by desire not for my new love, but for Leslie, whom I would leave and whom I would love for the rest of my life, heart and soul and flesh. I had to bend my head so the women wouldn't see me changing color.

"It's so beautiful," Jane said thoughtfully. "You'd think we'd all had a wonderful time."

"But you're all right," Polly said firmly, willing recovery. "You're both going to be all right."

I did not answer.

Jane's face was pink, suffused by unshed tears, but she gave Polly a wavery smile. "I kind of guess I have to," Jane said.

We lost sight of Zack, who had moved into the barn. Instead we focused on the ground he had just walked over, looking for ghosts: the seeded place where the burned-out shack had been bulldozed—all Zack's summer's efforts gone, beginning with his script; the movie that was never going to be a movie was a dead issue now. I heard the words ripping out of me. "Poor Lucky!"

What Jane said next startled me. "Lucky. It's so odd. I'm about to say something terrible. The grief. You know, somebody had to do it for us," she said, in an astounding moment of prescience, or was it prophecy that I will remember all my life. "I'm just sorry it had to be him."

I was even more surprised by what I said next. "They should have been more *careful*."

Jane whirled. "Who, the kids?"

"Leslie and Cal."

"Leslie and Cal." Jane's head was cocked; I should have been warned. She said in a level tone, "Careful not to get caught?"

I shouted. "Careful with our lives!"

FALL

The light changed; in seconds, it was fall. Sitting with my friends in the still, sunny kitchen, I thudded into a new level of consciousness.

For the first time, I comprehended my own death.

But Jane got up. She put her hands on my shoulders and when she spoke her voice was gentle. She could have been talking to an invalid. "Let's go," she said. "I think we're finished here."

20

Lucky

It was all my fault. The crash and the fire. Everything.

Something ugly marched into me and took over like an alien army. I was poisoned from the inside by the beginning change. Becoming what I was. If I thought drawing some stupid comic and making him read it was going to fix things between me and Dad, that's how crazy I was. He was so bummed by his birthday that it got to be Saturday and he still hadn't looked at it. By dinnertime I was bummed too. I got the comic from the living room where he'd put it down and forgotten it and put it on his chair. Goddammit, *there*. When Dad sat down on it without even looking I pulled it out and rolled it up and stuck it under the edge of his plate.

Chad. He just blinked and said, "What's that?"

"You forgot your present," I said. It was getting battered from being left lying around. Beer spilled on it and some of the colors smeared. Pretty soon it would be garbage. "Please."

But Daddy just took it with that pale blue, absent smile. "Oh, thanks."

All through dinner I kept watching him. *Two days and he hasn't looked at it. He hasn't even looked at it:* three weeks drawing in eight colors, I'd put in everything I wanted to tell him and was scared to say in person, guts and ganglia laid bare and strung out in colored Pentels, living map of Lucky, as Visible Man. Like a drawing of my soul. Dad left it behind like the French dessert that Mrs. Darrow had brought to the table with tears standing in her eyes. When I followed him into the living room and gave the comic back to him *again,* he just said, "Oh thank you, son," in that sweet, absent way and went on talking to Mrs. Peterson.

It was only a comic, what did I think was going to happen? Did I really think he'd understand?

It was Mom's fault. Leslie forced this party when she knows he hates birthdays. No wonder Dad was bummed. Chad hates birthdays. He hated being forty, I know. But Mom believed in parties the way some people believe in facelifts, or heart transplants. I heard her saying through locked teeth, "For God's sake smile, Chad. This is for you." So he had to sit on the sofa holding the goddam mylar pinwheel she thrust on him and trying to smile while they sang Happy Birthday one more time. When they proposed a toast he groaned and blundered out and I thought: *OK. He'll read it now.*

But he'd left the comic behind. There was a yellow stain on the cover from the curry. I had to take it to him before it got worse so I followed him into the kitchen when I knew all he wanted was to be alone. He was backed up against the kitchen counter with his fingers hooked in the rings under his eyes.

"Dad, you forgot your present. Dad?" See, I had to keep giving it to him. If I didn't, he'd forget. Then he'd never look at it, and if he didn't look at it, he'd never know.

"This isn't a good time for me, OK?"

Everything Alfred said in the barn bubbled up in my throat. I choked it down and other words came up. "It's your goddam special comic that I made you, OK?"

"Please Lucky." He really was pleading. "Not now."

"Aren't you even going to look at it?" In the other room the other parents were partying while Dad hid out. Fixed another drink. Sloughed me off without looking down. "Lucky, not now!"

"I'm sick of people saying, Not now."

He reached for my hair and missed. "Sh-sh, Lucky."

Inside me, Lucky fought the last battle with the alien forces and the alien forces won. It was awful. Green rot started in the palms of my hands; black hairs began to sprout. I was the thing I had been becoming. The monster said in a new, ugly voice, *"Dad, I'm warning you."*

"We'll talk about this later, son."

When you do certain things, you see only the moment. You never imagine there is going to be an afterwards. I snarled. "We're going to talk about it *now*." I was driven, eaten up from the inside out. I thought it really was about the present. God I was angry. "Why won't you look at it?"

"Oh, this? I did," Dad said without looking. "It's really nice."

Two whole days and all he could find to say to me was: nice.

"That's all? That's all you have to say?" I was foaming at the mouth. "Come on, Dad. Open it. Show me which parts you like."

"What?"

"Was it the part about the brothers or the part about the cave?" He was so bewildered that I got even angrier. "Which part was it, Dad?"

He was dragging his fingers down, stretching the skin under his eyes. He shook his head. "I'm sorry Lucky, I can't right now."

So it all piled in on me—his dopey, preoccupied smile, the horrible uses of the day, the weight of the whole summer. It was too much. On top of everything was knowing Alfred knew. Knowing what Alfred said I should do. The responsibility. Knowledge stuck in my ribs like a dagger, twanging every time I moved: *your mother;* the pain made me scream, "Then you can go to hell!"

"Shh, son. It's late. Don't, OK?"

God damn Alfred. *Well, aren't you going to do anything?* Like it was my responsibility. The monster stirred and flexed. There was green rot everywhere. "Then give me back my fucking present."

"What present?"

"This present!" The fangs stretched my gums, fixing to pop. "I worked weeks on your goddam present and you don't even care."

"Oh, Lucky." Dad did the unforgivable. He lied. "Of course I do."

"Like you care what fucking Mr. Darrow is doing with Mom."

He didn't see what I was saying. He didn't remind me to watch my language. Whatever it was with my father Chad Burgess that night, he was too far gone to deal. "Lucky, I love you, but I can't talk about this right now."

"OK, when?" *My own father and he won't even look at me.*

But dumb Dad, he just looked into his drink. "You heard me," he said. "It's late," as if it was just another day.

I don't know if I cared more about what Mom and Mr. Darrow were doing, or getting Dad to make them stop. Maybe I only wanted to lash out and hurt. Or to make him hurt me, so we could forgive each other and hug and cry. Black hairs crept up my arms and popped out on my throat. "Well aren't you going to do anything?"

"When things are better," Chad said, and put the comic on a shelf. So I had to turn on him. I bared my new fangs like a dog. "What do you mean, better?" The thing stirring inside me elbowed and pushed its way to the surface. It was getting huge. I had to make him face the facts here. I was sick of being alone with it. *Listen, Alfred. I was ready. I would have found a reason if there'd never been a you.*

"You mean when Mr. Darrow stops screwing my mom?" Then I smacked my hand over my mouth, too late.

I saw him move through a three-beat silence: Thud. Thud. Thud. I felt a *click* and something inside my own head moved into a safe corner and sat there, purring: *There.*

Chad went: Oooof. His face was awful. "Oh my God."

It felt good; it felt terrible. "Oh Daddy, I'm sorry." I was but I wasn't. Let Dad carry it for a change.

"You poor kid!"

I should have ended it then and there so we could get out in one piece but the fangs were growing, new ones knifing through my gums. I could feel black hairs crawling out of my collar and up my face. *Yes there's something wrong with me.* The pain was so bad I groaned. "Well, are you?"

Dad's face began to change. "Don't, son."

"Going to do anything?"

"Please don't."

I punched him in the chest. "Or are you going to let them keep on Doing It?"

To my eternal shame he heard me. He looked into my fury straight-on and did not budge. He did not ride out and do vengeance. He only shrugged. My father.

Couldn't he *do* something, now that he knew?

"Dad?"

He said quietly, "I think you'd better leave me alone."

So we faced each other in guilty complicity. *Shit. He already knew.* Like me, Dad knew perfectly well that Mom and Mr. Darrow were Doing It. We had both known all along.

"Oh, Dad!"

"That's enough, son."

We'd known all summer and neither of us had said anything or done anything because we were scared of doing anything that started the change. This is what left me wrecked. It was the responsibility. The terrible responsibility, not of knowing a thing, but of having somebody say it out loud.

So you can't keep on pretending it isn't going on.

My God, I thought, my *father*.

How could I guess what I'd just started? What gears were clicking into place? "Oh God, Daddy, what are you going to do?"

"Shh, honey. That's enough." Chad's head shook, but his face was smooth. He just cupped his hand around the back of my head. "Now go to bed."

My teeth were rattling; I was scared shit. For the moment Timothy a.k.a. Lucky Burgess and his father T. Chadbourne Burgess were the only two people in the world. For maybe the first time Daddy was looking right into me and I was so ashamed that I couldn't stand to have him see my face.

OH GOD WHAT HAVE I DONE.

He reached out. I ducked my head and bolted. I ran away from him. I didn't know what would happen, or when. Only that it would.

The crash jerked me awake.

I woke up scared. I sat up with my chest tight and my throat clicking with the dry swallows. Gabe and Kofi were first out of the shed chamber, then Speedy with her pale hair wild, then Mr. Peterson and the Darrows came yelling, then me, all six of us crammed into the stairwell bashing and punching, everybody crazy to be the first one down to see what was happening out there: who knew? They ran outside. At the last minute I hung back. Spinning in place. I wanted it to begin. I was afraid for it to begin.

The front door was wide and kids ran out in their underwear even though it was late August and cold, but I stood in the doorway; it was too hard! On the far side of the driveway Mr. Peterson's studio shack was on fire and so was Dad's Mercedes. It was like witnessing a death. The car was maybe the first thing I remembered about my life—Mom and Dad in front with me snug in the leather back seat, riding along half asleep with Leslie and Chad in front; they were in charge; I was the son of Leslie and Chad and our lives hummed along like the motor, purring as they drove and drove and drove. The Mercedes was on fire— finished, trashed—and oh my God, Daddy was lying in the grass. I freaked; I wanted to run out and thump Daddy's chest and breathe him back to life but then he shook himself and sat up and I couldn't bear to have him see me just then. People were running back and forth in the orange light and, poised on the stone steps, I looked and looked but I didn't see Mom. Then there was a noise up on the hill and I looked up.

There was this stir at the door of the utility shed—a pair of figures tumbling out. Beautiful Mom with a wild face and. And! Her hair was streaming and all her parts were pale and glistening, my mom naked before everyone. When I saw her like that, everything changed. Life tilted. All those running figures stopped being people I knew.

They were crazy sihouettes, writhing in the firelight; it was like watching movies of hell.

Knowing is one thing. Seeing is another. I ran into the turnaround and started spinning in the firelight; I was crazy, itching and filled with it:

What I saw.

WHAT HAVE I DONE.

When Dad crashed the Mercedes into the wrong shed, everything was exposed: grownup joinings, betrayals, the end.

I got so scared! If grownups can get caught *in these awful poses,* what's going to happen to me?

We were all in terrible danger. Parents, kids. Poor Frieda, where was she? Me, who made Dad bring it down.

The thing inside me flexed and took over. Guilt made me crouch like an animal and run away because. *I did it. I did this. Me.* Guilt came in like a message on a flaming arrow. *Thock.*

This.

When it came down, I was glad.

I was squirming and rubbing myself, scared and excited, puking with disgust. I had to run away. I crashed through the woods, heading for the road. I was hideous, revolting and terrible, transforming and sick with what I was becoming.

Already was.

21

Chad

Sitting in the rubble I'd created on that terrible weekend, I was afraid. The barn door gaped like the opening to a yawning grave. My ruined car was still smoking. The ambulance was gone. The clearing had emptied out but I was still flat on my butt in the dirt where I had folded up after I convinced the paramedics I was fine. Right, fine. My guts were trembling. I wanted to find Lucky and apologize for everything, what I'd done that night, what I'd failed to do, but I didn't see him right then; when a kid gets really pissed at you, he doesn't want to see you. I knew exactly how he felt, but still. I tried to call but my ribs were cracked so I couldn't produce enough breath to shout, and I was too shaken by the wreck I'd caused to get up, much less walk.

All I wanted to do was run after him but by the time I could stand up, he was gone.

In the kitchen Lucky had sobbed and groaned as if Leslie's affair was all his fault. I could have told him it was mine, for being an asshole about Luann. I should have grabbed him and made him stay. I should have told him, "Don't. Don't cry, It doesn't have anything to do with you," but I was so messed up that I couldn't stop him when he tore away from me. I should have followed him upstairs and made him listen, I should have yelled after him, "I love you, kid," but my jaws rusted open and my mouth dried up. If I'd done any of the things I was supposed to, maybe we could have hugged and cried together and started to feel better. Maybe I could have saved us from ourselves.

But I was frozen like the Tin Woodman, stiff and creaking. And Lucky wanted action, *action*, turning that fierce, blotched look on me. "Aren't you going to do something about it?"

All I could see was all our oversights written on his face—Leslie's and mine. I couldn't handle it. Maybe if I'd been stronger, but I couldn't stand to have him see how weak and stupid I really was.

"Or are you just going let them go on Doing It?"

I hit the fan and blew all over the place. I hated Leslie for being so careless. She hadn't wasted a dime's worth of effort keeping people from finding out. She didn't care who knew she was boffing Calvin and messing up a dozen lives. When Lucky told me he knew, the top of my head blew like an uncapped oil well. Right there in front of him I went through all the stages of realization, rage and despair in Fast Forward, which meant I overshot resignation and acceptance and went spinning, hurtling out of control.

Or are you just going to let them go on Doing It?

Was I?

"Go to bed," I told him, because I couldn't let him see how messed up I was.

And then I turned in on myself and chewed through all my material, getting naked from the inside out. So it was crazed, ruinous, foul and misbegotten, but maybe what I did was some kind of halfassed tribute to the kid. To his absolute view of things. The kind of kid integrity that demands action.

I thought about shotguns, spotlights and confrontations. I thought about beating the shit out of Cal. The truth? I was too poleaxed by grief to fight. I waited until they were all asleep. I waited until I thought I heard the happy couple sneaking out. Then I got into the Mercedes and headed up the hill and when I got to the top I turned the big old car around and started to coast. Then I hit the gas and roared down on them, dead drunk and screaming, *revenge*. It was like being on a high-speed escalator. I couldn't get off and I couldn't stop.

What was I trying to do that night, turn the adulterers out of the shack like the jelly out of a smashed clam shell, or did I want to flush them so I could plow into them and mow them down where they stood quivering in front of my headlights? Or was I going to do an Ethan Frome and bash myself to a pulp against that tree?

What did I think I was doing, anyway? Maybe I was too drunk to think. Maybe I wanted to show the kid he had a father he could be proud of, big laugh. Or else I was only trying to scare the shit out of somebody, but who? My wife and my best friend? Me?

I did the dumbest thing.

I hit the wrong shack. I wrecked my car. I should have known better. But God, I was miserable. God, I was drunk! And—God, Lucky shamed me into it; the kid, with his absolutist judgment and that crazy flaming need for conclusions, solutions. Ends of stories. Absolute truth.

By the time I grappled the door open and fell out of the car I had totally lost it. What I was trying to do there, what in God's name I'd had in mind. All I knew was that whatever else happened that night, I had to find Lucky and make it up to him somehow. I needed to put my hands on his skinny shoulders and sit him down somewhere quiet so I could apologize, and after Lucky forgave me, we could go find some island where no mothers came and live on coconuts and fish while I tried to explain.

So this was the worst thing. Not what I did, but what happened afterward. In the middle of the fire and confusion, I completely lost track of him.

I didn't know where he was!

But there was too much going on. There were too many particles. The car was wrecked. The shed was on fire. My head hurt and my lungs were tight because of the smoke. Jane, who had always been our rock, was moaning as if the world had come to an end. In our own ways, Leslie and I were both hideously ashamed. Then there was Dave, and everything else got lost in our discovery in the barn. There was trying to bring Frieda back and knowing there was no way even as we took turns sitting on her chest and pumping, trying to make her breathe. There were already too many irretrievable losses that weekend; we couldn't bear another one. But there was the death. There were the police. We were wild, so eaten out over Frieda that nobody really heard what the kids were trying to tell us, that after we ordered them away from the barn because we had to spare them, we had to *spare* them, they went looking for Lucky. So we didn't even know Lucky was gone. If they told us, we couldn't absorb it. We had exceeded the national average of bad things for the week, just the seven of us, and we'd done it in one night. People were saying things to each other that we couldn't bear to hear. You don't want whole human beings to see you when you're that messed up. Especially not kids.

Maybe we did hear them say, "Lucky isn't anywhere." Maybe we said what you say when you can't bear to have children see your adult grief, "Why don't you guys go off somewhere and look for him?" Anything to fob them off. Or spare them. Which?

Even when the kids came back from the outbuildings, fretting because they couldn't find him, my remaining friends told each other Lucky was just hiding, he'd turn up. I was so trashed I didn't know what was going on. I was lurching around with a skull-crunching headache. It was the least of what I felt.

So the realization came to us in stages, like a messenger crossing the desert on horseback.

By the time we understood that Lucky was not among us, the state cops were finishing up and it was almost dawn. They told us not to worry, he was probably hiding, which was not unusual in these cases—our private firestorm and these New England kids with their grave faces, playing grownup in their cop uniforms are reassuring us, going: In these *cases*. They said be patient, give the boy a few hours to come back on his own, he was probably hiding in the woods at the edge of the clearing or somewhere in the house, where it was safe. They said not to worry, if Lucky didn't come out now, he would show himself the minute it got light. If by any chance he didn't, by all means call them and they'd come back and institute a search.

By then I was so stupefied by trauma and the stuff the ambulance guys had given me that I let my friends drag me into the living room and put me to bed on the sofa. I was not in my right mind. "Lucky," I said, and tried to sit up. I was so upset that good old Zack offered to go out in the dark that minute and start looking, but it had been a long night and he said it without conviction; everybody was used up. I tried to get up again but they pushed me back. Almost morning, they said. They said, We'll find him as soon as it gets light. My friends made assurances while I lay there with my head drumming, not from the collision but from fear, because earlier that night when Lucky and I faced off in the kitchen, we said certain things to each other that I couldn't exactly remember but would always regret.

I wanted to turn my face to the wall. I should have grieved for him but I was too close to dying of remorse. If I could have closed my eyes and self-destructed, I would.

Yes I wanted to die.

In the deep sick self inside of me I probably knew Lucky was not temporarily mislaid, and he wasn't holed up somewhere playing a kid's game of hide-and-seek with us, but that same sick self was thinking: God, how do you wake up in the morning after this? He must hate me after what I did. I was so agonized over how I was going to face him that I lost track of where he was.

I should have lunged into the night and gone looking. I should have raked the woods with lights and called for helicopters to comb the mountains; I should have sent miners to check the ditches and troops to search the woods and divers to drag the reservoir because Lucky was in terrible danger, but I did not know this and at the moment I was drugged and too weak to move.

For the last time I tried to sit up.

Zack snapped, "Careful!"

Weird—I couldn't even lift my head. "Lucky!"

Jane said, "Lie down."

Polly said, "Don't worry, he can probably see us right now."

Calvin said without knowing, "He's fine. I'm on top of it, Chad." Calvin said a lot of other things; he promised this, promised that, anything to make me forget so we could keep on being friends, while all the time at some level my erstwhile best friend and lifelong rival was giving me the finger: you think you're so goddam smart with your options and your TV documentary, well I have been sticking it to your wife.

Leslie was crying. "He's hiding to punish me."

Then Jane, Jane who had more to grieve over than I did because she *wanted* her marriage; Jane Darrow, who wanted her sad marriage to that unfaithful rat, put her hand on my forehead and said not to worry, Lucky probably needed space right now, we needed to give him the privacy to work things out. "It's almost morning. We all need some sleep."

I tried to sit up again. "Lucky wouldn't just . . ."

"Sh sh." She pushed me down. "Yes he would."

God help me I didn't know him well enough to know what he would do. "But we'll go looking as soon as it gets light."

Somewhere beyond my line of vision Leslie fluttered. Her voice spiked. "Don't you think we should . . ."

Jane's cold authority surprised us. "I think you'd better shut up."

And Leslie? She ran upstairs so she wouldn't see me and Jane, waiting for her to explain.

I didn't sleep. I kept seeing Lucky waving goodbye on a dozen important occasions and me, Chad Burgess, busy writer and unwilling father, walking out of the frame.

OK, Lucky, I was a shitty dad.

It shamed me to remember what I'd secretly thought of him: *You could be more like other kids, if you'd only fucking try.* After Les co-opted him I was never easy with the kid, which might be why Lucky got so twitchy, hard to hug. The first day she brought him home from the hospital she handed the baby over like a little time bomb. *"There."* She made me hold him. I didn't want to. He was squalling. He was so little. I was scared. I did the best I could with the newly commissioned mother watching me like a cop. My wife scowled and hissed until I fixed my lips and kissed the top of the baby's head. "There," Leslie said, "that's better." She was so stern. He felt so *different.*

Look, I was just getting noticed after years of nickel-and-dime police stuff, writing my first major series. I was flying, in no way ready to get married, when I met Leslie. Too soon my gorgeous girlfriend said she was, God! Pregnant. It brought me down with a thud. The woman I liked because she was smart and funny and in spite of this dressed as if looks were all she had. Oh by the way, would you rather have Towle French Provincial for our wedding silver, or something simple, like 1812? I thought she wanted to be a careerist, like me, but it turned out I was the career. And, gulp. She turned out not to be pregnant at all.

We don't have to do this, she said, but we'd already set the date and told our friends. To her credit Leslie was more embarrassed by the error than I was surprised, but like it or not, you hold that kind of mistake against a person. You can't not.

So I married her because she was almost pregnant. Maybe that's why she wouldn't quit until she was. Biological clock she said, when the alarm was in no way set for twenty-three. She was begging for something I didn't even know I wanted. She campaigned until she won the contest. Contest. That's what it was. My will. Hers.

Of course I loved the baby. Wasn't he part mine? Not the way Leslie acted. *We,* she said, excluding me. She meant her and the baby. He stayed where she put him and did what she wanted.

No wonder she loved him. She fussed so much that the kid got, touchy, hard to *like*. I just couldn't get used to him. *Me, a father? You've got to be kidding. I'm only a young guy.* The truth? I looked at Lucky and saw myself, Mr. Success, failing at what comes naturally. *Some father you are. You can't even do this.* One of life's most basic assignments and I couldn't handle it. How was I going to succeed in real life when I couldn't handle this?

Kids are little yardsticks, measuring you off. The time clock. Tick tick. I'd be crashing on some project that might or might not fly—the newspaper series that was nominated but did not win a Pulitzer Prize, or the script I wrote from my first book, that died in development hell—I had all these daily failures chipping away at me and I couldn't even stop a baby from crying the few times Leslie left him alone with me. And in my weakened condition I would look at this undersized product of my genetic encoding and see my failure spelled out.

He got big. I felt like the same young guy, but I had this *growing kid* to remind me we were both getting older. *You are running out of time.*

But we got by.

Until that summer, we got by.

We were OK, I think, the Burgess family. We probably would have made it anyway, Lucky would have made it, if Leslie hadn't forced the issue by sticking us with that godforsaken farm. The waste! My wife knew what she wanted, and it wasn't Brook Farm. What she really wanted, she could have done anywhere. But Leslie has never been content to put a bare face on her intentions. A lady's legacy, straight out of Lavinia Poulnot Austin of Charleston and East End Avenue. If she wanted to fuck Calvin behind my back why didn't she just go ahead and do it? Why did she have to construct this elaborate device for fooling around?

I probably could have lived with Leslie's affair. We've forgiven each other for worse things. Without the crash and the fire, we might have squeaked by. In other circumstances we might have seen it through and lived to fight another summer, but Lucky— kids don't compromise.

Kids—they live on the front lines; they are on the front lines every living minute.

And all I could think of to do for him was wreck the car.

So wherever Lucky was, it was because of me. It was up to me to find him and I didn't even know where to look. Aching right down to my molars, I lay there in the dark, trying to think the way Lucky did. I was ashamed because I didn't know!

What I did know was that he'd tried to show me with the homemade comic book and I hadn't thought enough of it to read it. Lucky wrote his heart out and handed it to me with that goofy love-me smile, and what did I do? Said thanks and put it down and forgot.

How could I tell him it wasn't the gift I was rejecting, it was the birthday? The hounds of winter were on my heels that year and I was running scared. One day you look in the mirror and you think, *Oh shit, I'm out of time.* There was Leslie stringing Japanese lanterns and buying party hats when I saw all the best parts of me starting the march toward death. Forty. The beginning of the end and she made a party. And fucked Calvin to celebrate: "Oh, and incidentally, look what I have, that you didn't know I had—" Or was it: Who.

How do you tell an eleven-year-old boy what you're really afraid of? Death.

God! Glued to the foldout sofa, aching and betrayed, with my face stretched tight and my cracked ribs tearing at me, I heard my teeth collide and my insides clash. Death. It was starting to look good to me.

What if it looked good to Lucky too? I had to get close enough to look him in the eyes—Leslie's eyes—and find out where he was with this. How he was. In all these years of confused love and near misses I'd never gotten close enough to see inside my son.

When I found him, I'd look him in the eyes and say—what? Eight million reasons to go on living. I only had one. It was funny. Doped as I was, foggy-headed and miserable, I could only think of one reason to stay around, and it wasn't what you think.

I had to stay alive for him.

I must have slept after all. My eyes clicked shut and when they clicked open it was light. I was dizzy; I ached in places that hadn't even been battered but I got to my feet and went looking for Lucky's present. I picked it up off the kitchen floor and brushed it off. It could have been Lucky there between my hands; I held the thing to my face, stroking the dog-eared paper: There there.

Then I took it outside. I sat down on the front steps of the house where the others were still sleeping and opened it. For the first time in my life I tried to go back in there, where my boy had begged and invited and failed to get me to go so many times. I was trying to get inside Lucky's head.

THE MONSTER FROM SCARTH CAVE, it said.

This is for you, Dad. Picture of this amazing monster. Listen, it could have been me. I was that ugly.

So I sat on the farmer's front steps with my head throbbing and dried blood scabbing my temple, dazzled by the bright colors and disturbed by the slouching were-brute my son had drawn with black hairs sprouting and eyes the color of his and Leslie's. I was honored and scared and frustrated to be reading this, squinting at the impenetrable speeches in crabbed script that overflowed the talk balloons.

I heard the others getting up. I laid back. The house belonged to them, not me.

Exiled, I sat on the steps outside while they straggled downstairs and clumped in the kitchen, asking each other whether they'd seen Lucky sneaking in or heard him talking to the kids, whether he might not be up there in the shed chamber with the others, rolled up in his sleeping bag. Polly even tiptoed upstairs to look. I heard her come back down into the kitchen and report while the rest of my friends asked each other whether Lucky was really going to come back on his own, and whether it would be right to call in the police or if seeing people in uniform would only scare him so badly that we'd never get him back. I heard them chivvying the kids, fobbing off their questions and complaints so when the farmer's wife came to get them off the scene, they'd go quietly.

I heard them making a list of places to look. The house, even though it seemed ridiculous. Crawlspaces and trunks in the attic and the basement. The barn and the outbuildings. The rest of the farm. The reservoir. In town.

Somebody said, "The cave," but Leslie, *my Leslie*, said, "He'd never go up there alone. The kids are afraid of the cave."

I sat there staring into Lucky's comic with tears running down my face and thinking: Dear God, why couldn't I have done this yesterday?

By the time I had turned the last page I was through weeping and it was time to start. I could hear the women inside, calling him, but I knew it was pointless. When they came out the kitchen door to search the outbuildings, I put my head down because I didn't really want to see any of them right then. My wife and Polly and Jane were so distracted that they sailed out and headed into the barn without noticing me. I might as well not be there. I hadn't been there much that summer, after all. The farm was their place, not mine, and if Lucky was lost on the farm they would find him. Stig and Calvin got in a car and headed off to check at the reservoir. If they saw me, they didn't signify. I knew they wouldn't want me to go with them and I didn't offer. If everybody wanted to blame me for what had happened, fine. All that mattered now was Lucky.

I knew where to look.

It was right there in the comic, it had been there all along.

I hoped to God he was still OK.

22

Scarth Cave

When I stood up I bumped directly into Zack. He was standing over me with a bagel and a cup of coffee, my big, shaggy friend. His expression was a puzzle. As if in spite of everything he still wanted what I had.

"Are you going to eat or what?"

"I can't. I've got to go."

"The police are on the way."

"Police!"

"Leslie's idea."

"Is she OK?"

Zack shrugged. "Not really. She thinks fate is paying her back."

"It's not that simple."

"Try and tell her that."

So Leslie felt the way I did today. Ugly, responsible. I wanted to get my wife someplace where nobody was around and hold her until we both forgot, but Leslie and I were beyond it by that time, we were beyond everything but reproaches and regrets. "I can't. Can I use your car?" I reached for his keys.

Zack was studying me. I guess I looked worse than I thought; he said, "No way. Get in. I'll drive. Where do you want to start?"

"It's in here." I tapped the comic book. I was already scared. "It's in here. He's at the cave."

"Shit! The cave. My fucking film. I . . . ." Zack was so busy getting me into the car that he let me see how upset he was. "I told them to be careful, but kids . . ."

"They didn't need you to find the cave."

"All I cared about was my movie." As he backed the car around and headed out Zack gave me a raw, unexpected look. "There was never going to be a movie."

I looked at the ruins of the shed. "I burnt your script."

I guess he saw his whole unmade picture flashing before his eyes because he shook his head. "I should have burned it."

What I said next surprised me. "You have to keep trying." I didn't know why this had become so important. No. My head shuddered. I did. This was me, laying down stepping stones so I could walk back into my life.

"But I fell on my ass."

"So big deal." It was as if my life depended on it, not Zack's. What was I trying to do then, what did I think? If I could sell Zack, did I think I could sell myself, and what was I selling anyway? The rhetoric you need to keep from dying. I said, more for me than for him, "If you don't keep trying, you're dead."

"I should have burned it," Zack said anyway.

"Maybe trying is all there is."

In tragedies, there's something about us that makes us all assume the blame. "I never should have let them go near the cave."

"It wasn't the movie that did this to us, Zack," I said. Then I said the strangest thing. "It would have happened anyway."

We left the car at the place where the dirt road up the mountain trailed off into a steep path. I wanted to go ahead by myself. I didn't want anybody to be there when I found him because I didn't know what I was going to find, whether Lucky was OK or not OK, and if he was not OK, whether God or nature had done it to him or he'd done it to himself. I needed to make my discoveries without anybody there watching, but Zack was a good friend. He set his jaw and wouldn't let me go alone. He wouldn't stay behind even when I yelled at him.

"Go away." I snarled, glaring. "Just go away!"

He just blinked and forgave me and followed. Then as we went up the tortuous path to Scarth Cave without any idea what we were going to find, my good friend Zack went on talking. Sometimes you say one thing to keep from saying another and I think that's what Zack was doing, laying out a tolerable sequence of things for us to talk about to keep either of us from having to think ahead to what we were going to find.

Zack just blinked in the morning sunlight and started talking as if we were two ordinary guys out walking on a perfectly ordinary day. "Funny, you know?"

"What?"

"That this should be happening to you," Zack said. "You always had everything."

I didn't take him back over the events of the night. "Nobody knows what anybody else has."

"I thought you were golden. We all did."

"I'm not golden, Zack, I'm not anything."

"You're a success. I don't resent it," he said anyway. "You deserved it. You worked like hell." We were going along through the woods without knowing whether Lucky was in the cave at the top or lying broken at the bottom of some underground crevasse and there was my old friend saying as if we were out for a walk in the woods on any old Sunday, "Do you know I really thought I was going to make this movie and it would make me famous?"

"Don't give up. It still could."

"No it couldn't," Zack said. "It's over. I'm done."

"Don't give up." I don't know why it was so important. I do. I was begging for Lucky, as if everything was tied up with everything else. "When you give up, you're dead."

Zack's expression was sweet. "I'm not giving up. I'm facing facts."

"That doesn't mean you have to give up." We were talking about something more than what we were talking about; in an odd, almost mystical way, I was rehearsing arguments for Lucky. Laying out stones on the path back to life. I said, "We're in this for the sake of doing it. God," I said. It was like being struck down on the path. How could I get Lucky hooked on life, on aspiration, when he may have come up here to die? Rehearsing my life, I laid it out for him. "Whether you write movies or teach school, the whole thing is doing it. Doing it is half the fun."

"Done is done." Zack sighed. "Maybe growing up is facing it."

Desperate, I overrode him. "It might be the only fun."

"That's all right for you to say. You've got what you want."

"Nobody gets what they want." I put my hands out like a traffic cop. "Don't, OK? Don't quit." *Oh Lucky, don't.* No matter what happens you have to keep running, get up in the morning, go ahead and keep doing it. This is what keeps you going— what you can still *be*. Even when—God, when does it happen—even when you realize your body may outlive your expectations, you have to keep on trying because trying is all there is.

"It's OK." Zack's tone was light and the sweetness in his voice was consistent with Zack over the years, as if all the time we were being young together, he'd spun out his life in premature regret. "We're only ever who we are."

And Lucky could be dead. "Oh my God."

Lives depended on it; I said, "Hang in, Zack. You can do anything you want, if you just hang in."

Then it came to me in a flash of panic that what the gods—or is it God—what God might want here was human sacrifice: my life for my son's. So I was not exactly praying, but this is what came as I blundered forward . . . *If you have to take somebody, take me instead. OK, God? OK?*

Zack said sadly, "It's this fucking farm."

"No it isn't," I said. I reached where I was going in stages. "I really fucked up, didn't I?"

"It wasn't you." Zack's voice was soft, sad. "It was everybody. But the crash. You were amazing."

"I was an asshole."

Zack said, "It was definitely not our best time."

The path was getting steep. Shale crumbled underfoot—the same stuff that made up the walls of the cave. Because I couldn't bear to think ahead I fixed on details: all the freight we'd carried into that summer; I needed the fax and answering machine and cellular phone to stay connected because movement isn't necessarily action, but it makes you think you're on your way. So there was that and then there were the girls I saw, OK, and I was not the only one, because the loudest sound in our lives that year was the ticking of the clock—pressure from outside to remind us how important it was to stay young.

Going into that summer, we thought it was about success, but what drove us was something more profound. When you're over thirty-five you're out of business in some circles, by forty you're halfway to Dead. At my age no matter how good you are, you're already under the gun, and this is one of the things that drove the eight of us—we had to change our lives before we ran out of time.

We lost track of who we were.

I was almost leveled by the pain. "What happened to us?"

"I don't know, I guess it was . . ." Zack's eyes were like mirrored kaleidoscopes, multiplying the details of the summer and giving them all back. Finally he said, "I guess our lives just caught up with us."

"You mean, that's all?"

He looked like a bull hit by the mallet. "I think that's all it was."

We'd come to the place where the woods gave way to a rocky clearing. We were at the cave.

I started to run. I ran past Zack's discarded lighting setups and the kids' abandoned props and costumes and I struggled over the wire fence that protected the mouth of the cave. It was like walking into a movie set: *spooky grotto*—unreal, like the caverns where Tom Sawyer hid from Injun Joe. The kids were right; it was a creepy, terrible place. I put my mouth to the boards.

"Lucky!"

Inside something stirred. Everything in me let go and I was gasping for breath; I realized I'd been too scared to bring it out in the open, but I had thought he was dead.

He was there.

"Oh, Lucky!"

Let him be OK. Please, God. OK? I was begging, no, bargaining with God. I made my last, best offer, it was pathetic. *Take me instead.* I called again. When he didn't answer, I knocked on the splintered, stained boards that covered the cave's mouth because I knew without having to think it out that Lucky had pushed them aside so he could squirm inside and then pulled them back in place so nobody would know, like a kid hiding in bed and pulling the covers up over his head. There was a faint light inside. My God, I could see a flash of white through the gap in the boards.

I knew he wasn't going to answer but I said, "Are you OK?"

He was sitting on a mattress—Frieda's mattress, poor fragile, dead girl, forced to lie down week after week with a lover she didn't want. Lucky shrank against the stone with his knees up and his back to the dank wall of that terrible place. He sat in the failing glow from his flashlight with his thoughts turned in on God knows what. I don't know if he knew I was there.

I called. "Lucky, it's me."

There was no response. He was fixed in terror like an insect in Lucite, fully visible but impossible to touch. There was my son whom I had somehow seriously damaged, snapped into a tight knot and backed into the wall. My loving, wistful, *overlooked* son crouched there, surrounded by pathetic piles of objects he had shored up against his ruin—books, extra sweaters, a pile of tin cans. These were the things my son had marshalled against the apocalypse. It was enough to make you weep.

I started clawing at the boards. I could see the despairing slope of Lucky's bony shoulders, the tender skin on the back of my son's skinny little neck. There was Lucky, who thought he was prepared for the end of the world in whatever form it took, crouched there, overwhelmed. He was huddled with his chin on his knees, so overcome by misery that he never heard me call and he didn't even hear me cursing and pulling at the splintered boards with my raw fingers so I could slip through and get to him.

"Lucky. Son!"

Daddy! He did not say this. It's what I wanted to hear. He didn't say anything. I kept waiting for him to stir, praying for his aspect to change. It did not.

I went to him. "Honey, it's me."

He was cold to the touch and redolent of the cave: the dripping walls, perpetual darkness, the bats.

"Lucky. Tim? Timothy?"

He didn't hear.

"It's Daddy, son."

He didn't move.

I was so stupid I thought maybe he was putting it on. I thought he was too angry to speak. When I hugged him he'd yield and we'd be OK. I reached out. "Lucky, it's Dad. I've come to get you, OK?"

When I tried to put my arms around him he gasped and then went rigid, so I had to grapple with Lucky's dead weight in the halfdarkness, struggling to get him closer to the light. If I could only get him outside I could rouse him. But dead weight was compounded by resistance born of terror. I couldn't budge him. I couldn't even warm his hands. All I could do was take him in my arms and sit on the ground and hug and rock. I whispered, into his hair, "Lucky, Lucky, please, it's not your fault."

His back arched and his body clicked into a knot.

But I kept on rocking. I did. I was crying. I said, "Son. Lucky, son. Here you *are* and none of this is your fault." Then I rocked and wept into his hair and held him so tight that finally his eyes snapped open and he looked at me in—it was not exactly recognition, but at least he looked at me.

Here's this: as soon as Lucky saw who I was, he ducked his head, as if in shame, when all the time it was me. I was the one who should apologize.

I would have done anything to make it up to him.

I said, "None of this was your fault."

I said, "These things happen, that's all."

I said, "There are just things you can't do anything about, you know? Nobody can."

I said, "If it was anybody's fault, it was mine." If I had to, I'd die making it up to him.

I said, into his hair, "What do you want me to do?" I would have done anything he asked.

I could hear Zack knocking on the boards. "Chad?" At the sound, Lucky started to vibrate.

"Shh, Lucky, shh shh."

"Are you all right?"

I barked, "Don't come in!"

I could hear anxious Zack crunching back and forth in front of the opening. "What's going on?"

"Nothing. It's OK."

"Is he all right?"

"Maybe not. I think so." The kid was jangling, quivering like a knot of hot wires. I said, for Lucky, "He'll be OK. Just maybe not yet."

"What's the matter?"

"I can't get him to come out."

Zack started working on the boards. "Hold it. I'm coming in."

Lucky convulsed and spat. I shouted, "No!"

"Do you want me to get help?"

"Not yet. No. I don't think so."

"Shit, Chad. What do you want me to do?"

All I wanted him to do was go away. "Nothing right now, OK?"

"Maybe I should bring a doctor."

Lucky was doing everything within his power to get away from me. It got harder and harder to hold him in place. If I didn't get rid of Zack I didn't know what he was going to do. "Just go back downhill and tell them he's OK."

"It sounds like you need help in there."

"Please!"

"OK," Zack said, backing off reluctantly, "if you're sure that's what you want." He left us by degrees. We heard him at increasing distances calling, "You're sure you're all right."

I wasn't. I said I was. When we couldn't hear him any more, my boy relaxed.

Then I sat there on dead Frieda's mattress with Lucky in my arms trying to figure out what I could do or say that would uncurl him and bring him back to me, and all I could focus on was my own poor, tattered discovery, that it wasn't what you did, it was *doing it* that made all the difference, I wanted to tell him and I didn't have the words.

It was damp in that place, the stone walls were cold and my legs were cramping under Lucky's weight. There was no sound now except for his breathing and mine and the unidentifiable slither of small things moving underneath the litter on the rocky floor but I was drifting by then, in pain but strangely joyful even though my wife was leaving me and my son was in terrible straits and I had thoroughly fucked up my life. I was moving toward something I couldn't quite identify. Then in my exaggerated state I saw it clearly—where my friends were in their lives, where I was, all of us flawed and struggling forward, and I was momentarily staggered by the fact, not so much of being, as of the struggle.

Distracted as I was, shamed and nearly leveled by my own stupidity, I would still get up in the mornings with the fixed idea that if I only worked on it hard enough, things would improve.

OK, my work would improve, because even then at my lowest I could not stop *wanting*, and trying my best to *be*.

And oh my God I wanted more than anything for Lucky to come back out of himself and *be*. Trembling, I fixed on this, discovering it all over again, and even now I can't explain why this occurred and keeps recurring any more than I can completely identify what may be the theological implications. I heard myself murmuring, "Listen, Lucky. It's not what happened to us yesterday that makes the difference." I couldn't know if he heard me or not. "Your life isn't the only thing you are. What happens to you isn't what's important. What matters is what you do about it."

If he heard, he didn't respond.

"It's all just life," I said. "What she did, what we did, and what matters now is how we take it, OK?" I was crunching toward something even I didn't quite recognize.

"It's what we do with it, OK? It's what we do in our lives." It came to me—what I'd been groping toward since last night. For me it's my work; couldn't sort it out—what I did, which was what I *was*. What Lucky might grow up wanting to do. "Everything is process, son."

The light from the flashlight went out. Sitting there in the dark, I kept trying to decipher what I knew. I didn't know if I was making sense but I went on anyway. "Maybe process is the only thing." I knew. I did! "Like it or not, we still have to *be*, OK?"

I wanted to rip it out of myself and hand it to Lucky whole— the terror and joy of survival. "And I just. What I want is for you to come out and *be* with me."

He moved in my arms. I looked down. He didn't look at me and he wouldn't speak. Instead he put his head into my chest, leaning hard, as if to bury himself.

"I don't know if you can hear me and if you do hear me, I don't know if you want to hear anything I have to say but I am your father and I love you, so I'm going to say it anyway, and if you love me even a little after everything, maybe you will listen." I was stumbling toward it, drunk on discovery.

"Oh Lucky, please. We have to stay alive for each other, OK?"

23

The Kids

We didn't find out until later where Lucky got to on the night of the crash and the fire. We didn't even know what had happened to Frieda until they told us the next day. When we woke up we went around tugging on people's elbows but they were too distracted to deal. We were kids, and all the big things went on somewhere far above our heads.

We could come in from playing and discover huge changes: parents not speaking to each other for some dumb reason, Frieda dead. The groanies never told us anything. We were only kids.

After the crash they sent us away before the fire was even out. I guess they didn't want us to see Frieda dead.

The groanies were too busy protecting us from the truth about Frieda to know what was going on with us, or care. Unless they didn't want us looking into their naked faces and seeing them the way they were. They sent us inside.

We started looking for Lucky in the house. Cabinets. Closets. Scary places in the attic and tight places under the stairs. We even looked in Frieda's room. Then we got flashlights and went looking outside. We would have searched the barn but the groanies wouldn't let us near the barn.

So we crunched up the hillside in the dark, calling for him; we were so little and stupid, we even looked for him in trees. When we couldn't stand not finding him we zoomed back down and

ran on past the house, going the rest of the way down to the
stone wall that marked the field. We fanned out for as long as we
could stand it, calling back and forth because we were scared. We
kept bumping each other and clumping, standing around trying
to think of other places he might be, until the groanies saw us
and said, "My God, are you still up?"

"What were the cops doing here?"

Some parent said vaguely, "Oh, it was about the car."

Alfred started crying first.

His father shouted, "You kids should be in bed."

Alfred just bawled.

Gabe said, "Shut up, Alfred. Mom . . ."

"Not now."

"We can't find Lucky."

Some mom said automatically, "Well Lucky should be in
bed."

Rocky said, "Dad . . ."

His father snapped, "I said, *not now*."

The paramedics were already slamming the doors to the
ambulance. Dave wouldn't let it leave until the paramedics let
him climb in back. Now that it was OK to go into the barn, we
were scared to go into the barn. The doors gaped like a dragon's
jaws, black and ringed with rotting teeth. Mr. Burgess lurched
around like a Civil War victim with his hurt arm tied up in a
bandanna and a bloody rag around his head. He and Mrs.
Burgess and Mr. Darrow were all yelling at once, while Mrs.
Darrow shuffled around in her fuzzy bathrobe with red,
rubbed-looking eyes, forcing people to drink cups of coffee
they didn't want. Speedy's dad was sitting on a rock with
nobody to talk to and Gabe's mom was standing next to his dad;
at least she'd buttoned her shirt.

Rocky grabbed Mrs. Burgess by the arm. "We can't find
Lucky."

Rosy light filled the clearing—what was left of the fire. In the
burned-out car metal and plastic cooled and snapped. Smoke

curled and made us cough. When Lucky's mom finally looked down at Rocky her eyes were like melted candy, smeared across her face. "Don't you worry about Lucky, we'll take care of him." She was crying. "Please go to bed."

To his own astonishment, Rocky punched her on the arm. "Aren't you going to *find* him?"

To our astonishment she pushed him hard, weeping as she said wildly, "I said go to bed. You've already done enough!"

"Shh, Les," Mrs. Peterson said and then she turned to Rocky and Gabe and the others, saying, "She doesn't mean it, but you guys have to go to bed."

Rocky was jangling. "But what about Lucky?"

His mom said, "Please go to bed, Rocks. We'll take care of it."

"Where is Frieda?"

"I *said,* go to bed!"

So the grownups were all in it together, the parents colluding to get us out of earshot for the worst parts, us running away to safety and ignorance in bed.

The mothers said, "Now that's enough." "Don't worry." "Lucky's fine." Every one of them told the brave, sad mother's lie. "Everything's going to be fine."

They rushed us inside so fast that we wondered what we'd done wrong. We thought we would never sleep again. In the next minute we were poleaxed by exhaustion. We dropped like stones. This, then, was how we got sent to bed in the middle of the worst thing in our lives.

When we got up the next morning, Lucky was still gone. After they broke the news about Frieda the moms rushed us all into a car without even listening to our questions and sent us into Eaglemont with the farmer's wife, who didn't like us much. All day we dragged around town, not knowing about Lucky, where he was or how he was. The only thing that helped was pretending to look for him.

Maybe he really had hitched a ride into Eaglemont. While the

rest of us were bopping around in the clearing Lucky had probably escaped and met a fast car up on the road. In just another
minute we would come around a corner and see him. Then
everything would be all right. Lucky could be hiding in the drug
store or the supermarket. When the lights came on after the
noon movie we were seeing for the third time, he'd be sitting
there. We tried to fill up the terrible, empty day with doughnuts,
hot dogs, ice cream sticks, disposable toys; even though she didn't
like us the farmer's wife said the sky was the limit when what she
meant was, the groanies would have spent anything to shut us up.
When it was lunchtime and we got so wired and frantic that
some of us started crying, she finally let us go home. On the way
home in the car, Gabe and Kofi had a fight and Kofi bit Gabe so
hard he would always bear the scar.

Back at the farm the groanies were running back and forth
putting stuff into cars like refugees in World War Two. You'd
think the A-bomb was just about to fall. They could have been
running ahead of some rushing black shadow; this pretty *place;*
they could hardly wait to escape.

"Where's Lucky?"

"It's OK, we found him."

"Then why are we leaving?"

Even though it was barely noon they were shoving pots and
pans and sleeping bags and all the appliances and sports equipment of the summer into cars. Nobody wanted to spend another minute at the farm. We were going to be back in the city
before we'd even figured out which toys we wanted to take with
us and which to leave behind.

We were going to be back in the city before we knew who
was coming and who was not. "Where's Lucky?"

"Don't worry, he's fine."

"If he's fine, then where is he?" The parents didn't exactly
answer. "Don't worry, it's only a matter of time."

And Lucky? Basically, the parents lied to us. They told us he
was safe, but they didn't say where. We said could we see him

and they said not yet. We said Why not, and they said Because. They said Mr. Burgess was taking care of it. When we said taking care of what, they said don't worry, the police are helping him and when we said we didn't want to leave without Lucky they said, hush now, we have to go. Hurry up, it's time to get into the car.

We were sick at our stomachs with it by that time, halfway between screaming and throwing up. When Mrs. Peterson tried to herd Speedy into the family Volvo wagon in hopes Gabe and Kofi would follow, Speedy started to cry.

"What's the matter?"

"Lucky." She was crying like she'd never stop and if we weren't crying, we were close to it because we'd spent a night and a day running too fast in ignorance, do this, do that, and nobody would tell us anything.

"Oh please don't." But Mrs. Peterson was crying too, and that scared us as much as anything, her telling us everything was OK and showing us that it wasn't, all at the same time. She had this *look.* "I think he's all right."

"Then why can't we see him?"

"You just can't. Not yet. Now get in the car, OK?" She said sort of hopelessly, "Zack?"

Gabe's dad said, "OK, Gabe, Kofi. It's time. Get in the car."

"Please, we have to go."

Nobody moved. It just felt *wrong.*

Finally she told us. "He's in the cave and he won't come out."

"Now get in the car," Mr. Darrow said. "Now."

Rocky set his jaw and dug in.

"Rocky." God he was mad at us. "Do what I say!"

Alfred stood behind Rocky with this miserable look on his streaked red face.

Mr. Darrow made an angry grab for him. "Move!"

Rocky was running in place, blowing up like a rubber toad. When his father reached out he ducked his head and rammed his father in the gut. "Fuck you."

Calvin dropped his hands and turned this red, sad, used-up face to us. Rocky broke free and started running uphill.

Alfred screamed, "Lucky!" as if he thought Lucky could hear.

"Lucky!" We were yelling too.

Even though they were trying to hold us back, we broke and ran uphill after him. We had to go. It was bad out that day. The thing had gone on too long. We hated not knowing what was the matter and not being able to do anything about it and we hated being pushed out of the way every time anything big was happening and we hated being eleven and always getting shuffled out of the way. Something terrible had happened and we were not going to let this one go by, not until we'd done absolutely everything we could do.

24

Lucky

When the change begins you'll do anything to prevent it, you can feel it coming and you don't want to be a monster, you don't! It is so ugly. I am. I'm so ashamed.

Nobody wants it. You scream, *Lash me to the bed.* Would do anything to get away from what you're turning into, chew your leg off like an animal trying to get out of a trap. Inside you feel the rot beginning, pretty soon it will split your skin. It's only a matter of time before everybody sees. My God. It hurts so *much.* Then you drop on all fours and start to howl, like a werewolf. Some gross monster that's even worse. You cover your head because of the shame. You don't want anybody to see what's in your face, not your mother, not your father. Not like this.

Not after what you did to them.

You get so crazy you try to run away, but you can never get away from it, and this is the terrible thing about the change. No matter how fast you run or where you go it will catch up with you—the guilt. What's happening to you. What you have become. You can run out of the house and scuttle away on bleeding knuckles and torn feet, but no matter how fast you slouch along you can't outrun the huge, misshapen shadow running alongside. What you did. The shape of the thing you have become.

Once it begins nothing you can do or say will keep it from happening, nothing will stop your nails from growing until they curve back into your fingers and nothing can keep your mouth from stretching until it cracks your face. Blood fills up your throat and the hairs begin to sprout in a black ridge along your back.

God! Watch out for me.

Didn't I try to warn you?

Everybody, watch out.

So ugly.

Be careful.

It's ugly. No. I am.

Oh please don't.

No matter how fast you run or how deep you go, it overtakes you—the change. Once it starts, it won't matter what you do to shake it off or where you try to hide.

You might as well stay out in the open and wait for it: the change will have you no matter what, but you run anyway, because of the shame. After what you did, you can't let them see you. You're even afraid to see them—*God, no more!* Something terrible happens to people who get too close. You hate what you're turning into.

Are.

I want to die.

Go back to the house and they are all in danger; haven't I done enough? Hide or you'll do something even worse. You can not want a thing and still do it anyway. *Bury me deep,* you think, this might do it, but who can you trust to bury you? Your friends are, like: "What's the matter?" and all the time you're pleading with them, *Lash me to the bed.*

There is only one place left for you.

If I can just go deep enough, I'll never hurt anybody again.

This is Lucky in Scarth Cave. Drawn into a knot in the cold hole in the mountain, crouched on a mattress whose function he knew but has forgotten in his confusion of pain. He is locked in fetal position with his head between his knees. Lucky has gone so deep inside and stayed there for so many hours that when his father calls he doesn't hear, and when his father touches him, at first he's hardly aware of it. His own mouth is too dry for speech; his belly's tight and his joints are frozen. He hasn't eaten or drunk for hours. He hasn't spoken. He's as good as dead.

Lucky wants to be dead but his father keeps putting words into the air, like breath into his mouth. "We have to stay alive for each other."

The words don't mean anything. Yet inside, essential Lucky is stirring. He hears his father say:

"We do."

Let him talk, I'm in so deep he'll never find me. His father's body is shockingly hot in contrast to Lucky's but it is heat without warmth. His father's voice is like light rain on a windshield; Lucky is aware of it but it might as well be falling on a glass dome somewhere far above. He doesn't feel anything except cold dread. He is waiting for the monster, whatever it is, to come out of the earth and get him because he can't change back and he can't keep going on the way he is.

But Chad just keeps on. "Son, we can't stay here."

Lucky goes rigid with determination. *I can't leave here.* Scarth Cave is dark and filled with crawling things, foetid, reeking of the monster. It is just right for him. From somewhere deep inside the mountain, Lucky thinks he still hears the lost farmer's boy trapped in the dark and crying for help. He's sobbing for breath now, hollowed out by terror, brittle and ready to shatter.

I want to break his hold and push him away from me but my body isn't taking messages.

"Lucky?"

I will it: *Go away.*

My father starts to cry. "I'm so sorry."

I wish he wouldn't. My fault!

My fault for not going deep enough. My fault I can't come out of the dark and silence long enough to say or do anything final. Something so gross that it will scare him away for good. I should have kept going until I was so far inside the cave that I could never find my way back, and nobody would ever find me. But last night the cave mouth was too threatening, covered with boards like gnashing teeth; when I pulled one aside I thought I heard the monster scream. But I went inside. I did. Just not deep enough.

Even with the flashlight the cave was rank and cold and I was shaking so hard I couldn't walk so I had to hole up on Frieda's mattress right here in the front hall of hell. I thought I would die of being alone here. I thought I'd die of being scared. I thought when the flashlight burned out, I would die.

It's all I ever wanted.

Anything's better than going on the way I am.

No wonder he found me. Any fool could have tripped over me. I stopped too soon. I should have kept going. I should have crawled in so deep, dragged myself back out of his reach but I was weak. I was scared. So he found me, and now it's too late to get away.

"OK, if you aren't ready yet, we'll wait." My father's warm breath makes the skin on my neck twitch.

Clamped in his arms, I go rigid. I am trying to be dead.

"As long as it takes," my father says. He's rubbing, trying to bring back circulation in my legs. If I'm not careful he'll try to hoist me to my feet. His voice quakes but he is trying so hard to sound OK. "After a while, maybe we'll try standing up."

No.

This makes me afraid for him.

Watch out!

If I get up now I will be terrible.

He can't guess how close the monster is, or that the monster has claws that will close on his guts and pull them out in knots. The monster has fangs that can rip the life out of his throat.

"If only you'd look at me." Cupping both hands on my hideous skull, he tries to turn my head.

I make a noise. It means, *Don't.*

I can feel him tremble. "Son?"

You don't want to look at me, I am too terrible. If I rake his face with my eyes the skin will scorch and fall away from his skull in shreds.

"Son?" God, he says, "Whatever you think you did, OK, you didn't. You didn't do it, Lucky, OK?"

It isn't only that I told. I am stiff and dead. Inside, I sound the cold warning. *You'd better watch out for me.*

"Lucky?" He wants to wake me up. If he knew the truth he'd want me to die. "I know you're in there."

I did it, OK? If my father saw what I was really like he'd throw me across the cave and run. *You have to guard your house and bar the doors against the monster . . . I did it because I was mad at him for letting it happen. Not mad at fucking Calvin for fucking my fucking mother, I was mad at my father. Hating the victim, no? Well some victims are guilty as hell. I couldn't stand it so I pushed my father's face into the truth and ground it in. . . . .* you have to hunt him down with pikes and torches, and run him back into the bowels of the cave . . .

The truth? I would have done anything to make it end.

How could I know he was going to crash the car and wreck himself? So it was me who brought down fire and destruction.

"Not your fault, son," goes the endless song my father sings to me. Rocking me like a baby in the dark.

It's all my fault. I brought it down. . . . *bury him deep so he can't hurt anybody ever again.*

Then the rest bubbles up in my throat like hot blood boiling until it almost chokes me and in another minute it will come spewing out—the truth.

This, then, is the shape of the monster that my father is holding: *When it came down, I was glad.*

As soon as I did it I was scared.

I was so ashamed I had to run away. I wanted to get lost in Scarth Cave and stay there forever, just like the farmer's son. It would serve me right if I starved to death in the dark inside the mountain, and if they rolled big rocks in front of the mouth to keep me in there for good and I screamed and screamed and they walked away, that would be fine.

I just didn't want to hurt anybody else.

So when I ran away from them last night, when I crossed the road and scrabbled up the mountain and ripped off the rotten board and snaked into the cave, it was for their own safety. I was finished. Just done. Used up.

I was ready for bears to tear me apart or vampire bats to suck me dry, I wanted to starve or die of cold and loneliness or being scared and I wanted it to happen fast. I had to get it over with before the whole world saw the murderer's tears in my mouth, the spit smeared around my eyes, the black hairs sprouting all over me, and recognized me for what I was.

I was so scared!

The trouble was, the place was so awful I had a hard time going in. As soon as I quit being so scared I really meant to crawl deeper, I would keep going down and back and further down into the cave until I got crushed by rocks or tilted into a bottomless pit; anything was better than going on the way I was.

After everything, the cave was right for me. It was cold and dripping, vile—the stink! I thought if I could just stay there in the dark and cold; if I could just stay there long enough, I would either die or get killed. Either way, it would end. I wouldn't have to face what I'd done.

But, God! I didn't die.

Nothing ended.

It didn't even change.

I was still me. My father came. He stayed even though I wanted him to give up and go away. We sat there for a long time, him rocking me and begging, me hiding from him *for his own protection*. Then something else happened.

I heard sounds that were not our sounds and not the monster, either. Everyday voices in the everyday light outside.

Somebody else was coming up the hill. My friends.

I heard kids calling, "Lucky."

Rocky. Gabe, I thought. The others.

They came for me.

Oh my God.

I flew apart.

"Shh." My father's arms pulled me back together and locked me in place. "Shh shh."

In spite of everything I did, in spite of me doing everything and killing everybody, they still came for me.

There was a rattle outside, somebody broaching the wire barrier. The dark thing inside of me was flapping. Drag the monster into sunlight and it dies. I had to get away from my father so I could go deeper. I had to get away from them.

Oh my God I . . . I was snarling and clawing, trying to free myself, but Dad! He wouldn't let go.

He said it again. "We have to live for each other."

It ripped out of me. "No!"

They were knocking on the boards. "Lucky, hey!"

"Mr. Burgess. Is he in there?" Rocky's voice!

Speedy said, "Is he OK?"

Oh, don't!

I wanted to groan and drag myself farther into the dark.

My father held me in place. His voice rumbled out of him. "It's OK, Lucky. It's OK."

It wasn't. *Just let me die.*

Somehow he knew what I was thinking; he raised his voice. "It's OK, kids, but don't come in right now, OK?"

I couldn't get away because he was holding me in place; I couldn't die because Rocky and Speedy were out there knocking on the boards and calling through the crack. Then I heard Gabe and even fucking Alfred, crying: "It's me, Lucky, OK?"

I was shaking all over.

Alfred bawled. "I'm goddam fucking sorry, OK?"

"Shh-shh, honey," my father said into my hair. To them: "It's OK, guys, give him time."

But there wasn't any time. I heard groanie voices coming up the hill—even the mother. Dad was OK but I didn't want to see her just then. If I went out I would have to face her. I'd have to face all of them.

I heard her hammering, "Lucky, for God's sake. For God's sake Chad, what are you *doing* in there?"

And that rumble coming out of him: "For God's sake, Les, relax!"

"Shut up Chad, I'm coming in!"

Then my father growled at her so loud that it made her back off.

I could hear them all talking in the clearing outside the cave, all my damn friends and all the damn grownups including the ones I was certain I had finished off yesterday, people I thought I had slaughtered and buried were out there in the daytime sunlight, everybody going on with their voices sounding the same and it almost rattled me to pieces: what I had thought I wanted. The way they were.

So I betrayed everybody and wrecked everything and nothing had changed. Outside the sun came up anyway. Outside the sun was shining and the world was just going on. The same people were just going on in just the same ways, same old scenes set for me, waiting for me to walk back in.

It isn't like a movie, with an ending; it isn't like a comic book. The world doesn't end with guilt and accusations, with obscene gestures and ugly betrayals; it doesn't even end with a crash and a fire. It just goes on.

My jaws were frozen. So were my joints. I couldn't move. But I didn't die.

I wanted to die and it didn't happen. I wanted to hide and my father wouldn't let me alone. He came after me and found me when I didn't want to be found. He called and tugged on me and wouldn't quit. He was tugging on me now. He held me close. I could feel his breath on my face. His voice was low. "I know you're in there, Lucky. I can see you hiding in there."

I covered my face. I wanted to keep hiding but he pulled my hands down from my face so I had to stay hidden behind closed eyes.

I could feel his breath on the lids. "It's time to come on out."

My jaws were creaking like rusty gates. "I can't." I tried to break free from him. I wanted to drag myself away.

He grabbed me by the foot and pulled me back. "You think you can't do this, but you can."

I think I said, "Don't you hate me?"

My father's voice was filled with something else. "Why should I hate you?"

So I told him. It came out so thin I didn't know if he could even hear. *When it happened, I was glad.*

Then my father's voice came out of a still, sad place. "Oh, you poor kid."

I started to cry. He pulled me back to the mattress and held me and wouldn't let me escape. The whole time he was rocking: me, him, in some kind of cosmic *there there.*

Locked in his father's arms, Lucky struggled against the flexing of the web, the gentle, insistent, unremitting forces pulling him back to life.

"Kid," Chad said. "Oh, kid."

Lucky waited for his father to go on but he didn't, or couldn't—Mr. Words, at a loss for once and filled to overflowing with things he felt but could not express.

Held in place like that, immobile and considering, Lucky understood that maybe he was not to blame for what had happened last night, and whether or not he was, his father had come looking for him anyway. He had come looking because he was Lucky's father and this bond canceled or negated the wrongs they might have done each other, Chad's slights, Lucky's guilt. It superseded everything.

Used up, drenched and trembling, he thought: *It was supposed to be over but he came for me. And like it or not, I'm here.*

All that, and I'm still here.

He's here and still alive; he has no choice! Which, Lucky sees now, means that if he could live through all that, he will live through this. Facing the people in the clearing. What he has done. Therefore, willing or not, ready or not ready, happy or unhappy, he can probably live through anything.

Lucky lets out all his breath at once.

Chad murmurs into his hair, "Son?"

He considers his father: What were you telling me just now? What do you hope for that you haven't got? In spite of him, everything in Lucky rushes out looking for the answers. He whispers to his father. "OK."

So Lucky is delivered whole at the center—the secret of his survival: the hands and voices of the others, who love him and insist on it. Unbidden, they pursue him even into dark places, intent on dragging him out. For as long as he lives these people he loves will follow him into his darkest retreats, calling him back.

Expanding in the darkness of Scarth Cave, T. Burgess who is not dead yet examines the blackness racing behind his closed eyelids, imagining night. Once again he sees stars, some close, some remote, souls blazing by the billions. He is amazed by the fact that even the longed-for night is in no respect completely still, nor is it black or empty. Instead it is quick and populous. Sparks arc across the blackness behind his closed eyelids in a progress that is beyond his power to stop.

In a state of heightened consciousness brought on by excitement and exhaustion, Lucky reads the sparks as lone stars and massed constellations coursing behind his eyes like exhibits in a cosmic planetarium. Pushed to the limit and focused on eternity as he is, he sees spots of light racing past at tremendous speeds and he understands now that the individual sparks of light and the constellations alike are patterned, people moving in configurations he cannot understand, much less deny or prevent. Invisible threads keep them moving in concert even when they seem most separate, and like it or not he is moving with them, all of them driven or propelled or drawn from left to right across the curve of the universe by a complex of love and fresh guilt and renewed forgiveness that binds and causes joy as well as pain.

The web of lives exists and like it or not, Lucky is a living part of it. With a sigh, he opens his eyes.

He hears his father sigh.

Stretching cautiously, shuddering under the weight of the renewed perception, or vision, Lucky wishes he could reach out and seize one of the others—one of the stars, or is it one of the people he cares about. He wants to tell Chad what he understands now, what not even his father, who has been holding him, knows he knows.

He understands now that he isn't the only one who was wronged this summer, or who did wrong; *nobody's that lucky,* he understands. He was never the only one trapped in guilt. But that isn't the important thing. Compressed in the dark, crouched and shaking, at last he truly comprehends it:

You will do anything to get out of the dark.

Even thinking he wants to die, even crouched here, Lucky has been waiting for them to come and deliver him.

Hiding from his father, he wanted to be found.

I love you, coming back to save me with your blind hopefulness . . . you just won't quit! Which may be why I can't quit.

Right, I've been waiting for you.

Outside the cave, the others are murmuring. Lucky thinks he hears his mother's voice stretched thin, and he understands that they have all been waiting for him.

He understands as well that they can't any of them escape this day without his help. Therefore he touches his father's arms and they spring open. He gets to his knees stiffly. With a series of thumps that restore circulation in sleeping legs in a string of electric shocks, Lucky gets moving and hitches out of the cave and into the daylight, weeping and joyful, emerging from the earth.

Feeling cleansed and loving, tearful and shaky, he moves forward even though he's terrified of what's coming—My God, the *rest of his life*. Using the rusting wire barrier for support, he pulls himself to his feet.

His mother gasps. Caught out, she's afraid to touch him. "Are you all right?"

He doesn't exactly answer. Instead he sweeps the clearing with a shaky, beatific grin.

His father says for him, "He's fine."

Lucky hears and his mouth floods. He can hear his jaws flexing, breaking the seal: *crack*. His face is smeared with dirt and blood and tears; his joints are stiff from hours in the cave and he is so deep in hunger that he can barely stand. There is dirt in his mouth and his throat is filled with sand but his voice has come back and grinning, he answers. Unshelled before them, tottering and grateful, Lucky gives more than he means to. More than he thought he had left.

He says, "I'm here."

How long have I lived in New England? Since I saw my first snow in New London when I was three years old. All the time I spent exiled in Florida as a child and, as an adult, in places as odd as Waukegan, Ill. Always wanted to live here, finally did, moving to New Haven and then Middletown with my mate when we came to Wesleyan University, don't ask how long ago. Friends from Manhattan and Boston thought Middletown was deep country and weekended with us.

Skidding into midlife crises, these same friends began moving to the country to save their souls. They invited us back. We visited establishments in western Massachusetts, Maine, on Block Island and the Vineyard and in upstate New York, so close to the Massachusetts border that distinctions blurred.

Events blurred too, changing and fusing to inform this novel.